– Liverpool –
MMXXV

BIG TIME

dead ink

All rights reserved.

Copyright © Jordan Prosser, 2024
All rights reserved.

The right of Jordan Prosser to be identified as the author of this work has been asserted by them in accordance with the Copyright, Designs and Patents Act 1988.

First published in 2024 by University of Queensland Press, PO Box 6042, St Lucia, Queensland 4067, Australia.

First published in Great Britain in 2025 by Dead Ink, an imprint of Cinder House Publishing Limited.

Print ISBN 9781915368881
ePub ISBN 9781915368898
Kindle ISBN 9781915368904

Cover design by Luke Bird / lukebird.co.uk
Typeset by Laura Jones-Rivera / lauraflojo.com

Printed and bound in Great Britain by
Clays Ltd, Elcograf S.p.A.

www.deadinkbooks.com

BIG TIME

JORDAN PROSSER

dead ink

For all my friends
Wherever they are

Maybe you'll make it
Maybe you won't
Maybe you deserve to
Maybe you don't
Maybe you'll stay here
But I promise if you go
The road ahead will swallow you whole, that's right
The road ahead will swallow you whole

– 'Big Time' by Julian Ferryman
  (Track 14, *THE MOTHERF*CKER MANIFESTO*)

PROLOGUE

On his last day in Colombia, Julian Ferryman killed a guy. Not a local, thank goodness – even Julian wasn't that inconsiderate a tourist. He didn't bother to find out who the man was – didn't rifle through his pockets, didn't even stop to call for help. Julian had been examining his left eye in the buckled metal mirror of a public restroom somewhere in downtown Medellín, peeling down his eyelid and tracing the bloody capillaries across the surface of his cornea, when the man lurched towards him from one of the stalls.

'You're him,' he rasped.

Julian smiled. Ignored. Turned away.

'You're him,' the man said again, reaching for Julian's shoulder. Julian had been in this part of the world long enough to know that guys like this weren't that uncommon. Separated from the rest of the lads. Stood up on a date. Too much coke, too much sun. Cut off by their parents. Couldn't handle the humidity. From the guy's strawberry-blond hair and lilting *r*'s, Julian figured Irish.

He batted him away, muttered a pretend apology. 'I don't think I am who you think I am.'

'Oh, but you are,' the man cooed in such a way that Julian had to pause for a moment to make sure they weren't acquainted.

'Take it easy,' Julian said as he made for the door.

The man's hand dropped firmly on his shoulder, and when Julian turned back, the fellow's pasty face seemed darker somehow. Spittle rimmed his sunburnt lips.

'You've seen it,' the man said, not letting go. 'You've seen what

BIG TIME

happens. I know, because – *I've seen you see it.*'

Seconds later he was on the tiles, a gash to his forehead leaking thin pink blood to a drain in the centre of the floor. It can happen that quickly. Slippery surfaces. Hangover brain. A push becomes a shove becomes a thud. That's when Julian could have stopped, and stooped, and checked, but didn't. Instead, he left, not knowing what became of the man. Did the lads find him, take him back to the hostel? Get him stitched up at a clinic, a shot of Ron Zacapa, that's that, right as rain? Did he come home from the trip, file a traveller's insurance claim, fire off a few photos of the head wound to prove it, years later sit back with arms crossed and a playful grimace as the story was recounted by the best man at his wedding to the young woman he put things on hold with right before he went away on that very same trip all those years ago?

No. He never came to. A mechanic on his walk home from a ten-hour shift found him there around sundown, skin cold, lips blue, blood like tree sap – dark, hard resin. The *policía* spent the night on the scene, canvassing the area, coming up short. The man was taken in a black polyvinyl bag to the local morgue, then the Irish Embassy. Rubber stamps moistened, phone calls made. Weeks later, an expensive repatriation flight in the cargo bay of a 737, stacked among the kayaks and the golf clubs and terrified, beady-eyed animals. A hometown funeral with a view of the Celtic Sea, tea and Jameson's at his mum's place afterwards. The young woman he put things on hold with right before he left, gazing out the window for a long, long time.

Julian finished the last of his cocaine on the way to the airport, bobbing around in the back seat of a cab. There was at least a quarter of a gram still in there, shaley stuff like mother of pearl. He alternated nostrils, digging it out with the spare key to his mother's empty apartment back home, then tonguing the bag and rubbing his gums. Then he nervously licked every peso in his wallet, remembering he'd had the bills up his nose just a few nights before and imagining an army of sniffer dogs waiting for him at the departure gates.

No sooner had Julian folded the wet notes back in his wallet than he was taking one out and drying it on his jeans to give to the driver, who was giving him a knowing look in the rear-view mirror.

JORDAN PROSSER

The cabbie's look reminded Julian of the girls he'd met the night after he got the gram off a friend of a friend of some local producer. When he'd offered them a bump, one of the local girls said he had no idea what cocaine had done to their country and stormed off. Julian had felt bad for about a minute – until the coke kicked in.

There were no sniffer dogs at the airport. He was waved straight through the check-in queue. A sleepy-eyed customs official stamped Julian's passport upside down, then he was on the plane. He could have kept the coke up his arse and saved it for home. It was so much better than the shit they got back home.

Trevor's the flight attendant stationed at the front of the economy cabin, always whipping the little velvet curtain separating business and economy back and forth like a bullfighter. During the safety demonstration, Julian's staring at Trevor's purple vest, his shiny wing-tipped name badge, his cow-licked hair, his pink shaving rash. With that quarter gram in him, Julian knows he's fixating a little, and Trevor keeps catching his eye. A few hours later, at thirty-nine thousand feet, Trevor slides a tiny tin-foil dinner onto Julian's tray table, along with a note saying to come and meet him down the aisle once the lights go out.

Julian finds him in the antechamber where the crew prepare meals, surrounded by those same velvet curtains. The light in there is almost UV blue.

'Did you dig Medellín?' Trevor asks in a Kiwi accent. Nasal, like he's from the country. A guy like Trevor probably didn't have too many friends in the remote New Zealand countryside.

Julian says: 'Yeah, but I went all over. Bogotá, Cartagena. Even Venezuela for a bit.'

'You're Australian,' Trevor remarks with a hint of surprise. 'Where from?'

'Melbourne.'

'Wowsers. You got out. And now you're going back?'

In Ciudad Bolívar, ten days earlier, Julian had received a message from his band's manager, Skinner. It said:

Beaches has gone platinum (!!) so Labyrinth wants to fast-track new album – Xander's little brother can sit in on sessions if ur not back in time. U well?

BIG TIME

Julian's immediate thought was that Xander's little brother was a total dickhead, so there was no fucking way he was going to let him sit in for him on the new album. With the last of his money, he bought a ticket on the first flight he could, from Medellín to Auckland. In Auckland he'd wait another twenty-four hours for one of the FREA's monthly, military-run repatriation flights to Melbourne, where he'd likely be the only soul on board.

'My band's recording a new album,' Julian says with a sniff, nonchalant.

'How cool is that?' Trevor grins, not letting on that he, too, has aspirations of stardom.

Julian sniffs again, trying to clear the drip at the back of his throat.

'I could tell you were still gacked when you got on the plane,' Trevor says. 'The stuff's real good over there, hey?'

'Yeah.' Julian shuffles his socked feet. He looks back down the aisle, thinking it might be weird if the two of them hang out too long.

'Don't worry,' says Trevor – the rest of the crew are asleep in their bunks. He always puts his hand up for the graveyard shift because the plane's dead quiet, everyone's got their eye masks on and everyone's loose with Ambien and herbal sleep remedies. He likes to get high and listen to the engines. Would Julian maybe like to get high too?

Julian shrugs like he's not fussed either way. Trevor says he's got a guy who works the repatriation flights to Botany, and that together they may have been personally responsible for bringing the first F to South America – maybe even anywhere outside of Australasia. Trevor reaches into his vest pocket and pulls out a glass vial with an eyedropper in it. He turns the vial in his hand and the liquid slips and pools about inside, oily and bright, rainbow-tinged like petrol. He offers it to Julian.

Julian says: 'After you.'

Suddenly, Trevor's beaming at Julian in his stovepipe jeans and loose-knit sweater and leather bangles. It's a big moment for a jaded country boy who still longs to be one of the band kids.

See, Trevor's realised that Julian doesn't even know what F is, so right now he feels like an intercontinental kingpin compared to this guy who got on the plane in Medellín with only a guitar case and a canvas duffel bag. Julian focuses on Trevor's sweat patches, his shaving rash, his cheap American Crew short back and sides, trying to concentrate on his flaws – but, whether Julian likes it or not, for the next few minutes Trevor the flight attendant will be his mentor. He says it comes mostly from far-north Cooksland – small bush towns, coastal communities with workable ports, old mining areas with disused airstrips. He says that locally you can get it quite cheap, a buy-local discount, which is nice for a change, seeing as how those charlatans (Trevor's word) in South America and the States have been marking up Australasia's coke supply by like 250 per cent since the 1960s. 'But that's the CIA for you.'

Outside the FREA, it's a different story. A priceless commodity. Rare as hen's teeth. Even though F's only been around about a year, Trevor says there's whole drug empires in North and Central America falling over themselves to get their hands on it. He keeps using the word *lucrative* and licking his lips which, to be fair, do look quite dry. That's why Trevor's decided to start smuggling the stuff. High risk, high reward. Trevor has grand plans, you see: places to go, things to be. He likes the graveyard shift, but he doesn't want to be working it forever. He wants to perform on huge stages. He wants to sit on couches and be quizzed by late-night talk show hosts. He wants to make his world much bigger than it is right now.

Julian's familiar with the kind of drug dealer Trevor represents – upper-middle-class squares who didn't smoke a joint until their twenties, clinging to the moral high ground while everyone around them snorted and huffed and fucked their way through uni. Then finally, when they caved one day, due to boredom, or peer pressure, or just a gradual and inevitable loosening of morals, it turned out they were actually a lot smarter and better adjusted than your average deadbeat pusher, so suddenly people higher up the ladder were choosing to work with them over anyone else, and these squares started climbing that ladder. They were guys who had functional relationships with their families. Guys who could do long division in their heads. They were HR managers, classical musicians, accountants, engineers, flight attendants in their forties wearing purple vests and Hush Puppies. Julian doesn't mind this kind of dealer, because their later-in-life arrogance tended to mean they gave you

BIG TIME

a lot of shit for free.

'One drop in both eyes,' Trevor says. 'Even if you decide to do more than that, it has to be the same amount in each. My Botany guy told me about a bunch of kids at a concert in Bassland – Wrecking Bones, is that the band? – anyway, these kids thought it would be fun to put five whole drops in their right eye only, and when they snapped back from their trip, they all needed microsurgery to physically untangle their optic chiasma.'

Julian processes this before asking: 'How long does it take to kick in?'

'Anywhere between thirty seconds and a couple of minutes, depending on your tolerance level,' which in Julian's case, Trevor cheerfully points out, is zero.

'And what's it feel like?' Julian asks, bracing himself for some rapturous exegesis on Trevor's legendary experiences with F.

But instead, the flight attendant asks: 'Why do you like to party?'

Julian hates it when people use that word like that – *party* – but he goes along with it. 'You mean in general?'

'Yeah.'

Julian stares impatiently at the vial while Trevor twirls it on his fingers, a miniature baton.

'It makes everything better,' Julian says. 'Cigarettes, sex, coffee, music, whatever you're doing that day. Even if you're not doing anything that day, it makes that better too.'

'And why's that?' Trevor asks.

'I dunno, man.'

'Sure you do.'

Julian scratches his stubble and hazards a guess: 'It helps you drop the fear. Helps you be in the moment.'

'Exactly!' Trevor snaps his fingers, and Julian worries for a moment that Trevor might want to be his friend after this. 'Your traditional high elicits an artificial sense of equanimity. Fulfilment in some cases. Enlightenment at most. Makes you feel like everything's going to be okay. But it's still artificial. You don't *know* that everything's going to be okay. Maybe nothing will ever be okay again! Maybe you're just fooling yourself.'

Julian shrugs. 'Maybe.'

'But what if you could know for sure?'

JORDAN PROSSER

'How's that?'

Trevor stops spinning the vial and holds it aloft. 'One drop in each eye. Then you should go back to your seat. Try to get there in thirty seconds or less, just in case. You don't want to be standing when it hits.'

'And when it does?'

'It's got some similarities to your garden-variety party drug,' Trevor says. 'But with F, that all happens really early and wears off really quick to make way for the main event. So you'll chew your cheeks. You'll get hot and cold flushes. You'll get goosebumps. You'll start to free-associate shapes, patterns, numbers and images. You'll hear things in layers and find intricate detail in objects where you might not have before. But that's why it's so important to take it through the eyes. The eyes are like a freeway to your brain, whereas your other orifices are … toll roads.' Trevor adds that another bunch of kids he heard about tried bombing it and shelving it in crystal form, but the results were mixed. Like, self-mutilation and internal haemorrhaging mixed.

'You don't take F so you can dance and fuck like a champ,' Trevor says. 'You take it for your brain. Like tuna.'

'Like what?'

'Tuna,' Trevor says. 'You know. Brain food.'

Julian tells him he doesn't eat fish.

Trevor says: 'The initial physical side effects can come and go in just a few moments before it all retreats to the brain. Like the ocean draining from a bay right before a tsunami.'

'And then what?'

'Then,' Trevor says, 'the tsunami.'

Trevor tells Julian: 'You're going to see outside yourself. You're going to see outside of *now*.' It doesn't even sound like he's trying to be showy here. 'Maybe you'll even see *everything*!' he says, then he laughs, like, *oh it's just so hard to explain!*

He tries it this way: 'Imagine that time is a needle on a graph, moving constantly forward at a fixed rate, scratching history on an endless ream of paper underneath it. The blank paper up ahead is the future. Where the needle's already been, that's the past. And where the needle is at any given microsecond is the present. But people talk about these three things – past, present, future – like it's an even three-way split when, really, the universe is cleanly cleft in two, with only the thinnest of boundaries in between. Compared to the relative infinities of past and future, the present barely exists. And it's constantly moving. Which is why *now* so often slips by unnoticed. We're building sandcastles while running on a treadmill!'

The UV blue dilutes with a whiter, calmer kind of light as the plane crosses into dawn.

Trevor extracts the eyedropper from the vial. 'F pauses the treadmill. Lets you skip ahead. Makes *now* a bigger place.' Trevor tilts back his chin and takes the dropper to his eyes, squeezing once above each, then blinking.

Julian asks: 'And what's the *F* stand for?'

Trevor smiles as his eyeballs shine. '*Future*. Duh.'

The two of them lurch gently as the plane fondles a pocket of turbulence. Trevor replaces the dropper in the vial and hands it over. 'Thirty seconds,' he says. 'Just to be safe.'

Trevor starts to back away through the curtains, leaving Julian with the vial, still half full.

'Wait – you sure?' Julian asks.

'Plenty more where that came from.' Trevor winks. 'Just make sure you ditch it before customs. *Viaje seguro*.'

Julian wasn't a big fan of people slipping foreign buzzwords into conversations like that – but Trevor had turned out to be not so bad after all. Plus, free shit. So whatever.

Alone in the velvet antechamber, Julian rests his head against one of the wall cabinets, pushes his body away, arches his back and tilts his eyes upwards. His arm hovers, and the technicolour juice shines at the end of the dropper.

If the needle on the graph, as Trevor had put it, were paused and expanded right then and there, Julian could have taken a lifetime telling you and me every detail of the moment right before he first experienced F: the drop swelling and softening as it breached his focal limit, the brilliant refraction of a dozen soft light sources ricocheting around inside it. Somehow, even above the A390's engines, he could faintly hear the sound it made splashing on his cornea, like a drop in an ocean on a world somewhere behind him. Then his skull starts to grow cold – not merely his head but the very bones beneath it – and he thinks about how rarely you get to sense your own bones.

Normally it's only when they're broken. Then Julian thinks he'd like to be able to stop and really appreciate this feeling, if only he weren't on such a strict timeline. He puts a drop in his other eye. The chill passes between his ears – *ice-cream headache* – and out through the base of his spine. His jaw clenches, grinding his fillings. The skin on his forearms prickles upwards and out. Already Julian's feeling a tiny little supernova in the centre of his solar plexus, and he imagines a steady whirring circuit-board powered by a million white rodents on a million metal hamster wheels, running and turning in perfect sync.

Should've started a timer, Julian's thinking. He fumbles with his watch, but the digits dance in front of him. He's only wasting time; it's already been at least ten seconds since his first drop. He yanks a velvet curtain aside and begins the long journey back to seat 46D.

Did I hurt that curtain? Do curtains hurt? Julian is perturbed by the thought. He wonders what its insides would look like if he slid it aside too violently and they came spilling out: more curtain? Five steps down the aisle, Julian encounters a holy great mess on the floor where someone's travel-sick toddler has heaved up a gutful of stewed apple. There are clothes, too: a baby's sock, surely the smallest sock ever to exist on Earth, resting at a very specific angle next to the strip lighting that runs along the aisle. Pinpoints of light like shining chalk, and this sock with its tiny, crooked elbow, like a human arm emerging from a well of half-digested apple and stain-resistant carpet.

Arms in the floor. What are the ramifications of this? His mind is reeling. This jumbo jet is towing around a secret aerial graveyard. It is packed so full of cadavers that their extremities have begun to breach the cabin floors. Fifteen seconds now. Julian thinks of the decades-old bullet holes he saw in the brick buildings on the outskirts of Medellín, the stories of whole families vanishing in the night. The bodies must be somewhere. People don't just disappear. *You have no idea what cocaine has done to this country.*

This all takes another second for Julian to process, then another second to realise he's processing it. The realisation of this processing takes at least another two, but by then Julian has decided it's necessary to carry out these complex sums while walking at the same time, so he focuses on his pelvic joint, knee, femur, hamstring, all the relevant lower accessories, and places one foot down, then mirrors that action

BIG TIME

on the other side, then repeats, and repeats, lurching his way back to seat 46D. He was in the habit of booking aisle seats in case there were cracks in the windows, invisible hairline defects overlooked by compliance staff in their high-vis vests, ready to shatter at just the right altitude and suck unwitting passengers into a hungry stratospheric vacuum. Not him. Not today. Julian Ferryman laughs as the carpet gently advances his body forward, a merciful ocean of tiny fingers, a divine travelator, and while he shambles, gurning, through porthole-sized pockets of azure pre-sun sunshine—

—would you like to know what's happening to his brain? I bet you would, but the science remains unclear. Minuscule amounts of the substance known as *trypto-lyside glutochronomine* have made their way overseas and been objectively analysed, but global peer-reviewed journals have all been blocked by AusNet. At home, government-sanctioned research has returned predictably vague results. One wannabe whistleblower, an ex-CSIRO public servant who was tasked with a cursory analysis of the drug for routine classification purposes, claimed the brainwave activity that F produced in rhesus monkeys most closely resembled the effects of a seismic, borderline-fatal epileptic event, but that the activity was isolated almost entirely to the right dorsolateral prefrontal cortex – the area of the brain concerned with the passage of time. There was barely any spillover into the wider frontal lobe or cerebellum – that is, until she upped the dosage by less than 3 per cent and the monkeys were dead in under a minute, pupils engorged, lips foamy. Knowing that the official channels – the state-owned newspapers, radio stations and television broadcasters – would find a way to bury or muddy her findings, the whistleblower was forced to disseminate them through that most loathed medium of rebellion telegraphy: handmade zines. She was promptly taken from her Darlington apartment and interned at Broken Hill. The next day those same state-owned media outlets announced that the 'rogue' scientist had partaken zealously of the illicit F she had been given to study, subsequently suffering a permanent psychotic break and killing the monkeys with her bare hands. *The National Telegraph* went so far as to suggest that she'd attempted to molest them first. Make of that what you will.

Either way, Julian really should have set that timer. Neither one of us could tell you how long it eventually took for him to find seat 46D, but somewhere in between those first drops of F and me telling you the rest of Julian's story, he will have found his seat and sat himself down, felt the humming, thrumming and bubbling pass, felt his teeth release his mangled cheeks, felt a cold vacuum start to collect and condense not simply in his own outer extremities but from the fringes of everything else as well, from all of it, from everywhere – he will have felt it gather and collapse in graceful slow motion like a piece of paper folded to infinity, folded over and over and over and over until it became a tiny shred of cosmic origami tucked away at the centre of his brain.

Then: tsunami.

In his last conscious moments in the *then*, Julian knew that Trevor had been right: the *now* in front of him was bigger than it had ever been, and it only kept growing, like an elastic landing strip. Whether or not Julian truly saw *everything* in that moment, as Trevor had promised he would, I can't say. I myself don't know what *everything* looks like so, no, I'm afraid I can't say.

But Julian did see something. In fact, he saw a lot. And now, let me tell you: this is what he saw.

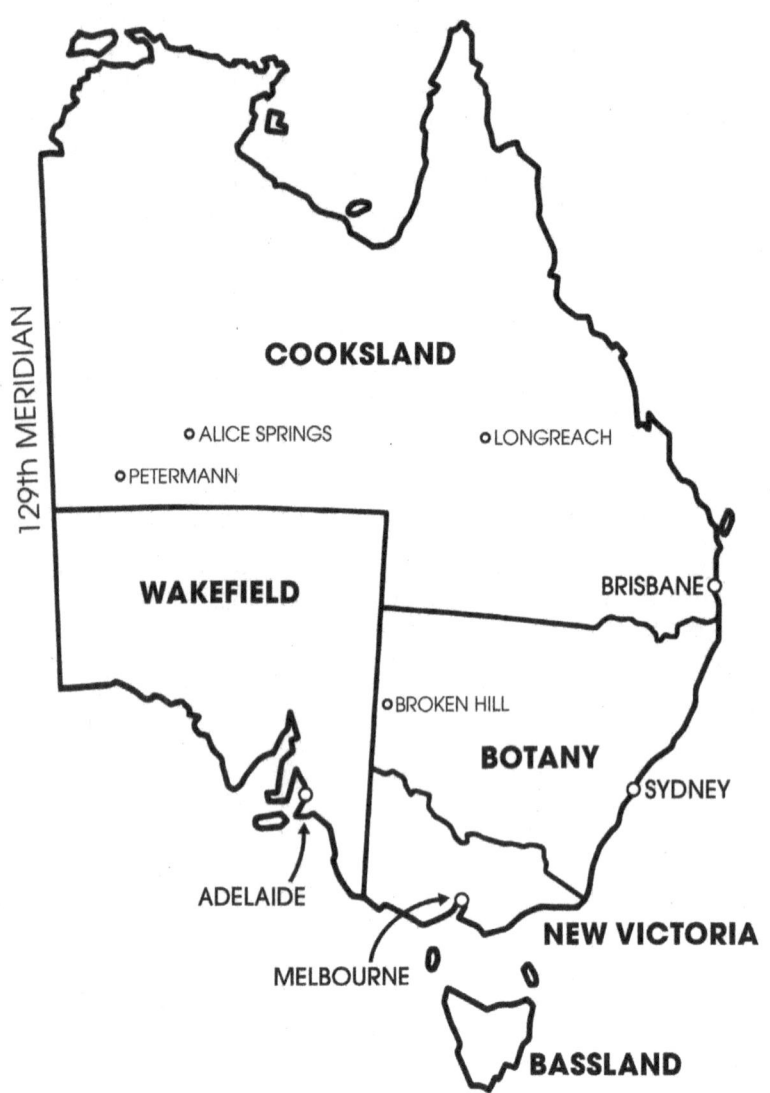

PART ONE

NEW VICTORIA

1

I'd really only met Julian a handful of times before he left for South America. We knew each other mainly through the music industry and mutual friends. We occasionally spoke at parties. I'd seen his band, the Acceptables, play a few times during the tour for their debut album, *Artificial Beaches on Every Mountain / Artificial Mountains on Every Beach*, and written them a good review. Mostly I knew about Julian in relation to Oriana and their on-again, off-again thing. I'd gone to school with Oriana Devereaux. We were close as kids. She came as Peter Pan to my tenth birthday party, and I went as a Minion to hers. She was the coolest girl I ever knew. I never understood what she liked about Julian.

But through the ages, the task has often fallen to good people, sidelined by history, to tell the stories of those lifted up by dumb luck and circumstance. And thus, the task of telling this story – the story of Julian Ferryman, of the Acceptables' sophomore album, of the ill-fated First Annual International Chronophenomenology Summit, of the fate of the Federal Republic of East Australia, and of *THE MOTHERF*CKER MANIFESTO* – falls to me.

There's a house party the day after Julian gets home. Red beer cups and a tub full of ice. Parquetry floors a patchwork of sticky sneaker soles. Hair ties on doorknobs and a spiked punch bowl.

Xander's little brother's saying: 'The women in my head have started to act like porn stars.' This is the dickhead Julian didn't want sitting in for him on the new album, and I'm sure you can see

BIG TIME

why. 'I blame AusNet,' he goes on, and a few heads bob in rueful agreement. 'Before AusNet,' he says, 'you had unlimited choice in the pornographic market. And that meant you had the ability to cleanse your palate and temper your darker urges with something more tame and respectable. Have a salad with your steak. But now, with AusNet, the only stuff you get under-the-counter is what smugglers and black-market weirdos *think* guys like us like – and I can tell you, they clearly have a pretty low opinion of us as consumers. I'm talking some of the nastiest, most twisted fucking stuff I've ever seen. I mean, I used to dig around, sure. I explored the four corners of the FreeNet while I could, to calibrate my tastes, and I did so successfully. Whereas now, all that's available to me is one singular corner, the corner where I only used to go if I was feeling really … what's the word? Impure, maybe. Something along those lines. The pirated shit you get these days, man … everything's *forced*. Forced blowjobs. Forced anal. *Skull fucking*. Like, you can't even refer to a person by their skin anymore, they want you to fuck a skeleton. It makes me sick. But hey. What am I gonna do?'

One of Xander's little brother's even younger friends chips in: 'Just don't look at that shit, man. If it's so horrible.'

'But that's what I'm saying, man,' says Xander's little brother. 'It's been so long since I watched anything above-board, like just some good, level-headed stuff, that now when I close my eyes, everything's hardcore. I can't even get off anymore without it being strange and violent. Sometimes I remember what I used to think about when I was younger. I used to think about the first girl I was crushing on in high school. I had this whole fantasy mapped out where our families ran into each other up at Batemans Bay, like, we were just accidentally holidaying in the same spot so we had the whole summer together, and even though she was always a little too cool to talk to me when we were at school – because she was in the year above me, see – when it was just the two of us, we really got to know each other. And then the night before her family went home, we went walking along the beach and when I turned around she was taking off her shirt. And then I was taking my clothes off, too, awkward as fuck. And she lays me down on the sand and we do it really softly, and part of the charm is that we're both unsure. And this is all in my head – this is before I'd ever even *had* sex, but this was how I was imagining it. I could even picture what the moon looked like. I was jerking off thinking about the fucking moon! You know what I get when I close my eyes these days? You know what's available to me? Jizzing in people's fucking eyeballs. Horrible, horrible, horrible shit. But hey. What am I gonna do?'

Another voice pipes up over the top of a plastic tumbler: 'Isn't Batemans Bay a work camp now?'

'Not the point,' says Xander's little brother, scratching his head, wondering how long he's been talking and whether he's said too much. He certainly didn't anticipate sharing so much with so many, but he's been drinking since 3 pm. 'It is, yes, but that's not the fucking point.'

Xander moseys over, saving his little brother from himself. 'You seen Julian?' he asks.

'Julian? Julian's back?'

'Apparently,' Xander says, taking the dregs of his beer into his mouth.

'Fuck,' the little brother goes. 'I was really hoping I could sit in for him.'

'We'll see,' says Xander, raising his eyebrows. His eyebrows say: no-one's even spoken to Julian in a year, so who knows if he's up to it. The one time they heard from him, via a heavily coded, heavily redacted postcard, he was in a boat off the coast of Panama, snorting coke that cost less than bottled water.

The scene, so to speak, now that I have a moment to set it, is Xander and Xander's little brother's parents' place in North Fitzroy. One of those warehouse renos where they kept the heritage-listed façade, but gutted the place and rebuilt the insides. With their parents at a legal conference in Cooksland, Xander and his little brother accepted their solemn duty as early adult miscreants and announced a house party. The text went out at 7 pm, the keg was flowing by 7:15.

'Same with music though, right?' says one of Xander's little brother's uni friends. 'Like, what you were saying about under-the-counter stuff. There's what you're getting fed commercially – which is basically trash – or there's what you can buy on the down-low, where there's zero quality control. There's this whole world in the middle you're missing out on.'

BIG TIME

Xander, only half listening, teases this out: 'Trash, huh?'

Xander's little brother's uni friend freezes up. 'Shit. No, I didn't mean—'

'It's cool. I'm fucking with you. Art's subjective. Or whatever.' Xander lurches off in search of more beer.

The Acceptables had formed about three years before this. At the start, it was just Ash and Julian. They met in third-year law, started swapping bootlegs of old Bloc Party and Killers and Yeah Yeah Yeahs albums, and were soon blowing off Criminal Law and Procedure B to jam in Ash's parents' basement. Julian could play both guitar and bass, but after Xander Plutos, who could play only guitar, joined by private invitation from Ash, Julian was relegated to bass – the first of many real or imagined transgressions against him. Tammy Tedeski rounded out the foursome on drums, having impressed Ash as a one-woman percussion unit at an underground rap battle series he frequented. The group's first album, *Artificial Beaches on Every Mountain / Artificial Mountains on Every Beach*, came about pretty naturally. Ash had songs. Julian had songs. Xander's guitar work was admittedly very good. They made space for solos from him, some flashy drum fills from Tammy, and on top of his songwriting credits, Julian nabbed a couple of bass lines that the DJ who introduced their first radio play had dubbed 'borderline iconic'. Which they weren't. Look, speaking to you from where I am now, all I can offer is my honest opinion: *Artificial Beaches on Every Mountain / Artificial Mountains on Every Beach* was a treacly, piecemeal, one-shouldered shrug of an album. The strained playground melodies of early-century glam-rock with the fuzzed-out wannabe arena musings of end-stage U2, all undergirded by a cavalcade of lyrics with the poetic and political aspirations of a diabetes prevention pamphlet you might absent-mindedly slide out of a wall-bracket in a GP's waiting room.

Here's the track-listing:

1. Artificial Beaches on Every Mountain
2. How U Move Me (feat. GAZELLE)
3. What Time Is Your Heart
4. Miracle Boy
5. Genevieve

6. Blueberry Afternoons
7. Fast Then Slow
8. Good Problem 2 Have
9. Artificial Mountains on Every Beach
10. Thief!!
11. What Time Is Your Heart (reprise)

And if I had to sum up the album's artistic credentials in one verse, it would be this, from the lead single 'What Time Is Your Heart':

What time is your heart
It's quarter to three
What time is your heart
Time for you and me
Ooh-ooh-wee
Ooh-ooh-wee

The liner notes simply state, *All tracks written by A Huang and J Ferryman*, so sadly we'll never know which one of them to thank for this particular lyrical gem. But hey, what do I know? Limpid indie nü-pop is a perfectly valid genre if you're looking for legal airplay and a record deal in an otherwise culture-snuffing kleptocracy. One live (entirely papered) gig and a homemade demo tape was all it took to get the Acceptables in with Labyrinth Records. The album was recorded in a week and their radio reign began the month after (not that hard when there's only three stations nationwide). A smattering of newspaper and magazine coverage, some guest hosting on weekend morning television, and a primetime spot during *Carols by Candlelight*. This was what constituted rock'n'roll stardom in the Federal Republic of East Australia.

So Xander you've met. Permanent purple circles under his eyes, jeans shredded to shit, platinum rings on each knuckle so chunky it's a wonder he could finger any chord at all. The only thing that made Xander more angry than the insane privilege with which he'd grown up was his parents' total cluelessness of his rebellion against it. They politely turned up at every Acceptables gig, nodding along in the

BIG TIME

front row. They framed the band's tour posters and kept a scrapbook of their media appearances. When 'Miracle Boy' played during Xander's father's favourite breakfast radio program on VIX 106.6, he came home that afternoon beaming, saying it was all the other blokes at the firm had talked about all day. The runaway success and mainstream popularity of *Beaches* might have been the worst thing that ever happened to Xander (until the bus ride to Botany in a few months' time – but we'll get to that).

Over at the keg, that's Tammy. Two black teeth and a shock of red hair skirting dangerously close to white-girl dreadlocks. During the *Beaches* tour, Skinner had embarked on a number of gentle conversations with her about the band's image, her own personal brand – and her personal hygiene. Tammy's answer was to walk onstage the next day wearing her actual pyjamas, carrying a meatball sub. Skinner shut up after that. No-one in the band had ever been to Tammy's house. I'm not sure anyone even knew where she lived. She wore a lot of camo and tactical vests, which Julian guessed was just cheap, army surplus stuff, but others suspected were hand-me-downs from her brothers, who'd been kicked out of the special forces.

Who else? Skinner's around somewhere. Bald, sweaty, bespectacled. An ex-fascist who's spent his forties getting inappropriate chest tattoos laser-removed and nervously making up for falling in with the wrong crowd at an early age. After landing a desk job at Labyrinth thanks to a friend of a friend nearly seven years ago, and spending most of that time tabulating paltry royalty cheques and sitting through unwatchable EP launches at the Grace Darling Hotel, he just happened to be at the right place at the right time: the Acceptables' demo tape landed on *his* desk. He brought it to the head of the label and had been embedded with the band ever since. With the news that Labyrinth wanted to fast-track their follow-up album (working title: *In the End It's All Okay, and If It Ain't Okay, It Ain't the End*), Skinner had been hovering around even more than usual – early-morning phone calls, late-night drop-ins – making sure everyone was ready for what promised to be a marathon recording stint.

In fact, here's Skinner now, scanning the living room while Xander's little brother talks his ear off. Xander's little brother, whose real name is Peter, but everyone calls Pony, goes wherever Xander goes. He might as well be included in the band's rider. He's spent the last year boning up on bass, not-so-secretly hoping that Julian would extend his South American sabbatical indefinitely. Other than that, you don't need to worry about Pony too much. He won't be around very long.

Anyway, just as Pony's thinking now's the perfect time to pitch Skinner one of his own solo projects, Skinner cuts him off and heads for the dining room. Ash has arrived.

A light 'Heyyy!' goes up from the crowd as Ash slips in, exchanging some handshakes, miming a small salute. A drink gets handed to him, which happens pretty much everywhere he goes. Frontman and foreman of the Acceptables, and the only child of wealthy, upwardly mobile immigrants, Ash is a label executive's platonic ideal of music industry stardom: handsome (but uniquely so), stylish (but not aggressively so), sexual (but not explicitly so) and talented (but not unmanageably so). There's a secret file in the label boss's desk drawer at Labyrinth HQ with a timeline for how long it might feasibly take to extricate Ash from the rest of the band and repackage him as a solo artist: ASH (all caps). Market research paints an unkind picture of the band's other members: uncultivated amateurs who only serve to mute Ash's indelible and indisputable mass appeal.

Ash barely makes it to the kitchen before Skinner's in his ear. 'Hello, Ash. Hello, matey. Have you seen him?'

'I just got here, Skinner.' Ash is smiling at someone up on the landing. He learnt a long time ago that there was no need to look directly at Skinner while speaking to him.

'Right, of course. Just thought I'd see how you're feeling about it all. Quick temperature check. What about Oriana?'

'What about her?'

'Is she coming tonight?'

'She's already here.'

Skinner removes his glasses to wipe the sweat from his eyebrows. Skinner's led a pretty motley life, done some pretty fucked-up things, and is no shrinking violet. But when he stands close to Ash, Skinner feels a quiet ache he's never felt before, a feeling it took him the entire period of *Beaches*' recording and touring to properly identify: standing next to Ash, he feels deeply un-beautiful.

BIG TIME

'Hey,' Ash says, 'want to see my new tattoo?'

Skinner almost swallows his tongue. Ash rolls his sleeve up past the elbow and twists his arm towards the light. Under a strip of cling-wrap, a black band of serif letters reads: *FREE TAIWAN*.

'WOW,' says Skinner.

'Yeah, Tammy put me on to this guy who does this really beautiful line work. Mostly political stuff.'

'WOW,' says Skinner.

Tammy appears, spreading the cling-wrap with her fingers to get a better look. 'Sick.'

'It is,' Skinner stammers. 'It is sick. It would be remiss of me not to remind you, though, that bodily alteration of any kind is technically a violation of your contract with Labyrinth. *Technically*. Personally, I love the tattoo. I used to have plenty myself, as you know, so I can certainly appreciate the artistry. Not to mention that I did, in fact, go to Taiwan once. So I sympathise with the cause. Beautiful place, beautiful people. So I sympathise. Nevertheless …'

'What are you doing here, Skinner?' Tammy asks.

'Running interference,' posits Ash.

Skinner forces a laugh and Tammy offers him her cup. 'Relax, man. Want a drink?'

The last time Skinner had a beer was during the secession night riots. He'd been drinking for almost forty-eight hours straight when the pub he'd taken shelter in was firebombed by a roaming gang of pro-WRA agitators. As he tried to escape, his synthetic pleather jacket had melted in the heat and fused with the flesh from his shoulders to his tailbone. He woke up a week later in a pop-up hospital in Sunbury with a fresh skin-graft replacing 73 per cent of the tissue on his back.

'No, thank you,' is all Skinner says. Tammy necks the beer instead.

'Tam,' Ash says quietly. 'Oriana's off somewhere. You got anything on you?'

'Mm-mm,' Tammy hums in the negative. 'Maybe Wesley?' And she stabs her chin over at me.

Yes, hello. That's me in the kitchen, leaning against the bench, speaking pugnaciously about Hollywood's debt to Jodorowsky to anyone who'll listen. While I'd only met Julian a few times, like I said, I had plenty of overlap with the rest of the Acceptables. Tammy and I dated once, ages ago, with things ending amicably. (No, even I never went to her house.) Xander, who was a bit older, had studied engineering with my brother for a couple of years. And I'd always liked Ash. After I filed that good write-up of their show at the Corner, very early on in the *Beaches* tour, Ash enjoyed keeping me around. I was a textbook enabler, always willing to follow him to whatever party or down whatever drug-fucked hole he planned on diving into. Especially when it came to F.

F had arrived in New Victoria during the Acceptables' downtime between albums, creeping its way from the deserts of far-north Cooksland slowly down the eastern seaboard. Ash in particular had developed a real taste for it and claimed that much of the material on *In the End It's All Okay, and If It Ain't Okay, It Ain't the End* – on which he was to be the only credited songwriter – was inspired by his encounters with the new drug.

Skipping ahead on F is a markedly different experience for everybody. Some people see their future in first person. Others say they can see themselves in the room. Others say they can leave their own selves behind and explore the wider world, unmoored, a spectre in time. For some, it's a full sensory experience – smell and sound, taste and temperature. For others it's a sequence of images like a Rorschach test, tableaus and friezes that might only make sense once you're out the other side. I've seen people snap out of their F-states and move like automatons, dutifully fulfilling every movement and mannerism required by their future selves. Others come to and just sit there, watching the world move past for what feels like the second time, recognising everything as it happens, letting their high play out as a form of passive, ecstatic déjà vu. In rare instances, people are still able to move even while they're under, their bodies chronologically separated from their brains, lumbering involuntarily towards reunion. With so many variables, it meant experimentation was rife; my friend Mia was particularly fond of F-centric chemsex. She would instruct her partner to go down on her shortly after she skipped ahead, foresee her own orgasm, then snap back in the middle of that very same orgasm. Mia speculated that seeing her future-self climax was what made her present-self climax. Self-fulfilling indeed.

BIG TIME

Some people trust the visions. Swear by them, even. They believe that these are their hunches brought to life, keen gut instinct made real and actionable. To that end, fortunes have been gambled, houses have been remortgaged, lives and livelihoods have been lost. You'll see a dozen slack-jawed F-heads lounging by the racetrack on any given day, heads lolling stupidly, pupils the size of meteors, silently watching their horses betray them.

But on the other hand, millions have been made. Lives saved and freak accidents averted. A junkie in a housing complex in Penrith snapped back from their F-state and immediately reached one long arm out the window, catching in mid-air a ten-month-old child who had fallen from the window of another unit six storeys above.

Then there was the question of tolerance.

I remember one night about nine months earlier. I'd been given a vial of the stuff by an old friend from my film school days. I was drinking beers with my housemates – Cleo Tigere, a fine artist; and Kyle Fennessy, a law intern – in the dingy courtyard where we spent most of our time together. Cleo enjoyed chewing dexies while sunbathing naked, and Kyle was a world-class pothead. But this was the first time any of us had ever tried F, so we were tentative at first. We splashed the juice on our fingers and dabbed it on our eyeballs manually, too scared the eyedropper might over-deliver the first dose (we'd heard about those poor fucks at that Wrecking Bones concert in Bassland). A person's F threshold, we discovered, was largely determined by the same common biological factors that dictated their tolerance for drink and other drugs. Which is to say: height, weight, age, metabolism, brain chemistry. Cleo's hardy, but small; it kicked in quick, and by her estimate she might have seen three to five minutes into the future. For her, it was fairly abstract – colours and shapes, she said. She tried taking more, tried to skip ahead as far as ten minutes, but she developed such a headache that she had to smoke a joint and go lie down in her windowless bedroom. This left me and Kyle, who's bigger than me in every direction – but I was piss-fit in a way he could only imagine. For years I'd been drinking red wine for breakfast, staying up until 6 or 7 am with one hand on a keyboard and the other in a desk drawer rattling with Modafinil. So I had the edge on him there.

JORDAN PROSSER

On our third or fourth drop we resolved to simply sit, facing the wall clock through the kitchen window, and report what time we'd seen the moment before we snapped back to the present. Kyle came back with 1:33 am – a good twelve minutes. But I came back with 1:41. We went another round – 1:57 and 2:23 respectively. I was gaining. Growing a muscle I didn't know I had. Ever since that night, it seemed the more I took, the further I could see. Mind you, my regular vision was getting worse. My optometrist even had to up my prescription.

There are bad trips, sure. One day we had to call Cleo an ambulance, mid-sunbathe. She'd skipped ahead and fallen into a seizure. But the close calls, the migraines, the double vision, the brain zaps – we believed it was all worth it. A moment stolen from tomorrow is worth a hundred paid out today.

Rumours abound, and reports vary. AusNet makes it hard to verify things. But one urban myth has persisted, about a man living in what used to be Byron Bay. A mystic of some kind, who claimed to be able to skip ahead days, even weeks. People flocked to see him, waiting outside his home to hear what the future held. But even mystics get greedy, so soon a week wasn't enough. He trained his brain. He clamped his eyelids open and developed a diluted F solution that allowed for constant, low-dose delivery. He started spending more time in the *then* than the *now*. He would be out for days, only stopping back for a minute or two to report on what he'd seen. His acolytes cleaned his shit off the floor and attached an intravenous feeding system to one frail limb. Rumour says, he woke up to say he'd seen summer and winter switch hemispheres, conservatively putting him some thirteen thousand years in the future. People wanted to hear what would happen between now and then, but he said there was still more to see. So he went under again, trying to find his way back to that future Earth on its unbalanced axis. But he never woke up, so no-one heard any more. Rumour says, despite the undertaker's best efforts, the mystic's eyes refused to be closed. A posthumous protest, having seen so much.

Rumour says, with enough F, you can see to the end of time.

*

BIG TIME

Just upstairs, at this very party, there's a bedroom full of loveable psychonauts committed to testing the duration and veracity of their visions. A simple case study with fairly few variables. The experiment is straightforward: four people sit in a circle and microdose F at the exact same time. Another person is designated timekeeper. Another person is there to take notes. And another person spins a bottle. This was all Oriana's idea and, in fact, she's there with them now.

It was Oriana who first thought of repurposing those little perfume samplers you get at department stores by filling them with F. Atomising the drug ensured a gentle, even layer across the eye; no more head tilting, no more eyedrops, no more uneven doses. And, discovered in a pocket or a handbag, they appeared relatively innocuous. Oriana had always had a knack for bootlegging.

The timer starts. The four subjects spray once in the left eye and once in the right. Then they put on blindfolds and make themselves comfortable. The notetaker notes the moment at which the drug kicks in for each of them. This is easy to spot: the shivers, the jitters, the mumbles. Then the tsunami. Once every subject is under, the spinner spins the bottle. Then everybody waits.

That's the real headfuck when it comes to skipping ahead: like me and Kyle watching our kitchen clock, it's not a 1:1 ratio. It doesn't take you two minutes on F to see two minutes into the future. I'd gotten to about 1:7 – pretty good, I thought. Some of the people here upstairs were batting 1:10. Some lucky fuckers, like that old mystic I suppose, skip ahead for one minute and snap back raving about next week. Age, height, weight, metabolism, tolerance, brain chemistry. Dumb luck and circumstance. As for Julian, well – we'll get to Julian. So, you've got four people under. The bottle comes to rest.

This time, it comes to rest pointing at Ludlow Reid, subject 1.

The notetaker notes this down. Ludlow's the Acceptables' official photographer, fond of ironic T-shirts and unfiltered cigarettes.

The timekeeper says: 'Two minutes, thirty seconds.'

Cleo's subject 2. She snaps back and coughs. This is normal. Your lungs are suddenly breathing air from a different point in time. Your brain's the one doing the travelling, sure, but it still takes a moment for everything else to re-adjust. Cleo's cough does seem particularly rough, though.

Blindfold still on, she wheezes: 'Ludlow.' She's telling everyone what she saw.

The notetaker notes this down.

Subject 3 is a guy named Raiph. There's not much point getting to know him. He sits up with a cough, shakes out his limbs and says: 'Ludlow.'

The notetaker notes this down. Oriana smiles.

The timekeeper says: 'Three minutes, thirty seconds.'

Subject 4 is Felicia 'Fizz' Hansen – we studied film together before I switched to journalism, but we never got along. I find her stuff too parochial, too patriotic, and she thinks I'm an insufferable dilettante. Anyway, Fizz coughs, then grins confidently as she says: 'It's me.'

A deviation. A few eyebrows tweak around the room. The timekeeper says: 'Four minutes—'

Then Ludlow snaps back, gasping for air, a hacking cough in their throat caught somewhere between *now* and *then*.

'It's me,' they say. 'It's me. But—'

Oriana takes Ludlow's face in her hands and slides her lips on to theirs, prying their mouth open with a dark tongue and feeling her way inside.

When she withdraws, Ludlow finishes their sentence: 'But Ash is about to walk in.'

Ash walks in. It's not the first time he's interrupted one of Oriana's experiments, and he doesn't bat an eye. 'Babe,' he says. 'Julian's coming.'

The timekeeper calls: 'Time.'

The notetaker notes this all down.

Cleo, Raiph and Fizz slip off their blindfolds. Oriana's still holding Ludlow's face between her fingers.

'Interesting,' says Cleo. 'Nice,' says Raiph.

'Fuck!' says Fizz, whose visions often seemed particularly off-base. She'd fractured her coccyx stage-diving at a Mandibles concert a few months back, having foreseen the crowd jubilantly catching her and safely depositing her on her feet. They hadn't.

This is what all of Oriana's experiments, no matter how amateur, were testing: were these premonitions or hallucinations? Constant or variable? Personal or collective? The distance you could see into

BIG TIME

the future was one factor, the length of real time it took you to see it was another, but by far the most pressing concern of even the most casual F user was the truthfulness of what they'd seen.

This round: three correlating results and one deviation. A 75 per cent success rate. Some nights were better, other nights were worse. Oriana wanted to understand how this could be. She wanted new conditions, new variables and new subjects. She wanted to know if it was possible for one participant's visions to influence or negate another's. Oriana wanted many things.

Years after all of this – somewhere very near the end of my own life – I received a contraband copy of *THE MOTHER-F*CKER MANIFESTO* from a sympathetic guard at the Broken Hill Detention Centre. I rolled my eyes at the thought of Julian's mawkish balladry sweeping through the FREA, maybe even back across the meridian out west, too. I listened to it a dozen times on an old record player one of my bunkmates had restored with stolen copper wiring, trying to make sense of it. Listening for something hidden in the lyrics, imagining that if I listened hard enough, I might hear Oriana's whispered voice in the background, sense her influence in the margins. Why, after all these years, was this album being released now? I pored over the liner notes. There were black-and-white photos of Julian, thin and bearded, posing in a deserted outback housing development, squinting in the sun. There were handwritten lyrics, xeroxed and blurry, the incoherent scribblings of a man who believes his every nascent thought holds a wealth of artistic merit. There was a short list of thank yous and acknowledgements (where he neglected to mention me). But nothing too out of the ordinary. Then I took the vinyl itself and held it up so its black grooves caught the light, and finally, it all made sense. I've had a lot of time to reflect out here, and I keep returning to one magical irony: for the only F-abstainer among us, Oriana might have seen the furthest of us all.

'Hey, Wes,' Oriana says to me, leaning back against the kitchen sink. I tell her that even HR Giger's *Alien* designs owed a debt to the French comic book artist Mœbius, and she says she knows, because I've told her before. Oriana says I'm a high-functioning alcoholic purely because it would be too embarrassing to be a low-functioning one.

JORDAN PROSSER

Ash hands her a vodka on ice, Tammy a beer, Skinner a soda water and me a glass of wine, and for a moment we watch a fight that's broken out in the backyard. Melbourne rich kids, Grammar kids with polo shirts and meth-head mullets. Big shoes, big cars, small dreams. Fuck knows what they had to scrap about.

Xander and his little brother squeeze in beside the pantry. Cleo's listening at the kitchen counter. Fizz hovers by the fridge. Ludlow puts a tray of potato gems in the oven, and the unofficial band huddle begins.

Tammy asks how they knew that Julian was coming. Nobody was sure who'd actually started the rumour.

'Has anyone even heard from him since that postcard from Panama?' Xander asks.

'I received one more after that,' Skinner says.

'Fuck you,' says Xander. 'When did that rat fuck send *you* a postcard?'

'A few weeks ago? It was a bit bent, also heavily redacted, but he said he'd booked flights. He sounded upbeat.'

Of course, Skinner wasn't being entirely honest; there was no second postcard. Skinner had a FreeNet burner phone he'd been using to check in with Julian periodically over the past twelve months, hoping to soften the blow when Julian came home and realised his own band had essentially tried to oust him.

'But will he *remain* upbeat?' I ask. 'Will he be upbeat about ... everything?' I'm waving my wineglass like a magical wand of context. 'Everything', of course, meant: the new album (conceived in secret), the musical arrangements (light on bass), the lyrics (with one sole credit) – and it meant Ash and Oriana.

Ludlow catches my drift. 'Yeah, I mean ... does he know about ... *everything* everything?'

'He knows,' Oriana says, kissing Ash on the temple. (She knew about Skinner's burner phone and had asked him to relay the information months ago.)

Pony suggests that the sessions for the new album are going to suck. He, like his older brother, loathes interpersonal tension, despite both of their abilities to generate a lot of it. Xander repeats something everybody there already knows: 'You worked your fucking arse off on these arrangements, Ash. So he can't just swan in and expect

BIG TIME

to have a say in everything the way he used to.'

'Nope,' says Pony.

'I mean he can't just rock up and expect things to be, like, the same.'

Skinner says: 'No, absolutely. And I think that, after we've had the chance to touch base and catch up, read the temperature, all our temperatures, had a chance to read the room, as it were, then maybe there'll be a frank conversation to be had.'

Again, Skinner's hedging. Labyrinth had made it very clear to him that at this stage, before they were ready to pull the trigger on ASH, a personnel change was to be avoided at all costs. You had to *earn* the sort of in-fighting and personal division that defined so many famous rock outfits. You couldn't just take it for a spin one album in. Labyrinth said it would make it hard for audiences to forge a 'meaningful association' with the band, compromising all the hard-earned good will from the first album. What this really meant was: they'd printed a hell of a lot of merch, and Julian's face was on it.

'We just have to stand behind the music,' Ash says. 'Simple as that. We have to say, yes, it's a new direction, but an important one. Right?'

'Totally,' says Xander, happy to have allegiances laid out so clearly.

'Absolutely,' says Pony, not really included in the question but keen to voice his support anyway.

'You're the frontman,' Tammy says.

'And Skinner's got our back,' affirms Ash, slapping Skinner on the shoulder. 'Plus – the label loves us.'

'They do,' Skinner says, happy to reiterate this much at least. 'More than merely Acceptable, they find you *essential!*' He's made this joke before.

'Cheers,' says Ash.

Everyone echoes, 'Cheers,' clinking their glasses. Then Oriana says: 'Julian.'

Because Julian is walking straight towards her, shoving Xander aside and crossing the kitchen floor, reaching for Oriana's wrist and grabbing it, slapping Ash away as he tries to intervene, ignoring Cleo's shouting and my loud *whoa whoa whoa*s, then pulling Oriana down to the tiled floor seconds before an ornate terracotta pot comes sailing through the windows above the sink.

JORDAN PROSSER

The glass shatters, the pot shatters. The clay cracks the floor tiles and dirt spills everywhere. Outside, one of the Grammar kids howls, 'Oh, shit!' and does a runner.

Oriana looks at the broken pot on the floor, unafraid. Oriana was very rarely afraid, preferring, whenever possible, to be curious instead. She looks up at Julian, who she met half a decade ago backstage at a battle of the bands competition and had loved almost immediately, but now has not seen for an entire year, and says: 'You saw.'

'Fucking hell,' Xander gripes, slipping about on the soil. 'You know how to make an entrance, don't you, mate?'

'Hey, Xan,' says Julian. 'Hey, everyone.'

Tammy goes in for a hug. 'Good to see you, man.' Ash says: 'Hey, Jules.'

Julian turns to him. They're sizing each other up for just a brief moment. Then they hug, delivering a couple of sturdy wallops to each other's backs, and the whole kitchen exhales.

This was the last house party any of the Acceptables would ever go to. Where blokes scaled the walls in the alleyway outside just to sit on the roof and get a view of the moon. Where girls on homemade acid gripped the walls of the 1970s bathroom, shrieking as the patterned tiles spread and bled before their eyes. Where Ludlow floated from room to room, snapping polaroids while handing out potato gems and spring rolls and curry puffs and mini meat pies. Vegan treats. East Meets West. Someone brought a panettone, two months before Christmas, and it got handed around and nibbled on sparingly before being repurposed as a football. Condom wrappers were fumbled in upstairs bedrooms and spilt beer was hastily absorbed via paper towel from Persian rugs. Poetry was read around backyard candlelight and vomit was swallowed mid-sentence. Out of everybody there, Skinner was the oldest, which meant he was most liable to know: if you ever find yourself wondering when *it* will happen, that means you're most likely in *it* already. The life that you've imagined is the life you currently have – stop looking ahead and start looking around. The party you were promised, the adulthood you craved, you're in the thick of them. Right now. You're already here.

BIG TIME

That night at Xander and Xander's little brother's parents' place – that was the youngest, sweetest and freest we would ever be.

Julian's talking to Cleo, who he's always had a furtive crush on, even when he was with Oriana. Our secret joke about Cleo is that one day she'll make a terrific rich old lady. Youth is wholly wasted on her. To see Cleo with a crop of short dyed hair, some flowing black calico robes, a pair of asymmetrical glasses and an ivory cane, berating the valet at some fundraising dinner would feel like a beautiful prophecy come true. Things being as they are, she's uncomfortable in her skin. Ideas too big for her body. A mouth too slow for her mind. Cleo wishes she didn't have to 'talk' to 'people' to 'explain' what she 'feels' – but sadly, it remained the foremost method.

Cleo recently got a grant from the Department of Transport, Infrastructure, Fisheries and Culture, but she's having second thoughts about her project.

'It's a video work titled *Self-Portrait Watching Titanic (Backwards)*. A self-portrait because I'm interested in watching the watcher. And *Titanic* because it's one of the defining entries in late-twentieth-century cinema, sort of the zenith of the artistry that emerged in the 1970s. And backwards because if you play a film backwards, there's no copyright infringement.'

Julian thinks she means that the audience for the piece is watching the entirety of the 1997 film *Titanic*, played backwards. Cleo explains that, no, the audience is watching *her* watch *it*.

'But it does go for the entire duration of *Titanic*. Three hours and fourteen minutes.'

'Cool,' says Julian, suddenly a little less than present in the conversation. He's noticed Oriana eyeing him off from the kitchen.

'And I'll be eating popcorn. And sour straps. And drinking a huge lemonade. Just stuffing my fucking face. That's what people used to do at the movies: just gorge. A feast for the eyes. A feast for the senses. A feast for the gut. Salt and sugar and artificial colouring and artificial flavouring and artificial people and artificial emotion. Melodrama! It's dead now. Now it's all social realism. But it used to be a thing.'

'So when are you making this … piece?' Julian asks.

'Fucked if I know,' Cleo says. 'Fucked if I can find a copy of *Titanic* anywhere. Not even backwards. It's old media, y'know? Probably redacted. Too individualistic, too libertine. Too sympathetic towards the steerage class. Plus, I told the DTIFC I was making a retrospective piece about *The Man from Snowy River*. They'd probably pull my funding.'

'Yeah,' Julian says vaguely. Oriana's walking over to him. 'Yeah, that sucks.'

'Can I talk to you?' Oriana asks, with the lightest touch on Julian's forearm.

Cleo knows she's been outranked. She scans the crowd and spots Fizz, a fellow film buff, and mumbles an excuse to leave Julian and Oriana one on one by the shale-rock fireplace.

'Firstly, hello,' says Oriana pleasantly.

'Hey,' says Julian, trying to sound aloof while his whole heart howls.

'Secondly, thank you for the save before.'

'No worries.'

'And thirdly, how was Colombia?'

'It was great,' says Julian. 'I crewed on a sailboat for a while off the coast of Cartagena. I spent a few months on the outskirts of Medellín. I even did some sessions for a guy I met there, who had this really cool studio in the hills. Got to pick up my guitar again, which was great. Wrote some new stuff of my own. Mostly it was chill, though. White beaches. *Playa blanca*. These guys would just walk up to you and ask if you wanted lobster, or cocaine, or both.'

'And it was both?' guesses Oriana.

'Almost always.'

They smile at the same time, like life's not all that bad.

'This is crazy,' Julian says with a laugh, 'but I actually thought I heard one of our songs playing on the radio, in a kiosk in the middle of the jungle. Impossible, I know. But it felt like a sign. Like I was ready to come home.'

Oriana's head tilts to the left, something she does when she's getting down to business. 'That pot plant. You knew, didn't you? You knew it was going to go through the window at that exact moment. That's why you pulled me out of the way. Is that right?'

'That's right.' Julian swills his beer, realising the pleasantries are over.

'So you skipped ahead, here? At the party?'

BIG TIME

'Nope.'

'Earlier?'

'Yep.'

'How much earlier? You didn't do it in Colombia, did you? That would be—'

'I never even heard of the stuff until I got on the plane to Auckland.'

'On the plane?'

'Yeah. The flight attendant, Trevor. We started talking, and he hooked me up.'

'Wait. So when did you see the pot plant?'

Julian looks right at her. 'On the plane.'

'And when did you get home? The repatriation flight?'

'Yesterday morning.'

'That doesn't make sense.'

'Why not?'

'Because that's an impossible ratio.'

Julian's unmoved. 'Okay, sure. Impossible or not. That's what I saw, and that's when I saw it.'

'You saw this whole party during an F-trip you took two-and-a-half days ago?'

'Yep.'

'And that was the first time you ever skipped ahead?'

'Yep.' Julian's beer's been gone a while now, but he keeps doffing his empty plastic cup.

Oriana's mind is racing. Whenever this happens, whenever she's processing new or vital information, she tends to hold one hand aloft, like she's conducting a silent orchestra. 'And when you saw it … did you see the pot plant hit me? Or did you see you pulling me out of the way?'

'I saw me pulling you out of the way,' Julian says, matter-of-factly. 'That's how I knew what to do.'

Oriana says it's incredible. She says something about Julian being in the highest percentile. She says the duration, and the ratio, and the veracity of his visions go well beyond anything she's personally encountered – particularly given his tolerance levels.

All Julian says by way of response is: 'I'd finish your drink if I were you.'

'Why's that?'

Julian bites his lip for a second, then says: 'Just between you and me, Skinner had been in touch. I hope you can keep that quiet, but he had. He told me how pissed everyone was. The others think I just left for no reason, so some of them wanted me out for good, but the label put their foot down. Skinner told me Ash was writing the new album on his own. He told me about you two. So I was prepared for all that. But still, part of me was dreading coming home. I didn't know what to expect. Now that I'm here though, I'm looking around ... and it's good, y'know? It's nice. I missed these people. I know I missed you.'

He waits for Oriana to say she missed him too. When she doesn't, he continues: 'The next little while might be tough, with the new album. So I wanted to let people have this night. Let them enjoy themselves for as long as they could.'

'Julian. What are you talking about?'

Julian looks over at a starburst clock on the exposed-brick wall. Dots for numbers. Dashes for hands. The clock used to sit in a newspaper office in the 1960s.

'We've got about seven minutes before a DID raid.'

Oriana's expression doesn't change one bit, but her breath slows down. The skin across her collarbones sinks a little deeper, wraps around them a little tighter.

'You saw it,' she says evenly.

'Mm-hmm.'

'Seven minutes?'

'Give or take.'

'Why didn't you say something earlier?'

'Because I didn't.'

'But why not?'

'Because I *didn't*.'

Oriana realises Julian means that when he saw this whole night play out during his trip, he saw that he didn't say anything. Which is why he hasn't until now.

'We'll be okay,' he says. 'It's just a spot raid. Only one person gets done. Some guy named Raiph.'

Subject 3 from Oriana's experiment upstairs. 'I was just with him,' she says.

BIG TIME

'You won't be able to find him, so don't bother trying. The way I figure, it's already happened. But we should go around and word people up.'

He jerks his thumb, like, he'll take that side if she takes the other.

Oriana has to ask: 'This was all from the plane?'

Julian nods, and Oriana smiles.

'This is big,' she says.

They break and do the rounds. Over the next six minutes, a prodigious amount of illicit substances are deposited begrudgingly into toilet bowls and down drains. Coke, F, acid, MD, dime bags of grass and all the corresponding accoutrement: hoon spoons and pocket bongs and hash pipes and rolling papers. Someone turns off the stereo, snaps the contraband vinyl into quarters and buries it under a hydrangea in the yard. Someone expends an eyedropper full of F in the fish tank, so the dozen or so guppies in there, brains all firing like little Roman candles, see what happens next before it even happens.

A dark convergence of SUVs on the street outside – a domino line of opening car doors – boots on the ground – a flurry of barrel-mounted flashlights – a squadron of thirty or more troopers in tell-tale dark-green Department of Internal Decency flak jackets turning on every light, turning off every speaker, rounding up every twenty-something, emptying every pocket. Conspiracy theorists would have you believe that these spot raids are targeted towards certain demographics, in certain areas, at certain times of day and on certain days of the week. But the boring truth was that one in every ten standard neighbourhood noise complaints was automatically slotted into the DID response queue.

Now there's a hundred stoned partygoers lined up on the lawn in five neat lines of twenty, all on their knees, zip-tied at the wrists, each pretending to be sober, each remaining more or less silent. Skinner, who's had more than his fair share of run-ins with the law, believes that one's assent should be clearly vocalised for the sake of legal transparency. He keeps saying, 'WE ARE COOPERATING,' over and over. 'WE ARE COOPERATING.'

Three months from now, there'll be a TGA-approved on-the-spot test for *trypto-lyside glutochronomine* – a handheld ultraviolet torch that, when shone in a subject's eye, can reveal trace particles of F up to six hours after absorption. But for now, for tonight, no such test exists. Tonight, it comes down to what is, or isn't, in people's pockets and on every person's person.

So Raiph gets pushed to the dirt, a knee on the back of his neck. Two finger-length vials of F in his windbreaker. He says they're not his. He says he doesn't even know how they got there. He says he's a med student. He says he wants to work with children. He says he's in love. He's about to propose. He votes conservative. His dad's a department man. Then a DID trooper slips a bag over his head, and his words stop making sense. Raiph is hoisted into the back of a van and is never seen in New Victoria again.

The guppies all die. The zip ties are cut. The sun comes up. Ash puts his arm around Oriana's shoulders and walks her home, turning back to Julian as he goes.

'Welcome home, brother. See you at the studio.'

And one drunken reveller, grass stains on his jeans, beer on his breath, limps forlornly down the street, shouting: 'They said it was a party! But is this what the party means? Is this what the party *really means*?'

2

When Ash said, 'See you at the studio,' what he meant was: see you at the abandoned church in the Belgrave rainforest that Labyrinth had fitted out as the band's new, state-of-the-art clubhouse.

'What was wrong with the Collingwood joint?' Julian asks on the first day of recording as they approach from the gravel car park. 'And how much of our advance did we sink into this place?'

'Don't you worry about that,' says Skinner. 'This is the label's gift, to help you breathe life into album number two!'

'If it's life you want,' Tammy says, wiping one finger along a lichen-stained wall, 'why'd you buy us a tomb?'

Ash argues that the church has meaningful provenance. Built by German Presbyterian migrants in the 1870s, it acted as a halfway house for orphans during the world wars before being bought by an affiliation of labour unions, serving as their headquarters (as well as a secret Socialist Alliance hangout) throughout the 1960s and '70s. It was an op-shop, then an art gallery, then a quarantine facility before being sold to developers and left in turnaround for nearly twenty years. One of the buttresses was half collapsed and the gargoyles on the roof were faceless, their features brushed smooth by time, bushfires and La Niña rain.

'It's responded to the world around it,' Ash says of the band's home for the next few months. 'It's moved with the ages. It's a traveller, a passenger – but a haven, too. It stands for something.'

'Like what?' asks Julian.

Ash places a hand on the cast-iron door knocker. 'Something real.'

JORDAN PROSSER

Downstairs, the nave had been gutted – the pews removed to make way for the mixing desk, a bank of monitors and a suite of tobacco-coloured Chesterfield lounges. An ocean of cabling snaked up towards the crossing and the transepts, where the band members would be arranged in an even line of four: Ash's mic, Tammy's kit, Julian's bass and Xander's guitars waiting for them at 10 am each day – primped, cleaned, tuned, rigged and ready. The altar was stacked high with amps and road cases.

It looked the part, but the acoustics were shit. Labyrinth plastered the floors with as many Persian rugs as they could find, and covered much of the brickwork and stained-glass windows with foam eggshells. Here and there, the translucent face of a dead saint poked through, serenely surveilling the band. The wooden beams above the nave were showing visible rot and termite damage, so they'd been painted a virulent yellow and braced with steel scaffolding.

Upstairs, the atrium and choir loft were transformed into a green room – more couches, pinball machines and pool tables, video games and daybeds, as well as a 'lacto' fridge, a dairy-free fridge, a vegan fridge and a beer fridge. There were speakers and a turntable and shelves of old albums Julian suspected were all redacted: the Drones, the Clash, Captain Beefheart, Camp Cope, the Peep Tempel, Minutemen.

'These go home with me at the end of each day.' Skinner winks. 'Just in case.'

Here's the track-listing for *In the End It's All Okay, and If It Ain't Okay, It Ain't the End*:

1. In the End It's All Okay (Prologue)
2. Boot to the Neck
3. Fuck Panic
4. My Futurist Bride
5. War Drums
6. Sun Gun
7. Apathy Headache (Interlude)
8. Tear It All Down
9. Puppet People

BIG TIME

10. If It Ain't Okay, It Ain't the End
11. Misanthropatopia
12. Scorched Earth
13. Seven Stitches (Coda)

The Acceptables' second album was more or less fully formed before the band even set foot in the studio. Ash had written all the lyrics, organised all the arrangements and recorded a full set of demos in his personal studio (which Labyrinth had paid for on the sly), playing scratch tracks for every instrument. He'd then tasked Skinner with tasking some poor Labyrinth intern with listening to the demos and transcribing them into sheet music, a uniquely time-consuming task for this particular album. Let me put it this way: every single track on *Artificial Beaches on Every Mountain / Artificial Mountains on Every Beach* was in standard 4/4 time and ran somewhere between two-and-a-half and four minutes. By contrast, the demo version of 'My Futurist Bride', the fourth track off *In the End*, was written in 17/8 and went for nine minutes and twenty-two seconds. 'Scorched Earth' was written in 10/4 and was only forty-three seconds long. The intern, who had done their best under the circumstances, stopped working at Labyrinth Records shortly after. *In the End* had no featured artists, no guitar solos, no notable drum fills and no 'borderline iconic' bass lines. Three of the tracks – 'Boot to the Neck', 'Apathy Headache' and 'Puppet People' – didn't have bass lines at all, 'Puppet People' essentially functioning as a spoken word track with some space for ambient guitar and the occasional shimmering cymbal. 'Apathy Headache' was just an excerpt from Foucault's redacted *Discipline and Punish*, read in exchange for a meat-free hot dog by a homeless person Ash had befriended in Carlton Gardens. And in case you needed any further evidence that Ash had no intention of resting on his band's comfortable pop-rock laurels, here are the lyrics to 'Misanthropatopia' (which Ash claimed to have written *during* an F-trip – snapping back to discover the lyrics magically appeared in his leather-bound notebook, as if having flowed directly from the future, through him, and out onto the page):

JORDAN PROSSER

There's thirty or forty or forty-four fun, flirty
Thorn-nosed young fuckers queueing for the stall
There's a UV tube stuck to every ceiling so that you can't feel
Any feelings at all

Let's see if this shit might stick to your skin
That's the sticky pink stuff that you're stuck in
With your erstwhile, puerile, cat-caught tongues
Filling your fucking cunt cheeks right up like chewing gum

I'm an agent of chaos, purveyor of fine sadness
Master of melancholy, misanthropy and madness
Patron saint of porcelain smiles
With a mind for malaise and putting talents to waste

And missed opportunity is my mistress, motherfucker,
She and I plan to rape and rage
And mix a coupla things up in our coupla minutes on stage—

'What the fuck,' Julian says a little too loudly. He's looking through the sheet music, which the intern had even gone to the trouble of binding. It's afternoon on day one in the studio.

Skinner's spinning in a chair at the mixing desk next to Solomon and Nat, the sound engineers, but when he hears Julian, he stops spinning. Tammy, who comes to rehearsals in full moisture-wicking activewear, slips her drumsticks in their sleeve and folds her arms and waits. Xander plays with his effects pedals and pretends he didn't hear.

But Ash heard. He's standing in the pulpit, annotating his own binder where he believes the intern screwed up. 'What the fuck what?' he enquires politely.

Julian flips through 'Misanthropatopia'. 'You've got the word *cunt* in here. And so many *fuck*s. I don't think we can say *fuck*, can we? Not unless we bleep it out. We definitely can't say *rape and rage*. I just …' Julian looks around for someone to back him up. 'I don't think we can say any of this.'

'*We're* not,' Ash says, meaning: *he* is.

Julian scoffs. 'Right. I get it.'

BIG TIME

Ash calls out: 'Skinner! What's the label's official stance on profanity?'

Skinner leans on the mixing desk, pretending he hasn't memorised the band's incredibly long recording contract back-to-front. 'Goodness, let me think. If I recall correctly, lyrical content is at the artist's sole discretion. We're not here to meddle with the music. We're just here to mix it and market it. No meddling! Right, Nat?' He squeezes Nat's shoulder convivially.

'Right,' says Nat.

Skinner was telling the truth, more or less. Section 2.4, clause 4 of the Acceptables' deal memo for *In the End* stipulated that neither Skinner nor anybody else at Labyrinth could hand down any musical or lyrical edicts. The band had been granted complete creative control. And while this might seem like a generous gesture, Labyrinth's reasoning was a little more calculated; having no creative input also helped indemnify them against any legal backlash stemming from the band's output.

Julian, still baffled, flips through the sheet music, scanning a page at random.

'Who the fuck do we know who plays saxophone?'

He could keep going, but doesn't, because of the itch behind his eyes. It had been there for a day or two, steadily getting worse – gritty like sand and hot like sunburn. Julian hadn't seen any of what was happening right then in the church. His visions from the plane had come to a close pretty much the morning after the party at Xander and Pony's parents' place. So right now he's in uncharted territory, feeling his way through the day like everybody else, craving another drop.

'You know what?' he says. 'Whatever.' He cracks a sponsor-provided beer.

'Let's take it from the bridge, then,' Ash says coolly. 'Roll it up.'

Julian doesn't say much during the recording sessions after that. He shows up at ten, stands in his spot and plays what he's told to. There are no jam sessions or lyrics brainstorms like there'd been with *Beaches*. There's certainly no room for improvisation. Ash drills bars with individual band members until he's satisfied. Other times he halts the session and storms over to sit with Solomon and Nat, listening to a particular riff or melody on loop before storming back from the nave and covering the band's sheet music with large black crosses and pencilled-in semiquavers.

'It's good practice for when we're out on our arses taking session gigs,' Tammy says with a sigh one afternoon, shooting pool in the green room with Julian.

Days often stretch into the early hours of the morning. Skinner brings pastries for breakfast, sushi for lunch, pizza for dinner – and for some inexplicable fucking reason, at about 11:30 each and every night, he puts together an exquisite charcuterie board teeming with grapes and figs and cheese and cured meats. The board inevitably sits collecting flies and condensation before being stashed away in the lacto fridge upstairs.

The church also features a busy rotating roster of friends, lovers and collaborators. I'm there a fair bit, getting a head start on a puff piece band profile commissioned by *DeadBeat*, the FREA's sole remaining music magazine. They were going to pay for me to travel with the Acceptables on their upcoming tour, so I'd broken the news to Cleo and Kyle and started packing all my shit in a storage unit, not realising the recording would take another five months and I'd be sleeping on an air mattress all summer. Pony is always around. He heard about Julian's objections on day one and appeared shortly thereafter, hovering, vulture-like, hoping and praying that either Julian would walk or Ash would banish him and he could ascend to his rightful place on bass, right beside his brother. Cleo's there from time to time, just to talk shit and raid the kitchen – if Skinner's charcuterie ever disappeared overnight, I could guarantee I'd find it back at my place the next day, all the cheese eaten but the figs untouched. And while Julian and some of the others had been on the fence vis-à-vis the church, Ludlow is in love with it. They're there three or four days a week, getting shots for my article and a hardback making-of coffee table book that Labyrinth plans to release to coincide with the album, buzzing through the space with their old Nikon whirring, drinking in the mottled light, the scaffolding and the candleholders, the yellow roof and the eerie depth of it all. Ludlow produces a frankly stunning series of oddly baroque band portraits, documenting week one, week three, week five, week ten and so on, marking the band's hairstyles changing, their roots growing out, their nail polish chipping, muscles popping out from under tank tops as they shed any excess weight, oily sweat beading on unkempt stubble, and the persistent looks of grim concentration as Xander and Julian and Tammy make the daily attempt to wrap their heads around Ash's new musical vision (which includes aspects of jazz, soul, hardcore, math rock, kawaiicore and folktronica, sometimes all within the same song). The tougher the session, the finer the photographs. Tammy in particular has never seen herself captured quite like that. She stares at Ludlow's proof sheets for a very long time, silently undergoing some sort of radiant self-reappraisal.

Julian's least favourite days are when Oriana rocks up with Ash and sits, motionless, on the Chesterfields behind the mixing desk, lit like a Renaissance devil under the cyan downlights. Sometimes smoking, sometimes drinking tea. Julian imagines Ash recording all those demos in his private studio with Oriana at his side.

But on the other hand, when Oriana comes, she brings F. By the end of that first year, we'd all started noticing plenty of the vials in general circulation getting watered down, cut with basic pharmacy crap like sorbitol, or nastier stuff like tropicamide – but Oriana's stash seemed like it came right from the source. All my hook-ups had stopped replying to my messages (I never found out what happened to them, but I could guess), so Oriana became the Acceptables' sole supplier.

Julian used to rely on black-market diazepam for his anxiety, but now he liked F better. The smallest hit from one of Oriana's perfume samplers could give him a full day's peace of mind – he could be sure that there were no more standoffs with Ash in his immediate future, and if there were, he'd know exactly what to do when he got there, because he had a script. F was the drug of choice for many bands and performing artists in the FREA for this exact reason. No more nerves. No more stage fright. Nothing left to chance.

3

Eleuterio Cabrera was in his seventies when he discovered the Anomaly. He wasn't a scientist. He was a football fan. Born in the Puerto Madero barrio of Buenos Aires to Maria, a seamstress, and Fidelio, a longshoreman, Eleuterio led a nondescript working-class life until a rare autoimmune disorder claimed the lower half of his left leg. At this point, the young Eleuterio stopped participating in the barrio's lively after-school football matches and became their designated umpire. Unable to play, he learnt to analyse, sitting in the shade on the sidelines while his friends and older brothers dribbled circles around each other, hollering 'GOOOOOOOOOOOAAALLLLLLL', kicking up beautiful shapes in the dust.

Secretly ashamed of his lame son, Fidelio would take Eleuterio to his favourite café on the quiet end of Avenue Azopardo every weekend to watch football on a small black-and-white television mounted in the corner above the bar. It was 1974 when Eleuterio saw his father's team, the erstwhile blue-and-white Club Atlético Temperley, defeat Estudiantes de La Plata 3–1 and qualify for the Primera División for the first time in thirty-seven years.

Fidelio was ecstatic. He wished his own father could have been there to see it. He plucked Eleuterio clean off his stool and swept him around the café, chanting 'Panizo! Panizo! Panizo!' in honour of the striker who had scored Temperley's decisive third goal in the eighty-first minute.

BIG TIME

*

That was the last time Fidelio saw Temperley play and the last time he picked up his son like that. He died a few days later in what the port authority described to Maria as a 'pinching incident', meaning Fidelio had been crushed to death between two large shipping containers full of black leather school shoes with tidy silver buckles.

Two years later, a coup d'état deposed the president and installed a military junta. Many young men, including two of Eleuterio's brothers, disappeared in the months that followed. A distant cousin of Maria's, who had emigrated years earlier, offered them a way out: a place to live and work in Falkirk, halfway between Glasgow and Edinburgh.

Maria packed one bag for herself, one for Eleuterio and one for his remaining brother, Isidore. They took a plane to Heathrow then a taxi to London then a train to Edinburgh then a bus to Falkirk. Eleuterio attended a Scottish school, worked in a Scottish tailor shop and saw the Scottish countryside. The first time he and Isidore visited Glasgow, they bought tickets to the Celtic v Rangers Premier League match in September 1978. Watching the game, Eleuterio felt he was home.

Life moves quickly – even more so for migrants. Soon Eleuterio was a postgrad engineering student at the University of Glasgow, living in Hillhead, smoking in shared apartments, slipping on ice during short winter days. He got a job with the government, optimising train lines. He fell in love with a woman, Lola, whom he married. Two children followed, Mary (after Maria) and Thomas (like the saint).

Thomas showed no interest in football, but Mary loved going to Celtic Park with her father on weekends. First, she sat on his lap, then she grew into the chairs, then before long she was helping Eleuterio up the steps to the members area. Mary was offered a scholarship at Stanford University, specialising in paediatric cardiology. Without his daughter to help him up the steps, Eleuterio stopped going to Celtic Park, favouring a pub at the end of Kelvin Way where he watched the football on a sixty-five-inch LED television mounted in the corner above the bar.

JORDAN PROSSER

This was how Eleuterio saw Celtic beat Rangers 3–1 on the day of his seventy-third birthday. Celtic's third goal came in the eighty-first minute. Roderick McAlister, a twenty-seven-year-old bow-legged, left-footed striker received a perfect pass from the right midfielder and curled the ball fifteen metres into the top-left corner of the net. As the stadium erupted in green and white streamers, Eleuterio was struck by a sudden, unshakeable sense of déjà vu.

On the subway home, he thought about McAlister, who, like many modern strikers, was renowned for a particular scoring technique – the McAlister Curve, they called his. Eleuterio spent hours at the local library, studying the striker's career, watching every goal of every game. Nothing quite resembled what he'd seen on his seventy-third birthday in the eighty-first minute.

Maria died from pneumonia. Isidore retired to Leeds. Thomas moved to the Western Republic of Australia. Mary stayed in California. When Eleuterio sold the family home in Falkirk, he found a pile of old suitcases in the attic and, in one, a paper coaster from the café on Avenue Azopardo. This was how Eleuterio suddenly remembered Buenos Aires: the taste of sweet cola on hot days, the chanting and flag-waving in the streets. He remembered being lifted up in his father's arms, spinning so fast he thought his foot might never touch the ground again. And he remembered Temperley v Estudiantes – the third goal in the eighty-first minute – Panizo, a bow-legged, left-footed striker, accepting a perfect pass from the right midfielder and curling the ball fifteen metres into the top-left corner of the net.

Eleuterio spent the next year searching for any record of the 1974 Primera Championships. Elderly fans in online forums still reminisced about the Temperley v Estudiantes game. With his rusty written Spanish, Eleuterio asked one Temperley supporter, a retired eighty-year-old bricklayer who still lived in the Virreyes house he was born in, if he remembered Panizo's decisive goal – but the bricklayer stopped replying to Eleuterio's messages. He had died, and his children had sold the Virreyes house to buy real estate in China.

With the help of his tech-savvy nephew, Michael, Eleuterio sifted through thousands of hours of grainy, digitised archival footage, but

BIG TIME

the Temperley v Estudiantes game had apparently never made its way online. Eleuterio told Michael what it had been like during the coup, when smoke filled the barrio and the electricity blinked on and off all day. Many of the television stations had fallen under military control, their executives disappeared and their archives destroyed.

Eleuterio lay awake at night in his Hillhead flat. When he did sleep, he dreamt of men in liquorice-green army fatigues pouring petrol onto piles of celluloid.

In desperation, he wrote directly to Club Atlético Temperley:

Dear Sir/Madam,
My name is Eleuterio Cabrera. I am Argentinian born, but write to you from Scotland, my home. Temperley has been my no. 1 football team ever since I was a child. I remember a 3–1 victory over Estudiantes in 1974. It was a game that was very special to me, and to my father, who is with God. Does your club keep recordings from this era? I recall it was a beautiful game, and I would very much like to see it again. Viva Temperley!
Sincerely,
Eleuterio Cabrera

Then he waited. Two Scottish winters came and went. Eleuterio even saw a full day of snow, though the ground was too warm for it to settle. He went to the railway museum and looked at the old engines. He visited Celtic Park but couldn't quite make it up the steps. Isidore died. Lola died. Michael moved to London. Mary had two of her own children now, quarter-Argentinian, quarter-Scottish, half-Americans with sandy hair and brown eyes who loved to surf. Eleuterio kept a photo of them on his fridge.

Then, one shimmering spring day, he got a letter. It said:

Dear Señor Cabrera,
Thank you for supporting Club Atlético Temperley for so many years.
We have some audio-visual material from the 1970s, though our archives have not been organised for some

time. If you ever find yourself again in Buenos Aires, you are welcome to come and look.
Kindly,
Anita Gonzalez, Executive Assistant

And so, on the eve of his seventy-sixth birthday, Eleuterio took a train to London then a bus to Heathrow then a plane to Houston then another plane to Buenos Aires, setting foot in Argentina for the first time in over six decades.

He asked his taxi driver to circle through Puerto Madero. The docks had been moved further up shore, away from the city. The place where his father died in a pinching incident was now a steakhouse. The café on Avenue Azopardo was a massage parlour. Eleuterio told the driver to take him to Estadio Alfredo Beranger, the home of Club Atlético Temperley.

Anita Gonzalez was a tall woman with thin lips and surprised eyes – surprised, at least, to find the old man who had written her a letter two years ago now leaning against the reception desk, asking to see the club archives. She made him tea and helped him to the basement, piled high with cardboard boxes on wobbly steel shelving. Anita explained that Temperley had gone into receivership between 1991 and 1993. What they were looking at now was everything the club hadn't catalogued from before then: receipts, ribbons, medals, merchandise and hundreds of thousands of photographs. Eleuterio thanked Anita, blew on his tea and got to work.

He spent his days in the basement and his nights at a small hotel off the Avenue Hipólito Yrigoyen. He sat up in bed with the window open, listening to the motor scooters and street vendors below. He felt the warm air and missed Glasgow's chill. He ate parrilla and missed neeps and tatties. He looked at his amputated leg on the bed. He had never missed his lower limb at all.

After months of sorting, filing, cross-checking and cataloguing, Eleuterio found an index card in a storage container referencing six reels of film from the 1974 Primera Championships that had been loaned out to the Argentine Football Association. Eleuterio shaved, ironed his shirt, then held Anita's hand as she helped him up the

BIG TIME

steps to the AFA headquarters. After twenty minutes of frowning at a computer screen, a tired archivist disappeared into another basement and returned holding a waterproof box. Inside: the only surviving footage of Eleuterio's game.

They gave the film to a man in an electronics shop who said it would take a couple of weeks to convert to a digital file. Eleuterio checked out of his hotel, took Anita to a lovely restaurant to thank her for her help, then took a taxi to the airport and a plane to Dallas then another plane to Heathrow then a train to London and a bus back to Glasgow. He walked along the Kelvin and waved at some familiar faces. He wrote Christmas cards to Thomas and Mary but heard nothing back.

When at last the file arrived, Eleuterio watched it through on a laptop in his kitchen, dabbing away small tears the whole time. In the eighty-first minute, after the stunning left-footed goal, he said to the empty kitchen: 'Panizo, Panizo, Panizo.'

As night settled, he found a recording of the Celtic v Rangers match from his seventy-third birthday and watched it from start to finish. Then he watched Temperley v Estudiantes again. Then he watched Celtic v Rangers. Temperley v Estudiantes. Celtic v Rangers. Focusing on different players each time, Eleuterio chronicled their every move on colour-coded Post-it notes that he arranged side by side along the sitting room floor.

As dawn broke and his windows blossomed with moisture, Eleuterio wrote to his nephew:

> If I send you two video files, is there a way you could line them up to play side by side? Or superimpose one atop the other, to be watched simultaneously? Will you indulge an old man who might be losing his mind?

Michael made the comparison video – a video that clearly confirmed what his uncle had discovered. Eleuterio wrote to FIFA and got a response from a robot. He penned very polite letters to the sports editors of the *Scottish Daily News* and the *Buenos Aires Times* but received no reply. So Eleuterio turned to his nephew again:

JORDAN PROSSER

What if we made the video available on the internet?
For more people to be able to see?

It took two days for the comparison video to catch the attention of a small online community of football analysts. From there, it got back to the clubs themselves and to bookkeepers, sports reporters and other industry insiders. After one week it was headline news across the globe. After two weeks it was the most-viewed online video of all time.

Plenty of football matches have ended with the scoreline 3–1. Of those matches, plenty still have had those goals scored in the twenty-sixth, thirty-first, thirty-third and eight-first minutes. Of *those* matches, a very small handful have had that eighty-first-minute goal come off the left foot of a bow-legged striker. The Temperley v Estudiantes and Celtic v Rangers games had all these things in common – but then they *also* had: substitutions at the seventy-first, seventy-ninth and eighty-fifth minutes; yellow cards at minutes nine and eighteen; one red card in the second minute of overtime in the first half; a 58.8 to 42.2 per cent possession split; four saves from each team; two and three offsides respectively; nine corners; and twelve headers from players in the exact same positions on the pitch at the exact same time.

The similarities ran deeper than statistics. Take Horacio Agostinelli (Temperley) and Colin McGraw (Celtic), both wing defenders. During their respective matches, the men moved as if mirroring each other through time. Twelve touches and eight assists at precisely the same moments. One yellow card at minute eighteen. At the sixty-first-minute mark, Agostinelli absent-mindedly ran his left cleat twice through the dirt then picked his nose with the middle finger of his right hand. So did McGraw. They thought no-one was watching and, at the time, nobody was. But soon people would be analysing every movement and mannerism, no matter how small, of all forty-four men across all four teams across both games, searching for the slightest deviation – and finding none.

The games were carbon copies, down to the very last detail. Not merely similar, but perfectly identical. It was the same game, played twice over, more than sixty years apart.

BIG TIME

An angry mob who'd lost money on the Celtic v Rangers match burnt down a bookie's in Finnieston. A class-action lawsuit was brought against the clubs by punters claiming the game must have been rigged. For their part, the Scottish Football Association put an immediate hold on all games and launched an official investigation, although what they hoped to find, nobody knew. Perhaps twenty-two well-paid athletes from two famously adversarial football teams had chosen that particular game to join forces and enact a highly orchestrated, rigorously rehearsed, utterly obscure practical joke that would take one septuagenarian Argentinian migrant three-and-a-half years to figure out? The investigation found no wrongdoing and the season was resumed.

Eight Scottish players checked into rehab facilities. One, Arthur Garrison, a twenty-nine-year-old forward, drove his Maserati into a pylon near the Auchenshuggle Bridge. After the funeral, his family discovered a secret stash of journals in which Garrison expressed a newfound belief that his actions were controlled by unseen forces. That his life was not his own. That none of our lives were, or ever had been – and that Eleuterio Cabrera had simply found proof. Garrison's journals sold at auction for £2 million. His family used the proceeds to create a not-for-profit organisation that helped struggling A-listers adjust to this new paradigm.

Worldwide, professional sports entered an erratic phase that lasted years. Nobody wanted to be the next Celtic v Rangers, or the next Arthur Garrison. Fearing themselves puppets in an invisible feedback loop, athletes acted out, intentionally defying their instincts and years of training. The final score in one Bundesliga football match between Bayern and Hoffenheim was 138–3. The Super Bowl drew 0–0. Wimbledon matches lasted thirteen days. Eighty-four compound fractures were recorded in a single NBA season. Water polo players drowned by the dozen. Olympic biathletes took potshots at each other. In the semi-finals of the US Open, reigning champ Tobias Marten simply stood at the service line, eyes closed, racket outstretched. After his 6–0, 6–0, 6–0 defeat to Japanese upstart Hideo Nakomori (ranked four hundred and twenty-nine in the world), Marten told reporters: 'If I were meant to win, I would have won.'

JORDAN PROSSER

Breakfast news programs and late-night talk shows crowded their couches with football analysts, sports writers, physicists, mathematicians, spiritual mediums and chronophenomenologists. The Pope gave a special interview on *Good Morning America* to temper the fears spreading through televangelist channels in the South, where children were disappearing from schools, squirrelled away in bunkers dug by their parents, reciting Hail Marys, eating tinned beef and counting bullets.

A psychic in Chicago had a column go viral, suggesting the Celtic and Rangers players had been possessed by the souls of the Temperley and Estudiantes players so as to relive a match from their glory days – despite the fact that three of the Argentinians were still alive (albeit in their late nineties).

Meanwhile, a loosely affiliated group of ecologists, etymologists and marine biologists published an opinion piece in the periodical *Science* suggesting that the Anomaly, as it had become popularly known, was little more than a testament to human vanity. Who, they asked, was to say that coincidences didn't occur at this scale quite commonly in the natural world? Who's to say that the migratory patterns of the elusive beaked whale, or the breeding habits of Amazonian cicadas, or just the general seasonal ebb and flow of life, already rhythmic and highly ordered, didn't frequently reach this level of exactitude, right under our noses? Perhaps if we paid as much attention to the natural world as we did to professional football, very few things would seem anomalous at all.

The physicists said an endless universe meant endless opportunities for coincidence; on a long enough timeline, everything would eventually happen twice. The mathematicians estimated the probability of the Celtic v Rangers match playing out the way it did at roughly one in 91318740165071305343578499026289409915286870712334149757552328627159494581955100508305179382839746328255758856551979423779065693323225164117190802680251243172444029891421150372188992192016104190488585102835448030125530081692587241346215685341825858059703946413579307319245162564465154201652920598270733480755506410178319161757751303474728317467931475004389845788823273699435787058179960498937936493848180574007088124284211156243642817335310312492546863235696223 37

BIG TIME

0857634000882873309077840285681334550908292820068363301988951819152901205258360180669557059589104664007980905156850087044739645991553096689365280174052462497633279673679907231250911387133278855959459314960681286515660262170922137092368215788997480630203767246354382656014560001988033845984305859682160196316905464812119647452030617289691607927939390181521413249429888029705634127368698728318444985548942116833088743350243767846507803420783243217421998807622165222247905367441938949962737231936083256620495785819722745645786006021842812547457244299690023584614674000425263865088389005662182521363982747293751732240003015613279534049917407230865644439148940178131923453104520492864454514043043214324631085930578006779083519635418974932310751384604464715346484505175794074104043137456877882660603765456859303393096093852592417142512417224804033200794584883002115697322628931708127324676348094018278512756280496672938519708829365028078075895969319473467984290951425449295129580941114965963790896422021231498939570787112213150197942035001484027859890341940656815058468209494950740137140410621377602987799081563105305806742058546930139876319855690167068153563418247944530014348006016359629173908474940392309132551783537282727150678612080653072780580458085910424503338081213823910024219729598789955703016212466924846000773989207045517033358419932444138184727094523741128394447806021690991108583556667195592306087855825844448730789072244052977569531581093792583514988034748787180460054101098174645878499905186420125255483414997902905635943603069748210782296740060843686312116038104902525871936276166569688894481932298313487855385438913813133857479581954523963739593089818430917950863484865809091711647397056536837277516689230373108138253297693237952974897414033675590198159610952313015880925155911680368818964734844028704625786045127934884546734822856281983680602145901737633004674128966404184163311201758527441961747907987845183179226047291774358333738277802686389438954614524512842071056971774056712308954733718709885

JORDAN PROSSER

2139053098721290529881234627127871127983920321686 0046
7761282070299087374704602239059665446756272910217 1754
1085903657781014082622794743606036771008280248265 9677
5055674230974303593748370387495509469859454889027 2643
0093182010092202418663626756663309304361309300527 911
9008525270326678   80596644833304055992150275421320 7274
4015774662948852151005410392450149942446999964000 6936
1987240965275172368488326122990797152123517095826 796
7992625302861034141419622538717235658402069324464 1618
3645110975398569834684215326718406213253164701039 2063
4461921004933009799945984973856373106340378740136 2706
7245349167558871049330734064642586066536245703539 0552
1504699797135397645698615609596869068837221035894 2080
9722137193129033113402899488901308981102041610654 8213
4928120945052908277650765711001731265405954797375 9547
0877663147114675482060171155400394365769581172771 5988
1301598888143715801555541664062791231977799402808 56251
7594639687452996423155755351760922615134868206031 1681
8928240101116503449821012693854716879642115524564 3257
8694213449942770921235313015745625564630338712208 3021
9539295401468048287041431149962672280500757634914 1303
6521485501166340423358124012881759047478266123104 5742
8510518069221203277044421736550851628235190275376 2964
8457513102844533965163557732316069735127576696497 2054
2618634284007799093282617783327384099127312086336 662
7599715378143989527818085635462869815013395840961 9869
7179922786920050261802595750042508670869203859493 9501
2964392353792309281080957581678991672853514748200 1146
4733169553245661126537210375217593335185936793775 4998
8469049190942359007853675549443366494790819318966 8374
9667337168417650345727332266667534531177130981488 5292
0108064143782283629668651055206145339938471405500 7595
6645395490378375867181856432669967542715751291986 7398
2184782798055093266862864603692854013859589750451 7999
7341755239456301750737381968687033116564875171413 0549
7027183043161123244229002522125000336473122012225 4628
3344341069856262605378268469792788032040504750285 3064
0416020111140219115943554602840018709970916347384 8643

BIG TIME

1789 05614695447363214303902383874878524521347449311491335945904315003370158799733375675261504569777365160141026536746176264411107904454419504477466774361941923747170556146208824657162274964102540390871782054392797798480599781313641061163890876150569677965615429741022997473448016228513658383062469475662696603682034081091594218503903991340071178963770231468322199412687236882458763618883985581731645809426163317091833603490162590455957027868378, which wasn't very helpful.

The simulation theorists just crossed their arms and smirked.

World leaders discussed the event at what was intended to be a climate summit in New Bangkok. Insurance companies overhauled their liability terms to exclude anything deemed an 'EXTREME COINCIDENCE'. Game shows sprung up in which football fans were tasked with re-creating other famous matches from throughout history. Players got book deals. Life rights were bought and TV movies were made. Managers, handlers and literary agents came pounding at the door of Eleuterio's Hillhead flat, offering money and representation. He never answered, even as printed cut-outs of his face were held aloft at doomsday rallies and his name was embossed on the covers of peer-reviewed journals – even as the Anomaly, known in scientific circles as the Cabrera Effect, fundamentally altered our relationship to time.

In a widely circulated, epoch-defining essay titled 'Time and Time Again: Why we should be worried', the controversial social scientist Demetrice Pham framed it thusly:

> The universe began in chaos and will end in order. This we are promised. We are also each promised one (1) birth, one (1) life and one (1) death, and that we will progress from each of these to the next at a regular pace, in a singular direction. During that journey, time guarantees us that nothing will remain the same. Time and change are axle and wheel – eternally conjoined, eternally spinning. Change is the universe's only true constant. But now – with the discovery of Eleuterio Cabrera's Anomaly – on a supposedly infinite timeline

of ceaseless churn, two things appear to be identical when they should not be. Make no mistake: this can be no mere 'coincidence'. Even the statisticians admit that the odds of such a thing occurring by pure chance are significantly outweighed by the odds that this points instead to a far greater, far more insidious reality: that there are no coincidences. That 'coincidence' is merely the mathematical panacea we've constructed to gloss over the terrifying truth that time has neither a regular pace, nor a singular direction.

Throughout history, we've worn the blame for our own time-related misinterpretations. Problems of perception. The proportionality of a lifetime versus the memory capacity of a human brain. Feeling a bit forgetful today! Hey, déjà vu! But now we're presented with the likelihood that the problem does not lie with us – the problem lies with time. We can no longer rely on it to carry us steadily forwards, because who's to say it won't, at a moment's notice, decide to repeat itself? Pause altogether? Or even go backwards – backwards towards chaos?

Time can no longer be taken for granted. Time, it seems, is now alive.

Eleuterio Cabrera died on his seventy-seventh birthday. Neither Mary nor Thomas made it back in time. But Michael, his nephew, caught a train from London and was there during his final hours. He brought him coffee from a machine when the nurses weren't looking and opened up the curtains to show him Glasgow at night. Michael told his uncle there was a candlelight vigil for him at the foot of Big Ben – people mourning before the biggest clock they could find.

In his last moments alive, Eleuterio was thinking of the game – of the café on the quiet end of Avenue Azopardo where he was lifted up in his father's arms. He wasn't bothered by the political, philosophical or ontological repercussions of what he'd discovered; it was a beautiful game, and he'd lived to see it twice.

4

Summer comes, and the church is a sweatbox. The Acceptables arrive on day seventy to find much of the sound cladding stripped from the stained-glass windows, century-old rainbow pietas shining down on them. When this happens, Ludlow's in heaven.

Ash is drilling Xander on a guitar overdub for 'My Futurist Bride', and Xander's struggling. They've been at it for hours. Ash has ordered him to remove all his rings, so you know it's serious. Oriana stays in the nave, listening closely, but Julian and Tammy are killing time in the green room with me and Cleo.

'I don't get why they told us. It's just so suss.' Cleo's talking about the Anomaly. Yesterday, it was front-page news in *The National Telegraph* and the lead story on *The National Broadcast* – in sync, for once, with the rest of the world's news cycle. 'They didn't even confirm the King had died for like, ten months. Why the transparency around this?'

'Maybe they're trying to get ahead of it,' I suggest. 'They know news this big makes its way to us sooner or later, and they'd prefer to be on the front foot. Control the narrative.'

'So suss,' says Cleo, who'd been up all night poring over the *Telegraph* article. 'So fucking suss.'

Tammy's playing pinball, but she's listening. 'I reckon they couldn't wait to tell us. Makes the rest of the world seem like an even scarier place. You read the last line of that article?'

Cleo recites it: 'Officials are closely monitoring global communication channels to assess any further threats.'

'So it's a threat now,' Tammy says. 'Time is a "threat". And even the slightest coincidence might be masking a defect in the fabric of reality. That's some good fear, man. That's some A+ fear.'

Cleo says: 'I don't think I can do *Titanic* anymore. I think I have to do something about this.'

'Reckon the DTIFC'll let you?' Julian says, poking at some sushi.

'What are you gonna do instead?' I ask. '*Self-portrait Playing Football in a Time Loop?*'

'It just feels like something's changed,' Cleo says. 'One of those line-in-the-sand moments, where there'll always be a before and after. It feels like an opportunity for something … really new.'

'Amen to that,' says Tammy. She tops out with a new high score and her pinball slinks towards the trough.

The band takes a week off in late January. Even after Labyrinth installed industrial reverse-cycle air-conditioning, the church was uninhabitable. The strings on Julian's bass were turning to spaghetti and losing their tuning in the forty-three seconds it took to play 'Scorched Earth'. The old wiring in the building fizzed and moaned anytime anyone turned on an amp.

Oriana asks Julian to meet her at the racecourse. There's a rose garden on a hill overlooking the tracks that no-one ever goes to. They're running horses year-round now, so the hot air smells like hay and sweat and fertiliser and tranquilliser.

'I wanted to see how you're doing,' she says.

'I'm good,' says Julian, picking at the wet grass. The sprinklers must have switched off only minutes before they got there. 'Just bored, more than anything. Does Ash know you're here?'

Oriana smiles. 'When we were together, did I tell you everything I did and every place I went with every person?'

'No, but I'm not a fucking control freak.'

'You are a little.'

'Okay, maybe a little.' Julian's got that itch behind his eyes. 'What do you think of the new music? Be honest.'

'I think it has an edge.'

'*An edge.* I genuinely do not know what that means.'

'I think it's something Ash needs to get out of his system. But I also think it could be useful.'

BIG TIME

'Useful?'

Oriana shrugs one shoulder. 'Societally.'

Julian almost laughs. 'You're out of it, man.'

Oriana isn't here to talk about the album, though. She wants to know about Julian's F-trips. How far is he seeing? Are the visions more detailed? Has he proven or disproven the accuracy of any?

'It just makes it more tolerable,' he says. 'I know in advance what we'll be recording that day. I know what sort of microaggressions Ash is gonna throw my way. And I know if you'll be there.'

Oriana nods. 'It's good when things are tolerable.'

They both stare straight ahead. A cheer goes up from the crowd downhill.

'Since we're talking,' Julian says, 'have you got any on you?'

Julian lies back on the wet, manicured grass and opens his eyes to the sun. Oriana takes out a brass vial with a surgical-grade glass eyedropper – custom-made, she says, a precision delivery system, she says, with an inbuilt purifying mechanism – and plants one perfect orb upon each of Julian's retinas.

'Not everyone would trust someone else to do that,' Oriana says. 'What if I just totally fucked up your brain?'

'Too late for that,' says Julian.

Julian's chest melts with a sweet, burning cold. His vision skitters. His jaw clenches. Then, within a minute, he's watching the afternoon unfold: he sees horses winning races, foam on their teeth. He hears the distant echo he recognises as the telltale sound of the future: timelines overlapping on a single audio track. Julian sees the sprinklers coming on again and soaking their clothes right through, before Oriana rolls over and kisses him on the mouth. But when he snaps back with a cough, she's already gone. It's the first time he's seen something and been wrong.

Day one hundred and twenty-two. The circuitry in the church has been completely rewired, the soundproofing replaced on the stained-glass windows. The brickwork on the walls and floor, blasted clean and dry by the summer months, has already repopulated with streaky tendrils of black mould. It's the Acceptables' second-last week in the studio, supposedly, but there's a handful of tracks still to go.

JORDAN PROSSER

I'm sitting on the couches behind the mixing desk with Oriana, chewing my pencil to a nub while I watch Fizz canter through the church, filming the band on her old 8 mm Bolex. 'She's doing it wrong,' I say with a frown.

Skinner's taken to wearing singlets – partly to fit in with the band, partly because he still gets too hot, even with the air-con blasting, even during autumn. You can see the tattoo-removal scars on his chest and the skin grafts from the secession night riots on his back. Nat's had to get prescription glasses. Solomon's lost about seven kilos.

'From the top,' says Ash. 'Roll it up.'

'Fuck Panic' is the centrepiece of *In the End* and by far the most difficult song on the album. At a relentless 190 BPM, it's the closest Ash has ever come to writing pure punk. It features some truly unpleasant, almost mutant funk riffs and some bold bass rhythms. Xander's fingers are in tatters and Tammy's activewear is yellow with sweat stains, while Julian, who's seen this whole day and knows what's about to happen, is just breathing deeply and playing his part. '*Fuck panic! I'll just do what they tell me / Fuck panic! I'll just buy what you sell me*,' screams Ash, smashing his lips against the pop filter on an expensive condenser mic.

Xander's D string snaps at the headstock, ricocheting backwards and splitting his cheek open. 'SHIT,' he hollers. Pony rushes to his side and Nat cuts the track.

'Good lord,' says Skinner. 'Solomon, grab the first aid kit. That was sounding terrific, folks! Keep it up!'

'Two minutes, Xan, then we're back on,' says Ash, dabbing his forehead with a towel.

'Oh, get fucked,' says Julian, right when he knew he would.

'Was that for me?' Ash knows full well it was.

'Let the guy get a Band-Aid, would you?'

'When we stop we lose momentum.'

'We wouldn't need that kind of momentum if you hadn't written this batshit fucking song.'

I can tell Fizz doesn't quite know who to film. In a moment of solidarity, I telepathically urge her: *keep it on Julian, keep it on Julian*.

'Like, when did we used to write stuff like this? Ever?' Julian prods.

BIG TIME

'We didn't,' Ash says plainly, curling his mic cable.

Julian won't drop it. He can't, because he knows he didn't. Therefore he doesn't. He rifles through the sheet music in front of him and reads: '"*Necktie hangmen sniffing in the dirt / Hard to eat your truffles when the world has gone berserk / Hard to check your balance when your bank is killing clerks / Hard to park your Lambo when the street is in the surf.*" Honestly – what the fuck is this?'

Skinner mops his brow and chimes in: 'I quite like "*Lambo*". Feels colloquial. That sort of vernacular really helps to geo-locate the music in the listener's mind.'

Julian clarifies: he's not trying to pick the song apart artistically. He couldn't give a shit about Ash's inner artist. What he wants to know is: are they trying to make the first album to get redacted before it's even been released?

'We've been at this for months now,' he says. 'Playing your music. Going along with your vision like we're hired hands. I get it, man. You're Ash. The label's got high hopes for you, I'm sure. But that's not what I'm talking about. I'm talking about the elephant in the room, the one with a spit hood and complete jurisdictional impunity. Whether it's good music, or bad music, or whatever, that doesn't fucking matter – what matters is: this is *dangerous*.'

Tammy's tried to stay neutral this whole time, but finally pipes up. 'Did you even listen to the demos, dude?'

Julian never had. Out of laziness or hubris, he wasn't sure.

'The label signed off on the demos,' Tammy says.

Skinner clears his throat and blinks the sweat from his eyes. Yes, Labyrinth had signed off on the demos. The tracks had been stripped apart, broken down, analysed, then put back together by a proprietary algorithm that claimed to be able to predict an album's week-one chart placement with 96 per cent accuracy. But Labyrinth didn't need a machine to tell them the new music was inflammatory – overtly political, in a sort of rough-hewn way. A bit unrefined, but bolshy for sure. The exact type of diatribe one might expect from a group of well-to-do suburbanites who made some money, felt bad about it, then dramatically overcorrected as they clicked into the real-world order for the very first time. *In the End*'s content wasn't particularly shocking or unexpected, but it might have been enough to put some of the wrong noses out of joint. Labyrinth's human analysts ran the demos past their lawyers and marketing experts, crunched the numbers, then presented a few possible scenarios to the board. Regardless of what happened to the band members themselves, there was no outcome in which a controversial follow-up album from a group of ingenues with strong cultural capital and a healthy fanbase didn't spell financial success for the label. Furthermore, Labyrinth's parent company was based in the WRA, where albums redacted in the east regularly outperformed any other release. The board had given their unanimous approval to proceed. They even upped the budget.

'It's time we took risks,' Ash says. 'It's time we stood for something.'

'Like your precious fucking church?' Julian marches straight up to him, waving one arm around at the parapets. 'It's just a pretty, empty building, Ash. Nothing here means anything, and you can't just pretend things mean something when they don't. What are you trying to do, exactly? Who are you trying to be? A beat poet? A soothsayer? You spend a few months mainlining F and now you're Henry fucking Rollins?'

'People listen to us,' Ash says calmly. 'Whatever we make, they're going to listen. When they do, what do you want them to hear?'

Julian's whole body trembles as he shouts: 'Fucking MUSIC!'

The word *MUSIC* takes a trip around the dome of the church, bouncing off the balustrades. Everybody there, for just a brief moment, makes the small mental concession that the acoustics really weren't so bad.

Julian reins it in a little. 'People want the bands they love to make more of the music they were making when they first fell in love with them. What's so bad about that? What's wrong with just making people happy? I thought that's what we did. I thought that's what we were.'

Ash reminds him: 'You bailed, Jules. You came back for this. No-one tricked you into being here. But when you left, you lost whatever say you had in what we are and what we're not.'

Remembering the morning he hastily packed his bags and fled Melbourne without so much as a word to the rest of the band, Julian falls silent. He flips through his sheet music to 'Boot to the Neck', then tosses it at Ash's feet and splits for the green room, spitting: 'Why don't you practise this one? There's no fucking bass in it anyway.'

On the final day of recording, it's just Ash, Xander, Skinner, Solomon and Nat. Xander finishes some pick-ups on a melody line for 'War Drums', takes a case of beer from the beer fridge, hops in Pony's waiting car and disappears into the hills.

Ash makes the engineers wait while he listens back to all his vocals. He re-records a few overdubs and tells Nat to tweak the reverb on his 'Misanthropatopia' chorus. Then he meets a Labyrinth chauffeur in the gravel car park and is taken to a nearby hot springs where he's booked in for a five-day spiritual cleanse and supervised vocal rest.

Skinner tells Nat and Solomon to take the rest of the day off, even though it's already 6 o'clock. They'd all be back after the weekend to continue mixing. Once he's alone, Skinner saunters down the nave, stepping carefully over the thick arteries of XLR cabling. He taps one of Tammy's cymbals with a dirty fingernail and considers singing something into Ash's mic, but doesn't.

Skinner locks up the church and walks to his car, an old 1983 Datsun lovingly restored by him and his brother in the double garage of their family home in Mulgrave, decades ago. Skinner hadn't held on to a lot from his previous life, but he'd kept this car. He washed it by hand every weekend and had a special mechanic in Geelong he took it to when it needed work. He wouldn't have it with him on tour, so he'd been driving it as much as possible, listening to the thrumming engine, feeling held by the leather bucket seats, drinking in the smell of petrol.

Skinner drives home from Belgrave, following the line of ancient hills, speeding along beneath ancient trees, canopies blasted by bushfires every couple of years, blackened trunks made new by faint, algae-like regrowth. At the foot of the mountains, right before the highway, there's a large LED billboard on a moveable trailer, parked on the shoulder. Skinner's seen it every night for the past five-and-a-half months, watching its message change with the seasons or the local authorities' concerns *du jour*. Sometimes it said *CATASTROPHIC FIRE DANGER* or *MICROSLEEPS CAN*

KILL. FLASH FLOOD WARNING, DRINK RESPONSIBLY THESE HOLIDAYS and so on.

Tonight, its orange letters say: *REPORT ALL EXTREME COINCIDENCES.*

PART TWO

WAKEFIELD

5

After a hundred and thirty-two days of recording and a month-long break during which the band members exchange barely a single word, the Acceptables depart on their second, and last, national tour. Labyrinth's plan was to drum up interest in the new album while it was being mastered, hitting a few key venues around the country for one-night-only shows, giving fans a taste of the band's bold new direction. First, they would head west for a Friday night headline show at the Thebarton Theatre in Adelaide. After that, the Enmore Theatre in Sydney and the Fortitude Music Hall in Brisbane, followed by a meandering three-week journey back down the east coast, popping in for a few surprise sets in Newcastle and Wollongong, before a triumphant return to their hometown of Melbourne, where they would play a weekend of shows at the Palais. Word from on high was that the set list should reflect a healthy mix of the radio hits from *Beaches* that audiences had come to know and love, with just a tantalising dash of new material from *In the End*. Naturally, Ash had other ideas.

After dropping a small fortune on the rainforest recording studio, Labyrinth had procured a staggeringly large, chromium-and-black tour bus that was waiting for the band early one morning in the empty carpark of a suburban hardware store; it was too big to pick anyone up in the city.

Everyone's arriving in cabs, walking circles round the bus like they're sizing up some dangerous ungulate they've encountered in the wild. I pull up with Cleo, who's bagged herself a spot on the tour after asking Oriana to ask Ash to ask Skinner really nicely.

BIG TIME

She says she needs a 'consistently dynamic creative environment' to be able to properly conceive and make her new work, whatever it ends up being. Two days earlier she'd loaded all her stuff from the sharehouse into my storage unit, leaving poor old Kyle to find two subletters.

'Fucking hell,' I say, rolling a cigarette as I crane my neck to see the vehicle in its entirety.

'You like it?' asks Skinner, alighting from the front steps. He's bought himself a visor and a bus driver's jacket.

'It's obscene,' says Cleo.

Skinner thinks this might be a compliment. 'Just wait till you see inside!'

Ash and Oriana pull up last, wearing matching tracksuits, which Julian ignores. Ash stands there a minute, toting an old gym bag, looking at the bus, admiring the hand-painted decal spelling out the vehicle's name: *Genevieve* (the title of one of *Beaches*' lesser ballads that Julian claimed to have written about an old girlfriend). Further down, in the same brushwork, is the album artwork for *In the End*, which Ash had already designed himself: a single human eye, open, ringed with fine eyelashes, the eyeball itself adorned with the markings of a clock, complete with a big hand and a little hand jutting out from the pupil, marking five minutes to midnight. Ash had shown mock-ups of the artwork to the rest of the band during their months in the studio when no-one had the energy to suggest any alternatives.

Tammy thought the whole thing was quite funny. 'Just in case it wasn't already obvious enough that we use illegal drugs – sure, let's put it on the side of a moving billboard,' she says as she hops up the steps.

Inside, Genevieve was more limousine than mass transport: leather armchairs with drink coolers in the arm rests; king single bunk beds with double block-out blinds on each; a cocktail bar; a small wine cellar; three separate lavatories (one with a shower, one with a spa); and a state-of-the-art sound system, including a gimbal-mounted turntable that could keep a vinyl steady during even the bumpiest ride. The turntable was gilded by shelves of store-bought, DTIFC-approved records, but Skinner had smuggled a lockbox of the redacted vinyls from the studio on board as well.

JORDAN PROSSER

Xander and his little brother were already in their seats, rolling their own joints (Xander had a weed plant he'd propagated that he believed to be ultra-pure, and he never smoked anything else), while the band's full-time roadie, Dante, was stacking amps into a luggage compartment with pupils that belied a lifelong (and happily active) amphetamine addiction. Dante was also their saxophone player.

With the exception of the Plutoses' home-grown hydro, the band's supply of narcotics was Oriana's responsibility. Stashed in an artificial compartment in the bottom of her emerald-green suitcase was almost three litres of F dispensed across fifty brass vials and eighty perfume samplers, as well as twenty grams of imported cocaine, five perforated cardboard sheets of LSD, five hundred grams of marijuana, a dozen sheets of Fentanyl, a hundred caps of pure MDMA and three hundred tablets of Captagon. There was a crippling shortage of baby formula in the FREA, never enough penicillin and a dearth of silicon chips required to run even the most basic IT infrastructure. There were any number of ways that the racketeers from Indonesia and New Zealand in their stealth ships and scuba gear might have made their fortunes – but the classics were classic for a reason.

It's a nine-hour drive to Adelaide. Once the Acceptables and their entourage have filed on board, draping hoodies and flinging shoulder bags, laying claim to bunks and chairs, it takes Skinner four attempts to leave the carpark without scraping the arse of the bus along the wall of the hardware store. Dante has to get out in mid-morning traffic and guide him. But soon we're on the freeway.

Xander and Pony are comfortably high, plucking at guitars. Pony loudly announces that he and his brother have got a little side project on the go, clearly wanting someone, anyone, to ask more about it, but no-one does. Skinner, Ash and Dante are discussing the tour manifest; Ash wants them to squeeze in one more show at each venue. Ludlow's jumped in a top bunk, headphones on, curtains drawn. Julian, Oriana, Tammy, Cleo and I are flipping through vinyls at a large foldaway table up the back, deciding what should be the official anthem of the tour.

'How about *The Sound of Silence*? In anticipation of the crowds,' quips Tammy, who's spent the past month growing increasingly anxious about playing live again for the first time in over a year.

BIG TIME

Julian picks up a Jackson Browne. '*Saturate Before Using*. You guys heard this one?'

Oriana nods. 'You bought me that album.'

'"*Saturate Before Using*" is a misnomer,' I say, pouring bourbon in my coffee. 'People mistook the album art for the album name.'

'So what's it called?' Julian asks, annoyed.

I shrug tipsily. 'Untitled? Self-titled?'

'Didn't the Ramones have a tour song?' asks Cleo.

'Yes. It's called "Touring". Bit on the nose.'

Julian puts on the Jackson Browne. Ash hears the opening track and flashes a look towards the back of the bus.

'AusNet was down last night,' Oriana says to no-one in particular.

'Bullshit,' says Cleo.

'It's true,' says Oriana.

Tammy slips off her combat boots. Her socks stink.

'Down how?' I ask.

'An attack. Highly orchestrated. It got patched up pretty quick, but for about three-and-a-half minutes, just before midnight, the FREA was open to the rest of the world.'

'I'll be damned,' Cleo says.

Julian asks: 'Who did it?'

'Bad actors,' I figure. 'Gotta be foreign.'

Julian notices Oriana's shifted her chair so she's facing away from Skinner, Ash and Dante. 'No,' she says. 'It was local. Somewhere in the east. Someone with the alias *Mal Vivante*.'

It wouldn't have been the first time. In the year it took to establish AusNet, it was a wildly unstable entity; for a while, it seemed like people were lining up worldwide to take turns at knocking it over. Lithuanian separatists, English anarcho-monarchists, Korean ransomware gangs, malware experimentalists from MIT, as well as wannabe hackers in every major city in the FREA. But once the Central Government ironed out the kinks and restricted tech imports, mandating brick phones, dial-up modems and government-issued servers, the attacks petered out. Externally, people stopped seeing the sport in it. Internally, it was a reminder of just how quickly people could get used to things.

'*Mal Vivante*,' repeats Tammy. 'Good band name.'

JORDAN PROSSER

Somewhere near Mount Gambier, Ash puts on the Millennium's 1968 record, *Begin*.

I'm asking, 'What are your personal hopes for album number two?' and recording his answers on a microcasette dictaphone so I can listen again later when I'm sober.

Ash sits opposite me. With one hand, he fiddles with a dog-eared, leather-bound notebook, containing the original handwritten lyrics for every Acceptables song. He says: 'I want this album to be a coming of age. I want people to know that the passion, the talent and the innovation we brought to *Artificial Beaches on Every Mountain / Artificial Mountains on Every Beach* wasn't just a flash in the pan. It wasn't some fluke. Surely that's top of the agenda for anyone making a follow-up. Right? If you do something once – then you set out to do it again – you want to best yourself. Right?'

'Right,' I say. 'Because it wasn't some fluke.'

'It was just the beginning,' Ash says with a smile. His teeth are like Tic Tacs, uniform and smooth. He's in that brief, golden window of your twenties when frequent drug abuse somehow only makes you look hotter. You can see why Labyrinth are banking so much on him.

'What can you tell me about making the new album? How has the writing process differed from last time?' Yes, I'm being a dick; Julian is within earshot. Sometimes I just enjoy seeing how people as suave as Ash manage to talk their way around things.

He answers: 'It was very different. I know I've put my ideas front and centre this time, and I know that's rubbed the others the wrong way occasionally. But I hope they understand that this is my gift to them. Besides, having an idea, having something to say, that's like, 1 per cent of the fight. Making it happen, bringing it into the world – actually saying it – that's 99 per cent. And that's where I need the others. I couldn't say anything without them.'

Not bad. Xander's passed out in his bunk, so he didn't catch any of this. Tammy hears it, and so does Julian, but their expressions betray nothing.

'And how did the ideas for this particular album come to you?'

Ash almost laughs, cupping a hand over my recorder. 'Do you want the printable answer or the real answer?'

BIG TIME

'Give me both and I'll write whatever's better.'

'Write whatever won't land us in a DID holding cell, thanks,' Julian chimes in.

Ash ignores him. 'The printable answer is: I'm a little older. I like to think a little wiser. I've seen things. I've had my mind opened by different people and experiences. I think this album, and the songs on it, are a direct response to my current worldview.'

'And how would you sum up that worldview?'

'Irate.'

I reach across and switch off the tape recorder. You can never be too careful. 'And the real answer?'

Ash thinks for a minute, casting his eyes towards the front of the bus, where Skinner's visor reflects the oncoming traffic in the day's dying light. Then he says: 'It was F. All of it was F.'

'Go on.'

'The real answer is: I only ever thought I had one album in me. Shit, I thought maybe I had half-a-dozen songs in me, tops. And after we finished *Beaches*, holy fuck, I was scared. Having that album do as well as it did? And then being expected to do it all again? I was terrified. And then, well … then there was Oriana.'

Right on cue, Oriana comes and sits on Ash's lap. He says this next bit directly to her, like she's the one interviewing him – but also in third person, as if she wasn't even there: 'She opened my eyes. Naturally, I was curious when I first heard about F. But she was the one who convinced me to try it. She made the space in our relationship for me to go to some really strange, new places. She knew there was something inside me that only needed to be unlocked.'

'And F unlocked it?'

'Some days, I'd snap back from an F-trip, and I would have seen myself write a new song. So I wasn't *thinking* about writing that song anymore – because I'd already written it. I was just transcribing something I already knew by heart.'

'But you did still write it.'

'Of course. It's a loop, yeah? Other days I'd snap back and – swear to god – the words would already be there in my book. Like I wrote them while I was under.'

'Do you think that this disassociation – the detachment from the intellectual process – has made the music more fundamentally *you*?'

JORDAN PROSSER

'Yes. That's exactly how I'd put it. Once you strip away thought, you can strip away fear, you can strip away ego. And when you circumvent all those things, what's left? Only you. All of you. And nothing and nobody else.'

Oriana kisses him on the temple, gets up and goes to the front of the bus, where she sits silently behind Skinner, watching the passing parade of highway reflectors.

I switch the tape back on. 'Ash Huang,' I put to him, 'do you stand by every word you've written on this new record?'

He leans in, eyes wide and gleaming. Ash has an answer for everything. 'These songs are my children,' he says. 'I would happily die for any one of them.'

At the Wakefield border, the bus comes to a halt and three uniformed, helmeted patrolmen from the Department of Internal Borders and Migration march up the steps. We hold out our ID cards as they shine ultraviolet torches in our eyes. Skinner explains our reason for travelling and shows them a printout of correspondence between the record label and the venue in Adelaide. The men lightly jostle a few pieces of hand-luggage. They fish around in Ash's gym bag, but skip right over Oriana's green suitcase. She doesn't blink, doesn't flinch. In fact, she smiles at them.

'These beds should only be used when the coach is stationary,' one of the men says.

Ludlow slips out of a top bunk, sweeping back their hair. 'My apologies. Sorry. Sir.'

The officers finish their inspection, noting the rack of guitar cases up back.

'You folks in a band or something?' one of them sniffs.

'They're the Acceptables,' I offer with a flourish.

'Never heard of 'em,' another officer says as they slouch back to the road, leaving mud on the steps.

Once we're in the clear, back on the highway, nearly everyone on board retires to a reclining leather armchair or the privacy of a bunk. Oriana dutifully hands out her perfume samplers, smiling beatifically as she fishes them from the secret compartment in her suitcase.

When she hands one to Julian, he asks, in a whisper, 'Where do you get so much of this stuff, anyway?'

BIG TIME

She whispers back: 'Maybe I'll show you one day.'

Skinner finishes the drive alone, in silence, while the rest of us feel the rush, the high, the pinch, the release, the cosmic origami folding in our brains. We see the evening and the night stretch out before us – minute after minute, mile after mile.

6

The colour fades as you enter Adelaide. Over many years, sulphur-heavy rain, born of the refineries along the coast, has stripped the paint from the buildings and turned the city bone grey.

Our accommodation is a sprawling block of serviced apartments on Hindley Street that used to be a prison and still felt a lot like one. After a middling buffet breakfast (Ash and Oriana ate their own pre-prepared açaí bowls, Tammy ate a dozen banana pancakes, Xander and Pony gorged themselves on streaky bacon, fried eggs and croissants, Julian picked at the pastries, Skinner ate only fruit, Ludlow had their usual breakfast of porridge and honey, I had hash browns and sausages, Dante had a little bit of everything, Cleo slept in late and missed out), we're gathered in one of the motel function rooms before the soundcheck at 5.

Ash hands around the set list for the gig that night:

1. In the End It's All Okay
2. Scorched Earth
3. My Futurist Bride
4. Fuck Panic
5. Good Problem 2 Have
6. War Drums
7. Boot to the Neck
8. Miracle Boy
9. Sun Gun
10. Puppet People

BIG TIME

11. If It Ain't Okay, It Ain't the End
12. Misanthropatopia
Encore 1. Thief!!
Encore 2. Seven Stitches

When he sees this, Julian, whose unusually light F-trip on the bus the night before had only shown him as far as the blueberry danish he'd eaten for breakfast, audibly sighs.

Ash gets on the front foot, saying: 'I know this is pretty *In the End*-heavy. But that's why I decided on this order – we put some of the more immersive tracks from the end of the album right up front, turn it into a real proof of concept. Try to educate people. Pique their curiosity but keep them wanting more. By the time we get to "Fuck Panic", fifteen minutes in, I think people will really be on board. I think if we can sell that drop at the end of the first verse, they'll be eating out of the palm of our hand.'

'Three tracks,' Julian says, half to himself. Ash waits for him to finish. 'There's three tracks from *Beaches*. And one of them's an encore.'

'*Beaches* went platinum. Remember? We don't need to sell it anymore.'

'But people don't know the new record yet. Isn't the worst part of any gig the moment when the singer says "Here's a new one"?'

'I think it's kinda exciting when that happens,' says Pony. Everyone ignores him.

'What if they don't like the new stuff, Ash?' asks Julian.

'Then they're welcome to not buy the record.'

Julian looks to Skinner. 'How does Labyrinth feel about "take it or leave it" as a sales strategy?'

Skinner puts on his best kindergarten teacher voice: 'Let's try the set list out tonight. We can always recalibrate as we go. Drop in more of the old music on an as-needs basis.'

Julian hasn't foreseen this particular argument, so he acquiesces. 'I just hope we're not relying on a cut of the bar,' he says. 'People are gonna be leaving in fucking droves.'

Theories are rife, even to this day, as to exactly when and why the Acceptables were placed on the DID watch list. Some say it was Tammy, on account of her brothers. Others say it was Skinner, who could scrub the villainous ink from his chest but couldn't scrub his record from a number of government databases. Others think it stemmed from Julian's re-entry interview when he returned from South America, the one-on-one screening with International Border Enforcement agents during which they confiscate any overseas-bought smartphones and interrogate you about your dealings abroad. Innocuous though Julian's intentions in South America were, it didn't take much to get flagged. A day or two in a city known for its libertarian leanings. A dinner with a friend of a friend of a known activist. One too many gallery visits, concerts, or poetry readings. At the end of the day, they could strip away your FreeNet tech, but it was much harder for them to make you forget the ideas you had, the people you met, the art you admired or the things it inspired in you.

No-one would have guessed that it was actually Oriana. She was always careful and covered her tracks well, but the sharks had been circling for a long time before she and Julian finally fled to the WRA. A number of her FreeNet aliases had been tentatively linked back to her. Burner phones were found with partial prints. A family vacation to France three years earlier had seen Oriana take a solo side-trip to Algeria, where she was photographed with a distant step-cousin who just happened to be part of the North Africa Liberation League.

The categories of the DID watch list, in order of increasing severity, are:

1. Person of Interest
2. Person of Concern
3. Watch and Report
4. Watch and Act
5. Wanted for Immediate Assessment

As the Acceptables finish their soundcheck onstage at the Thebarton Theatre on Henley Beach Road in Adelaide, Oriana is filed under 'Watch and Report'. That's why, as Julian looks out at the empty auditorium, picking up the blinking island of the sound desk at the rear, watching the bar staff run to and fro, filling sinks with

BIG TIME

ice and topping up margarita machines with salty green slush, he spots two men perched in one of the far balconies. Motionless. The kind of clean-cut, sure-footed, steady-handed, broad-shouldered, narrow-eyed squares that would seem out of place in the thick of a rock concert even *after* the official starting time, let alone conspicuously early with the best seats in the house.

Julian catches Tammy's eye while the foursome take turns testing the reverb on 'War Drums'. 'Tam. Check out the Brothers Grimm.'

Tammy's eyeline follows Julian's chin to the balcony. She watches the men without seeming to watch them, all the while keeping time with one foot on the kick-drum.

'The label?' she mouths.

'Don't think so,' says Julian.

'Promoter?'

'Not with those haircuts.'

Ash shouts at the sound tech across the empty venue floor: 'Too wet, Liz. Way too sloppy. You need a mop for that reverb.'

The men in the balcony stay for the entire soundcheck. They stay even once the Acceptables leave the stage, the houselights come down and the crowd starts to trickle in. They don't check their beepers, they don't write any notes, they don't take any photographs. They just sit there, watching, as it ticks over 9 and the support act, a small army of synth-pop idiots called Vocabulyrix, takes the stage.

Ash had fought Skinner tooth and nail over the inclusion of Vocabulyrix on the bill, but Labyrinth insisted. The eight-piece group had been strategically stitched together from a round of open auditions, and they were in desperate need of some live audience experience. Thankfully, the Adelaide crowd was a generous bunch; a good number had arrived in time to catch the opening act, milling around the sides of general admission, tapping their feet and swilling overpriced beer. A few even had the good grace to get in there and dance to Vocabulyrix's only widely released single so far, an aspirational quasi-reggae number called 'Believe 4 U'.

Julian's hovering in the wings, smoking a cigarette he bummed off the stage manager, stealing a glimpse at the haircuts in the balcony, when Oriana appears beside him, sucking on a vape.

'They're DID,' she says.

'How do you know that?'

'I've seen them before.'

'What are they doing here?'

'I doubt they came for the von Trapps.' Oriana jerks a thumb at the lead singer of Vocabulyrix as he leads a quarter of the crowd in a half-hearted clap-along to the chorus motif: '*Trying to fly / It'll be alright / Just don't fight / It'll be alright!*'

'Fucking pop-aganda,' mutters Julian. 'Should we tell Skinner?'

'If you want to give him a heart attack.'

'Then what do we do?'

Oriana shrugs and blows a cloud of bubblegum steam past Julian's shoulder. 'Play the hits?'

'It's your boyfriend who needs convincing of that, not me.'

She gives a little nod. She knows this. She's just playing.

'You know,' Oriana says, 'me and Ash …'

'You and Ash what?'

Oriana reconsiders whatever she was about to say. 'Nothing. Another time.'

'Believe 4 U' wraps up with a snappy drum riff. The keytar player wails: 'WE ARE VOCABULYRIX THANK YOU FOR HAVING US NEXT UP IT'S THE BLOODY ACCEPTABLES!'

Julian's head turns when he hears the name of his band – a band he still cares about. A band he would like to say he still loves. Hearing two thousand people hollering ecstatically at the mere mention of it pricks him with pride. He turns back and sees Oriana slinking off to the green room.

In the lull between sets, the crowd starts chanting: 'AC-CEP-TA-BLES! AC-CEP-TA-BLES!' and then: 'WHY ARE WE WAITING / SLOWLY DEHYDRATING?' and so on. Right at the front, pressed up against the steel barricades that separate the audience from the stage with a moat of security guards in between, there are representatives from the band's national fan club, each wearing a T-shirt emblazoned with the face of their favourite Acceptable. There's a young man wearing a shirt featuring Tammy, her hair smoothed by Photoshop, curled, coiffed and combed. On other T-shirts, the screen-printed Ash looks distinctly less Asian. Xander's facsimile has a chin like a gladiator. And Julian's has eyes like an anime idol.

'AC-CEP-TA-BLES! AC-CEP-TA-BLES!'

'In the End It's All Okay' – the first of two title tracks, the first track on the album and the first track of the band's live set – opens with about forty-five seconds of slowly building, ambient distortion. It does the trick of quieting the crowd down. The noise swells to fill the Thebarton. The haircuts peer down from their balcony as Ash begins to sing from offstage:

This is a cold drop of truth in both eyes
Lean your head back and don't act so surprised
Thought you'd be good but it never came right
Never even tried, you never even tried

Then the theatre floods with light as the Acceptables take the stage. The screaming crowd drowns out Ash's next lines, which might have been good for them to hear:

I'm not here to continue the tradition
I am here to hold your hand and dance you towards sedition

Except it's hard to dance to a song you don't know – especially one written in 11/8 time. Julian glimpses a few eager punters giving it a go, trying, flailing, failing, then standing still and simply listening, mouths ajar, invested but confused.

Fan Club Tammy looks at Fan Club Xander with a hopeful shrug, like, *maybe this is good?* Two Fan Club Julians scull their beers and head back to the bar.

The song finishes and a wave of warm, hopeful applause washes over the stage. Ash grinds his lips against the mic and says: 'Thank you for coming out tonight. I hope you're here because you really want to be. I hope you made an active choice. Tell me – when was the last time you all thought for yourselves?'

Someone shouts: 'Play "What Time Is Your Heart"!'

A ripple of laughter. Ash smiles patiently. 'That song will not be featured this evening.'

No-one in the audience can tell if he's serious or not. 'What Time Is Your Heart' was number one on all three east-coast radio stations for eleven consecutive weeks. It had been licensed for a car commercial, used as the playout anthem of that year's AFL season and adapted for the opening credits of a new soap opera. Twenty-seven people in the two-thousand-strong crowd had some excerpt or variation of the song's lyrics illegally tattooed on their bodies. They'd expected it to be the opening number. Or possibly the closer. Or at the very least, an encore.

Ash barrels ahead: 'This one's called "Scorched Earth". Every year the FREA mines and exports three hundred million tonnes of coal, despite international trade sanctions. This is about that. Three, four!'

The live version of 'Scorched Earth' had been expanded from its original forty-three seconds into a generous minute twenty. A dirge of sorts, which sees Tammy, Julian and Xander all tossing their heads as Ash half-sings, half-shouts:

Our friends out in the country
They will crackle and burn
They will suck pockets of oxygen from canopies of fire
Over ill-advised in-ground pools

When the song finishes, the haircuts stand from their balcony seats and exit through the fire escape. A number of other people start to leave as well. Ash can see it. Julian knows he can.

'There's no going back!' Ash laughs with a little shake of his head. 'Not for you, not for any of us. Hit it!'

'My Futurist Bride' required Xander to exercise his meagre keyboard skills, which at least gave his diehard fans in the front row something to swoon about. They squeeze each other's hands as Xander throws his greasy mane of hair back, striking a rock-god pose as he struggles to find C minor.

Ash sings:

To me and my forward-thinking futurist bride!
How the hatred of antiquity gleams in her eye

BIG TIME

I'm standing with Cleo and Pony in the GA section. Cleo's chewing her fingernails, eyes darting back and forth between the stage and the steadily dissipating audience. People are discarding plastic schooners still half-filled with beer. Pony picks one up and drinks it.

'More for me!' he says.

*On our wedding day we rape whole worlds away
And pollute old museums with new, sharp-edged names*

There's shouting backstage. Julian can't quite make it out over Tammy's snare. There's movement back there, too, shoving and pushing. Ludlow sees it from their vantage point at the foot of the stage, in the moat of security guards – it's Skinner and a man with a moustache, yelling at each other.

Seven minutes later, 'My Futurist Bride' finishes with a loud 'C'MON!' from Ash. The amps go quiet. The reverb from Xander's keyboard quickly fades. The Acceptables find themselves surrounded by deathly silence. Maybe fifteen hundred people are still there, watching them, glassy-eyed.

Ash begins to stalk from one corner of the stage to the other. Ludlow follows him with their lens. Ash reaches one side, raises the mic, thinks – then shakes his head and walks back the other way.

Finally, he says: 'Growing up near Warrandyte, I used to go bushwalking with my father. One day, we saw a snake. A deadly brown snake, lying right across our path. I stood there, frozen. But my father wasn't afraid – he picked up a stick and shooed the snake away. I said to him, "Dad, I hope I never see a snake again." And he said that even if I never saw them, they'd always be there. Millions of snakes. Hiding in the grass. Under the dirt. On the banks of every river. He said, if you averaged it out, there was one snake for every five square metres of the Australian mainland. That's a snake for every room in your house. A snake for every car in every driveway and every aisle in every supermarket. After that, I saw them everywhere I looked, even if I couldn't actually *see* them. And I was afraid.'

He's standing right on the apron of the stage, teetering over the bald head of a security guard.

JORDAN PROSSER

'Once you see something, you can never *unsee* it. Even if you ignore it. Even if you pretend. It will always – *always* – be there.'

Metres from Ash, every single member of the Acceptables fan club is unironically playing Snake on their phone. Ash wipes his face with a towel, throws the towel into the wings, whips the microphone cable back over his shoulder and rounds the stage, huffing: 'Let's do this. FUUUUUUUCKKKKKKKKK-KKKKK—'

Ash's relentless drilling of 'Fuck Panic' during the band's recording sessions was about to pay off. As soon as Ash screams 'FUUUUUUUCKKKKKKKKKKKKKKK—', the Acceptables kick into high gear, playing smoothly, relentlessly, riding in each other's slipstreams. It's unbelievably tight. No oxygen, no errors. If the dwindling crowd at the Thebarton Theatre hadn't been quite so aghast, so violently put off by this change in artistic direction from their one-time favourite band, they might have realised that this was easily the best the foursome had ever sounded together.

During the first verse, Ludlow also took the best photos that would ever be taken of the band: Ash, howling at the microphone while the veins threatened to burst from his neck; Xander, his bandaged hands a blur against his Stratocaster's steel strings; Tammy, eyes closed, having lost a stick twenty seconds in, using one bare fist to attack the high hat; and Julian, straining and seething, bass guitar swinging against his knees, arms pumping, ape-like, collarbones popping from his scoop-neck T-shirt. This was one of the last times Julian would play a gig without having seen it on F beforehand – one of the last times he would feel the rush of a live set, the thing that made him fall in love with making music in the first place.

Ratfucker, starfucker, tell me what you see!
Tried to turn the market but the market's on its knees!

It was coming – the drop at the end of the first verse.

Tried to love your family but your family's a disease!
Tried to please His Highness but His Highness is displeased!

BIG TIME

At the sound desk, Liz is pushing up the levels, hoping to turn the night around. Her colleague on the lights is cueing up a particularly wild chase they'd programmed specifically for this moment. The stage is inundated from all directions by roiling plumes of haze.

Over sixteen bars, the track builds and builds. The fan club has put their phones down. People are pausing at the exits, turning back and listening to see where this is going.

Tammy's locked into a steady build: *thump-a-thump-a-thump-thump-a-thump-a-thump-a-thump*. Julian's in lockstep with her. Xander's fingers are hopscotching down the fretboard. Ash's baritone is swelling, billowing:

Panic panic panic …
Panic panic panic …
Panic panic panic …
PANIC PANIC PANIC …!

What's meant to come next is the triumphant opening salvo of the Acceptables' all-new, paradigm-shifting, anti-establishment anthem:

FUCK PANIC! I'LL JUST DO WHAT THEY TELL ME!
FUCK PANIC! I'LL JUST BUY WHAT YOU SELL ME!

But as Tammy stands from her stool, fists held high, and as Xander springs mid-air to prepare for a resounding downward chord attack, and as Julian sinks to his knees, bass lifted towards the heavens, and as Ash's knuckles turn white around the mic, and as Liz tops out the PA system, and the canopy of LEDs turns a violent red, pivoting and locking onto the band, all we hear is:

FU—

—before it all goes dead. The sound drops out with a pop and a whine. The lights blink off. The crowd whispers, then chuckles, then wails. Beer cups hurl and arc through the dark. From the auditorium, Cleo and I can just see the band, but the band can't see shit;

retinas burnt and blinded by the thousands of watts of hard electricity they'd been staring straight into only seconds ago.

The man with the moustache was Billy Hoffman, the venue's general manager. As Ash hurtles off the stage and into the wings, Hoffman and Skinner are still in the middle of their stoush.

Ash growls: 'I'll give you five seconds to explain what the fuck just happened.'

Hoffman is half-livid, half-embarrassed. 'Look,' he says. 'It's nothing personal. We just can't have this kind of music here.'

'What kind of music is that?' Ash wants to hear him say it.

'You know ... inflammatory.'

Skinner flicks away a wave of sweat. 'This is a gross breach of contract. If you don't let them finish their set, you'll be liable for our travel costs, accommodation costs, the full performance fee—'

'Check your contract again,' Hoffman snarls. 'Check the bit where it says that "artist" – that's you – hereby indemnifies "presenter" – that's me – against any liability, damages, penalties, claims, or losses resulting from "act". I've lost a quarter of our Friday night crowd fifteen minutes in. I've got cops at the box office asking to see my liquor licence. They want to see the fucking set list! It's *you* who's in breach of contract, mate.' He stabs Ash in the chest with a hairy finger.

Ash chews his lip. Skinner paces.

'Nobody here wants any more trouble than we've got already,' Hoffman says. 'If I were you, I'd leave quickly and quietly – while that's still possible.'

He turns on his heel and heads directly to the green room. Vocabulyrix is still there, drunk on free beer, listening in horror to the PA system. Hoffman tells them they're needed for an encore.

Skinner addresses the rest of the band, who are hovering listlessly, still plugged into their amps. 'Alright then. Let's shake a leg. Dante can come back for the gear.'

On the *Beaches* tour, the Acceptables grew accustomed to multiple encores, to gifts and bouquets and booze in their dressing rooms, to young men and women waiting in backstage hallways with come-hither eyes and whispered suggestions of where the night might take

BIG TIME

them. They were used to piling out the stage door and taking twenty minutes to reach the tour bus, wading through an army of shouting, shaking, fainting fans. They would sign records, T-shirts, foreheads, breasts. They would pose for photographs and record messages for ailing relatives. Everywhere they went, they found themselves the endpoint of someone else's pilgrimage.

But tonight, the Acceptables traipse through an empty loading bay. A family of stray cats fish around in a dumpster. A handful of tech crew smoke cigarettes by the side of the road, and when they see the band, they turn their backs.

Once everyone's on board, Skinner fires up Genevieve. 'Who's hungry?' he asks.

Nobody says anything.

'I could eat,' says Skinner.

7

The night sky above Adelaide turns a dark pewter before tossing down nitric rain in heavy, uneven waves. The stormwater drains fill up instantly. Mountains of subterranean trash slalom through the city-wide network of gutter deltas, rounding the freeways then spilling out to sea. Pedestrians scatter, rolling down their sleeves and tucking the hems of their trousers into acid-proof gumboots.

The deluge licks at the windows of the Happy Star Chinese Restaurant, where we sit, still wet with sweat and rain, spinning a lazy Susan and stabbing scrappily at dim sum, piling our plates high with Mongolian beef, Kung Pow chicken, and pork and prawn money bags.

Skinner never learnt how to use chopsticks, so he's eating fried rice with a spoon. 'I'll speak with the label first thing in the morning,' he says. 'Make sure this doesn't happen again. I remember the days when bands just showed up, nothing in writing, smashing equipment, throwing champagne bottles at the audience. And the audience throwing all sorts of things back! A real riot, used to be. Now you put one toe out of line and you're tossed out like a pack of criminals. Yes, I'll be speaking with the label first thing tomorrow morning.'

'And what can they do?' Xander asks, dunking one end of a spring roll in a vat of soy sauce.

'They can make alternative arrangements, if necessary.'

'I get the feeling it's gonna be like this everywhere,' grumbles Tammy.

BIG TIME

'Excuse me,' says Ash, pushing out his chair. He takes something from Oriana's hand, then navigates through the dim assortment of half-empty tables and disappears into the bathroom.

Cleo waits until he's gone before saying: 'I did this installation once, where I wanted to use human bones to reconstruct the first colonial dwellings. Farmhouses, outhouses, stuff like that. The gallery said that using actual bones would have violated Department of Health and Productivity guidelines, so I had replicas made from fibreglass. Even if something looks a little fake, you still get the meaning of it.'

'I don't,' says Xander, who's never been the biggest fan of Cleo as an artist or person.

'I think she's saying we should change the lyrics,' Tammy says.

'Not change,' reasons Cleo, ' just … substitute. Keep the interior, swap out the chassis.'

'I like the lyrics.' Ludlow shrugs.

'For real?' Julian says, wincing.

'For real. Some of it's a bit brutal, but it's clever. There's some good wordplay in there.'

'It's not the alliteration freaking people out,' says Tammy. She flags down a waiter and orders two more lagers.

'So we change them,' says Pony, getting on board. 'Just a few tweaks here and there. A little less "fuck the man", a little more "crazy times, amirite?"'

'Who's this *we*?' Julian prods.

'Oh, suck it.' Pony swats a hand at him. 'I'm trying to help here.'

Cleo slurps down a noodle. 'He does say "rape" a lot.'

'Yeah, but like, in the biblical sense,' I rationalise. 'Like when people talk about "raping the earth". It's not *sexual*.'

'Not exactly sing-along material either though, is it?'

'We spent five months recording these songs,' spits Xander. 'You wanna change the fucking lyrics? Go ahead and change them.'

'It's not up to us, is it?' says Julian pointedly. Everyone looks at Ash's empty chair, then the chair next to it. At Oriana.

She gets what they're getting at, and she already has her answer: 'No.'

'You're the one person he might actually listen to,' says Tammy, drinking one of her beers.

'It's true,' says Julian.

'I refuse to play Yoko with you guys,' says Oriana. 'Besides, I can already tell you what he'll say. He'll say the music doesn't work without the lyrics. And vice versa. You can't just swap out one part and expect the rest to retain the same meaning. They're intertwined. Yin and yang.'

Tammy burps. 'That does sound like something he'd say.'

On the way to the restaurant – just as the heavens opened and the streets liquefied – Julian had put one of Oriana's perfume samplers up to each eye and spent the next seven minutes seeing about seventeen hours into the future. That's why he's kept relatively cool throughout this dinner – and why he knows what he's about to say. He also knows what Oriana will say in response, but he wants to hear her actually say it. So he says: 'You like the new music, don't you, O?'

Even with every single eye on her, Oriana holds Julian's gaze. She knows what he's doing, and she won't be drawn. 'I do.'

'You think it has an *edge*.'

'I like its ambition.'

'You didn't think *Beaches* was ambitious?'

'In its own way. But once you do something once, doing it again isn't ambitious anymore.'

'Can't argue with that logic,' I say, sucking the meat from a chilli prawn.

Julian taps his tongue against his teeth, waiting for the clock he has ticking away in his brain to tell him when the time is right to say: 'You told me there were DID agents there tonight.'

For a moment, no-one's eating anything.

'The fuck?' says Xander.

'Jesus,' says Tammy, polishing off beer number two.

Julian detects a smile at work on Oriana's lips. 'No fair,' she says. 'You've seen this.'

Skinner's still catching up. 'There were DID agents at the gig tonight?'

Julian keeps looking at Oriana as he says to Skinner: 'She even said she's seen them before.'

Xander wants details. 'When? How far back?'

'A while back,' says Oriana.

BIG TIME

Skinner stares into his fried rice. He's thinking of the prisons he's been in before and the things he's heard about the new generation of work camps. Days spent stirring vats of chemicals, manning production lines in blazing heat and bitter cold. He's imagining his mother, sitting alone in the nursing home he quietly pays for, waiting by the phone, wondering why he hasn't called.

'I'll mention this to the label,' he says.

Here's one thing that caught Julian a little off guard when he skipped ahead earlier: right now, in this moment, he's supposed to say, 'Ash, be cool,' even though he's facing away from the bathroom, out towards the street-facing windows and the rows of aquariums full of dazed, doomed fish. He's supposed to say, 'Ash, be cool,' even though he hasn't seen Ash come back from the bathroom yet. So which version of Julian knew to say it? The version taking a face full of F on the bus forty-five minutes earlier? The version that version on the bus was watching? Or the version sitting here now, facing the aquariums, saying, 'Ash, be cool'?

The paradox is ultimately irrelevant, because by the time Julian does say, 'Ash, be cool,' he knows exactly why he was always going to say it: Ash has returned from the bathroom, picked up a knife – the only one on the table, for dissecting the duck in orange sauce – and placed it lightly but decisively against Julian's neck.

'I know what you're doing,' Ash hisses.

Cleo and Ludlow stand from their chairs. Xander coughs out his food. Oriana's eyebrows dip inwards and down, but apart from that, she doesn't move an inch.

'Ash, be cool,' Julian repeats.

'Ash, what the fuck?' I hear myself shouting.

'I saw,' Ash says. 'I saw what's going to happen in just a few minutes. The windows caving in. The restaurant emptying out. A whole squad of DID troopers dragging us into the street. And I saw them leaving *him*' – an emphatic press of the knife into Julian's Adam's apple – 'untouched. I wonder what that could mean?'

Skinner can't stand because he can't feel his legs, so he moves his arms twice as rapidly to compensate. 'Ash, nobody understands what you're saying! Please, pop the knife down, and let's go back to the hotel and talk, okay? We can call the label!'

'I don't wanna call the *fucking label*!' Ash wails. 'I want to know how long this fucking rat has been spilling our secrets to the DID!'

'What secrets?' says Julian. 'You think I'm gonna dob you in for being an F-head just cos I don't like the new album?'

'When did they get to you? What have they got on you? Did you do something while you were away? Did they bust you on the way back in?'

Tammy's trying to convince the restaurant owner not to call the police. 'Ash,' she shouts over at him, 'if you're trying to *not* get arrested, you're doing a shithouse job.'

'So you skipped ahead just now, in the bathroom?' Julian calmly plants his hands on the table, fingers evenly splayed.

'Sure,' Ash says, coughing involuntarily as if to confirm the fact. 'Why not?'

'Tell me everything you saw.'

'What?'

'In detail. From the moment you saw yourself coming back to the table and doing this.'

Ash looks around. 'I saw us say what we're saying now.'

'And then?'

'And then I saw an armoured car pull up—'

'No, you said that was in a few minutes. Give me something smaller, something between now and then.'

Ash grits his teeth, mind dancing between timelines. There's a certain fogginess that comes with extended, devoted F use. Fake memories. Brain slippage. Double déjà vu.

'I ... I'm standing here. And somebody tries to come into the restaurant. But Tammy turns them away.'

'What then?'

'Then ... three people walk past and look inside.'

'What do they look like?'

'Why does that matter?'

'Because I've seen them too. What do they look like?'

'Two women, one guy. The women are dressed in black. The man has a—'

'A green jacket,' Julian finishes.

Ash swallows, surprised but not surprised. 'Yeah. He's wearing a green jacket. And they're all trying to fit under the one umbrella.'

BIG TIME

'So we're neck-and-neck. What then?'

'A crash outside. A fender bender. The lights change, and a white car accelerates too fast and drives into the back of a blue car. The people get out, and they argue.'

'What then?'

'While we're watching them argue, that's when the van pulls up. We try to go out the back, but they've surrounded the place. Xander gets hurt. Tammy tries to fight.'

'Too fucking right I do,' says Tammy.

'They zip-tie our hands, throw hoods on our heads. They put us in the van.'

'What then?'

'That's as far as I got.'

'I saw it differently,' Julian says. 'The white car doesn't crash into the blue car. It accelerates, the blue car doesn't, and there's *nearly* a crash, but the driver slams on their brakes just in time. They honk their horn and shout something out the window, then accelerate around them and drive through the intersection. Then you put down that knife, and Tammy says something. Tammy says something that makes us all laugh. We go back to the hotel, and tomorrow we drive to Botany.'

'Fucking liar,' growls Ash.

'You can't both be right!' Cleo's hopping back and forth, wanting to turn and run, wanting to stay and watch.

'So we wait and see,' says Oriana. She couldn't have asked for a better experiment.

The restaurant manager's got the phone in one hand, watching breathlessly. The cop shop's only two blocks away.

A small handful of late-night diners have congregated around one banquet table for safety. The cooks have stopped cooking and are watching through the service hatch.

'You ever seen something happen that then didn't happen?' Julian asks Ash, trying to swallow, feeling the blade kiss his neck as the spit goes down.

'Couple of times,' Ash says. 'What about you?'

Julian thinks of the wet grass at the racecourse, the smell of genetically modified roses. A kiss from Oriana that never happened but he remembers nonetheless. 'Only once,' he says.

JORDAN PROSSER

A bell *dings* above the front door as a woman loaded down with shopping bags tries to sidestep her way inside. Tammy races over, takes her shoulders and turns her around, apologising as she physically expels her from the premises before shutting and locking the door.

'Whoa,' says Ludlow.

'The fuck else was I gonna do?' says Tammy.

Pony wonders aloud whether Tammy turned away the customer because she'd chosen to, or because Ash had told her she was going to.

I shoot him a look. 'Chicken, meet egg. What difference does it make?' I wish there was more wine.

Meanwhile, Tammy's skirted around the fish tanks to get an angle on Ash. She catches Skinner's eye with a flicker of hers. She's saying: *I can take him if I need to.* He clears his throat: *not yet, for goodness sake.*

Oriana reaches into the middle of the lazy Susan, takes the last curry puff and dissects it with her teeth.

On the street outside, a trio of forty-somethings – two women and one man – two black dresses and one green jacket – all squeezing in under one umbrella – their extremities absorbing an industrial amount of rain-borne chemicals – jogs past. They look inside and see us, a curious tableau: oily plates drying under lamplight, a young man at knifepoint, a *Last Supper*-worthy line-up of aghast, rigid, watchful characters, all framed by the sickly blue fish tanks. They drink in the sight then disappear in the downpour.

'Two for two,' Cleo says, letting out a too-loud laugh.

Xander worries: 'What if they're the ones who call the cops?'

'They're not,' says Julian.

'Just tell me what you did, Jules,' Ash demands. 'Tell me what they've got on you.'

'Nothing, man. I'm squeaky clean.'

The colour changes on the white tablecloth – a red light outside. Tammy, Xander, Pony, Cleo and Ludlow press their faces up against the windows. At the table, Ash, Julian, Oriana, Skinner and I turn our eyes to the intersection. A blue car pulls up. A hatchback. A white car pulls up behind it. A people-mover. The roads are soaked. Even coming to a regular, steady halt, the people-mover skids a little on the bitumen.

BIG TIME

'How long?' asks Ludlow.

'Depends on traffic, I guess,' says Pony.

Nobody moves. Nobody says anything. Julian thought that maybe Ash's hand might shake in hesitation – but it doesn't. For a moment, and only a moment, Julian considers that if what he saw was wrong, and what Ash saw was right, he will shortly bleed to death on the floor of a Chinese buffet restaurant in Adelaide. And he's not even twenty-seven.

The lights go green. The white people-mover accelerates too fast, then brakes again, hard, wheels spinning, its big rear fishtailing slightly as it comes to stop only inches from the rear of the blue hatchback. A piercing *HONK* draws the attention of a few pedestrians, hustling home under flimsy umbrellas. From inside the restaurant, we hear the driver shouting 'Eatshitmotherfuckerrrrrr!' through an open window as the white car steers around the hatchback and accelerates through the intersection.

Two seconds later the blue hatchback, having stalled at the lights, restarts its engine and crawls gingerly ahead. Only then does Julian feel the knife start to tremble in Ash's hand.

'Oh god,' he says.

'That's that, then,' Skinner says, sweat condensing at the tip of his nose. 'We're all agreed? No accident. No police van. Is that ... how this works?' He looks around desperately, hoping for verification.

'It could still happen,' Xander speculates, glued to the window, eyes darting up and down the block. 'Maybe we should wait.'

'It's over,' Oriana says.

Pony's not convinced. 'How can you be so sure?'

'The futures they each saw deviated at that moment, splitting off like branches on a tree. Now that we've gone down one branch, it's highly unlikely that the version we're in – Julian's version – will dovetail once again with the false version.'

Ash looks straight at Oriana. More than anything, he seems insulted by the word *false*.

'Ash?' Julian prompts. 'Would you mind?'

'Sorry, mate,' says Ash, voice trembling.

The second Ash removes his grip on Julian's shoulder and lowers the knife, Julian stands from his chair, grabs Ash by the shirt, lifts him clean off his feet and hurls him down on the banquet table.

JORDAN PROSSER

It's a mess of limbs, downed crockery and cold chow mein. Skinner is closest, so he tries to get between them, shielding Ash's precious face from Julian's flailing paws. Then Xander races over and tugs at Julian's collar, like he's yanking a dog from a fighting pit. I'm standing, shouting at them both, and Cleo's shrieking over by the fish tanks, while for some reason Pony's started doing laps around the table, utterly confused about what he ought to be doing and where his allegiances lie. Oriana steps back and watches.

Clearly, Julian left this part out when he'd recounted his version of future events. He knows precisely when to land one terrific right hook on the side of Ash's face, leaving him with a black eye he'll have for the rest of the tour (and the rest of his life, for that matter).

'OI!' shouts Tammy, loud enough that even over the din of fleeing patrons and shattering porcelain, everybody halts and turns to face her.

When she shouted 'OI!', Tammy didn't necessarily know what she was going to say next. All she knew was that it broke her heart seeing Ash and Julian like this – seeing what had become of the band she'd once hoped would be her life. After Ash approached her at an underground gig and asked her to try out for a spot in the Acceptables, she'd practised for thirty-six hours straight on an electric drum kit in the attic of her family home, headphones glued to her temples in a late-April heatwave. Nobody had ever really asked her to be a part of something before.

So she shouted 'OI!' for the sake of her past-self in that attic – but also because Julian had said she was going to say something. Something that would make them all laugh. At the time she shouted 'OI!', she had no idea what that might be, so she just said the first thing that came into her head.

'Is this what the party really means?'

In that split second between thought and speech, her mind returned to last year's party at Xander and Pony's parents' house, stumbling away from the DID raid, hearing that one forlorn partygoer decrying the night.

Skinner snaps: 'This is not a party, Tammy! This is clearly a very serious band matter!'

In response to that, and despite all present circumstances, Ash and Julian begin to laugh. They're face to face, almost on top of one

BIG TIME

another, so now they're laughing in each other's faces, cheeks bruised and red, eyes bloodshot and slick with tears.

'Is THIS,' Julian croaks, 'what THE PARTY ... *really means?*'

Ash cackles in reply: 'Is this what "the party"' – air quotes – 'really means?!'

'I don't get it,' says Pony.

Julian slides off the table and waves a hand around at the restaurant. 'Is this.'

Ash wraps a fistful of ice from a wine cooler in a napkin and presses it to his eye. 'What the.'

I stand up fast, knocking over an assortment of empty beer bottles. 'PARTY.'

Cleo giggles with relief, hugging Oriana, who seems tentatively pleased with this outcome. 'Really ...'

Tammy holds an imaginary microphone to Pony's lips. 'Means?'

'Heyyyyyyyyy!' Ash and Julian cheer.

Ludlow takes a step back with their camera and captures the moment. Skinner takes the company credit card over to the horrified restauranteur and keys in an enormous tip.

'Bunch of fucking lunatics.' Xander lights a cigarette before he's even out the door.

One thing Julian had noticed with his F-trips: the further he went, the less he felt. If you see yourself stub your toe twenty seconds into a trip, you could just about feel it happening. But if the toe stubbing wasn't scheduled for an hour, a day, or a week down the line, you could probably *guess* how much it would hurt, but the feeling itself was out of reach. Skip ahead far enough and all you're experiencing is raw data.

When Julian had seen the outcome of the band's dinner at the Happy Star Chinese Restaurant, it was cold and remote, devoid of emotion or any genuine sensation. Yes, he knew that his life would be threatened. He knew that he would hurt his old friend. And he knew that in the end, it would be okay. But now, he and Ash and Tammy and Cleo and Ludlow and I are all linking arms with Skinner, reciting our new mantra over and over, experimenting with different inflections on every word, imbuing it with comic gravitas. And now that Julian's actually living it, he can feel it, too.

JORDAN PROSSER

It's good to feel things, thinks Julian Ferryman, as our conga line spills out into the poisonous deluge. He felt a bit like the driver in that blue hatchback; having narrowly avoided disaster, he had the whole night ahead to reflect on how close things had come to being so much worse.

8

Yumi Atako and Ren Hashimoto met on the first day of elementary school. Their relationship began as many do at that age: Yumi approached Ren near a set of steel benches in the gymnasium and politely asked if she would like to be her friend. Ren was embarrassed; she already had a friend, the son of one of her father's work colleagues. Yumi assured her that you were allowed to have more than one. Ren was relieved and gratefully accepted. This brief interaction set the template for their relationship well into adult life – and beyond life itself.

Yumi was tall for her age, and bookish, with a pair of round glasses and a gleaming lunchbox with a cartoon owl on it. Ren was much shorter, almost always a little grubby, and brought her lunch to school in a crumpled brown bag. The moment Yumi outgrew her uniform – a navy-style *seifuku* with black leather shoes with tidy silver buckles – she was bought another, while Ren remained in the same dirty *fuku* until her arms were nearly bursting through the stitching. The first time Ren went to Yumi's house for dinner, she was astonished by the food. A private chef bowed deeply to each of the Atakos as each course was served, and gave Ren a bowl full of shaved ice, coloured green. Yumi's parents didn't exchange one word throughout the meal, preferring to read the financial papers; Mr Atako was the Niigata regional manager of a national logistics company. Months later, Ren was deeply embarrassed when she realised that her father's lowly job was in one of Yumi's father's shipping yards.

JORDAN PROSSER

On their first school camp together, Ren and Yumi traded a significant amount of Pocky with classmates to end up in the same bunk. Yumi's long legs meant she always slept up top. Both fancied themselves burgeoning adventurers; Ren was obsessed with ancient Egypt, while Yumi had become fascinated by the natural world, volcanoes and earthquakes and deep-ocean exploration. They snuck out before dawn one day to track down a hornet's nest they'd spied the afternoon before. Ren threw pebbles at it while Yumi read from an illustrated encyclopedia of insects. One of Ren's pebbles landed squarely in the middle of the hive – a direct hit! – as she was often accidentally good at things. The girls screamed as they fled back to their cabin and refused to leave for the rest of the day, feigning stomach aches.

At camp the next year, in the second grade, Ren claimed to have discovered a new species of beetle, and Yumi gave it a Latin name: *hashimotus renisectus*. In the third grade, when their class took a bus along the winding roads near Naeba, Yumi was motion-sick and vomited in Ren's lap. As Yumi cried and moaned, Ren made her laugh by impersonating the macaques perched atop the concrete barriers along the mountain highway. In the fourth grade, the duo won a talent competition – Ren sang, and Yumi played keyboard in a rendition of the folk ballad '*Sakura Sakura*'. In the fifth grade, Yumi contracted meningitis and was flown to Tokyo where she lived for months in a hermetically sealed room. Ren went to school camp alone, writing Yumi letters every day she was there.

Yumi-chan,

Today Haruto tried to impress me by eating a worm. I told him I used to eat worms all the time, but he didn't believe me, so I picked up four, right out of the dirt, and ate them in one go! He was grossed out but very impressed. I felt horrible afterwards. I wouldn't have to do this kind of stuff or even talk to Haruto if you were here.

What's it like in hospital? What do you get to eat? Do you order off a menu or is it decided for you each day?

Ren

BIG TIME

There was a menu at JR Tokyo General, but Yumi didn't get to tell Ren about it until she was discharged three months later and six kilos lighter. The doctors discovered that her sickness had triggered an unexpected mutation in her genes. She could now no longer eat fish.

'I wish you could have visited,' Yumi said to Ren when they saw each other again, hugging tightly, noses pushing into each other's hair.

'Me too,' said Ren, not telling Yumi that she'd tried. She'd walked around Niigata for days, passing out handwritten résumés, hoping that a café or convenience store might find it in their hearts to hire a ten-year-old for just a few shifts a week, after school or on weekends, just enough so that she could afford a return ticket to Tokyo.

In the sixth grade, Ren asked Yumi if she liked being bitten, and Yumi replied that she didn't really know.

Ren asked: 'Want to find out?'

Yumi pulled down the neck of her T-shirt. Ren closed her teeth gently around one collarbone. After she pulled her mouth away, Yumi could feel her friend's saliva drying on her skin.

'It's okay,' was her assessment. 'Want me to do you now?'

At the end of that year, the unthinkable happened: Yumi's father was promoted, and he announced they would be moving to Tokyo.

Ren organised a going-away party in a local park. A few other girls from school came but didn't stay long. Ren and Yumi had been each other's only real friends for the past seven years, and the idea of embarking on something like junior high school without one another was so horrifying that as night fell, and the parents tried to lead the girls to their separate cars, their separate homes, their separate lives, Yumi and Ren linked arms and dug their nails into each other's skin, screaming and refusing to let go. By the time Mr and Mrs Atako and Mr and Mrs Hashimoto finally managed to pry their daughters away, the young girls' forearms were banded with blood.

Having swapped ghost stories in sleeping bags, discovered new insects, won talent competitions, exchanged dark secrets, eaten until they were sick, danced until they fainted and sampled each other's skin with their teeth and tongues, Ren and Yumi were reduced to mere pen pals.

In the seventh grade, they wrote almost every other day. By the eighth grade, it was once a month. By the time they entered upper secondary, they rarely corresponded beyond birthday cards.

In Tokyo, Yumi had attempted to make friends the way she once had with Ren – but the girls in Tokyo were a different story. They wore their *fuku* differently, and had colourful hair and strange jewellery, and listened to music that even Ren would not have enjoyed. Yumi spent most of her time in the library.

Back in Niigata, Ren kept to herself as well. She cut off her hair, smoked cigarettes but didn't enjoy them, and by the tenth grade she had a boyfriend: Haruto, the kid who'd once tried to impress her by eating worms. They experimented thoroughly with each other, mostly in parks and parked cars, as the Hashimoto family were still all crammed into a three-bedroom house and Haruto's parents were devoutly Catholic. But the town felt different. When Yumi was there, Ren had felt as though adventure was waiting at the crest of each hill; every beach a blasted moonscape, every construction site a nefarious Yakuza hideout. Now, life felt distinctly unadventurous.

Shortly before her eighteenth birthday, Ren sat in the back of Haruto's Suzuki as his hands unbuttoned her shirt and explored her torso. She reclined her head all the way back so she could see through the rear windscreen, up to the desert of stars flung out far above her.

'I'm going to leave this place,' she said, just as Haruto was starting to unbutton her jeans. 'And I don't want you to come with me.'

Throughout high school, when her parents would pressure her to decide on a career, Yumi's mind would return to that hermetically sealed room where she'd lived for three months in the sixth grade. Even through her feverish fog, she had asked the doctors for more details, more data, relying on the comfort of facts. She asked the doctors to explain everything wrong with her body, and she trusted every word they said. She liked the idea of someone trusting her like that. So, the spring after graduation, Yumi began a Bachelor of Medicine in the hope of one day becoming a doctor at Tokyo General.

Yumi moved to a campus dormitory to fully immerse herself in university life (and create some distance from her parents). In her

BIG TIME

first week of study, Yumi's roommate, a girl from Osaka named Sara, dragged her along to a party in another dorm where the second-year boys chugged heavy cans of beer while eyeing off the freshman girls. After losing Sara in the crowd, Yumi hovered politely, still not all that adept at making friends. Thankfully, that night, she didn't need to be. Just as Yumi was preparing to slip out unnoticed, Ren appeared with a shout, sprinting down the hallway, lifting Yumi up in her arms and spinning her around so fast she nearly knocked over a trophy cabinet.

Ren had made good on her promise to leave Niigata, and Haruto, and everything and everyone else behind. She had worked at the 7-Eleven near school every weekend for the past year, studying for exams behind the counter while her supervisor unloaded pallets in the storeroom. Ren's parents didn't understand their daughter's desire to leave their hometown but saw her off at the train station nonetheless, her mother handing her an enormous stack of homemade bento for the journey (it had been so long since Ren's mother had travelled to Tokyo, she didn't realise the trip now took less than two hours). Ren had moved into a women's boarding house not far from the university. And now, in this new place, with Yumi serendipitously restored to her side, life felt like an adventure again.

Yumi took Ren to the Metropolitan Art Museum and told her all about high school – about the half-decade of lonely afternoons in the library. She showed Ren her parents' place in Roppongi, where Mr Atako spotted Ren and bowed politely before retiring to his study, clearly not recognising her. Ren insisted they spend a full night in Harajuku, playing pachinko, drinking bourbon in American-style jazz bars. Ren told Yumi all about Haruto – 'Worm boy?!' Yumi exclaimed – and her six siblings, who had all started families of their own and taken jobs at the port, like their father. Both girls were envious of the others' high school experience; Yumi longed for their seaside town, whereas Ren wished she'd come to Tokyo years earlier. She felt addicted to the city, obsessed with it, so much so that she almost flunked out of university halfway through her first year. She was studying English literature but barely even opened any of the course's assigned readings. Luckily, because she was Ren, she'd already read them all behind the counter of that 7-Eleven.

JORDAN PROSSER

While Yumi was dissecting cadavers and observing rotations at Tokyo General, Ren was exploring the city and hooking up with boys she met at more dorm parties. This was where she met Jiro, a beat poet and saxophone player who fronted a rockabilly quintet Yumi sometimes saw playing opposite Tower Records in Shibuya. After a couple of months, when Ren tried to break things off with Jiro, he hit her. Yumi called the police, had Jiro arrested and asked Sara if Ren could stay in their dorm room for a little while. Sara didn't mind – she was returning to Osaka for the summer anyway. She then fell pregnant to her high school boyfriend, having rekindled their romance, and never returned to Tokyo, which was how Ren and Yumi became full-time roommates.

Any friend who's ever moved in with a friend can tell you that companionship is different to cohabitation. For the first time ever, Yumi and Ren got on each other's nerves. Once-charming quirks became irritating foibles. Ren argued that Yumi had been 'indoctrinated' by her parents, who themselves valued success above pleasure and quiet respect over candid truth. A little weed, a little sex, a little leisure could only do her good. Yumi conceded, yes, that may be the case – but she had chosen her path and was determined to walk it. Weed and sex and leisure could wait until after she'd graduated.

Yumi had had sex – once – with a boy whose name she couldn't remember. She met him with Ren at one of their bourbon bars in Harajuku. They were celebrating Yumi passing her second year with full honours, and for a brief moment, Yumi could see the appeal of Ren's general MO. After chatting with the boy for nearly twenty minutes, she gestured to the restrooms. It wasn't until they were in a bathroom stall, with his pants around his ankles and her skirt above her waist, that she realised she had no idea what she was doing. The boy didn't mind. He was tender but determined. She bled and apologised. He wiped everything away with a fistful of toilet paper, kissed her wetly on the mouth and went back to the bar. Yumi waited for the pain in her abdomen to subside, and for her legs to stop shaking, before she rejoined Ren and their other friends at the table. Ren took one look at Yumi and wrapped her arms around her, pushing her nose into her hair.

BIG TIME

If Ren believed this incident marked the debut of a different, more carefree Yumi, she might have overestimated. A few weeks later, Ren stumbled home with a boy she'd met at a protest. The door to the dorm room sighed open and they fell on her bed, shedding clothes and trussing tongues. By the time Yumi thought to clear her throat, or say something, or simply get up and leave, it was too late – she was entombed in her duvet on the opposite side of the room, facing the wall, listening to the smack of skin on skin. The next morning, lover departed, face down in the pillows, Ren woke to find Yumi standing over her bed. Yumi had never shouted like that before – didn't believe she was even capable of it. But she shouted and shouted, calling Ren names, calling her a slut and a terrible friend. Ren apologised – said the bourbon had got the better of her – but she refused to be embarrassed. Yumi's voice was hoarse. Ren's head hurt. They could agree on one thing: it would be best if Ren found somewhere else to live.

That night would be the last time they saw each other for almost two decades. Ren returned late from another rally, tiptoeing through the door. She packed her belongings, lay down in bed, turned off the light and heard Yumi start to cry.

Ren said it would be alright; they would always be friends. Yumi peeled off her covers, crossed the floor to Ren's bed and let herself in next to her, spooning her, burying her nose in her hair. Ren told her about a writer's program in upstate New York she'd been accepted into. She would be leaving the following week. Yumi said it sounded like a terrific opportunity, but even she was barely listening to her own words. She was focused on her fingers, resting on the soft skin of Ren's stomach. The fingers moved, raking the fine hair around Ren's belly button.

'You must be excited,' Yumi said, as the sweep of her fingers broadened in both directions – further towards Ren's chest, further towards the elastic band of her shorts.

'Not really,' said Ren, pushing back against Yumi, filling her concaveness.

'Why not?' asked Yumi, brushing her bottom lip across Ren's shoulder.

'Because you won't be there,' Ren said, taking Yumi's hand in her hand and pushing it below her waistband.

They didn't speak another word – not then, and not for a long time. Ren pulled Yumi around her like a shawl. When Yumi hesitated, Ren pulled her tighter, rolling over to face her friend, her pen pal, her roommate, her Yumi, kissing her wetly on the mouth. They slid their clothes down and kicked at them, expelling them from the single bed, taking turns on top, biting and licking and holding and touching and tasting all the parts of each other they'd never explored.

When Yumi woke up on Ren's side of the room the following morning, she was gone. The sheets still smelt of her – bourbon and tea and dry shampoo. She had moved out, as promised, and moved away soon after that. On the day Ren took a plane to JFK airport, Yumi was presented with a female cadaver in class – small and pale, about her age. Ren's age. For the first time in her medical studies, Yumi looked away. Not from death, but from the young woman's nakedness.

The people in your life are a form of time travel; knowing them, then losing them, is like pausing the hands on a clock. The time between Ren and Yumi parting ways and finding each other again – the time they were paused – that time certainly happened. There was love in there, failures, graduations, marriages, further studies, vacations to white-sand beaches in Thailand in Yumi's case, and in Ren's, at least one arrest.

In America, Ren embraced the life of an expat. She loved the way her mere presence conjured the same adventurous awe in others that she admired in herself. In the writer's program and beyond, when stubble-chinned, floppy-haired men leant an inch too close and asked, 'But really, where are you *from*?' and Ren replied, 'Japan,' the response was always the same: 'Japan. I've *always* wanted to go,' their voices gesturing towards internalised teenage fantasies of short-skirted, big-eyed anime girls, neon sex clubs and pale genitalia.

That all definitely happened – as did Yumi's specialisation in oncology and her first day on rotation as a supervising doctor at Tokyo General. She met a woman whom she loved and could rely upon. That happened. They moved to Roppongi, not far from Yumi's parents, and bought a dog with long ears and fur like golden felt. That happened. Yumi watched her mother, then her father, succumb to different forms of cancer. She spent years guiding them each through arduous chemotherapy, short-lived remission, painful bone marrow transplants and then finally humiliating, lung-rattling death. That absolutely happened.

That was what prompted Yumi to begin investigating alternative medicines. She was quickly mocked, then censured by her own department as word of her extracurricular interests spread among the staff – but as long as Yumi maintained the highest ethical standards during work hours, there was little the board or the Chief of Oncology could do about it. Yumi became an active member in the alternative medicine lecture circuit – a rowdy cavalcade of international doctors who bandied about all sorts of hypothetical cures, some based in irrefutable scientific fact, others clear flights of fancy. Yumi spent her annual leave writing papers on amygdalin and altering the pH levels of volunteer patients in small trials. In Dubai, she delivered a rousing keynote address on the topic of ozone anti-aging procedures, which was met with derision from her colleagues back home but hailed as revolutionary by those on the circuit. Yumi stopped short of ever claiming any of these treatments 'worked', per se – but she believed it was a doctor's duty to remain curious. She was approached by numerous global pharmaceutical companies, Pfizer and Roche and Gilead and Bayer and Biogen and Otsuka and Vertex and Ipsen and STADA, each asking her to be the poster child for their experimental cancer treatments: ultraviolet T-cell therapy, *Clostridium novyi* tablets, anti-fungal itraconazole peels, telomerase inhibitors, tumour suppression sound baths, targeted radioactive acupuncture, epigenetic stem cell propagation and in one case even a full-body transplant procedure. Yumi was cunning in her dealings with them. She read the preliminary findings and gleaned what she could, sapping each army of earnest corporate scientists of their learnings before inevitably turning down the lavish fortunes they were offering. She would be champion of no cause other than the ongoing pursuit of knowledge.

Yumi was in her forties when she first visited America. She'd been invited to present at a symposium and had taken two weeks' leave, telling her colleagues at Tokyo General she was bound for a distant relative's wedding. She kissed her partner on the cheek and boarded a train to Haneda airport. Plane travel was a nightmare; the lankiness, the long-limbedness that had defined Yumi's adolescence was still a source of constant inconvenience. Her thin frame made cold winters difficult to tolerate, and her knees ached and her back sighed daily with the effort of keeping her towering stature upright. But as soon as Yumi touched down in New York City, she was glad she came. It looked a lot like the place she'd seen in movies growing up, but many of the bookstores and brownstones had been replaced by teetering, featureless apartment buildings. She took a taxi round the verge of Central Park and saw horse-drawn carriages cutting furrows through the fallen leaves. She ate out for every meal, preparing lecture notes at tables for one in diners across Manhattan, gorging on birria de res tacos in Jackson Heights, fried yardbird in Harlem, empanadas in the Bronx and bagels on the Lower East Side. She liked the loudness of New York. In Tokyo, it was the city itself that was loud – the wiring and the infrastructure. Here in America, it was the people.

The symposium was held in a rented-out lecture theatre near Greenwich Village, a stuffy grey box with no raked seating and one small projector screen framed by faded velvet curtains. Yumi sat in the front row with the other speakers and listened to her peers from across the globe, whom she normally only ever interacted with over email, dryly expound on the beneficial cytotoxic effects of cold atmospheric plasma treatment. Yumi had had friends in her life, but never much of a community. She liked these people. This was why it was always worth getting on the plane, she reminded herself.

Taking the stage to a bout of warm academic applause, squinting as she stepped accidentally into the beam of the projector (she was never the most adroit public speaker), Yumi began her disquisition on oncolytic viral therapy, sharing her findings from a small study co-facilitated by Lund University. Two minutes in, as she pressed the clicker to change the slide and the projector went dark for just half a second, Yumi saw her: Ren, seated in the far corner of the back row. Yumi fumbled her words, shuffled her index cards, then forged ahead as Ren watched with an uncanny smile, the hands on the clock picking up right where they'd left off.

BIG TIME

*

During the afternoon break, Yumi found Ren at the catering table. She couldn't tell whether she looked older or even younger; her face was still that of a woman in her twenties, but her hair was much shorter, cut close to the scalp, and her skin was white like talc. They tried various forms of greeting, both overly formal and overly familiar, before laughing at their own efforts and falling into an embrace.

They went to Ren's favourite hole-in-the-wall Italian place on Carmine Street. Yumi ate carpaccio, tortellini and gnocco fritto, while Ren picked softly at the bread bowl. She confessed that her interest in the symposium was two-fold: she knew Yumi would be there, but also, she'd been frequenting such conferences for months.

'What stage are you?' asked Yumi.

'The last one,' said Ren. She was diagnosed with lymphoma in her early thirties and had spent the last ten years in and out of remission. But now it was back – in her bones and blood and brain. She could feel it when she moved, when she breathed, when she blinked. Her doctors had told her there was no further treatment available to her.

Yumi said she was sorry and told Ren about her parents – the years she spent watching them die.

Ren said that *she* was sorry – then laughed. 'I guess if we're both sorry, neither of us needs to be.'

By the end of the meal, Ren was feeling faint. Yumi paid for dinner and took Ren back to Flatbush, where she lived in a one-bedroom apartment on the seventh floor above a bodega. She said the family who ran it had been kind the past few years, running up ready-made meals and groceries and dropping them at her door. Yumi put Ren to bed and watched her fall into the heavy but fitful sort of sleep she'd seen in a thousand patients – bodies pulled down into the mattress, air pulled from their throats, life pulled from their lungs.

On a desk by the window, Yumi found a folder stuffed with paperwork – palliative care pamphlets and assisted dying brochures with titles like *WHAT NOW?* as well as Ren's latest test results: blood work, cell count, nitrogen and haemoglobin levels and so on. Yumi had hoped, perhaps a little arrogantly, that by scouring the data herself she might find some gaping loophole, something blindingly obvious which her American counterparts had missed. But she could tell their prognosis was accurate.

Yumi wrote a note:

Ren-chan,
I'm here for two more days. I'll come see you tomorrow.
Yumi

Then she looked across Ren's bookshelves, hoping to find some trace of herself there – a trinket, a photo, some impression of their time together as girls in Japan. Finding nothing, she eased the front door closed and took the B train back to her hotel.

On the second day of the symposium, a team of researchers from New Zealand discussed a new, controversial synthetic hallucinogen supposedly being manufactured in the Federal Republic of East Australia – scientific name: *trypto-lyside glutochronomine*; street name: F. Though it had only been a decade since the FREA shut itself off from the world, it was impossible to get a complete picture of just how prevalent the drug had become, or what its repercussions for the global medical community might be. It was also all but impossible to obtain. One PhD candidate from the University of Otago was working on a paper hypothetically advocating for *trypto-lyside glutochronomine* in end-of-life care, using anecdotal accounts of the drug's effects from FREA refugees and defectors. She argued that a glimpse into the future could help ease the emotional toll on patients and caregivers by giving them some degree of certainty as to what the next hour, day or week might bring. Even beyond palliative care, she said, the ramifications could be profound: imagine seeing test results days in advance. Imagine a surgeon telling a family the outcome of their loved one's procedure before they even scrubbed up. Imagine being able to plainly demonstrate to a suicide risk that, despite what their brain was telling them, they would definitively still be here tomorrow.

The session ran overtime. The young woman's mic was unceremoniously cut and the scientists were clapped offstage. A brain surgeon

BIG TIME

from Boston, whom Yumi was friendly with, leant over with a chuckle, saying: 'Clearly they've never dealt with insurers. Still, cute idea.'

The conference concluded with the MC thanking everybody for their 'perpetually open minds'. Yumi raced out, grabbing the young PhD student just as she was bundling into a cab. Yumi said she was fascinated by her presentation and wondered, hypothetically: how might someone obtain a sample of *trypto-lyside glutochronomine* to carry out their own research?

The student looked Yumi up and down. 'Hypothetically?'

'For a friend,' Yumi said.

The young woman sighed kind-heartedly. She said she wished she could help. Her team in Dunedin tried for months to procure some for their own trials, but there was too much red tape.

'You won't find it through any official channels,' the young woman said. 'It's not in any vaults at the WHO or the CDC. Not yet anyway. Your best bet is to look where things get lumped before the law knows what to do with them. The black market.'

Then she smiled, handed Yumi a business card and disappeared down Christopher Street.

Only hours later, around 3 am, Yumi was waiting in the stairwell of a tenement building in the southern guts of Brooklyn. She was there to meet Rango.

Yumi had gone straight from the lecture theatre to Ren's apartment and asked, point blank, whether she knew any drug dealers. Ren said that was a fairly vague term which could be used to describe much of her social circle. Yumi specified: someone with overseas connections. Someone you might go to for the newest, weirdest designer stuff. Ren asked what she was up to.

Yumi replied: 'Are you afraid of dying?'

'Same as everyone.'

'I want to help with that.'

'So it's not a cure for cancer?' Ren laughed softly.

'We might cure the fear of it first,' said Yumi.

Ren gave her an address and told her to knock seven times at apartment 5B. Yumi did as instructed and waited one very long minute before the door opened a few inches, catching on a safety latch. Two green eyes stared out from inside.

'You're Ren's friend?' the eyes asked.
'Yumi.'
'She never mentioned you 'fore tonight.'
'We didn't see each other for a very long time.'

The door closed, the chain rattled away and the door re-opened. Yumi was ushered into a low-ceilinged apartment by a shirtless man covered in tattoos. When he turned to lead her down the hallway, she saw a hefty tree trunk etched down the length of his spine, its branches and roots spreading out along his limbs, encasing him in an exoskeleton of ink.

She sat on a pleather sofa while Rango hovered near a large marble table covered in baggies and bottles and industrial scales.

'What are you after?' he asked.
'Trypto-lyside glutochronomine.'
Rango squinted.
'F?'
Rango nodded, impressed. 'You done it before?'
'It's for Ren.'
Rango nodded again, slower. 'She's real bad, huh?' Then he laughed. 'Well, die doin' what you love, they say.'

For the next five minutes he spoke at length in his southern twang, partly to Yumi, mostly to himself, lamenting how Australia used to be such an easy market, lax border protection and incredible markups, but now, well, different times, different times indeed. And that was just getting stuff *in* – getting anything *out* from there was even harder. Smuggling F was a prohibitive business. People had died trying to get even half a gallon out into the world.

With that, he removed a small, insulated steel cylinder from a wine fridge in the kitchen, placed it on the marble table and unscrewed the lid. Inside, it brimmed with rainbow-tinted fluid.

'Powerful shit,' he said, delicately measuring a few millilitres into a blue glass vial. 'That'll be seventeen-fifty.'

Yumi didn't blink. She'd stopped at an ATM on the way over and taken out five thousand dollars. She shoved a fistful of cash at Rango and was pleasantly surprised when he gave her change.

'Give Ren my love, wouldja? And go easy with it. Start out small. Gotta be the same amount in each eye, too. Heard some pretty gnarly stories 'bout what happens if there's an imbalance.'

BIG TIME

'Thank you,' Yumi said, her hand closing around the vial, her heart pounding, her brain on autopilot. Forgetting where she was, she bowed deeply towards Rango, and without missing a beat, he bowed back.

When Yumi returned to Ren's apartment, pale dawn light was sliding through the skylight. Yumi sat by the bed and told Ren what she was holding in the blue glass vial.

Ren asked how much it cost, then laughed when Yumi told her. 'Cheaper than my health insurance.'

Yumi helped her lie back on the futon.

'Does this mean you're my doctor now?' asked Ren.

Yumi said she wasn't sure what she was. But Ren said she knew. Yumi gently pried Ren's eyelids open, administering a single drop to each eyeball. As Ren waited for the feeling to find her, she asked about Yumi's return flight – wasn't it meant to be today? Yumi said she didn't mind missing it. She liked New York. She could always go home a little later.

Yumi missed her flight that afternoon, and one the week after, and one the week after that. She checked out of her hotel and relocated to Ren's apartment, where she slept on the daybed under a thin wool blanket. She promised her partner back in Tokyo she'd be home soon. Then one day, they had a fight on the phone. Ren could hear it in the shower, even over the din of the hot water pounding down against her shoulders. After that, Yumi ignored her phone. She extended her leave from Tokyo General until she used it all up – first her paid leave, then her unpaid leave, then her sick leave, then two more weeks of carer's leave she fought to claim. She argued her case for a medical sabbatical, saying she'd embarked on a potentially ground-breaking research project. She was forwarded a formal letter of termination the next day and offered a modest severance package.

But Yumi couldn't go home – not since she'd started treating Ren with F. When she first skipped ahead, Ren had seen herself sleeping peacefully through the night, waking the following morning and walking down the street to get bagels and lattes – then she'd snapped back and they'd done just that, together. She saw the good days and knew they were there to look forward to. She saw the bad days – days spent in bed, or days with urgent hospital visits, Yumi wheeling Ren through the emergency room, telling the doctors what she needed (because Ren had already seen it happen and told her what to say) – and knew to be prepared for them. She developed a tolerance for the new drug quite quickly (it helped that she'd been party-fit her whole life), so her trips grew longer, her visions more vivid. Ren knew that Yumi would stay with her even as her life in Tokyo slipped further away, and that knowledge alone helped more than any pamphlet or pill.

With Ren's permission, Yumi had started documenting her F-trips, taking notes and filming as she recounted her visions. Then, after Yumi checked Ren's vitals and stopped recording, they would forget about the future and talk about the past. Yumi learnt all about the twenty-plus years that Ren had lived in America – mostly in New York, but Austin for a spell and California for a couple of months, 'playing house' with an art dealer and his teenage daughter. Ren was glad to have given motherhood a test-drive so she could know it wasn't for her.

What about Yumi? Had she ever thought about children? Yes, but for whatever reason, she could never picture having them with the person she was with – and then time made the choice for her.

Ren took her hand, fingers light and bony, tilting her head back on a cushion, ready to receive her daily sacrament. 'Would you like to know what we'll be doing tomorrow?'

By spring, Ren was seeing close to a full week ahead in startling detail. Yumi had a standing engagement at Rango's, every Wednesday night at midnight, where she forked over more of her severance pay in exchange for more blue glass vials. She knew which corner stores made the best coffee – which pizza place sold the best pepperoni by the slice – and when Ren was napping, Yumi would show herself around Brooklyn, pretending to be a local, wondering what the difference was between pretending and actually being one. When her academic visa expired, three months after she touched down at JFK, Ren suggested they take a taxi to the council chambers and get married on the spot. Yumi was granted a spousal bridging visa. 'Soon you'll know what it's like to be a widow,' Ren said on their way back to Flatbush, kissing Yumi on the cheek. Yumi could feel the effort it took for Ren to even move her lips.

BIG TIME

*

It was late April when Ren snapped back from a trip, coughing violently, pointing to the bathroom, unable to form words or stand on her feet. Yumi carried Ren to the toilet – she must have weighed less than forty kilos – and drew circles on her back as Ren vomited into the bowl, trembling with the effort, eyes watering and teeth chattering. As the nausea passed, Ren turned her head to find Yumi's eyes.

'Yumi-chan. I'm going to die next Wednesday.' It was currently Friday.

Yumi didn't say anything. She'd known this would happen eventually, soon even, but hearing it felt different.

'There's more,' Ren said.

Yumi helped her back to bed and placed a wet washcloth on her forehead. She hooked up a new bag of fentanyl to Ren's IV, picked up her notepad and pressed record on the video camera.

'What did you see?'

Ren took a deep breath. 'It happens in the morning. I'm sorry to say, but it happens when you're out. You go to get us breakfast. Bagels and lattes. I lose my breath and I start to go under. I'm in a coma for two or three minutes before my heart gives out.'

Yumi bowed her head. 'Ren. I'm so sorry.'

'Don't be. I said there's more.'

'What do you mean?'

'I saw what comes next.'

Yumi sat forward in her chair. 'Next?'

Ren nodded, finding it too absurd to say. Finding it almost funny. 'I saw what happens after I die.'

Yumi and Ren didn't leave the apartment for the next five days. With the remaining F, Yumi showed Ren her own death again and again. Ren wasn't fazed – in fact, she grew strangely accustomed to the idea. She could describe it like an ad on television she'd seen a hundred times, letting the idea of it wash over her without really absorbing its meaning.

And after death – what then? When Yumi asked Ren about the afterlife, she described a great shopping mall, many storeys tall, filled with hundreds of stores, its floors covered in brown and white tiles, buffed to oblivion. A glass-walled elevator. A circular stairwell connecting all the floors for those who wished to walk. Consistent and reliable air-conditioning. Vaulted windows arranged above the thoroughfares like the roof of a cathedral. Militant rows of fluorescent lighting. A food court with loving approximations of many international cuisines. A fountain spewing into a chlorine-blue pool, the bottom dappled with different denominations of coins from people making wishes. Stoic and watchful security guards. Clothes for every season in every size. Free parking with every purchase. Indeterminate weather outside. And all the time in the world.

'It sounds like a dream,' posited Yumi. 'A dream of childhood.'

Ren said she was correct, in a sense – the shopping centres in Niigata had always felt like a safe place. 'I remember our whole family would go sometimes, when we needed a new washing machine or rice cooker. While my parents spoke with the shop attendants, my brothers and sisters and I would jump on the beds, recline on the couches, throw pretend dinner parties on the outdoor furniture settings. Because – you remember – some days my parents would yell at each other day and night. We had nothing to eat and no new clothes. But then other days, we were shopping for appliances, all of us together. Even when I was little, I guess I knew that if we were shopping for washing machines, life couldn't be all that bad.'

'So your mind is returning to that moment,' said Yumi, helping Ren sip water through a straw. 'To a happy memory.'

Ren gripped her hand. 'This isn't a memory, Yumi. It's an actual place. I die, and I go there. I'm me, like I am now. But I'm also not any specific age. I'm sort of ... all ages. And when I walk up to the concierge desk, where you would normally go to ask directions to a particular store, and I ask the woman at the desk what time the mall closes, the woman looks at me, and her face is glowing. There's a ring of fire around her face, except she can't see it. Only I can see it. As it burns, she smiles at me and says there is no closing time, because there's no time at all. And she's right – the closer we get to Wednesday, and the longer I spend in that place, the more I feel it: there really is no time there.'

Looking down at her notebook, Yumi found a triptych of tears mingling with the ink of her pen.

BIG TIME

'What you're describing, Ren ... do you think of it as heaven?'

'I think it's *my* heaven,' whispered Ren. 'And I know that sounds stupid. A shopping mall. But it's not about that. It's about being someplace where time never runs out. Where there's no time, you'll always be safe.'

Early Wednesday morning, just after midnight, Yumi helped Ren to the roof of her apartment building. Even with the cloud cover, even with the light pollution of Brooklyn and beyond, they could see the desert of stars and space junk flung out far above them.

The clinician in Yumi had to ask: 'Has it made it any easier? Knowing what's ahead?'

'Not really,' Ren said. 'Knowing what's ahead doesn't change the fact that you won't be there.'

Just before dawn, Yumi Atako carried Ren Hashimoto – her friend, her wife, her patient – back to bed. She tucked the blanket in around her knees, plumped the pillows, adjusted the blinds, dipped a washcloth in the sink, squeezed out the excess and laid it across her forehead. Then she buried her nose into Ren's short hair.

Ren tried to speak – lips chapped, eyes heavy. Yumi said she didn't have to say anything. She would be right back. She was just stepping out to get them some breakfast.

9

Eager to bail on Wakefield, the band retires to their old prison block hotel just as soon as they stumble from the fracas at the restaurant. They sleep for eight hours, wake up at 10, pack their bags, pile onto the bus and settle in for the twenty-hour drive to Sydney.

Skinner entrusts Dante with the occasional shift at the wheel so they can complete the journey without stopping. The first time Dante settles into the driver's seat, Skinner hovers over him like a dutiful dad, pointing out the road signs, gently suggesting the appropriate time to shift gears, mouthing *whoa whoa whoa* any time Dante approaches a set of traffic lights. Dante, for his part, has an industrial trucking licence and had driven buses part-time during TAFE, but he wasn't about to deprive Skinner of his fun.

Dante had also slept the night before with a gun under his pillow. He'd missed out on dinner at the Happy Star to sneak the band's gear out of the Thebarton and was sitting at the hotel bar when they'd all come traipsing in. Cleo joined him for a nightcap and told him all about the DID agents and Ash's meltdown. None of it was what Dante, with his naturally paranoid inclination, wanted to hear. When Cleo asked if he wanted another drink, Dante turned her down – he was thinking about the large pack of methamphetamines stashed in the vent above the bathroom door in his room upstairs. He was thinking about the small 9 mm pistol jammed beneath the mattress. He'd bought it off the brother of a friend of his brother's. In the FREA, possession of an illegal firearm was punishable by immediate and indefinite detention, but the rush Dante felt carrying it – the jolt of knowing he was the most dangerous person in any given room – still outweighed the fear of being found out.

So Dante's at the wheel with Skinner by his side. To avoid a double border crossing, we've decided to go the long way – heading north-east, further inland. Soon after the checkpoint at Cockburn – standard procedure, UV lights and ID screens – Dante turns us onto the Broken Hill Bypass, a pocky stretch of dual carriageway hastily built to give interstate traffic a suitably wide berth of the FREA's biggest gulag. Everyone goes quiet. Pony presses his face against the windows to get a better look at the smoggy citadel on the horizon: the spewing smokestacks, the tiny metallic specks of combine harvesters, the kilometres of electrified fences and booby-trapped wasteland between here and there. The rest of us look away.

By the time we rejoin the highway near Little Topar, the sun's setting behind us, basting the A32 sorbet orange and bubblegum blue. Everyone finds a bunk or reclines in a chair and settles in for the night. Then Oriana visits us one by one, vial in hand, a dream diviner in torn tennis shoes. One by one, she puts us in a trance. One by one our skulls grow cold, our skin bubbles with gooseflesh and our breath quickens, before it all condenses down to the size and the weight of a pinhole black hole, and we spend the next however long floating forward in time. We see the sun set before it sets. We see townships pass before we pass them – Wilcannia and Noona and Cobar and Canbelego. Skinner nods off as Dante steers us through Dubbo. We're just over halfway there.

Besides the designated drivers, only Julian refused Oriana's visitation. After the restaurant, he said he'd seen enough for a while. He's at the fold-out table near the back of the bus with a guitar in his lap, plucking something out. Once the band and everybody else has been seen to, Cleo and Ludlow and Pony and myself included, Oriana comes and sits beside Julian and listens.

'What's that?' she asks.

'A song,' he says.

'No shit. What's it called?'

'Hasn't got a name yet. Trying to unpack a few of the things that came to me while I was overseas.'

'It's nice. Simple.'

'*Simple*. That could be taken one of two ways.'

'I mean it in the sense of: *pure*.'

Julian tunes his guitar down half a step and tries the melody again.

'You contemplating a solo career?' Oriana asks.

'Would you blame me?'

They sit for a minute, Julian playing, Oriana swaying with the movement of the bus as Dante hugs a shoulder. He's a good driver. Better than Skinner. The air-conditioning hums above them and the wheels rumble beneath, but Julian's guitar cuts through.

'Are there lyrics to that?' Oriana asks.

There were, but Julian felt awkward about singing them. He glances down the aisle, checking on his unconscious travelling companions.

'Don't tell me you're shy,' Oriana teases.

Julian laughs softly. Then he says, 'Lyrics,' psyching himself up. This song would eventually become the opening track on *THE MOTHERF*CKER MANIFESTO*. It was called 'Quiet Boy Freak-out', and it went:

Tender and laughing and quiet and kind
Love is down the phone lines, baby
Love ain't blind

Tender and pungent and pale and sublime
Love is down the phone lines
Maybe love comes from the spine

Flat-footed, funny, and old-school and mine
Skin-coloured, two-legged, with one-track mind
Beautiful and breakable and small and divine

Love is down the phone lines, baby
Love ain't blind

'Hmm,' Oriana hums.

Julian stops dead, B string pinging off his fingernail. 'What?'

'Nothing. Sorry. Keep going.'

'You don't like it.'

BIG TIME

'I didn't say that.'

'You said it was pure.'

'I said it was simple.'

'And what else?'

Oriana breathes out placidly. She knew her inclination towards brutal honesty was a sticking point for many people, but she knew no other way.

'It feels very ... familiar.'

'What's wrong with that? Nostalgia sells.'

'Nostalgia is inherently conservative.'

Julian laughs. 'I feel I stumbled into the wrong lecture or something. Are we talking about the same thing?'

'I think so.'

'It's just a song.'

'Why does it have to be *just* that?'

Julian turns his face to hide his scowl. There's a whiff of Ash in this. 'Not everything has to *mean* something, y'know.'

Oriana shrugs. 'I just think you can't espouse progress while simultaneously fetishising cultural artefacts.'

'*Artefacts?*'

'Two years ago, two thousand years ago, doesn't matter. The past is the past. If you want to move forward – *really* move forward – you have to let go of every single thing behind you. No cherry-picking.'

One of Julian's least favourite tracks on *In the End* was 'My Futurist Bride'. Right now, he's looking at Oriana, thinking, *How the hatred of antiquity gleams in her eye*, wondering whether Ash wrote it about her. He wonders about all the things Ash knows about her that Julian never will. You don't always give the same parts of yourself to everyone.

'Tell me something from your trip,' says Oriana, expertly changing the subject. 'An adventure you had. Or something you saw.'

'Okay.' Julian sets his guitar aside. 'The night I left for home, I was taking a taxi through Medellín. I looked out the window and there was this group of kids – I say "kids", I dunno, maybe teenagers. Late teens. Riding on scooters. Every boy had a girl sitting behind them, hands around their waists. There's no helmets or anything like that there. It was late at night, and these kids were out just joyriding. They kept speeding ahead of me, then circling back, swarming round my cab like a school of fish. The whole group of them expanding and contracting as the road narrowed then opened up again. We stopped at a traffic light, and I looked out and locked eyes with this one girl, and we just smiled at each other. Perfect strangers. I wondered what their lives were like, these kids. I wondered if they felt as young as they looked or as old as they were trying to be. It's funny how you never quite feel the age you are. It's all relative, I guess. But watching them, I felt old. I felt like an old man, staring out at some perfectly manufactured picture of youth. I almost wanted to roll my window down and tell them.'

The bus slinks downhill through a dark pastoral valley, and Julian and Oriana feel their stomachs swing upwards half an inch. One of Ludlow's arms comes plonking out of their bunk, limp and anaesthetised.

Julian looks down the aisle. 'You've really got 'em all lined up, don't you? Willing guinea pigs.'

Oriana smiles, then jumps up to the record player and unlatches Skinner's lockbox. 'What are you feeling? Public Enemy, Public Memory, Prince, Phil Collins ... Phil Collins was redacted? Why?'

'Excessive percussion?' Julian guesses. 'Who knows. Chuck it on.'

'When we're in Sydney,' Oriana says, sliding *Face Value* from its sleeve and placing it delicately on the turntable, 'there's someone I'd like you to meet.'

'Like, a producer?'

'No. They're not in the industry. But I've told them a little bit about you, and they'd like to meet you.'

Julian shakes his head, sealing his guitar back in its case. 'When did everything become so cryptic with you?'

'Not cryptic,' Oriana says. 'Just careful.'

The bus fills with a sudden, echoing chorus of coughs – everyone snaps back all at once then shouts in perfect unison: 'LOOK OUT!'

They'd seen the cow. A lone cow that somehow managed to saunter over a cattle grid from a nearby property and make its way into the left lane of the dark highway. Everyone on F had seen it before Dante did – so they also knew that no matter what he did, and no matter what they said, he was going to hit it.

Dante swerves right, spooking the beast, who kicks up its hind legs and flees the wrong way, galloping directly in front of the bus, its amber flanks shining iridescent in Genevieve's headlights before its body is flattened. Its bones break, its legs detach and its innards stretch across the bonnet. In death it makes its mark, shattering a headlight, detaching half the front fender and leaving a dent the size of a small boulder in the bus's chassis. A hairline crack spreads like quicksilver up the centre of the windshield as Dante slams the brakes, locking his elbows and deftly controlling the enormous vehicle's sudden, heaving deceleration.

Ludlow and Cleo are thrown clear from their bunks. Ash, Tammy, Xander, Pony and I cop a face full of headrest. Pony's nose implodes and his mouth fills with blood. The luggage lockers above us swing open, raining hand baggage and sound equipment down upon our heads. Ludlow's camera gear lands with a sickening crack, and Oriana's precious green suitcase goes flying, tumbling, sliding halfway down the aisle.

'Is everyone okay?' Skinner shouts once the sounds of rending metal and dying cattle have settled.

'No!' shrieks Pony. Xander's holding him in his chair, trying to calm him while Ash fishes around for a first aid kit.

Skinner immediately blames himself for falling asleep, but Dante says it wasn't that. The cow ran right in front of them. Nothing to be done.

'That was incredible,' says Oriana, who's landed on her knees by the fold-out table. 'Synchronised hallucination. Conjoined visions. They woke up in unison, in response to imminent, real-time danger.'

'You alright?' Julian asks her.

Oriana grins ear to ear while the Phil Collins record skips across the same iconic drum fill, over and over.

'Ow ow ow ow ow,' whines Pony as Xander presses an icepack against his nose. Tammy flexes her right wrist, worrying she might have sprained it. Ludlow inspects their bag full of dented lenses.

'We'll pay for that,' says Ash.

'Let's wait a moment before we start doling out compensation,' Skinner cuts in. 'There's insurance for this sort of thing.'

'Random act of livestock,' I mumble to Cleo, who doesn't find this funny. I feel like shit. Lately I've been making the mistake of skipping ahead while I'm still half-cut, so I get to live through my hangover twice. And getting pulled out of a trip like that – none of us had ever experienced it before. It felt like waking from a dream with a slap to the face.

Oriana gets to her feet and shouts over the murmur: 'So you all saw it? You all saw the cow?'

'Not now, O,' Ash growls.

The cabin fills with red and blue light.

'Shit,' says Tammy.

'Fuck,' says Xander.

'Where did they come from?' Cleo wails.

Julian guesses correctly: 'They must have been following us.'

Seconds later, a department cruiser pulls up beside Genevieve. Two patrolmen get out, trudging through the cow guts and knocking on the door to the bus. A third sets up a basic perimeter of witches hats and reflective signage, even though there's no traffic for miles in either direction.

'Department of Internal Borders and Migration,' says the patrolman on the other side of the tinted glass. 'Open up.'

Oriana dives for her green suitcase and hauls it back to the table with Julian. Everyone does what they can to improve their immediate appearance: Xander flicks a roach out the window on the far side, Dante pulls a cap down low over his eyes, Ash throws on a cardigan to hide his *FREE TAIWAN* tattoo.

'We'll be fine,' Skinner says, with all the resolve of a person who's been hospitalised seven times after various encounters with law enforcement.

'Borders and Migration! Open up!'

Skinner gives a nod and Dante throws the lever, opening the doors.

The patrolmen mount the steps. Dark Kevlar with embroidered insignia, tactical helmets with perspex face shields lit green from within, belts hung heavy with zip ties and artillery.

The patrolman who was knocking, whose name patch reads *OFFICER BARNES*, says: 'You folks made a real bloody mess out there,' sticking his thumb back at the cow smeared across the bitumen.

Skinner laughs heartily. 'Yes, poor thing! A horrible shame. Unavoidable, sadly. It got a fright and ran right out in front of us. And then we got a fright! And then ... well ...' He trails off and hangs his head in mourning.

BIG TIME

The patrolman behind Barnes, whose name patch reads *OFFICER HICKS*, says: 'Nice set of wheels you've got here. Except for the bunged-up front.'

Dante stares straight ahead, dead still, hands on the wheel. 'Yeah, she goes alright,' he says.

'Your destination?' asks Barnes.

'Sydney,' says Skinner.

'And where did you depart from?'

'You mean you don't know already?' Ash interjects with well-practised innocence.

Hicks sneers at Ash, then says to Dante: 'You're not driving under the influence of any alcohol or narcotics, are you, son?'

'No, officer.'

'And you've got your heavy vehicle licence?'

Skinner's ready to jump in with some long-winded excuse, but there's no need; Dante flips open his wallet and hands over a perfectly legal, perfectly valid heavy vehicle drivers licence.

Hicks says: 'If you'd like to step out of the vehicle, Mr Tolentino, we'll perform a quick routine breathalyser and ocular inspection.'

Dante says: 'Of course, officer.' He stands and follows Hicks out, readjusting his jacket at the back to better conceal the pistol tucked into the waistline of his jeans.

Barnes shouts out to the third patrolman: 'Officer Lee! Full vehicular inspection, please!' Then he says to Skinner: 'My colleague's gonna give your rig a once-over to make sure she's still roadworthy. I would recommend booking in for a full service as soon as you get to Sydney.'

'Absolutely,' says Skinner. 'Consider it done.'

Then Barnes turns his greenish-whitish face to the bus's other occupants. He stands in the aisle, drumming his gloved fingers on the back of an empty seat.

'Anybody injured?'

We shake our heads and shrug, offering an assortment of 'nah's and 'all good's.

The patrolman looks at Pony. 'What about you, son?'

Pony's shivering with the effort of controlling his pain, holding the icepack against his nostrils. 'Just a blood nose, officer. Get 'em all the time.'

'Righto, then,' Barnes says with a nod.

But he keeps standing there. Fingers tap-tapping like he's forgotten something. Or like he's waiting for something to happen. After another full minute of thinking and tapping, he says: 'Well, we won't take up too much more of your time.'

From where I'm sitting, I can see Ash's, Xander's and Pony's shoulders drop. Behind me, I can hear Cleo, Tammy, Julian and Oriana exhaling.

But then Barnes says: 'Just a quick sweep and we'll get out of your hair. Daisy! C'mere girl!'

For a moment, in my stupefied state, I think – I hope and almost pray – that Daisy is some new recruit, a rookie who still gets called things like 'girl', and that Barnes is bringing her aboard to show her the ropes and help her conduct her first highway check. But Daisy wasn't a rookie. Daisy had actually been with the DIBM for about as long as Barnes. They worked very well together. And now Daisy was loping up the steps and clambering down the aisle, nose to the floor.

Julian almost chokes. 'Fuck.' He truly hated sniffer dogs.

Daisy is a nine-year-old German shepherd with fur like a bear and eyes like Beelzebub, strapped into her very own Kevlar harness. Combat gear for canines. Cute. She's inhaling the floor of the bus through her wet, black nose, going seat to seat, row by row, not missing an inch.

'Good girl,' says Barnes. Then to us: 'Just keep nice and still. She's friendly. I promise.'

I know I shouldn't have, but I couldn't help it – I turned and looked back at Oriana. Oriana, who I'd known since primary school. In all that time, I'd never seen her look more afraid than she looked right now, clutching that emerald-green suitcase to her chest, knowing that its contents – the sheer volume and purity of it – could have her dragged off this bus and put in front of a firing squad before dawn.

Julian's sitting next to her, wishing like hell that he'd skipped ahead with the others. Then he might have seen this. He might have known what was coming. Instead, all he can do is reach across the seat and take Oriana's hand, squeezing it tight.

Daisy gets a nose full of Ash's old gym bag. Then she pauses beside Pony, smelling blood. She turns to Xander. Sniffs. Turns back

BIG TIME

to Pony. Sniffs. Then proceeds towards the bunks.

'Thank you, Mr Tolentino,' we hear Hicks say outside, and Dante returns to the bus. He takes one look at Daisy, then one look down the aisle. He sees Oriana gripping her suitcase and his spine turns to steel. His muscles tense beneath his jacket. He clears his throat and leans, ever-so-casually, against the dashboard. Watching. One hand scratching his stubble. One hand hovering behind his back.

'You know,' says Barnes offhandedly, 'I've got a niece named Genevieve.'

'What a coincidence,' Tammy says.

Barnes turns cold. 'Careful, love. We don't joke about that kind of thing anymore.'

Struck by the urge to appear somewhat more respectable, I stand abruptly, and Daisy growls, showing me her yellow front teeth.

'I said nice and still, mate!' calls Barnes.

'Sorry,' I say, trying not to vomit. 'Sorry, Daisy. Good girl.' The dog loiters at my ankles for two seconds too long, then forgets I exist and pivots towards Cleo, who closes her eyes and balls up her fists and waits for the whole thing to be over.

Daisy traipses straight past Tammy as though she were invisible. I'm the only one close enough to hear her mutter: 'That's right. Keep walking. Scooby-Doo Nazi motherfucker.'

Ludlow, who I guess likes dogs even when they're filthy snitches, gingerly offers the back of their hand. Daisy sniffs it coolly then moves on, directing her attention to the back of the bus.

With his eyes on Oriana, chest heaving with uneasy breath, Ash says a bit too loudly: 'Is this going to take much longer?'

'It'll take as long as it takes,' Barnes chides. 'But she's nearly done. Good girl!'

Hicks reappears at the front of the bus, standing almost shoulder to shoulder with Dante.

'Good girl,' says Hicks.

Daisy finishes inspecting the lavatories and the wine cellar, then turns to face the fold-out table where Julian and Oriana are pressed against the bench seat, trying to press all the way through and out the other side and down the highway and back to Adelaide.

'Bad girl,' Julian says under his breath.

The dog stops in her tracks. Her sharp sniffs become long

inhales. Even from the other end of the bus, Barnes can sense the shift. 'What is it, Daisy? What have you got?'

Dante adjusts his footing.

Daisy starts to growl.

Barnes marches down the aisle – past Ash and Xander and Pony, past me and Ludlow and Cleo and Tammy. He arrives at the fold-out table and looks down at Oriana. At her suitcase. But he doesn't ask her to open it, and he doesn't tell Daisy to attack. Rather, Barnes cocks his head to one side, like a thought's just occurred to him, and says: 'What's that sound?'

It can't have been more than six or seven minutes since Dante hit that cow. But in that six or seven minutes, what with everything else going on, nobody thought to turn off the record player.

'I know that sound.'

Barnes has got that famous Phil Collins drum riff in his helmet – the riff the record's caught on and has been playing over and over in a booming, unpleasant staccato. The patrolman peels his eyes off Oriana's suitcase and turns to the stereo, watching the vinyl spin on the gimbal-mounted turntable. He yanks it off. The drums die. He reads the label on the record, then kneels and inspects the spilt contents of the lockbox. Cosmic Psychos. Dead Kennedys. N.W.A. Amyl and the Sniffers.

'Heel, Daisy.'

The dog returns to Hicks at the front of the bus, sitting obediently, panting amicably.

'Who owns these?' asks Barnes, holding up the sleeve for *Face Value*.

Technically, the records belonged to Labyrinth. Banking on an eventual return to the old world order, their archivists had amassed an impressive catalogue of redacted albums that were kept in a fire proof vault in the basement of the company's Melbourne headquarters. Skinner had loaned them out from the illegal library, citing them as part of the Acceptables' rider.

Barnes stands and proclaims: 'Right now, everybody on this bus is in direct contravention of section thirty-two of the Cultural Purification Act. Unless somebody claims responsibility for this illicit audio material, your vehicle will be impounded and you'll all be arrested and taken in for questioning.'

BIG TIME

Dante stands up straight. Skinner notices, knows that Dante's thinking about doing something and knows he has to stop him from doing whatever he's thinking of doing if he wants to keep the band alive and the tour on the road.

'I'll give you ten seconds to think it over,' says Barnes.

Here's what I know: in the less than ten seconds that follow, some barely imperceptible physical cues reveal who's willing to throw their lives away for the other people on that bus. Xander takes a deep breath, ready to make a fraudulent but heartfelt confession. Ludlow's eyebrows reach up to their hairline in pre-emptive surprise at what they're about to say. Cleo begins to wince, a life-changing lie curled up on her tongue. Even I shake my head from side to side, wondering if this was what I was for. But it wasn't my time – my time would come.

Pony beats everybody to it.

'They're mine, pig!' he shouts, leaping out into the aisle.

Barnes orders Hicks: 'Take him.'

Hicks seizes Pony by the back of his shirt, shoving his bloodied face into another seating bank and zip-tying his wrists. Xander and Ash take a reflexive step forward, but Daisy starts barking and frothing at the jaws.

'You are hereby detained under the authority of the Central Government of the Federal Republic of East Australia,' Hicks drones, reading Pony his rights, which were none.

'Fucking fascists! Fucking philistines!' Pony screams, landing a feeble kick against Hicks's reinforced shin guards. Daisy bites Pony on the leg. Xander shouts and kicks the dog. Barnes pulls a baton and strikes Xander across the face, perforating the cornea in his right eye. Tammy catches him as he falls. I vomit in a bunk bed.

Dante pulls the pistol from the back of his jeans, but Skinner grabs his wrist with astonishing strength and holds the weapon out of sight, keeping Dante in the clear. Xander shakes off Tammy and lunges for Pony as the patrolmen drag him down the aisle. Dizzy and half-blind, Xander trips on some luggage and falls to his stomach, crawling after his little brother, crying, 'NO NO NO.'

'It's just music, you idiots!' Pony howls with laughter. 'It's words and music! Melody and harmony! It can't hurt you! The music can't hurt you!'

Hicks hurls Pony down Genevieve's steps, into the mud and bovine blood, then tosses him in the back of the patrol car. Daisy follows them out with a shit-eating yap.

Barnes pauses at the top of the steps and points his baton down the aisle, right at Oriana and her emerald-green suitcase.

'You'll keep,' he says.

Some people would have you believe there's an invisible ledger that must remain balanced – all of us beads on the galaxy's infinite, immutable abacus. They believe that when people disappear – obviously or inconspicuously, by means natural or unnatural – we ought to be grateful, because those people keep the rest of us in the black.

But there is no formula for who gets to stick around. Not in war time, peace time, hard times or good times. It's just dumb luck and circumstance. Xander's little brother wasn't the first name on any list. He wasn't the bravest, the dumbest, or the most deserving. So what was he?

What can you say about someone you never really liked but will always sort of miss? They're gone, and that's that. The sun comes up tomorrow.

PART THREE

BOTANY

10

The First Annual International Chronophenomenology Summit was the brainchild of two Oxford-based researchers who had been studying the ongoing ramifications of the Cabrera Effect, synthesising the findings from two dozen Extreme Coincidence Hotlines set up around the globe to determine whether or not these coincidences did indeed point to some deeper flaw in the fabric of time, and to assess whether said fabric was – to continue the metaphor – getting thinner. Had it been left too long in the wardrobe without any mothballs? Had it been forgotten in the washing machine, soiled by mildew, folding over itself and developing permanent new wrinkles? Had it been subsequently ironed too vigorously, made crisp and delicate? Was time still opaque, or was time becoming sheer, possibly even see-through on a sunny summer's day? Could time still be relied upon to keep us safe and warm, and to protect our modesty, or would we soon need to pop on another layer? The findings thus far were inconclusive.

Just as the Cabrera Effect news cycle was hitting its peak, new rumours emerged of a Japanese doctor whose patient had witnessed the afterlife through the application of *trypto-lyside glutochronomine*, the fabled 'time travel drug' from East Australia. Video recordings of the now-dead patient describing the tangible, physical realm that awaited us all on the other side had spread online like wildfire. The Pope was forced to make another appearance on *Good Morning America*, assuring Catholics worldwide that the Vatican's official stance on heaven had not changed – i.e. in the church's view, heaven had never been, and was not currently, a shopping mall.

BIG TIME

To complicate matters, a German dark web alt-science collective calling themselves *Neue Götter*, or 'New Gods', established their own underground testing program in which volunteers, after intensive screening and psychiatric evaluation (designed to prove both their sound state of mind and a willingness to die for science, two things that apparently did not cancel each other out), were administered a hard-won portion of this 'F', reported back on their hallucinations, then were executed on camera by a randomly selected *Neue Götter* henchman. The execution was necessary, of course, to ensure that the future the subject had envisioned earlier definitively included their own death (and whatever came after).

Much to the frustration of scientists and clergy alike, so far seventeen of the eighteen volunteers had reported exactly what Ren Hashimoto initially described: a shopping mall that never closed. In their descriptions, the stores, the signage and the food in the food courts were all German, but the rest was consistent, down to the concierge with a ring of fire around their face.

The eighteenth volunteer had changed their mind at the last minute and begged not to die upon snapping back from their F-state. They claimed they had once gotten lost in a shopping mall when they were very young and the memory still traumatised them – they did not want to spend all eternity feeling like a frightened child. They were killed anyway, shot twice in the chest and once in the temple. Their data was struck from the study due to 'unscientific bias'.

One of the Oxford researchers, a man named Abel Finnigan, had been sent the latest *Neue Götter* dispatch video over an encrypted messaging service from an associate in Brazil and was watching it as he ate his cereal in the lab cafeteria: another trembling blond German waxing lyrical about the great shopping mall in the sky before holding up a copy of that day's *Berliner Zeitung* and getting shot in the face.

'What about in developing countries?' huffed Abel. 'What about in remote parts of sub-Saharan Africa? Or those tribes in the Amazon, you know the ones. What does heaven look like to a person who's never been to a shopping mall?'

His colleague, Edwina Abbakar, chewed on a protein bar. She was always trying to eat more protein. 'You're saying you'd like to introduce an untested psycho-hallucinogen to a closed-off indigenous Amazonian society, then execute them to collect the data?'

Abel almost spat out his cereal. 'Obviously that's not what I'm saying. What I'm saying is: this is getting out of hand.'

Abel, like Edwina, was a chronophenomenologist, splitting his time between a private research foundation and the Oxford University Department of Physics. You might think he'd be happy that his chosen career in a historically overlooked field of science was suddenly having its time in the sun – but you'd be wrong. Abel had been invited to appear on countless TV news programs to offer his commentary in the aftermath of the Cabrera video and he'd turned them all down, having witnessed his fair share of scientists getting eviscerated on breakfast television. On the contrary: Abel had chosen his career quite deliberately in the knowledge that chronophenomenology was obscure, ineffectual and unprofitable. He was playing the long game, with one eye on the studies in front of him and the other on a long, cushy, inconspicuous career in academia. A few barely read periodicals, a book published by some little-known college press, then tenure at a nice, rural university somewhere in America. Maybe Minnesota or Wisconsin. The simpler the people, Abel imagined, the less he'd have to explain himself and the easier it would be for him to just skate by.

But now, alas, his field was blowing up. His student intake had tripled in the past two weeks. Theology majors were transferring out of their third-year classes and into first-year physics.

Even Abel wasn't immune to the growing hysteria. Just the week before, there'd been a power outage at his home. He'd left his phone at work, the microwave was dead and then somehow, inexplicably, his watch died at the exact same time – his analogue watch, which usually needed its battery replaced once every six or seven years – so for a four-hour period, Abel didn't know what time it was, or if there even was any. He got his watch battery fixed the next day, but still, he was torn – the power going out and his watch dying at the exact same moment? What were the odds of that? He spent the day agonising over whether or not to report the event to one of the Extreme Coincidence Hotlines he'd helped establish but decided against it. He tossed his watch into the upturned beanie of a homeless man and bought one of those kinetic ones, but he'd been in a bad mood all week.

'What I'm saying is,' Abel repeated, thinking about his old watch, 'there must be a rational explanation for all this.'

'I agree,' said Edwina. 'Though I'm not sure we'll find it on our own.' By the time they'd finished breakfast the kernel of the idea for the summit had been formed.

The foundation where they worked was supportive in theory but reluctant to draw too much attention to themselves. The chair of the board muttered words like *pseudoscience* and *bandwagon*, suggesting that the investigation into the potential collapse of temporality was merely a craze. They agreed to provide silent funding up to 25 per cent, but no more than that. The UK Government had problems of its own but offered a few thousand pounds to appear to be supporting the public interest. The Minister for Science suggested seeking out an international partner to cover the shortfall – after all, this was a topic of significant global concern.

But the Danes said no. The Swedes had their own thing in the works. The French were under the thrall of a devout, right-wing president. Abel and Edwina tried fifteen different universities in America, all to no avail. Then, just as they were about to shrug off the prospect and return to their everyday research, an email arrived in Abel's inbox.

'It's from the emissary for the Federal Republic of East Australia.' He laughed. 'I didn't think they still did science there.'

What the FREA did was keep its enemies close. The fledgling country had almost entirely withdrawn from the international stage, severing all but its most lucrative trade deals and recalling ambassadors from nearly every country worldwide. Their representative on the UN Security Council had been summoned home, found guilty of foreign collusion and publicly executed. But the nation did maintain one emissary on each continent, mostly ex-private sector bigwigs who attended all the diplomatic parties but stood alone in the corner, suspiciously eyeing off the canapés. Nobody knew what to say to anyone from the FREA anymore, and the emissaries never looked as though they wished to be approached.

JORDAN PROSSER

Two days after receiving the email, a black town car ferried Abel and Edwina from their lab to the European emissary's quarters in a quiet cul-de-sac in South Kensington. They were told to wait in a sitting room beside a large marble bust of Captain Cook. A faded Eureka flag was framed on the wall, alongside imitation pastoral artworks of eighteenth-century settlers and a needlepoint of Banjo Patterson. The emissary, a fat man with orange sideburns who used to run the electricity grid in Bassland, appeared and greeted them coolly before informing them that the Central Government of the FREA was willing to both generously fund and physically host their summit at the International Convention Centre on Darling Harbour in one month's time. Edwina said that was very soon. The emissary responded that the situation appeared to be evolving rapidly and that time, as it were, was of the essence.

He gave Abel and Edwina twenty-four hours to consider his proposal, then sent them away in the black town car.

While Abel's career aspirations pointed towards a feasible mortgage and possibly a cat, Edwina was far more ambitious. Growing up in the public school system in Brixton, from a very young age she showed a prodigious proficiency for advanced mathematics – her sixth form science presentation concerned the second law of thermodynamics (the most under-appreciated of the four, she said at the time). She completed high school two years early and was fast-tracked to a Doctorate of Philosophy in Theoretical Physics. Much to the dismay of her lecturers and supervisors, Edwina chose to pursue a career in chronophenomenology, arguing that the least explored fields of science would inevitably be those with the most left to discover.

'Maybe this is an olive branch from the FREA to the rest of the world?' Edwina posited in the cafeteria the next day, eating a poached chicken salad she'd brought from home. 'Maybe this is about rehabilitating their image?'

'If that's the case,' Abel replied, 'I'm even less inclined to go along with it. The ground feels shaky enough as is without us becoming the meat in some political shit sandwich.'

But Edwina talked him around, arguing that the opportunity was too good to pass up. And besides, this could be the perfect fodder for that one dusty tome Abel wanted to pump out before retiring to the Great Lakes at the ripe old age of forty-five.

Edwina informed the emissary they would be honoured to accept their offer. A name was chosen – The First Annual International Chronophenomenology Summit (much to Abel's dismay: 'There's going to be a second?') – a website was thrown together, and invitations were fired off across the globe. Many declined the RSVP, citing safety concerns. But by the cut-off date, more than a hundred theoretical physicists, quantum mathematicians, experimental electromagnesis PhD candidates and sub-thermodynamic temporal fissure analysts had responded in the affirmative.

Suitcases packed and hearts full of hope, they boarded a chartered plane to the FREA.

Leaving was the easy part. Touching down at the disused international terminal of Sydney Airport, Abel and Edwina were immediately led to a locked holding room where they waited five hours as their luggage was broken open and methodically sorted through. They had their cell phones seized and were told they could purchase replacement 'bricks' at most electronics stores – late-twentieth-century-style burner phones with a button keyboard and no cellular data connection. Abel had the airport paperback she'd bought for the journey impounded, and a number of other European scientists who'd hitched a ride on the same plane complained of missing laptops and literature, and in some cases even 'redacted' fashion items.

The International Border Enforcement officials had no knowledge of the summit or whether the chartered plane and its passengers had even been cleared to arrive. Abel was permitted one long-distance phone call which he used to contact the emissary's office back in London, where it was currently 6 am. He left a message, then waited another three hours for the workday to begin in the UK, at which time the emissary sent word and the holding room was unlocked. The dishevelled academics were ushered onto a bus, where they found all the other international attendees who had arrived throughout the day and had been kept in their own holding rooms, dealing with their own bureaucratic bungles. On the bus they met their handler, a woman from the Department of

Transport, Infrastructure, Fisheries and Culture, who apologised for the confusion and handed out manifests for the two-day conference that would commence the following morning.

'Unfortunately, the welcome dinner originally scheduled for this evening has been cancelled. We've been given special dispensation to travel after curfew, so we'll be taking you directly to your hotel.'

'Curfew?' asked Edwina.

'Yes.' The handler looked at her plainly. 'Tonight, we suggest you simply relax and unwind in your hotel's luxurious three-point-five-star facilities. For your own safety, we would not recommend you attempt to venture out into the city.'

Abel asked what everyone was thinking: 'Can you tell us why?'

The handler smiled. 'Since word got out about the summit, and your imminent arrival, there is ... There has been—'

Her search for words was cut short by a ziplock bag of pig's blood exploding across one of the windows. A throng of men and women were parked outside the arrivals area, showering the bus with improvised projectiles — rotten vegetables, chunks of cinder block, flaming tennis balls.

'There has been unease,' the handler concluded, finding her seat at the front of the bus and not looking back.

The scientists arrived at the Buchanan Hotel just before 9 pm. It was a tall concrete building with uniform blue windows, stocky and plain in such a way that it looked like a child's rendering of what an inner-city hotel ought to be. The semi-circular driveway was blocked at both ends by manned police barricades, holding back a seething, swelling crowd of white-eyed Botanians. They hammered on the sides of the airport bus as police officers held them back, opening one barricade just wide enough to let the vehicle through.

The driver parked at the top of the turning circle and left the engine running. Bell boys were summoned and hastily dragged the scientists' luggage into a huge pile in the middle of the lobby floor, as if stacking it for a bonfire, then promptly disappeared.

'What on Earth is going on?' asked a very sweaty Abel, trying to dig his suitcase out of the pile.

'There have been some very concerning coincidences in the past forty-eight hours,' their handler replied, handing out room keys to

BIG TIME

all the attendees. 'I dare say you'll have some lively debate at your show tomorrow.'

'It's a summit,' said Edwina.

'Of course,' said the handler. Then she nodded goodbye, and as she trotted towards a rear exit, she removed her official-looking government lanyard and dropped it in a bin.

'That's odd,' said Abel.

Almost all the scientists, terribly jet-lagged and already thoroughly regretting their journey Down Under, retired to their allocated rooms. Some looked over notes for the panel discussions and presentations they were due to give the next day but would never actually give. Others ordered room service, turned on their television sets and scanned the paltry selection of local content on the hotel's in-house cable channel (footy tipping, home renovation, paedophile hunting, docudramas about single-term prime ministers). Some barricaded their doors and tried to call home but discovered there was no outside line.

'A woman gave birth on her birthday.' I said this.

Abel and Edwina turned towards the bar, where I'd been planted ever since the Acceptables and their entourage narrowly made it back to the hotel about an hour earlier.

'Excuse me?' said Abel.

I repeated: 'A woman gave birth on her birthday.'

Even Edwina was beginning to think that a room service meal and a nice, barricaded door sounded like just the thing. She said, 'Congratulations,' and began to carry her suitcase to the lift.

'No,' I said, laughing, 'I mean, thank you, but nothing to do with me. The "very concerning coincidences" your friend was talking about. That's one of them.'

Abel scoffed. 'But that's not particularly out of the ordinary. That's a one-in-three hundred and sixty-five chance. That would happen multiple times per day, every single day, everywhere in the world. It'll happen again tomorrow.'

'It was triplets,' I said.

'Okay, fine,' Abel indulged me, doing the maths in his head. 'Triplets, that's about one in ten thousand ... so a one-in-three million, six hundred and fifty thousand chance. Slim, but not inconceivable. There's about four hundred thousand babies born worldwide every day, so that would still happen once every ten days.'

'The mother was a triplet herself,' I said.

Abel sighed. 'One in thirty-six billion, five hundred million, then. Once every … two hundred and fifty years. On a planetary scale, that's a blip.'

I sank a significant mouthful of Bassland whisky and held my empty glass up at the bartender.

'And what if I told you that the mother – and her two sisters – had been born on *their* mother's birthday as well?'

Abel blinked. Edwina was listening, poised by the elevator, re-opening the doors every time they tried to automatically close.

Just then, the hotel's head of security came stalking past, muttering into a lapel mic, sweating through his too-tight collar. He called in the doorman, then manually shut the glass sliding doors at the main entrance and locked the on/off switch with a key that he pulled from his belt on a retractable wire. He whispered something to the concierge, who then marched along the floor-to-ceiling windows at the front of the hotel, closing all the blinds and dimming the lights.

The dozen or so people in the lobby bar went quiet. As soon as they did you could hear the roar of the mob outside. Getting bigger.

'Does this mean you're closed?' I asked the bartender. He shrugged at me.

I sipped from my fresh glass and turned back to the scientists. 'You folks fancy a drink?'

11

With his little brother in the back of a DIBM cruiser, it took me, Ash, Tammy and Julian each pinning down one of Xander's limbs to stop him leaping off the tour bus and doing something that would get him interned too. He spat and shrieked until the lights of the patrol car had dipped westwards in the direction of Dubbo. Only then did we let Xander stand, and once he stood, he took Genevieve's interior apart with his fists, tearing the curtains from the bunks and demolishing the sound system. His heavy punches were even clumsier than they might have been, given his perforated cornea and his sudden loss of depth perception.

After ten minutes of this he sat on the edge of the highway, sobbing into his bleeding palms, black jeans slick with cow guts. We each took turns trying to get him back on the bus. Oriana said it wasn't safe to stick around; they could send more cars for the rest of us. Tammy said they'd get his brother back, knowing this was a hollow promise. I mumbled something about how Pony would have wanted the band to forge ahead and play the next gig, and Xander took a half-hearted swing at me but missed.

Finally, Ludlow sat with Xander in the long grass by the side of the road, lit by Genevieve's one working headlight.

'I won't try to be that person who, the moment something unspeakable happens to you, tries to tell you about the most unspeakable thing that ever happened to them,' they said. 'But I've had people snatched away from me just like that. Some of them I saw again, most I never did – and even if I did, they weren't the same. Right now, you're this big ball of barbed wire, because you're thinking to yourself: "What did I do wrong? What should I have done differently?" etcetera, etcetera, etcetera.'

Julian was listening in, smoking a cigarette halfway down the side of the bus. He was thinking about how Pony was a dickhead, but the kind of dickhead you got used to – even came to appreciate. He'd also been the only one who still seemed genuinely excited about what the Acceptables could be.

Ludlow went on: 'The kind of moment you're in right now … sometimes I feel like I can almost hear it. To me, it sounds like heavy chains, dragging across the bottom of the sea. An old anchor plummeting away from you, slipping through your fingers. I think that's the sound of infinite possibility shrinking down to a single outcome. Happening so fast that it's already happened. Plop! Finished. So you see? The choice has been made for you. It was never really up to you. You have to give in to that. It's what we all have to do before we can keep going. First, give up. Then we can begin.'

Xander put his head on Ludlow's shoulder and wept. The adrenaline that shot through him like a ripcord minutes ago had left him cold and clammy, while the pain in his right eye pounded like a hot hammer. After a while, Ludlow helped Xander back on the bus.

Skinner stood a moment in the middle of the empty highway, looking one way then the other. 'As soon as we get to Sydney,' he said, before returning to the driver's seat, 'I'm calling the label.'

When the band arrived at the Buchanan Hotel, shortly after dawn, a small crowd was already waiting outside – but not for them. Maybe on the *Beaches* tour, they would have been there for them. But this rabble was on the lookout for an international delegation of so-called scientists who had recently come under intense scrutiny in both *The National Telegraph* and on *The National Broadcast*. There had already been one small riot outside the Convention Centre where the First Annual International Chronophenomenology Summit was set to take place. Nothing outrageous – a trash can through a window and a few spray-painted grievances. But later that day, when police tracked one of the rioters to their apartment building in Parramatta, they unwittingly stumbled across a large drug lab. After a nine-hour siege, three police and seven civilians were dead, including a twelve-year-old boy who lived in the neighbouring apartment and had been hit by a stray bullet when the police moved in. At a vigil held the next day, a rumour spread that the dead twelve-year-old had an older brother who had also been killed by police. Another rumour said that this older brother had known his killer: a crooked cop who sometimes demanded protection money from the older brother and his family. And a third rumour suggested that this crooked cop had a younger brother – also a cop – who had recently been assigned to the tactical squad in Parramatta and sent out on a raid the day after a small riot at the Convention Centre. The younger cop had inadvertently murdered the kid brother of a man whom *his* older brother had already killed.

To make matters worse, two days after the twelve-year-old's death, *The National Broadcast* broke the news of Wilma Garrett, the triplet who'd given birth to triplets on her birthday. The thirty-six-degree autumn heat, coupled with this fresh slew of suspect serendipity, caused the ongoing vigil to turn violent. Police tried to disperse the crowd with fire hoses. More people were killed, many arrests were made, and the work camps bloomed the next day.

Which is why, just before midday, Skinner gathered the band in another nondescript function room on the eleventh floor, overlooking a choked-up tollway.

Cleo was the last to arrive, running in, dripping wet. 'Sorry! Sorry I'm late.'

'Where have you been?' asked Oriana.

'The pool! There's a pool on the outdoor mezzanine level. It's so nice.'

'Why didn't you stay out there?' Xander growled. 'Like, why are you even here?' His eye was plugged with gauze, his head wrapped in bandages. He'd been on the phone to his parents all morning and hadn't slept.

'Don't be a cunt, Xan,' Tammy said affectionately.

'Is that a fire?' asked Ludlow, looking out the windows. In the distance, a tornado of black smoke pointed down towards a warehouse district on the other side of the harbour.

'Probably,' I said. 'This city's fucked.'

Finally, Skinner, who'd been huddling with Dante on the far side of the room, patted the roadie loudly on the back and strode over to the main group.

'I just got off the phone with the label,' he said, a vein of untapped worry in the back of his throat.

'What did they say?' Xander gasped. 'Did they find him?'

'Not yet,' replied Skinner. 'But they assure me they've got their best people on it. Their very best. No, actually, the call was about the show tonight.'

'What about it?' said Ash.

'They've just announced a curfew for Greater Sydney. Effective as of 8 pm.'

'We don't go on stage until 10.'

'I know,' said Skinner. 'I know that's what was originally planned. But the label has spoken with the venue, and they agree it would be better to push ahead with the show tonight rather than postpone it. We're just going to bump up the set times a little.'

'For fuck's sake …' Ash slipped into a chair at a conference table and looked out over the bay. Ludlow surreptitiously took a polaroid of him in that moment, perfectly out of place in the corporate milieu, one dirty boot hitched up on a clean white tablecloth.

Skinner summarised: 'Petit Revenge start at 4 pm. You'll be on at half past 5, finished by 7 and back here well before 8. Safe as houses.'

Xander paced the length of the room, fiddling with his bandage. 'Hey, I've got an idea. Why don't we play the Domain, hire a few jumping castles, make it a real all-ages affair? Fuck it, why don't we sit this one out and get the Wiggles to headline instead?'

I thought this was quite funny and laughed out loud.

'Shut up, Wes,' snarled Ash.

Skinner wiped his brow and shoved his hands in his pockets. 'I realise this is less than ideal, but it's the best we can do under the circumstances.'

'That means we've only got a few hours,' said Julian.

'That's right!' Skinner clapped his hands, mistaking Julian's assessment for enthusiasm. 'If we hurry, perhaps we could even hop on a ferry, do a lap of the harbour. Bit of an impromptu photo shoot, just like the old days?'

'I mean we've only got a few hours to get high,' Julian clarified.

Skinner frowned.

BIG TIME

Tammy patted Julian's shoulder as she made to leave. 'I like Jules's idea better.'

The rest of the band agreed.

By the time the Acceptables took the stage at the Enmore – at the very rock'n'roll time of half past five, to an almost empty house – they knew exactly how the evening would pan out. They'd helped themselves to Oriana's green suitcase before leaving the hotel, with the exception of Xander, who was down to one workable eye (and had naturally heard the horror stories about those poor bastards at that Wrecking Bones concert). Instead of skipping ahead, Xander had partaken of half a gram of coke and a fistful of Captagon tablets. He'd smashed the mirror in his hotel room and ordered up two bottles of vodka which were empty by the time he arrived for the soundcheck.

Petit Revenge was a four-piece all-girl electropop act from Newcastle, who wore matching cherry-red outfits and performed elaborate dance routines at their concerts. Their best-known song was a cutesy, bubblegum love anthem called 'Shut Up and Crush on Me' – the track that eventually toppled the Acceptables' 'What Time Is Your Heart' off its record run in the number-one spot on the national charts. Ash had hooked up with Petit Revenge's drummer during the *Beaches* tour, but things ended badly. She glared at him in the wings for almost their entire opening set at the Enmore.

'I forgot about her,' said Oriana, wrapping her arms around Ash.

Out at the bar, I was surveying the small clutches of skinny, wide-eyed high schoolers hovering at the sides of the cavernous venue.

'Xander wasn't wrong about it being an all-ages gig,' I muttered to Cleo.

She nodded. 'They're babies. Must have been in fucking preschool during secession. They've never known anything different. This shit is like the Stones to them.'

The ticketing company sent out a slew of desperate text messages at 3 pm advising patrons of the adjusted set times, and this was who could make it to the earlier show. The situation wasn't much improved by the time the Acceptables went on at 5:30. There were maybe a hundred and fifty punters in total, embarrassed to be at a gig so early, embarrassed to be part of so small a crowd.

It wasn't just the change in set times, though. The city's rail network was struggling in the heat, train tracks buckling all over town, replacement buses backed up at intersections for miles. Plus, there was still rioting throughout central Sydney – Enmore Road, right outside the theatre, had been heaving with protests and counter-protests all day. Shortly after lunch, a group of anti-fascists had mistaken a group of fascists for their own faction and joined their march for an hour or two before being ambushed by their own anti-fascist friends. They were all soon overcome by a wall of capsicum spray and an advancing platoon of Emergency Incident Response officers. Some tried to run, escaping into oncoming traffic and causing a seven-car pile-up on King Street. Others were arrested, transported and interned, living and working the rest of their lives shoulder to shoulder with members of the opposing group who they'd originally taken to the streets to condemn.

The crowd inside the Enmore was so small and quiet, and the fracas outside so tumultuous, that any time the band finished a number the noise of civil disobedience would immediately flood the venue, drowning out whatever modest applause they'd earned.

Other than that – and compared to Adelaide – the show proceeded with little incident.

'When was the last time you all thought for yourselves?' Ash asked – his new favourite provocation. A few patrons shuffled to the bar. Nobody said anything.

'This one's called "Scorched Earth". Every year the FREA mines and exports three hundred million tonnes of coal, despite international trade sanctions. This is about that. Three, four!'

Fucked out of his mind on bourbon, blow and Middle Eastern party pills, Xander struggled to keep up with the rest of the band, especially during the tracks with particularly unruly time signatures. Halfway through 'War Drums' he snapped two strings on his guitar and lay down in the middle of the stage while Dante fetched him a replacement. During the wild frenzy that marks the end of 'Misanthropatopia' – a special live arrangement that went for six and half minutes and nearly broke the venue's sound system – Xander threw up four minutes in, gushing puke down his vintage Strat and into his pedalboard. He kept playing. I think Ludlow even got a photo of him, vomit mid-stream.

BIG TIME

The lighting grid flashed hot and yellow as Ash howled his final lyrics, and the Acceptables' set finished to a few polite cheers. Xander unclipped his guitar strap, letting the instrument clatter to the floor, and lurched offstage, followed by Julian, Tammy and Ash, each projecting the kind of zen resignation that can only come from knowing exactly how bad a show would be before you even played it. They finished at 7 on the dot. There was no encore.

The house lights came on immediately, and an announcement blared over the PA system: 'WE WISH TO REMIND PATRONS THAT THE CITYWIDE CURFEW COMES INTO EFFECT AT 8 PM – ONE HOUR FROM NOW. THE BAR IS CLOSED. THERE IS NO MORE ENTERTAINMENT. PLEASE GO HOME.'

The hundred or so punters who'd stuck out the show made their way towards the exits, but opening the venue doors was like opening a car window underwater, as the crushing hordes of protestors on the street outside spilt back in on them. Bandana-clad anarchists tousling with bare-chested nationalists came heaving into the lobby, swinging flaming torches and jousting at each other with homemade tasers. The Acceptables had gone out the back and hopped right on the bus – they had no idea that by the time the curfew kicked in an hour later, the Enmore had become a valuable territorial asset in an escalating guerrilla war. Riot police with see-through shields swung batons and crushed skulls underfoot as they tried to expel a growing number of violent blackshirt chrono-conspiracy theorists who'd fortified the dress circle bar. When a Molotov cocktail caught on the stage curtains and flames began to engulf the venue, the authorities made a tactical retreat, locking the main doors and barricading the fire exits. By 10 pm, the century-old theatre was a blasted façade and a pile of ash – as were the two-hundred-odd agitators trapped inside. More people than had been at the gig.

Half an hour later, I'm in the bar at the Buchanan Hotel, buying rounds for my new best friends, Abel Finnigan and Edwina Abbakar. I'm on the whiskies, and I assumed Finnigan would approve given the provenance of his surname, but it turned out he was a gin man. Edwina, hesitant to join at first, is now two-thirds of the way through a bottle of cab sav. We may have lost a lot of the good whisky when the borders closed, but we still had our wine.

'This is good,' Edwina says, topping up her own glass after telling the bartender to leave the bottle.

'So is it always like this?' Abel asks with a touch of hesitancy.

'What?' I say.

'Life,' he says. 'Here.'

'Ohhhh,' I say. He's referring to the violent mob surrounding the hotel, holding up placards reading *STOP KILLING TIME*.

I clarify: 'Is it always such a hopeless vortex of existential dread, political delinquency and poor taste? In a word, yes.' I finish my drink and order another.

'I came here on a family holiday when I was little,' Abel says. 'Many years before ... before it all changed. It was different. It was beautiful.'

'It was okay,' I say with a shrug. 'Whatever's bad about it now was there before. It just became the law of the land.'

A young woman with a hard-cropped fringe is waving at us from the other side of the bar.

'You know this chick?' I ask.

'No,' says Edwina. 'But she's got a lanyard.'

'Bad guys can have lanyards,' Abel says, and I nod enthusiastically. 'She's pointing. She's pointing over here. I think she wants to come over.'

The woman approaches, fluttering her hands. She comes in peace. She asks if we're with the summit and whether she could join us.

'Which institution do you represent?' Abel quizzes her. Edwina tells her to pull up a seat. The woman's name is May Minnow-Chen – Minnie to her friends – a PhD candidate from the University of Otago studying the use of psychoactive hallucinogens in end-of-life care.

'I've always been a big advocate for getting completely fucked up right before you shuffle off,' I say, endorsing her entire field wholeheartedly.

Minnie arches her eyebrows. 'Well ... I think you're talking about recreation and escapism, which certainly have their uses. My field is more concerned with chemically altering the human brain's relationship to mortality.'

BIG TIME

'Wait a minute,' Edwina says, wagging a friendly finger at Minnie. 'I've read some of your research. You're the one studying that time travel drug.'

Minnie goes stiff like she's stepped on a landmine. Her voice drops twenty decibels. 'Yes, that's me. But I'm not sure we ought to be—'

'D'you mean this?' I ask, pulling a full vial of F from my coat pocket.

'Jesus!' hollers Abel, grabbing my hand and shoving it and the vial under the bar. Admittedly, I'm being a little reckless. But Minnie's awestruck. She'd spent the last year sparring with her university's accounts department, trying to find some legitimate way of using faculty funds to smuggle even five drops of the substance out of a hostile foreign country. I once put a tube of the stuff through the washing machine by accident.

'Where did you get that?' Minnie asks, entranced.

'My mate Oriana. She basically has it on tap. I can hook you up if you want.'

Abel's still gripping my hand. 'Please,' he says. 'We're trying as hard as possible not to put so much as a single toe out of line while we're here.'

'All good, man. I'll stash it.' I return the vial to my coat, winking drunkenly at Minnie. 'More where that came from, though.'

We order more drinks – Minnie takes a hard seltzer – and Edwina asks her: 'So given your field of research – what's your take on this Atako woman?' to which Minnie shakes her head and smiles, almost wistful.

'My take is: I'm the one who told Yumi Atako to seek out *tryptolyside glutochronomine* to treat her friend.'

'You're kidding,' says Edwina.

'We were at a conference in New York together. We barely exchanged a word. But I pointed her in the right direction, I guess.' Minnie taps her glass and exhales. 'Probably the biggest regret of my life is not following up with her – sticking around, even. Being a part of it all.'

'Don't worry, love,' Edwina says, patting her on the back. 'You'll have your moment. It's a growing field.'

Mere months after the Cabrera Effect, Yumi Atako's 'Heaven

Tapes' were front-page news in the FREA. I put it to the group: 'What do you all think? Is heaven a shopping mall?'

Abel rolls his eyes. 'Please.'

'I believe it's a sort of shared hallucination,' Edwina says, taking the question a little more seriously. '"Heaven", as we refer to it, if it exists at all, is more likely a loose neurological state, something the brain passes into after the point of biological death. A predefined template with a range of variable settings. My guess is that the lived – or rather, the *not*-lived – experience of it would normally be different for everybody, because of course, no-one ever returned from that place to tell the rest of us what it looked like for them. But once Ren Hashimoto saw her version of that template – what *her* brain projected onto those settings – and came back to report on it, I believe it triggered a sort of mass confluence where everybody's "heaven" is now informed by hers. People are highly suggestible when it comes to these things.'

'What do you make of it all?' Minnie asks me.

I burp and think. 'I'm quite a depressive person,' I tell her. 'I think I wouldn't know heaven if it was written in neon right above the gates.'

'Or the revolving doors, as the case may be,' Abel laughs.

'The escalator beside the water feature and the artificial palms,' I offer.

Edwina sings something about paving paradise and parking lots.

I say I haven't heard that one in a while.

12

Ash and Oriana had the penthouse suite, so that's where the party was. I convinced Abel, Edwina and Minnie to join me up there after a few of the protestors managed to sneak past the barricades and started lobbing roof shingles at the hotel windows downstairs.

Let me set the scene: a palatial three-bedroom suite with a glass-walled balcony overlooking Botany Bay. Two main bathrooms and an additional powder room, each now with an assigned purpose: one for stashing booze, one for doing drugs and one reserved for use as an actual bathroom. An open-plan kitchen with a marble galley-style bench opening out towards a conversation pit replete with deep right-angled stairs, a gas fireplace and creme-and-brown shagpile carpeting. The lights are low. Every surface is covered with bottles, candles and vegan snacks. It's close to midnight, and the band's been at it since the second they arrived home from the gig.

I knock at the door with my scientist pals – and who should answer but Felicia fucking Hansen. Fizz. What a starfucker. Took a plane to Botany but got detained at the airport when a security guard thought her camera gear was prohibited surveillance equipment, so she missed the gig. But now she's here, sipping tequila from the bottle, about as annoyed to see me as I am to see her.

'Figured you'd show up eventually,' she says, bristling. 'Did they run out of appletinis downstairs?'

'Ignore this one,' I say to my new friends as we let ourselves in. 'She's uniquely small-minded.'

Ash is half-cut, holding court in the conversation pit with Oriana at his side, sermonising about universal income and how he'd like to make album number three free, or at least pay-what-you-can. Skinner's not there to hear this, thankfully, because he's milling politely on the balcony with Julian and Tammy and Cleo. They're all asking Cleo how her project's coming along, which is about as well as my article. Dante's just standing in the kitchen, tossing back shot after shot, riding high off his public saxophone debut earlier that evening, while Xander lurches back and forth between the three bathrooms, making full and graphic use of each. Skinner disposed of our box of redacted records after the incident on the bus, so we were reduced to listening to local radio – a late-night 'party mix' of Catholic rock and country disco.

I clear my throat loudly. 'Guys! Let me introduce you to Abel, Edwina and May – but her friends call her Minnie. They're here for the summit. They're all chromo ... shit. They're all ...' I try to say 'chronophenomenologists' about seven different ways but the whisky's got my tongue.

People turn and nod. Xander pauses by the kitchen bench and looks Abel up and down with his one good eye, then stalks off towards the guest bathroom to rail some more MD.

'Is he okay?' asks Abel, pointing at his own eye in reference to Xander's. 'That looks infected.'

'He's self-medicating,' I say, then I make us all drinks and escort the scientists to the conversation pit.

'Welcome, welcome,' says Ash. 'Welcome to our refuge in the sky. Where do you hail from?'

'Abel and I are from England,' says Edwina. 'May, you said you were from ...'

'Dunedin,' says Minnie. 'In New Zealand.'

'I went there once,' says Oriana. 'Does it still have the steepest street in the world?'

'Ooh, no, I'm afraid not.' Minnie winces like it's her fault. 'They levelled it out.'

'Pity.'

'So that's your fan club down at the barricades, is it?' Ludlow asks, not unkindly.

Abel frowns. 'Apparently.'

BIG TIME

'Just to clarify, I'm not actually a chronophenomenologist,' says Minnie politely. 'I wish!' A cute laugh.

'She's a psychiatric PhD candidate hoping to alter the human brain's relationship to mortality,' I offer. 'Namely through *tryptolyside glutochronomine*.'

'You're studying F?' Oriana looks at Minnie.

'Yeah!' she replies, happy and humble. 'Well – trying to. It's a bit like studying unicorns.'

'We had a scientist doing that,' says Fizz as she joins the group. 'Studying F, that is. Not unicorns. They called her a monkey fucker and threw her in prison.'

Minnie's smile drops.

'I hope that none of you take this the wrong way,' Ash says to the scientists, 'but, like – why do you think you're here?'

Edwina thinks he might be joking, so she laughs, but he isn't, so she stops. 'For the summit,' she says.

'Yes, but why do you think the government – *our* government – the same government that shuttered the CSIRO and now only offers "hobby sciences" as an elective class in public high schools – why do you think they chose to personally invite a hundred scientists within their sovereign borders for an incredibly well-publicised convention on a topic that's already causing deep social anxiety? Feels a little like pouring fuel on the fire, doesn't it?'

Minnie swallows heavily. Abel stares into his drink.

'We took it as a positive sign,' says Edwina, clearly shaken. 'An olive branch. I'm a big believer in science as the highest form of diplomacy. But when you put it that way …'

'Do you think we've been set up?' asks Abel. 'Be honest.'

Ash holds up his hands, like, *I've already said too much.*

'I think it's good you're here,' says Oriana. 'I think it's good for people to open their eyes a little wider. Even if it hurts.' Then she checks her watch, kisses Ash on the cheek and says to the group: 'Excuse me.'

Edwina's gripping the shagpile carpet, then letting go. Gripping, then letting go. She's realising she's a very long way from home. These people are nice enough, but they're not *her* people.

'Hey,' Minnie says, a hand on her shoulder. 'We'll be okay.'

'Of course you will,' I say vaguely, keeping one eye on Oriana as she heads towards the balcony. She's on a mission, and I want to know what it is.

'Do you party?' Ash asks the scientists.

'Isn't that what we're doing right now?' says Abel.

Ash smiles. 'No, I mean – do you *party*?'

Xander's in the guest bathroom, crying out of one eye, thinking about Pony. Thinking about how he'd never been a particularly affectionate or dependable big brother. He never got to do many of the things big brothers were meant to do for their siblings, like guide them, or inspire them. Or protect them.

He's banging his fist down on a bank card, crushing up a pastel assortment of ecstasy tablets. The pills look so innocent and friendly on the marble vanity, like a bag of mixed lollies. But Xander's sick of trying to feel better – sick of chewing his cheeks and slurring his words and lurching past his friends like a sad marionette. He wants to feel something more. He wants to know that tomorrow will be easier than today. Maybe Skinner will get a call from the label, or Xander will get a call from his parents, who might have gotten a call from one of their high-powered lawyer friends with department ties. He wants to skip ahead to a few days from now, to when his eye – and his heart – don't hurt so fucking goddamn much.

So he lifts a half-full vial of F from an open ziplock bag on the bench top, unscrews it, tilts back his head and empties the contents straight into his left eye.

Out on the balcony, Tammy's necking a bottle of champagne, staring fourteen storeys down at the tennis court and the pool. Cleo's talking to Skinner, trying to describe a redacted video work she once saw in an underground museum in Bassland that had since been filled with concrete.

'That's the sensibility I'm going for, I think. A kind of new Gothic.'

Skinner's nodding, listening politely. Julian offers him a joint and Skinner smiles *no*.

'I'll take a drag,' says Oriana, appearing outside.

BIG TIME

Julian lights up, puffs a few times to get it going, then passes it over.

'You know why I'm here?' Oriana says through the smoke.

Julian nods.

'You know what I'm about to ask?'

Julian nods again.

'What else do you know?'

'I know I'll go with you. We'll try to sneak out, but Wes is going to cut us off and insist on tagging along.'

'That's fine. Do you know where we're going?'

'I just know there's a car waiting for us downstairs. Nothing after that.'

'What a thrill for you,' Oriana says, picking a strand of tobacco from her lips. She hands the joint to Tammy, who sucks it halfway down in a single breath.

'You guys gonna be okay?' she asks with a cough. 'Curfew and all that.'

'We'll be fine. Thanks, Tam.' Oriana takes Julian's hand and pulls him inside.

'How does Tammy know where we're going?' asks Julian.

'Tammy knows a lot more than she's given credit for.'

I've been reclining in the conversation pit, trying to get comfy on the awkward shagpile stairs, handing round a mirror with a dozen chopped-up lines on it. When I see Oriana pulling Julian towards the door, it's the perfect excuse for me to stretch my spine. I make it to the kitchen quickly, feigning the construction of some elaborate cocktail while getting perfectly in their way.

'Going to the afterparty, you two?' I whisper cattily. 'Naughty naughty. Ash is right there.'

'I'm taking Julian to meet a friend,' Oriana says.

'Music friend? Drug friend?'

'I'm taking him to meet a man who's going to overthrow the government.'

I blink at Julian, who might have been as surprised as I am if he hadn't already seen this happen.

'Can I come?' I ask.

'Sure,' says Oriana.

JORDAN PROSSER

If I had known what I was leaving – if I had known where I was going – I would have sobbed, and laughed, and held my friends close. I would have kissed each and every one of them on the lips, and rested my temples down on their shoulder bones and danced a slow dance. I would have drunk the place dry. If only I had known that this was it. But then, we never do. That's what makes it so *it*. Y'know?

So I abandon my half-arsed cocktail and follow them out the door, feeling Ash's eyes burning into the backs of our necks. The door clicks shut during the space between songs on the radio, so the scientists look up just in time to realise I'm gone.

'Is he …?' Minnie sniffs, rubbing her nose as it burns from the blow.

'It's cool,' Ludlow says to her. 'You're welcome to stay here as long as you like.'

'Of course you are,' says Ash, sucking on generic-brand Valium to level out his high. 'Now tell me,' he draws his fingers in little circles, playing eenie-meenie-minie-mo with the three academics. 'Which one of you has a working theory as to what the fuck's going on with … *the big T?*'

'You mean *time?*' asks Edwina, snorting dramatically and passing the mirror down.

'Dead simple,' says Abel, tonguing his gums and speaking even faster than he normally would. 'Frequency illusion. A mass Baader-Meinhof phenomenon.'

'For those of us playing at home?' prompts Fizz, resting her head in Ludlow's lap.

'You know when you think to yourself, *I'm going to get a new car* – say you want a new Volkswagen. Suddenly it seems as though there are Volkswagens everywhere! But there hasn't been some magical influx, it's just that you're subconsciously looking for them. You're tuned into that wavelength.'

'You can't get a new Volkswagen here,' Ludlow points out. 'Local manufacturing only.'

'I don't drive,' says Fizz.

'But you can appreciate the metaphor.' Abel smiles thinly. He says the Cabrera Effect brought to the foreground something that had previously only ever been background – the omnidirectional

BIG TIME

flow of time – and now that people were paying more attention, of course they were bound to see more of the same: coincidences and other time-based anomalies both great and small.

'Maybe you even see a car out of the corner of your eye,' says Abel, 'and because you're so attuned to Volkswagens, you *think* it's a Volkswagen, even though it's not. Either way, it's not the cars that have changed. It's you.'

'It's us ...' Ludlow says in a mystic tone, spreading their fingers towards the ceiling.

'The institution where we work,' Abel says, thumbing Edwina, 'tasked us with setting up Extreme Coincidence Hotlines in major cities around the world, for "scientific research purposes". And let me tell you' – he rolls his eyes – 'there is nothing scientific about 99 per cent of the data they capture. And the 1 per cent that does mean something? They're still just coincidences! They've always happened and they always will. Our simple desire for them to mean something more does not and never will magically generate that meaning.'

'But what about the triplets?' Edwina taunts.

Ash howls with laughter, delighted to see dissent within the scientists' ranks.

'So you know about the triplets,' Ludlow says. 'Pretty wild, hey?'

'I think so,' says Edwina. 'I think that's something.'

'You're also forgetting,' grumbles Abel, 'that we're living in an overly documented world, and that as a species, humans are incredibly self-centred. Animals don't celebrate birthdays, yet many have triplets. What happened earlier today happened to a human in the twenty-first century, so of course we perceive it as having disproportionate significance. Wild dogs in Jakarta could have been having entirely albino litters every Harvest Moon since the tenth century BC, it's just that nobody knows or gives two shits about it!'

Fizz clutches her stomach, laughing so hard she rolls over and tumbles down the steps of the conversation pit.

'You don't think probability can create meaning?' asks Minnie.

'Probability is about smaller or greater,' says Abel. 'It is not about better or worse.'

'But a one-in-a-trillion chance. Is that not *better* than one-in-ten?'

'Absolutely not. It's simply rarer. And again, we humans convey an inordinate amount of significance on the *rare*. Rarity fluctuates and can be artificially manufactured. *Rarity* is actually nowhere near as *finite* as its definition implies.'

'Hey Xan!' Ash calls across the room.

Xander's stumbling between bathrooms like he has been all night. But now he's lurched into the kitchen bench, knocking over my abandoned cocktail shaker, spilling blue curaçao on a biscuit-coloured rug.

'Easy, man. Skinner'll have a conniption if we don't get the deposit back for this place.'

Xander's moving strangely. His head's leading his body. He doesn't seem to hear Ash. He doesn't even look up.

Ludlow says to Minnie, by way of explanation: 'He's dealing with a loss.'

'Oh, how awful,' Minnie says. She calls out to Xander: 'My condolences!'

Xander swivels towards the front door.

Minnie looks back at Ludlow, her big pupils and tense jaw making her skin look tight around her skull. 'Should I have said that? Maybe I shouldn't have said anything.'

'Don't worry about it,' says Ash, before hollering: 'Dante! Mate! You know how to make a Manhattan?'

Xander's in the future, but he's also here and now. His legs are moving because he thinks his legs have moved. His head is time's arrow, carrying the rest of him in its slipstream, dragging every limb and scrap of flesh inexorably forward. His feet move, then stop, then find their balance, then move again, scraping unnaturally down the argyle carpet along the hallways of the fourteenth floor. Behind his wasted eye, his right dorsolateral prefrontal cortex is a ball of white light, hijacking neural pathways and blocking enzyme inhibitors. Xander is sleepwalking, torn between two different time zones. Part of him is back in the bathroom. Part of him is already downstairs.

'You want to know what I think?' asks Edwina.

'Hell yeah,' says Ash, sipping his Manhattan. Everyone in the pit leans forward to hear.

Edwina gestures towards Dante, who's currently got the coke mirror, with a little *over here when you're done with that, love* wave of the hand. He passes it to her and she hoovers up two lines in rapid succession. Abel looks at Edwina, taken aback. His research partner was full of surprises tonight.

'Have you heard of the "observer effect"? In physics?' Edwina asks.

'Nope,' says Fizz.

'Heisenberg's uncertainty principle,' Abel interjects.

'Not quite,' snaps Edwina, before turning back to Ash and the others. 'In quantum mechanics it's widely acknowledged that the simple act of observing a particle, say, an individual electron, can alter that particle's behaviour. I believe this can be extrapolated to encompass entire objects, forces and systems. Now, roughly when was it that some mad genius in some gangster's basement far north of here first combined the chemical ingredients to create *tryp-to-lyside glutochronomine*?'

'Hard to say.' Minnie racks her brain. 'Reports vary. A few years ago, at least.'

'Four years,' Ash says, repeating something Oriana told him.

'Four years,' confirms Edwina. 'And roughly how long ago did they play that football match in Scotland that Mr Cabrera then discovered was a carbon copy of that other one?'

'Four years this July,' offers Dante, who watched the Premier League each year via an illegal FreeNet uplink at his uncle's house.

'Perfect,' says Edwina. 'Imagine that. After fourteen billion years – or more, depending on when you personally believe that "time" began – after fourteen billion years of having total run of the joint, flowing in the same direction at exactly the same pace, with very little to no tinkering or interrogation from any of the countless trillions of organisms living within its boundaries, suddenly, one sunny day in ... wheresitcalled ...'

'Cooksland,' says Ludlow.

'One day in Cooksland, the contents of one pipette are combined with another, and BOOM.'

'What are you getting at?' Abel asks, rubbing one of his eyes red.

'We turned the tables! We got the drop on it! The first time somebody actually took some of the stuff and saw a few seconds more than they were naturally meant to see, they were sticking their nose where it didn't belong, weren't they? It was an unprecedented violation of the natural order of the universe.'

'So now,' Minnie follows, 'time is acting differently ... because of the drug?'

'Shortly after its invention, we're treated to the most extraordinary chronological anomaly ever recorded – a coincidence so statistically improbable that it could *only* be the result of an irregularity in the flow of time. And since then, we've started witnessing more and more such phenomena. And yes, Abel,' she laughs, wagging a finger in his face, pre-empting his next words, 'I realise that what I'm saying is the literal definition of confirmation bias, frequency illusion, you and your bloody Volkswagens. But that kind of improbability *does* mean something. It simply has to! The Cabrera Effect, and these triplets, it's not like spotting a Volkswagen just because you decided to buy a Volkswagen, it's like ... it's like—' She's standing on the lip of the conversation pit without even realising it, at the mouth of a volcano, a font of revelation. '—like spotting a Volkswagen in space, a trillion lightyears from Earth, a billion years from now. It's not just numbers. It can't just be numbers!'

'Fuck the numbers!' Minnie screams.

'We have tampered with the natural borders of our existence and understanding – borders guarded by time. Ren Hashimoto witnessed the afterlife! Just think about that. We each have one life. One eighty-year slice of those fourteen billion years, with no peeking before or after. Those are the rules. But then she goes and bloody peeks! She just waltzes into the afterlife and skips straight back, transgressing the most fundamental rules of both physics and theology in the process. And she does it a dozen times! If I were time ... I would be freaking out.'

'Edwina,' says Abel. 'You talk about time as though it were a living thing.'

Edwina leans in to her audience, punching out her words: 'Because I think it is. And I think it *knows*. I think it knows that we're fucking with it. I think it knows it's being observed, tampered and tooled with. Explored, stretched and desecrated. And I think we should expect it to become more and more erratic as a result.'

'I wish I'd recorded that,' Ash says to Dante.

Abel shakes his head and drinks his drink.

'I want to try some,' says Minnie. She's been listening to Edwina, balling her fists, building up the courage to ask: 'Can I?'

BIG TIME

'Some …?' prompts Ludlow.

'*Trypto*-fucking … some fucking F!'

'Really?'

'Yes!' Minnie explodes. 'It's all I think about! It's like I've been studying some exotic animal without ever seeing it in the wild, basing my entire life and my whole career off other people's safari photos. I *need* to try it. I need to see for myself.'

Ash stands. 'Dante,' he says reverently. 'Get your saxophone.'

Dante salutes and sprints out of the penthouse, down two floors to his room, to the bed, to the leather case hidden underneath, to the red-flocked interior and the battered brass Yamaha his grandfather gave him.

Ash circles the bottom of the conversation pit. 'I grew up in a religious family,' he says to Minnie, who's looking up at him with wide eyes. 'I attended mass every Sunday until I was eighteen years old. And never once did I feel moved. The words washed over me but never soaked through. Then, soon after we finished touring our first album, Oriana showed me F. And the first day I tried it – I found my religion. Lie down on the carpet.'

Minnie lies down. Dante returns, panting, clipping his neck strap to the back of the sax. He starts to play a minor-key version of the brass line from 'Born to Run'.

'Everybody gather 'round.'

Ludlow, Fizz, Abel and Edwina form a loose square around Minnie.

'Put your hands by your sides,' Ash tells her. 'Breathe out. Force a sigh. Now tilt your head back.' He's done this for a few people – administered their first trip. This is Ash at his most sage-like, and his most insufferable. He proceeds to give Minnie a similar spiel to what Trevor gave Julian on that flight between Medellín and Auckland: the warm, tight chest. The cheek-chewing, the free association. Then the sudden rush, and the sudden sight.

'I've never really hallucinated before.' Minnie giggles.

'And nor will you now. These are not mirages in the desert. This is your brain experiencing the universe without the tyranny of temporality.'

Abel laughs sardonically and Edwina flicks him on the ear. Ash doesn't notice. He's laser-focused on Minnie, and there's something sensual about the way he opens his jacket to retrieve one of Oriana's specially engineered brass vials.

'Keep your eyes open, that they may stay open,' he says.

Then he removes the glass eyedropper from the vial and runs the tip around his mouth, dampening his lips with the drug. Ash bends over and kisses Minnie's eyeballs – first the left, then the right. She blinks with the speed of a butterfly's wings.

'We'll be here when you get back,' says Ash.

Tammy finishes Julian's joint and stubs it out in a potted palm. Cleo's talking Skinner's ear off, her voice fast and monotone from a combination of uppers and downers. Tammy considers butting in, rescuing Skinner from his own good manners, but she doesn't.

Cleo's talking about the galleries in Botany – how they used to house some of the wildest, most transgressive artworks in all of Australia, even the world. Giant mutant creatures cradling plasticised children. Stacks of standard-def televisions playing the names of murdered asylum seekers on a loop. Flags soaked in blood, assault weapons dipped in gold. Slow-motion video of guerrillas in Congolese jungles, the foliage turned pink by ultraviolet film.

'I quite like the, uh, the Ned Kelly series I saw last time I was here,' Skinner mumbles.

Cleo looks at him like she wants to punch him.

'I did!' he insists. 'I liked the brushwork.'

'If I see one more fucking painting of that guy …' Cleo shakes her head and stares into space. 'That was the beginning of it, y'know? Of the great myth that ended up eating us all. The loveable rogue-morphosis. The plucky larrickin-ating. The valiant Anzac-ification. Put a petty criminal on your fifty-cent coin and no-one'll ever suspect you're a pack of uber-capitalist neo-Nazis.'

Skinner smiles at her blankly.

'Oh,' Cleo says, remembering. 'No offence.'

'None taken.'

Skinner never spoke much about his life before secession, and the band had never really asked. Sometimes he longed, in private, to come clean about it all – to share with somebody every cruel detail of that life. But it occurs to him that Cleo is not that person.

'It just kills me,' she says. 'It's like all we're good for is working or fighting or dying. Heaven forbid we should have a single beautiful thought in our heads.'

Skinner says: 'I went to the Louvre once.'

'You lucky fucker,' Cleo says, slapping him playfully on the arm instead of the face.

'And the Tate. And the Centre Pompidou. Some friends and I scrounged enough money for flights to Europe, to follow this hideous punk band around on tour. While my mates were off trying to ingratiate themselves with the lead singer, finding him drugs and girls and that sort of thing, I thought I'd see the sights.'

'Well, look at you. An appreciation for the finer things in life. I believe every one of us has the soul of an artist, simply trying to break through.'

'Oh, I don't know about that. I've never had much to say about anything, myself. But I guess I have always gravitated towards those who do. Leaders wouldn't be leaders without followers, would they? I suppose we all have our parts to play.'

'Yes,' says Cleo, suddenly teary-eyed. She leaps at Skinner and wraps her arms around him in a too-tight hug. Skinner stands very still, but doesn't discourage her.

'Guys.'

Tammy's leaning over the handrail at the edge of the balcony, looking down.

'Guys,' she says. 'Is that Xander?'

Minnie jerks awake on the floor of the conversation pit, hacking up a lungful of alien air.

'It's okay, you're okay,' says Fizz, rubbing small, soothing circles on her back.

'So,' Ash sits beside her, cross-legged, chin resting on his fists. 'What did you see?'

Minnie's trying to say something but can't stop coughing. 'Your— Your f— Your friend—'

'Dante, get her a drink.' Ash beckons to the roadie to bring a glass of water.

Minnie drinks, blinking, coughing. 'It's unbelievable,' she says.

'What? Tell us!' Ash is giddy.

'Your friend …' Minnie downs the glass and starts to breathe again, touching her face and chest to make sure she's all there, that every bit of her made the return journey. 'Your friend, with the injured eye.'

'What did you see?' Ash asks again with a hint of concern.

Minnie's still processing it all – images from her future and sensations from her present colliding in real time. She knows she doesn't have long. She knows she's woken up as the bearer of bad news. But as far as she knows, the future is still fluid. So where does she begin? Talk about a bummer first trip.

She says: 'Does this hotel have a pool?'

13

Xander's body is carving through time. He's right beside the tennis court. Now he's right beside the pool. Without ever breaking his strange, zombie-like stride, he shuffles down the steps and into the water. The bottom of the pool is set with pink tiles, a shimmering gullet. Xander is feeding himself into the mouth of a waiting whale.

A mathematics problem: Alexander Plutos is six-foot-four. Let's say his mouth, nostrils and general breathing apparatus sit at around six feet. The hotel pool is fifty feet long, the shallow end is four feet deep and the far end is eight. Xander has been travelling at roughly three feet per second, but the water slows him to a crawl of one or two. How long until Xander starts to drown?

Tammy, Ludlow, Ash, Fizz and Cleo are sprinting down the fire stairs five at a time. Skinner, Dante and the scientists are in the elevator, jabbing at the button panel with balled-up fists.

Xander's nearly halfway down the pool, chlorine blue lapping at his shoulders. How his body feels is: warmed by the year-round solar-heated water. Kissed by the chemicals, already beginning to prune.

'Xander, wake up!' Ludlow shouts as they emerge from the stairwell on the mezzanine level.

Ash vaults over a sofa in the cocktail lounge. Tammy shoves aside a bus boy, so hard they go spinning into a water feature.

'Xander!' cries Skinner, squeezing through the elevator doors the second they chime open.

Now they're sprinting past a row of floor-to-ceiling windows looking out on the recreation area. Through a manicured row of hedges, past the empty tennis court, they can see Xander – and then they can't. His head slips below the waterline, and a spasm of bubbles leaves him there.

'Xan!' wails Tammy, ramming the double doors open with her shoulder and leaping over the hedge. She and Cleo and Fizz and Ludlow and Ash and Dante are charging across the tennis court, bare toes on the fluoro-green acrylic. Tammy clears the service line and in one clean motion she kicks the gate open, jumps, dives and spearheads to the bottom of the pool, hoisting Xander's flotsam body over one shoulder and kicking back up to the surface.

Ash and Cleo dive in after Tammy, helping her ferry the body to the edge. Xander's not breathing, not moving, not blinking, the blood from his bad eye soaking through its saturated bandage. Ludlow, Skinner and Fizz hug the edge and haul Xander out like a hunk of aircraft debris, waterlogged and heavy as a tomb. Abel and Edwina watch from the tennis court, but Minnie – her eyes still flashing with sporadic, F-induced afterimages – skids along the wet cement to Xander's side. She checks his pulse, checks his breath, tilts his head, feels around inside his mouth.

'Roll him!' she cries, and the others roll him. A stream of pool water escapes Xander's lips, but not enough.

'Roll him back!' They roll him back, and Minnie knits her fingers on his chest, interspersing every thirty compressions with two open-mouthed sighs into his slack-jawed mouth. But there's nothing going into him and nothing coming out of him. His body is a sealed-off habitat. And in his mind, the trip has ended. Xander found his way to precisely where he was headed all along.

Cleo's pacing, tugging at her hair. Tammy's kneeling beside Xander, watching Minnie work, nodding along, waiting for the moment when he coughs up a lung of hotel pool, coughs his way back in time to them. Skinner's looking up at the hotel balconies, populated by curious onlookers, business travellers and honeymooners and would-be attendees of the First Annual International Chronophenomenology Summit, poised in their pyjamas, frozen in shadow, nightcaps in hand, watching Xander die. In time, Skinner will have to make his way from room to room, buying these people off, humbly requesting then paying generously for their silence. After Ludlow returns to the penthouse and flushes every remaining ounce, gram, drop and tab of contraband, after the police examine Xander's body and demand to search the suite, they will also go room to room, asking: had these musician types demonstrated any antisocial behaviour? Any idea what might have transpired here tonight? They'll get the same response from every guest: one too many beers and a tragic accident playing Marco Polo. That's not a crime, is it officer? One too many beers? Why, that's practically our mantra. Words to live by. One too many beers. A fine young man. He held the elevator for me when I checked in this afternoon. Skinner's slush fund, the kitty provided by Labyrinth in case of such emergencies, will be drained dry.

But right now, Edwina is whispering to Abel: 'Fascinating, isn't it? The effect of the narcotic imbalance. Right eye, left brain; left eye, right brain. Like a car with one headlight – half at your destination, half still in the driveway, with you in the middle, stretched between the two. He was pulled in both directions – pulled quite tight – then it's as though the tension released and he was slingshotted forwards, towards … I don't know, exactly. But he made his own way there.'

'Death by paradox,' says Abel.

'Suicide or self-fulfilling prophecy?'

Minnie's fists have seized up. 'I can't,' she says. Tammy takes over without missing a single compression. Minnie backs away, pressing up against the chain-link fence around the tennis court, her face stretched in what looks like agony but feels like enlightenment, her brain a devilish cocktail of cause and effect. When she skipped ahead, she had seen Xander die. She had seen herself sitting where she is sitting right now, mouth twisted in a silent scream, wondering if this was all her doing. When she skipped ahead, for a moment it had just been her and the dead man, Minnie and Xander alone in all of time – but now only she was left. When she skipped ahead, Minnie knew that before the night was through she would watch a man die, suspect that she killed him, lose a part of herself she would never get back, wonder if this was what it meant to be a god, and wonder whether we were all one now.

Poor girl. I almost feel bad I ever met her.

The paramedics take three hours to get to the hotel because the streets of Sydney are a war zone tonight. When they do arrive, they perform a perfunctory vitals check, ask for Xander's ID, then zip him up in black vinyl and wheel him away. Cleo gets a glimpse inside the ambulance. There's at least four bodies in there already. Apparently, the city morgue is so full they've packed body bags with ice cubes and had to hack the thermostat. Many remains will never be identified, because the only people who could identify them are in other bags in the same room. Progressive blood, far-right blood, it all looks the same when it's being washed off the sidewalk with a garden hose.

'Xander always hated Botany,' Ash says as they watch the ambulance crawl away past the barricades, through the still-swollen throng of protesters holding placards saying *TIME'S TIME IS UP*.

'But he loved swimming,' says Tammy, teeth chattering even though the water in her clothes is warm and the air is muggy. 'Don't try to make something of it.'

Edwina's standing at the shallow end of the pool, the cuffs of her slacks rolled up above her ankles. She steps into the water.

'Edwina,' says Abel, who's caved to a decade-old craving and scabbed a rollie off Ludlow.

'It's okay,' she says, taking another step down.

Cleo and Fizz and Dante and Ash are all sitting along one side of the pool, dipping their feet. The refraction makes their legs look small, acute and strange. Skinner's in the water, floating on his back, staring up at the night sky, all the stars muted by pockets of red light from fires in the city surrounding them. Everyone's drawn to the pool, even if it feels somehow haunted now – but then, people are often drawn to such things.

'I've got a great idea,' says Skinner, 'for your next project.'

Edwina, who's closest, figures he might be talking to her. 'My work is mostly research-based.'

'Everyone's so preoccupied with seeing what's next,' says Skinner. 'But I've got a grand idea, and you're welcome to have it. I won't even patent it. Like the polio vaccine. I'll give it away for free, for the good of humanity.'

'Okay,' says Edwina, cautious but kind.

'We've cracked the future. So what's the next logical step? What's

BIG TIME

the next hot ticket item that pharmaceuticals and junkies will want to get their hands on? It's obvious: a drug that lets you go backwards. More powerful than memory. Something that really takes you there. I'm no chemist, but it must be possible. Could you simply invert the formula for the opposite effect?'

Edwina pushes forward into the water, towards Skinner. He's crying, but you can't hear it in his voice. You can't see it either, because his eyes sit only an inch above the waterline. Chlorine swallows salt.

'I'm so sick of the future,' he says, quieter. Maybe he knows everyone's listening. 'I'd like to go back. Back to last night. Back to that morning we all arrived at the bus. Back to the recording – it was hard, wasn't it? It was a real slog. But I'd take it, in a heartbeat. And this new drug, maybe it could work the same way: the more you take, the further you go. So with enough in my system, I could go back to the first tour. I remember one morning we were late for a media call, in Hobart, I think, and I arrived at the accommodation, and I couldn't find them anywhere. The house was a wreck, they'd been partying all night. Then I tiptoed up to the master bedroom and there they all were, curled up on the bed. A "cuddle puddle", someone called it. Ash, Julian, Tammy and Xander. All in it together. Dusty as hell. I had to drip-feed them coffee. But I'd go back to that. Or to those very first recording sessions for *Beaches*, watching them find their feet, hearing them discover their sound. Those moments when we'd be struggling with a track, and then suddenly, it all clicked. I think that feeling is why I'm alive today. I think that's why I didn't die in a fire one night, years ago. But while we're at it, could I go back to that time, too? I would un-throw every punch, stitch up every wound I inflicted. The apologies we feel we owe people now, what if we could simply offer them at the time? God, the regret. It's the bloody regret. I wish I could clear it from my mind. I wish I could go back and turn the dial in a slightly different direction. The sleep I would have now. The way I would hold my shoulders.'

He's at no risk of sinking, but nevertheless, Edwina puts one hand beneath the small of Skinner's back and holds his head in another, catching him mid-baptism.

'But then,' Skinner says, his voice finally cracking, 'the mistakes we make in an effort to be loved – can we really call those mistakes?'

Edwina's treading water. She kicks herself up to look Skinner in the eye.

'What do you think?' he says. 'Will it sell? Could you move some units?'

'We can certainly look into it,' says Edwina.

Abel's ashing his cigarette and making his way inside. Minnie's lying motionless on the tennis court. Dante's thinking about a boy he kissed before leaving Melbourne, wishing he'd got his number. Felicia's puking in a hedge. Ash is beginning to sober up and wishing that he wasn't. Cleo has a cough, which she thinks is from partying but in three months' time will discover is the first indicator of an aggressive carcinoma in her left lung. Ludlow's disappeared upstairs, crying in the shower.

Tammy's trying to box-breathe to stop herself from shaking. Breathe in. Count to four. Breathe out. Count to four. She grips her phone tight and checks the time. She was meant to hear from Oriana by now.

14

When I stupidly follow Oriana and Julian out of the penthouse, down in the lift, through the hotel kitchen and out into the staff car park, there is, as Julian had predicted, a car waiting. Oriana ushers us into the back seat, then slides in after. In the driver's seat there's a bald man with diamond earrings. In the passenger seat there's a kid, no older than seventeen, turned around to face us while casually nursing some sort of machine pistol.

The kid says: 'He puts some thorn in the thicket and the ire back in fire.'

Oriana says: 'He's an unbeatable poet and a first-class liar.'

The kid nods. 'Let's go.'

The diamond-eared driver puts the car in gear and snakes it past an unmanned barricade. Seems the rioters didn't think to check for a rear entrance.

'So nice to meet everyone,' I say. 'That was a cute little exchange. Are we all part of the same book club?'

The driver makes the introductions. His name's Holiday, and the kid's is Biggs. They're friends of the friend Oriana's taking us to meet.

'Any friend of hers,' I say, already wishing I was back at the party. Then again, if I'd stayed and been there for Xander drowning himself in the pool of a three-point-five-star hotel, I probably would have wished I'd come here instead. You never can win.

'Will we be okay out here?' asks Julian. 'With the curfew?'

'Should be,' says Biggs. 'This ride's got diplomatic plates.'

'Don't take this the wrong way,' I say with a smile, 'but you folks don't seem all that diplomatic.'

Holiday's eyes flick up at me in the rear-view mirror. 'Neither did the bastards we nicked it off.'

I stop smiling, opting for a solemn nod instead.

The car glides along the one-way streets of inner Sydney. For every quiet block, lights off, peaceful and unpopulated, there's another three swarming with improvised barricades and pockets of militia. As we pass Liverpool Street, a band of insurrectionists in paintball armour have ambushed a stray police patrol and are chasing them into the guts of Hyde Park, brandishing machetes. All of this necessitates a few detours, including one minor confrontation: when some gurning, Eureka-flag-wearing fuckwit takes off one of our side mirrors at an intersection with a baseball bat, Biggs rolls his window down quick enough to stick his pistol right under the idiot's chin, sending him packing down an alleyway full of burning rubbish skips.

After a few more minutes taking in the chuckle of the diesel engine and the tapping of Holiday's knuckles on the brown leather steering wheel, we pull up next to a darkened pocket of greenery. A sign tells us it's *HARMONY PARK*. Biggs gets out first, checks the street both ways, then guides Holiday and me and Oriana and Julian towards a tall sandstone building with a glass façade. I can just make out a crop of orange café umbrellas on a rooftop deck high above, blocking out the moon. The doors are guarded by two towering mercenary types with combat goggles and AR13s slung across their shoulders. They stand stock still as Biggs shows us inside and through the lobby. I assume we'll be taking an elevator up to the umbrellas – but instead Biggs leads us down a dark flight of stairs and into an underground venue with green walls, plush seating and a mid-century bar made of curved blond wood. More mercs mill about inside, tipping their chins at the sight of Biggs and Holiday – and Oriana. Like they're pleased to see her. Like it's been a while.

I'm thinking of her dressed up as Peter Pan at my tenth birthday party. Apparently, she'd been so insistent on having Peter's shadow as a prop, she'd demanded that her stepfather cut a perfect silhouette from the curtains in their living room with textile shears.

BIG TIME

'O.' An older woman, poised at another set of double doors, hugs Oriana as though their reunion means the world – hands open, palms pressed against each other's backs.

'Sita,' says Oriana, squeezing her tight. Then she jabs a thumb at the doors. 'Is he inside?' The older woman nods.

I look at Julian. 'Do you have the faintest fucking clue what's going on?'

'No,' he says, shaking his head. 'Feels safer in here than it does out there, though.'

'It is,' says Oriana, walking back over. 'But Wesley' – she holds my arm – 'you're never going to write or share a word of this with anybody. You know that, right?'

I offer a salute. 'Yes, ma'am.'

'You've always been a good friend,' she says, putting a hand on my cheek. That hand on my cheek might have been why I did what I would do a little later. I'm a sucker for affectionate proclamations like that. The soul-baring stuff. I've never been good at it myself, but I like it when I see it in others. I especially like it when it's meant for me.

But then Oriana says: 'I need you to stay out here.'

I'm about to kick up a fuss – I don't really feel like killing time in the cantina with her black-ops pals – but then I glance at the bar and spot a bottle of actual, legitimate Japanese whisky.

'Here if you need me,' I say, planting myself on a stool and reaching for the Yamazaki.

'He's ready to see you,' Sita says, pointing Julian towards the double doors.

'Cool,' says Julian, starting to get a little shitty at feeling so out of the loop. 'I guess I'm ready to see him too.'

Sita pulls the doors open, letting Oriana and Julian into a small, rundown cinema, with mahogany armchairs in rows of ten and curtains the colour of English mustard hanging each side of a disused silver screen. The middle seating rows have been forcibly ripped out to make way for an enormous array of computer hardware – blinking server racks sitting at the heart of a mess of cabling, twisted together like black jelly snakes. A man with silver hair is leaning in towards the main console, the LED sheen from a row of monitors picking up flecks of dandruff on his shoulders. When Oriana enters, he turns.

'O,' he says, weathered face split by a grin.

'Hello, Charlie,' Oriana says as they embrace.

Then Oriana turns to Julian and presents the man, saying: 'Jules. I'd like you to meet Charlie Total.'

The man steps right up close and offers his hand. 'A pleasure to meet you, Julian.'

Julian shakes Charlie Total's hand. His fingers are bony, but his skin is soft.

'Hi,' says Julian. 'Oriana tells me you're trying to overthrow the government.'

Charlie blinks – then begins to howl with laughter. 'Did she!' He turns and points at Oriana, who smiles slyly. 'Cheeky lass. What you must think of me! She's not wrong, though. No, she ain't wrong. Please, sit.'

Julian folds down one of the chairs and slumps back against its plushness. The rear of the seat in front of him bears a plaque: *FOR K, FROM C. MI AMOR.*

'This used to be a cinema?' Julian asks in an effort at small talk.

'Correct,' says Charlie Total, leaning back against one of the seating banks. 'Real good one, back in the day. Showed all sorts of stuff. French New Wave. German Expressionism. Guilty pleasures, too: erotic thrillers, pagan horror. Plenty of Aussie stuff, back when they had a clue. You know, I've always thought the word *retro* is much too cheerful. But then *retrospective*, which, of course, *retro* is short for, is far too stuffy. When we look back at what we used to be, I reckon I'd like the experience to be a little bit of both. Wouldn't you? Syrupy and salty. Sweet and sour. Take the good with the bad. Like those places you used to be able to get both kinds of popcorn, mixed up in the one box. You need a little spoonful of sugar to help the medicine go down sometimes, don't you?'

'Depends on the medicine,' says Julian.

'Right you are.' Charlie nods, his silvery beard brushing his chest. 'After all, it's just stories. Which is what I wanted to talk to you about.'

'What's that?'

'Stories,' repeats Charlie. 'I'd like you to tell some for me.'

Julian glances over at Oriana, who lingers by the door like a soldier at ease.

BIG TIME

Julian asks whether Charlie knows he's a musician. A bass player, professionally. Guitarist and lyricist in his own time.

Charlie settles back into a computer chair and reaches for a bowl of pistachio nuts that he proceeds to crack open with his teeth. 'This isn't really about that.'

Julian's at a loss, shrugging his shoulders. 'Then what is this about?'

'You'll have to forgive me!' says Charlie, rightly sensing Julian's frustration. 'I can come across a bit cryptic. I was an actor in a past life, so the drama still really does it for me.' He laughs, downs a fistful of nuts, then goes on: 'So. The past is all stories. Some true, others embellished. But at the end of the day, all of human history's just a story we remember and pass along. Doesn't matter whether it's a story round a campfire or a stack of encyclopedias. And given that this is how we experience history, it's how we imagine the future as well: as a story we're yet to hear. A film for which we've only seen the trailer. That is, until the big day arrives and we get to experience it for ourselves. Before that, we're left to fill in the blanks with what little information we have. A few clues, a good hunch or two, but the rest ... imagination.' He clears his throat. 'Oriana tells me you have a gift.'

'My bass?'

'No,' Charlie says with a laugh. 'Your music is good, though! Don't get me wrong. Even if I liked your early stuff better.'

'You and everybody else.'

Charlie's tapping one boot in some strange rhythm only he knew the melody to. He seems restless, cracking open nuts faster than he can chew them. Julian wonders if Charlie lives down here, in the abandoned cinema – whether he curls up beneath the console after a long day's work and sleeps on and off until dawn. Or maybe he lives in the building above, sunning himself on the rooftop, surrounded by orange umbrellas.

Charlie asks Julian: 'What's the furthest you've ever skipped ahead?'

Julian finally starts to catch up. He looks at Oriana. 'You smuggled me across town in the middle of a civil war to be interrogated about my drug habits?'

'Hear him out, Jules.'

'Can you answer me, Julian?' says Charlie. 'Can you tell me how far?'

Julian sighs, a little performative, because the fact was, deep down, he was also somewhat proud. 'The first time I ever took F, I was on a plane coming home, and I skipped ahead three days. Over the summer, while we were recording the new album, I think the furthest I got was ... a week? Ten days? I really needed it at the time. But I was starting to feel sort of ... rubbery. Like I was spending too long out there. So I cut back. I stuck with the perfume samplers Oriana gave us, microdosing instead, so I was skipping more often, but seeing less when I did – half a day, maybe a day at most.'

Charlie Total chews, then spits half a pistachio shell out on the floor. 'Good boy. That's smart. That sort of self-control is very admirable. But what I would like' – a generous gesture towards Oriana – 'what *we* would like, is for you to take that self-control and chuck it out the window.'

'What?'

'We want to see how far you can go, boy! The further you go, the more useful you'll be.'

Julian doesn't know what this means. He just knows he didn't like the sudden downswing in Charlie Total's voice when he used the word *useful*.

'Oriana told you I'm a man who's trying to overthrow the government,' Charlie says, his head crowned by the monitor array bleeding white light into the auditorium, 'but I am one of many. A nationwide network. Men and women just like me, and Oriana, and – in time – like you. People doing what they can. A rebellion, a resistance, call us what you will. We're the light that shines through any time a crack appears – when they paper over the crack, we force another elsewhere. We're the sewage beneath the sinkhole, see? We're a lever waiting to be pulled, and right now, all we lack is a fulcrum. A flashpoint. A defining spark to set the tinderbox ablaze. We're waiting with our toes on the starting line, and we'd like for you to be our starter pistol.'

Julian feels nauseous. He has the sudden urge to be very polite. 'I'd like to go now, please,' he says, trying to stand, making to leave – but Oriana is behind him, putting a gentle but steady hand on his shoulder and pushing him back down in his seat.

BIG TIME

Charlie says: 'One day soon, Julian, you'll have an opportunity to leave East Australia. When that opportunity comes, you'll take it. Of course you will. Because by then, there'll be nothing here for you. I can tell you with absolute assurance that the DID is building a case against you, and all your friends, at this very moment. And not just a standard snatch-job, no, my boy. They'll be rolling out the red carpet for each and every one of you. So you'll leave. Grand. Oriana will be there to help you along. You'll be compensated and catered to. It might even end up being quite a nice life. All we want you to do in return is take more F. We want you to skip ahead, then come back and tell people what you've seen. Tell them the truth.'

'We've never encountered anyone with your level of tolerance,' says Oriana, her lips close to Julian's ear. 'There was Edmond, up in Byron Bay. We thought he was our best shot. But it went to his head. The old coot went and killed himself just to see some stars explode.'

Charlie's back to chewing pistachios as he speaks, hand-to-mouth. 'We have a PR firm in the WRA already working on your media persona. We're thinking international broadcasting. One-on-one consultations with influential individuals. With the right publicity, our guidance and your charisma – which Oriana assures me you can command when necessary – you could go global. A modern-day Nostradamus. You'll tell people the things you see, then they'll see them happen. All you need to do is tell the truth. And then one day – one fine, special day, when we tell you that the time is right – you'll tell one lie.'

Julian moves his lips but can't unclench his teeth. 'What's the lie?'

'Dead simple!' Charlie throws his hands in the air, scattering pistachio shells among the server cables. 'You'll say you've seen the fall of the Federal Republic of East Australia. You'll say you've seen the Central Government overthrown and its departments disbanded. You'll say you've seen the Leader flee, hunted, eventually presumed dead. That's it. Then you're done.'

'So I just make some shit up?' splutters Julian, hot-cheeked. 'What's that supposed to achieve?'

'The news will leak back east,' Oriana says. 'We believe that's what will set the wheels in motion.' She touches his shoulder. 'Self-fulfilling prophecy.'

'A bloodless coup,' says Charlie. 'A *coup d'voila*.'

Julian shakes his head. His head shakes his body. 'This isn't me,' he says. 'I don't know what you've heard. Or what Oriana told you. But I'm not some revolutionary.'

'I thought you were an artist.'

'I'm just a bass player, for fuck's sake!'

'Isn't it every musician's dream to be the soundtrack to revolution? This way, you get to be the revolution itself.'

'I write pop music,' says Julian. 'Three-and-a-half minutes of up-tempo bullshit, ten times every two years.'

Charlie comes closer, pressing his hands down into the seating bank right in front of Julian. His breath smells like the green of pistachios, the blue of spearmint, the brown of old gums.

'My dear Julian,' he says. 'Every single day you are surrounded by other people's pain. Don't you feel it?'

Julian jumps up, too quick for Oriana to stop him. He backs away down the aisle, Charlie's eyes following him like a painting.

'I'm going back to the hotel,' Julian says. 'I'm going to finish this tour. Then I'm going to go home and pretend I never heard any of this. But if you ever try to rope me into this shit again …' he stabs a finger at Oriana, 'I swear to fucking god, I will turn you in.'

Charlie sucks his teeth. 'I personally believe there's only one meaningful binary in life: are you free, or are you not? If you are free, you fight every day to keep it that way. If you're not, you fight every day to change that. Either way, you're fighting. Do you think you're free, Julian?'

'Free enough for me.'

Charlie exhales quickly. A puff of disrespect. He turns back to his monitors, as though he's lost interest.

Julian makes for the double doors. He wants to be out in the night air of Surry Hills, 3 am, smelling like freshly baked bread and unexploded bombs. But Oriana's there again, blocking his way.

'Let me out,' he says.

She looks at him calmly.

Julian scoffs. 'So the groupie's now a freedom fighter. Guess I underestimated you.'

'Maybe I overestimated you,' says Oriana.

'Before you go!' Charlie Total hollers from the console. 'Ever been to Ireland?'

BIG TIME

Julian holds Oriana's gaze as he says: 'No.'

'Me neither,' laments Charlie. 'Always wanted to. But did you ever meet a man from there named Brayden Byrne?'

'No.'

'What about an Inspector José Muñoz Rojas?'

'No.'

'Funny,' Charlie says with mock bewilderment. 'Because our intel says you killed one of them – and the other's been looking for you ever since.'

There's a face staring out at Julian from one of Charlie's screens. A yearbook photo. Strawberry-blond hair and brown freckles. Then next to that, an autopsy photo of the same face from a Colombian morgue. Strawberry-blond hair stained crimson, freckles black against dead marble skin, stitches on the scalp, slack-jawed and shut-eyed.

You're him, the man had said.

Next to the autopsy photo is a loop of grainy footage: an alleyway outside a block of public restrooms in downtown Medellín. Brayden Byrne going in. Julian going in. Julian coming out.

'We acquired this footage from a pet camera in an apartment across the street,' Charlie hums, stroking his beard, watching it for the hundredth time. 'Inspector Rojas has never seen it. I'm sure he'd like to, though. I'm sure he'd love to put an end to the whole international incident. I'm sure Brayden Byrne's family in Ireland would love to put a name, and a face, to the young man who killed their boy. Might help them move on. Don't you think?'

Julian stares at the screen, watching himself entering the restrooms then walking back out, trying to hail a cab to take him to the airport.

'He died,' Julian says.

'Head trauma triggering a brain bleed,' Charlie tuts, bringing up the coroner's report on another screen. 'Wouldn't necessarily have been fatal – but he was left there for a number of hours.'

'It was an accident,' says Julian.

'Murder two at best, I'd say. Can't think of many countries in the world who wouldn't extradite somebody over something like that – even the FREA.'

JORDAN PROSSER

*

So that was that, then: the moment Julian Ferryman stopped being free – even free enough for him. He'd tried so hard, his whole life, to get by without ever giving anybody anything on him. He'd never been a snitch, or a sycophant, but he'd always been careful. He'd always known that a person's free will was more or less dependent on their ability to keep their nose clean and remain factionally unentangled.

But Julian had entangled himself without even knowing it. All because he hadn't bent down to check for a pulse in the young man's slender neck. In the months since, recording with the band, setting out on tour, Julian had held on to the precious thought that he could walk away from it all at a moment's notice. Go somewhere new. Become a different person.

Brayden Byrne's final words had been to tell Julian that he'd seen *it* – but whatever *it* was, it wasn't this. Now, there were shackles. Now, Julian was tied down. Now, he'd lost something irretrievable – the blessed ability to turn one good, blind eye.

If Charlie had intended on proving his point further, he didn't need to, and nor does he have the time. As Julian hovers at the monitors, hollow-eyed, watching his past-self haunt the streets of Medellín, an explosion sounds somewhere outside – far enough to sound like thunder, close enough to shake the mustard curtains.

Out at the bar, I see it ripple in the surface of my Yamazaki. A bad omen. I drink it all.

The doors to the cinema fly open, revealing Oriana, tense and alert, and Julian, pale and shellshocked. Sita starts relaying something she's hearing through an earpiece. All around me, Oriana's mercenary friends begin gearing up, tightening their bootlaces and strapping on flak jackets.

'Hey fellas,' I say, 'I'm starting to feel a little underdressed.'

Holiday's at the stairs, saying: 'Twenty seconds. Cars are waiting.'

I gravitate towards Oriana but get distracted by the silver-haired man standing next to her. 'Hey,' I say, 'weren't you in that old Ivan Sen movie?' Charlie Total winks at me.

'Fifteen seconds,' shouts Holiday as another explosion, closer

BIG TIME

this time, makes the chandeliers shake and the bottles on the wall behind the bar shimmy sideways. Oriana catches a rifle from one of the grunts and offers it to Julian, but he shakes his head, looking like he's about to throw up. She offers it to me and I laugh.

'Five,' says Holiday. 'Four. Three. Two.'

Biggs leads us out, machine pistol braced against one arm. As we file back into the lobby upstairs, the mercs make a flying V, with Charlie Total, Oriana, Julian and me at the centre. The windows are open and there's smoke in the air. There's fire on the wind.

'Move,' says Holiday, holding the lobby doors open. There's a convoy of armoured cars, no doubt also stolen, engines idling, just at the corner, no more than fifty metres away. Biggs makes a run for it, then falls mid-step. I think that he's tripped. It seems so incidental, like he's lost his footing. But there's a bullet in his back and the kid is dead.

I never got to ask Oriana what we came there for that night, who Charlie Total was to her, or how Julian was mixed up in everything. I just knew he was important. I never got to hear the same speeches he did, never had Charlie asking me about other people's pain. But sure, I knew all about that. Hell, I'd felt it for half my life or more, and I'd done everything I could to drown it out. But then sometimes, somebody's dead right in front of you. On the same street as you. And there's no drink in the world for that.

A squad of military police are advancing out of Harmony Park, pinning our group between the sandstone building and the waiting convoy. I kind of want to cry, kind of need to burp. Kind of wish I could just lie down on the pavement and let the ground have me. I look at Julian Ferryman, frozen in place beneath a streetlight, and think: dumb luck and circumstance. In case I haven't yet made it abundantly clear – I never really liked that guy.

'STOP SHOOTING,' I scream, getting to my feet. 'STOP SHOOTING, PLEASE. I SURRENDER.'

Oriana whispers something, but she's already miles away. I wander out into no man's land, hands held high. 'I DON'T KNOW THESE PEOPLE. I'M SO LOST. PLEASE DON'T SHOOT ME.'

JORDAN PROSSER

One of the troopers tells me to drop to my knees with my hands behind my head, but instead I keep walking.

'I'M NOT EVEN FROM HERE. I DON'T KNOW WHERE I AM, AND I'M SCARED.'

Stop walking, the trooper says.

'CAN YOU HELP ME?'

Stop walking.

'CAN YOU TAKE ME HOME?'

Get down on your knees.

'FUCK YOU, PIG.'

I'm always faster when I'm drunk. My plan is to lead them on a merry chase along Liverpool Street – at the very least divide their attention and buy Oriana some time. A few car windows explode in gunfire behind me. I can hear Holiday and Sita shouting, boots scraping, the doors in the convoy opening and closing. Maybe that did the trick. Maybe I was good for something.

Another pop and I'm on the ground, right in the middle of an intersection. Boiling hot lead searing through my shoulder, melting the muscle even as it cauterises it. I can only laugh as it takes four troopers to pin me down, zip-tie my wrists and ankles and pull a hood over my head. Sometimes all you can do is laugh.

So technically, this is where I leave you. But like so many others who have gone before me, I'll still be around. Even if you can't see me. Even if nobody ever hears from me again. Out of sight, out of mind. Out of world, out of time.

PART FOUR

COOKSLAND

15

Olenya Panchenko had a dog named Lotto. By the time Olenya was seven, the black spots on the Dalmatian's coat had begun to turn a lustrous grey, and his eyes reflected the blue light of the family television with the glassy beginnings of cataracts. He was also going deaf, something apparently quite common in the breed. Olenya's parents, Karina and Yegor, bought him off a farmer who'd been left with a whole litter of the things and had no idea of Lotto's precise genetic provenance. This was when Karina and Yegor were living in the small rural town where they first met and married. After Olenya was born, they moved to the city, into a two-bedroom apartment on the fourth floor of a concrete, Soviet-era apartment tower, one of four in a crowded complex that overlooked a slightly sad playground with one working swing and a slippery dip that made you go even faster on mornings when it was covered with ice.

This is the apartment where Olenya grew up, where her first memories, and her first words, were of Lotto – of the too-big beast with its spotted limbs doing three-point turns in the cramped corridor, rearing back and leaping up on her bed first thing in the morning, last thing in the evening and any time there was thunder outside. Olenya insisted on taking the dog with her everywhere, out in the freezing snow and onto crowded subway carriages. One time she attempted to take Lotto to school with her, hoping nobody would notice. And when Olenya couldn't take Lotto with her, the dog would wait by the front door for hours on end, forgoing any food or water, staring with his blurry blue-and-brown eyes at the

BIG TIME

brass door handle, waiting for the tiniest, most minute indication that Olenya was about to arrive home. And when she did, after a flurry of leaps and licks to the face, after nearly bowling over Karina with her brown paper grocery bags or Yegor with his family-sized takeaway dinners, Lotto would patiently follow Olenya from room to room all night, looking up at her, sometimes dolefully, sometimes playfully, extending a paw when he wanted it held, inserting his head between her arm and torso when he wanted it scratched. There was no feeling in the entire world Olenya liked more than the feeling of Lotto's chin, bony and warm, resting heavily on her thigh.

On the night of the first air raid, Lotto clung to Olenya and buried his snout beneath the duvet, his entire body quaking from what must have sounded like endless, muffled thunderclaps. Olenya stroked his head and kissed his eyebrows and sang him a song Karina used to sing to her. This continued for a week. Olenya stopped going to school. She heard her parents whispering through the open crack of their bedroom door, listing the names of distant cousins and old high school friends in towns close to the border. The kitchen filled with stacks of tinned food. It was no longer safe to go for afternoon walks or even down to the playground with its solitary swing, so Olenya's full-time job became looking after Lotto. She read him books and massaged his cramped legs. At dusk, when the sirens started, Lotto curled up into a ball just as small as his angular joints would allow, and Olenya would smile down at him beatifically, her awkward monochrome companion, their shadows on the wall from the flickering nightlight looking much bigger than either one of them felt.

One day before dawn, after another night of heavy shelling, Olenya's parents wrapped her in so many quilted jackets she could barely rest her arms at her sides. They loaded their Peugeot hatchback with all the tinned food and one small piece of luggage each. Olenya helped Lotto into the back seat, where his thick brow bumped against the roof. Yegor kept the headlights off, driving slowly from the half-empty resident's carpark and through their blasted neighbourhood towards the highway, passing old four-wheel drives and repurposed delivery vans, their roofs stacked high with bedding, antique furniture and waterproof crates full of family photo albums. All the traffic was heading in the same direction: west. The only vehicles in the opposite lane, those heading back towards the city, were armoured supply trucks and a trio of forty-year-old battle tanks, grinding along so slowly that Olenya locked eyes with a young blond soldier reclining by an access hatch, smoking a cigarette, assault rifle pointed benignly at the sky.

Soon after they reached Yegor's cousin's house, news arrived that men aged eighteen to sixty were no longer permitted to leave the country. Instead, they were being ordered to report to the nearest military barracks for rapid training and deployment back east. Olenya sat in the back of the Peugeot, its engine still running to keep the heater going, stroking Lotto's back, watching her parents pace back and forth in a muddy field beside the house. Karina was screaming something. Yegor was trying to hold her head in his hands. Eventually, Yegor marched up to the car, opened the back door and kissed Olenya fiercely on the forehead. Lotto licked his chin. Then Yegor went into the house. A minute later, Yegor's cousin's wife, a textile maker named Olga, emerged with an armful of belongings that she stuffed into the boot of the car along with Olenya's and Karina's. The women took their seats up front, and Karina wordlessly returned the car to the highway.

Olenya had never travelled that far from home, so she couldn't tell you what it used to look like – but now it reminded her of a cartoon she'd once seen which was set on the moon, grey and rocky and pocked with craters. She knew there was no air on the moon, and therefore no wind, but nevertheless she felt there was something distinctly lunar about the swirls of ash and mist that kicked up in the empty fields on either side of the highway. She saw clusters of civilians moving on foot, dragging suitcases with broken wheels. She saw one man with a bloodied forehead and pale cheeks clutching nothing but a small terrier, a brown-and-white thing bundled into an old fire blanket. She saw churches turned black, their stained-glass windows blown out and scattered like confetti. She smelt the wet of fresh mud and the nefarious whiff of strange meat. She heard the radio station changing every hundred miles as her mother drove them in and out of pockets of reception, heard the measured tone of field reporters reeling off body counts and damage reports. She felt Lotto's chin on her thigh.

BIG TIME

They came to another town. All the buildings on the left side of the main street were razed to the ground, while the buildings on the right remained perfectly and inexplicably intact. At the end of the street was a bridge, freshly blasted to oblivion by some retreating platoon, sheets of broken bitumen piled up like ten-tonne jigsaw puzzle pieces in the roaring river below. Only the bridge's steel scaffolding, twisted out of shape and gnarled like an old tree, still tenuously connected one bank to the other. A crowd of concerned travellers stood at the verge, weighing up their options. The next workable bridge wasn't for twenty miles downriver and it had been claimed by enemy soldiers. A consensus was reached that the women and children would attempt to cross the broken bridge the following morning on foot.

A man in a wheelchair told them there was shelter in the school gymnasium. Olenya, Karina and Olga found a spot in a corner. They ate some tinned food with a hunk of bread and unrolled the sleeping bags Yegor had bought the year before, imagining he might soon teach his daughter about erecting tents and lighting fires and other such wholesome, outdoorsy things. Olga sang a song to herself. Karina said nothing, staring out through the white windows of the gymnasium. Lotto was curled up heavily in Olenya's lap. She patted his head and whispered in his ear. When Olenya looked up, her mother was looking at the dog, a twitch at the corner of her lips.

That night, Olenya dreamt she was camping with her father, but couldn't lift the axe they'd brought to chop wood. Her father shook his head ruefully, saying that without a fire, they would freeze to death. Then Olenya woke up on the gymnasium floor, trembling from cold. There was a halo of warmth around her knees where Lotto had been when she'd fallen asleep. He wasn't there now. Her mother's sleeping bag sat unzipped and empty.

Pulling on boots and her thickest jacket, Olenya paced softly down the aisles of makeshift campsites, whispering her dog's name. Then, by a closed side door, she heard what sounded like an argument outside. It was Karina's voice, saying: Go. Get out of here. Go now. Stupid thing.

Olenya opened the door and saw her mother in track pants and a singlet top, standing barefoot in a fresh fall of snow. Lotto sat in front of her, head to one side, tongue lolling about goofily as he puffed big gusts of frozen air. Olenya thought that Lotto looked beautiful there in the snow, beneath a pale moon. She thought about how if it weren't for his spots, you might not have seen him at all.

Karina was saying: Go boy. Get out of here. She was pointing across an empty field towards a murky beech forest that ran along the river. Lotto eagerly rearranged his footing, then looked back at Karina with the same adoring gaze.

Olenya stepped out and her mother turned. Get back inside, she said.

Lotto yapped happily, his tail making a *pap pap pap* sound as he batted it about in the snow.

Go, Lotto! Karina commanded. The dog jumped up briefly, pranced about, then sank down on all fours, ready to play.

Stupid thing! Go on now!

When Olenya tried to run to Lotto, calling out the animal's name, Karina swept her up in her arms, saying: I'm sorry, sweetie. Lotto can't come with us. He has to stay here.

Lotto growled happily, rolling about in the powder, his big glassy eyes reflecting the round of the moon.

Someone will take care of him, said Karina.

I will take care of him, said Olenya.

No, said Karina. Not anymore. We have to take care of ourselves.

Lotto trotted after them. Karina shouted: Stay! The dog sat back on its haunches and waited. Then Karina carried Olenya back inside the gymnasium and shut the door behind them.

Olenya began to cry, throwing her fists at her mother's face. Karina held her tightly. Claws pattered on the concrete steps outside, and there was a scratch at the door. Lotto started barking – a shrill, confused sound.

Olenya screamed so loud that people began to wake up, rolling over in their sleeping bags and flicking on their torches. Karina looked around apologetically, then placed one firm hand over her daughter's mouth.

He'll be okay, she said. Someone will find him. Someone will love him just as much as you do.

Impossible, thought Olenya.

BIG TIME

Lotto barked in his off-key way, trotting around the side door, scratching at the walls. He must have barked for five minutes straight. The sound grew hoarse and dissolved into whimpering. Olenya screamed into Karina's hand: Lotto, I'm in here. Lotto, I love you.

Olenya had fallen asleep that night with Lotto curled up at her knees. Now she knew she would never feel that warmth again. The scratching at the door stopped, giving way to a minute's silence. Then came the swish of soft, clawed feet, trotting down the concrete steps and into the snow, which crunched and crunched before swallowing the sound.

The next day, Olenya looked everywhere – in every room of the gymnasium and in every ruin on the left side of the street. She held her mother's hand as they tiptoed like tightrope walkers across the iron struts of the broken bridge, carrying just her backpack and one extra jacket. If only she were a little older and a little bigger – if only Lotto were a little younger and a little smaller – she could have carried him with her over the freezing water. She would have carried him all the way.

At train stations across Europe, Olenya and her mother were met with the pitying expressions of people crowded against the barriers, holding up cardboard signs stating how many spare rooms they had and how many people they were willing to take. Long-haired art students in Vienna, bespectacled tech workers in Berlin, pearl-necklaced mothers in Paris. Olga was taken in by a baker and his family in the sixteenth arrondissement, while Olenya and Karina were each given a room at the back of a florist's shop in Belleville, where they slept in single beds and woke every morning to the smell of hot coffee and freshly cut tulips. The florist, a woman in her early fifties, had pink cheeks that popped from her face and lovely hazelnut eyes. She had two adult sons who were studying in England – hence the empty rooms – and said she was grateful for the company. But Olenya doubted whether she and her mother were particularly desirable house guests. For one thing, they'd barely spoken a word to each other since the night Karina let Lotto go. And while Olenya played in the flower shop and helped the florist make crepes for breakfast on the weekends, Karina lay in her room for hours on end, drifting in and out of sleep, or simply staring at the thin band of sunlight between the patterned lace curtain and the windowsill.

Olga's husband called with the news that Yegor had been killed by a mortar while defending the airport. Karina didn't leave bed for a week. The florist made her and Olenya beautiful funeral bouquets of white roses and lilies, but Karina's sat on the floor by the door to her room and died within a few days. Olenya asked Olga to visit, and finally Karina emerged. She and Olga stayed up all night, drinking wine and smoking cigarettes. They broke some beautiful porcelain plates, which the florist swept up patiently the next morning, smiling at Olenya as she asked her to put the coffee on. Olenya ate breakfast and returned to her room, where she thought about her father. Then she thought about Lotto – his chin on her thigh – and cried for the rest of the morning.

Olenya started classes at the public school down the road, as well as one-on-one remedial French with a tutor three nights a week. Karina got a job cleaning houses in the wealthy seventh arrondissement, where she was taught to avoid making eye contact with any of her clients. But it seems one day she must have defied her training – because this was how she met Remy.

Olenya suspected something when her mother started returning later and later from her shifts in *le septième*, leaving the florist to make dinner and put Olenya to bed. Hours later, Olenya would hear the front door open, hear her mother's wedge-heeled shoes clatter to the floor, hear a fresh bottle of wine being uncorked, and hear the two women arguing softly in urgent, broken English. One of these nights ended with Karina storming into Olenya's room, packing all her belongings into the same backpack she'd brought from home and announcing that they were going to live in the Eiffel Tower. The florist could only watch and wave goodbye as Olenya's mother dragged her outside and into the back of a cab.

Of course, Remy Devereaux didn't really live *in* the Eiffel Tower – but to the seven-year-old Olenya, he might as well have. His fifth-floor apartment on the Avenue Charles Floquet looked out across the *Jardin de la Tour Eiffel* and lit up every hour of the evening when the tower began winking its canopy of golden lights. It had nine bedrooms with a working fireplace in each, polished parquetry floors and walls decked with old oil paintings of men in powdered wigs and women petting lithe Italian greyhounds. It had a doorman named Patrice and a private elevator to the lobby. Olenya had been there a whole week before she fully realised it was her new home (she and Karina still rarely spoke).

Similarly, it took Remy some time to adjust to the young girl in his apartment, crayons splayed across the hearth in the drawing room. But on the night she first arrived, Remy had bent down to give Olenya a kiss on each cheek and handed her a small stuffed toy – a cheetah. Would you like to go to the zoo sometime? he asked, and Olenya nodded. He was an older man, maybe twenty years her mother's senior, with a thick knot in his eggplant-coloured tie. He smelt like expensive leather, and when he smiled his ears crept up the sides of his ruddy face. He enrolled Olenya in one of those international schools, where she began to develop the same nondescript mid-Atlantic accent that signified the children of bankers and magnates the world over. Olenya liked Remy, but she never saw much of him. He worked late and travelled quite a bit. Sometimes she would glimpse him on the balcony, reading the paper with an espresso in the morning, or drinking cognac by the fireplace late at night. But more often than not, it was just Olenya quietly avoiding her mother in the nine-bedroom apartment while Karina drank champagne from the bottle and bossed around the new cleaners.

For Olenya's eighth birthday, Remy made good on his promise and took her to the zoo. Karina couldn't come, owing to another of what Remy and the house staff had begun referring to as her 'episodes' – phases of boozy catatonia during which Karina would languish in bed for days and throw a magazine at anybody who tried to speak to her. At the *Parc Zoologique*, Remy showed Olenya the real-life cheetahs, as well as the snow leopards, giraffes, meerkats and hippos. Then he took her to the *DOWN UNDER* section, where koalas clung to eucalyptus trees and wallabies bounced off rocky outcrops, and asked Olenya how she would feel about moving to Australia. Olenya had never given much thought to the place and had grown quite accustomed to simply going wherever other people took her. But the marsupials seemed friendly, so she shrugged and said *oui*.

The next day, removalists began to pack everything in the apartment into padded cardboard boxes, pulling the oil paintings off the walls and tenderly wrapping Remy's family crystal up in thick sheaths of butcher's paper. Karina stalked about in her nightgown, a celery stick in one hand and a bottle of Dom Perignon in the other, shooting deathly glares at the hired hands. She was not anywhere near as amenable to the idea of moving to the other side of the planet as Olenya was. But Remy had been given an important new job – he would be chief of his logistics company's Asia-Pacific branch, negotiating long-term trade agreements and lobbying politicians.

The day before leaving Paris, Remy took Karina and Olenya to the passport office. Instead of heading to the main reception desk, Remy showed them to an empty backroom where an immigration officer kissed him on both cheeks, took a large wad of euros from Remy's steady hand and pulled down the blinds before making two new passports, right there on the spot. Remy elucidated briefly on the current political climate in their soon-to-be new home, explaining it would be preferable if Karina and Olenya's names were modified to something less obviously indicative of their refugee status – something a little less Slavic, more full-blooded Western European. This is how Karina became Caterina – and Olenya became Oriana Devereaux.

For the next decade and a half, the Devereauxes occupied the penthouse of a towering casino building on the shores of the Yarra River in Melbourne. Remy's company paid for it to be fully furnished, not anticipating that the Frenchman would insist on bringing many of his own heirloom pieces. This meant the place was horribly cluttered from day one, with sleek, low-backed daybeds jutting up against ornate baroque chaise lounges, and Remy's gilded oil paintings fighting for space on the walls beside minimalist, mass-produced catalogue artworks. Oriana could see the whole city from her bedroom window. With a good set of binoculars, she could peer right into the saltwater crocodile enclosure in the aquarium on the opposite bank.

Caterina, meanwhile, hated everything about the place. She hated the unpredictable weather, the clanging of the trams, the wide-eyed tourists shambling along Southbank. She bitterly chastised Remy for bringing them there, reminding him (loud enough for Oriana to hear) that he was exorbitantly wealthy by birth and did not *need* to work a day in his life if he didn't feel compelled to. But Remy was compelled. He enjoyed his work. As it turned out, he enjoyed being a stepfather, too. Remy and Oriana bonded over their shared love of exotic animals and spy movies. He taught her to play poker, reasoning that if she were going to try her hand at gambling one day (which their home address all but guaranteed) she might as well be given a fighting chance at it.

Oriana came to know and love all three floors of the casino at the base of their apartment building, its elliptical caverns and undulating hallways. She made friends with all the pit bosses and a number of the house regulars. She was there when a woman named Connie won the jackpot on a slot machine called *WHERE'S THE GOLD?!* – a victory Connie attributed to the positioning of Jupiter and Oriana's lucky aura. She gave her fifty dollars as thanks. Oriana loved to watch the security guards move in perfect, furtive synchronicity any time a high roller hit a conspicuous lucky streak, or when some hapless idiot on a three-day bender sidled up to a cashier with the half-baked idea of knocking the joint over. One time Oriana thought she saw a dead man, broken by bad luck, being wheeled into a secret corridor near the prayer room, and a wall with no handles gliding silently closed behind him.

Fearing the casino would turn her daughter into a reprobate, but equally suspecting that another international school might turn her into a snob, Caterina insisted Oriana attend a regular school in the suburbs – and although she would never confess as much to her mother, Oriana was grateful. Being away from all those diplomats' daughters, with their equestrian competitions and designer backpacks, made it much easier for her to relax, blend in and simply get on with life. To forget herself, even. Oriana played soccer, sang in a choir and went to birthday parties on the weekends. One time she insisted Remy cut a silhouette of fabric from the curtains in their casino apartment to accompany her Peter Pan costume. The drapes stayed that way until they abandoned the place, many years later.

Just as Oriana's adolescence was beginning to approach some sort of normalcy, however, the country around her was sliding into a strange and ominous retrograde. The trouble had started long ago; in the mid-'00s a hot mic captured a promising prime ministerial candidate calling a war veteran – who also happened to be a high-profile survivor of a recent overseas terrorist bombing – a 'whinging rat-fucker'. The candidate had lost the battler vote and roundly lost the election, clearing the way for almost half a century of calcifying conservative rule. The country suffered through a global economic crisis, a fifteen-year recession and a viral pandemic, each of which the ruling party used to further convince its citizens that they were better off on their own, insulated against the shocks and uncertainty of free markets and open borders. Things reached a tipping point when Oriana was in year ten; there was a spate of political assassinations, a contested election, then the Red Referendum, which led to the secession of the west. Citing domestic security concerns, the newly minted FREA constructed a ten-foot wall along the length of the hundred and twenty-ninth meridian, from Kununurra in the north down to Eucla in the south (at great expense to eastern taxpayers). The territories were abolished, the states renamed and their boundaries redrawn. Long-established laws were tossed out, and new ones that had been percolating for decades in the desk drawers of neoliberal apparatchiks were implemented overnight. The Central Government, with its many new and expanded departments, gave sweeping powers to police and law enforcement. The borders crept closed. Immigration and tourism trickled to a standstill. Planes sat empty on airport tarmacs. Internet speeds were slowed, then choked, then cut off completely, replaced with the brand-new, fully siloed AusNet. A mandatory buyback program replaced all smart devices. Analogue TV and radio channels were switched back on, broadcasting only state-approved or -operated programming. International sanctions came thick and fast, leaving the FREA with a massive resource shortfall. Prisons were modified into manufacturing plants, and work camps were constructed in agricultural areas, or deep in the outback, to cover the sudden deficit by way of free, forced, invisible labour.

Arriving at drama class one morning, Oriana was informed that the entire arts faculty at her high school had been let go and replaced with a new team of chaplains. Sciences were cut, literature was cut, history was to be 'overhauled'. Having chosen to study the life and influence of Jandamarra, a nineteenth-century rebel of the Bunuba people, ahead of her end-of-year exams, Oriana was told that the new, compulsory subject of her final essay would be Abel Tasman's discovery of Van Diemen's Land. Leafing through her newly-printed textbook – the *Illustrated Official First Edition of East Australian History* – Oriana failed to see a whit of anyone with anything other than pale European skin.

Oriana had never thought much about Remy's job. From his title – Vice-President for Asia-Pacific Expansion – she assumed it to be deathly boring, filled with board meetings, teleconferences and spreadsheets with many decimal places. But after secession, as the international borders were grinding shut and the supermarket shelves were running dry, it dawned on her that Remy really must have had his work cut out for him. His job existed wholly to facilitate the smooth import and export of global goods, and now he was stuck in a remote and wildly paranoid jurisdiction that seemed hellbent on cutting off virtually all contact and commerce with the outside world. The Central Government maintained only a small handful of trade agreements (coal, plastics, petroleum, some frail and genetically modified livestock) with countries who were privately willing to profit off of prison labour despite their public anti-FREA stance.

Remy had always worked late, even back in France – but in France, he would arrive home with a twinkle in his eye and a box of macarons to leave at the foot of Oriana's bed. Now, he would limp in at midnight from the penthouse elevator, shoulders slouched, tie askew, sitting wordlessly on the balcony for hours at a time, staring out at the plane-less sky.

He also began to keep strange company. On more than one occasion, Oriana came home to find Remy in his study, consulting with an array of bizarre and wholly out-of-place characters. Always pointing at maps. Always speaking in whispers. There were two men with bright orange hair, deep facial scars and thick military vests. There was an older woman who once had a briefcase handcuffed to her wrist. When Oriana attempted to walk slowly past the study, slow enough to lean in and listen, Remy would inevitably spot her and grant one fond wink before shutting the door tight.

Remy never knew this, but one night, Oriana followed him. Instilled with a heady mix of Caterina's obstinance and Remy's natural inquisitiveness, there was nothing Oriana hated more than feeling left out of the loop. She had graduated from high school and was floating through a succession of part-time jobs she loathed. She worked at a tattoo parlour before it got shuttered by the newly minted DID (citing 'self-defacement' as a detentionable offence). She pulled pints and pedalled doughnuts. She got a job as an usher at the casino auditorium, and one Saturday evening, as she ripped tickets for another Best of Cold Chisel tribute concert, she spotted Remy darting across the casino floor to a waiting car outside. Oriana whipped off her uniform vest and followed him, hailing down a taxi and instructing it, with mild embarrassment, to tail the car in front. This led her to a dilapidated furniture store in Footscray, brimming with ostentatious salmon-coloured dressers and imitation Parthenon pillars. Oriana followed Remy through a back entrance. The red-headed twins were there, as was the woman. At the back of a storeroom, they examined an extraordinary array of artworks lumped beneath a heap of unassuming painters' drop sheets: pieces by Tiepolo, Gleeson, Namatjira, Turner, Brack, Ufan, Dürer, Clarke, Carvalho, Delaunay, possibly even Caravaggio. Oriana couldn't name them all, but she'd seen them years ago on school excursions to the major galleries.

What Oriana didn't know then, but would come to understand later, was that Remy had, in a sense, taken Caterina's advice: he wasn't working anymore. Yes, he left the apartment at six in the morning and returned at all hours of the night, but it was months since Oriana's stepfather had been Vice-President of anything. Instead, he'd taken his international contacts, leveraged his professional influence and committed himself to a new cause. Yes, the embargoes placed on the FREA, coupled with the new nation-state's own strident import bans, had turned Remy's once-cushy job into a logistical and political nightmare, and yes, commodities had plummeted – but Remy no longer cared about gold, iron, cocoa or coffee. Now he was concerned with life-saving medicines, the insulin injections and anaesthetics and antibiotics and PrEP treatments that were being stopped at the border and expiring at sea with no way of being manufactured locally. He was concerned with the women getting sent to work camps for protesting the country's new contraception laws, the writers disappearing after publicly criticising the Leader and the teenagers forfeiting their lives over a single, trumped-up possession charge. He was concerned with the centuries of art and culture, both Indigenous and European, being gradually but definitively scrubbed out of existence. For a little while, Oriana assumed that Remy had stolen the artworks she saw that night in the furniture store, when in fact, he was risking his life to ensure they were safely transported out of the FREA. Oriana's stepfather wasn't some high-flying art thief or war racketeer – he was a deeply connected, highly calculating, remarkably well-resourced bootlegger of artefacts, medicines and imperilled human beings.

In this capacity, Remy was something of an artist himself, as his smuggling operations often had a whiff of the theatrical about them. He once transported a truck full of New Victorian activists to a guerrilla port in Cairns by having them all placed in a medically induced coma and convincing multiple DIBM patrols that they were the cadavers of captured dissidents being transported to a government morgue. He buried priceless Rodin sculptures in the bottom of coal shipments bound for India. He baked antiepileptics into plaster casts and laced sneaker soles with propofol. He infused corn cobs with ciprofloxacin and plastic piping with pyrazinamide. He'd enlisted a whole team of renegade scientists in far-north Cooksland who could alter the chemical state of just about anything, powdering it or freeze-drying it or atomising it so as to hide it in plain sight – in meat and vegetables, fabric and textiles, in the thickest block of Bassland pine or the finest pages of a Bible. Then it could be transported, broken down, extracted and reconstituted once it reached its destination. Remy knew all the checkpoints along the meridian wall where the FREA still ferried its modest international freight, and he bought off border guards by the hundreds in order to use those roads. He exploited many other unguarded gaps, hand-carved tunnels and sabotaged stretches of the wall, as well as remote seaside ports all along the coast to get his precious cargo out of East Australia and to keep the things its citizens so desperately needed flowing in.

JORDAN PROSSER

*

So when Oriana fell pregnant at the age of twenty-three, she turned to Remy for help. The boy in question – the would-be (but never-would-be) father was a bass player, part of a clique of rock musicians that Oriana had been hanging around ever since meeting them at a local battle of the bands competition the year before. He was thoughtful but moody, clever but critical. Oriana loved him, but there were plenty of things she loved more.

After inexhaustibly decrying the casino for the first few years of living there, Caterina was now well and truly in its thrall, spending most of her days (and often whole nights, for there was no real way of knowing what time it was down there) oscillating between the roulette table and her favourite row of 'lucky' pokies, one arm crooking incessantly on the lever, eyes flitting suspiciously between the rotating symbols, searching for patterns or pointers as though examining portentous tea leaves. This made it easy for Remy to whisk Oriana away for a long weekend, first to Port Fairy, then across the Wakefield border to Streaky Bay, then finally to an abandoned outpost town in the far-western section of the Nullarbor, where they waited in Remy's air-conditioned SUV until a pair of women pulled up alongside them in an old Volkswagen Beetle.

One of the women said: He puts some thorn in the thicket and the ire back in fire.

Remy said: He's an unbeatable poet and a first-class liar.

There was bedding and a pillow laid out in the Beetle's trunk, along with snacks and bottled water. Remy handed Oriana a bag of belongings he'd packed for her, including the small stuffed cheetah. *Pour la chance*, he said.

The women drove for half a day and almost a full night before they let Oriana sit in the back seat of the Volkswagen. They must have crossed the meridian at some point, but Oriana wasn't sure when. The following morning they arrived at a small clinic on the south side of Busselton where a doctor with sandy blond hair, looking more like a surf instructor than an obstetrician, calmly explained the procedure to her. Oriana never had to give her name, never had to pay a thing – but she could sense the two women, who she would never see again after this, moving in the background,

BIG TIME

doling out information and compensation as needed. The blond doctor helped Oriana lie down on a table and told her everything she would feel – a sharp sensation followed by a dull ache. If she wanted to, he said, it might help to think of something else. Something that made her happy.

Oriana closed her eyes and thought of Lotto.

She was still thinking of Lotto on the drive back to the border, where Remy was waiting to meet her, thanking the women and returning Oriana to the climate-controlled comfort of his vehicle, then on to Melbourne, where her mother barely noticed they'd been gone. After that, Remy began to take Oriana with him everywhere – to more late-night meetings at the furniture store, to rendezvous at condemned ports near Warrnambool, to quote-unquote business trips to Botany and Bassland. She formally met the red-headed twins, the Tedeskis, ex-special forces grunts turned racketeers and fixers, and even became friends with their kid sister, recommending that her boyfriend and his writing partner consider her as the drummer for their new band (she spent a lot of time at the Tedeskis' house, listening to the twins' horror stories from the secession night riots and their sister's horror stories from band rehearsals). Oriana met the older woman, Sita Chandra, an ex-hedge fund manager turned black market money launderer. And one day she met a man named Charlie Total, an ex-actor, ex-government programmer who taught her to code, taught her to leap over firewalls, taught her to slip in and out of even the most secure networks without leaving a single digital fingerprint. Oriana found herself part of a nationwide network of everyday people seeking to turn back the political tide which had so suddenly and violently turned against them.

She thought of Lotto when she went on quote-unquote family vacations to New Zealand and France and Algiers, where Remy entrusted her to make vital connections with the North Africa Liberation League, brokering a deal to bring urgent medical supplies and weaponry to rebel-controlled Cape York. Back home, she thought of Lotto during the recording and touring of her boyfriend's band's debut album. The night after their sold-out final show at the Palais Theatre, Oriana, her bass player boyfriend and the band's lead singer stayed up until dawn, just the three of them in a luxury hotel room, smoking pot and sculling vodka and laughing about what the future might bring. When the lead singer started kissing her, and her boyfriend simply stood there, watching on hungrily, Oriana decided to go along with it. She'd always liked the frontman, who was brash and arrogant but oh-so-very passionate in an only slightly obnoxious way. The three of them went to bed together, but after a time it seemed the boys were more interested in each other than her, so Oriana sat back on the sofa, comfortably naked, rolling and lighting a cocaine-tipped cigarette while she watched the other two have their way with each other. Two days later, wracked with secret dismay, her boyfriend announced that he was spending his entire (not insignificant) split of the tour's profits on a hard-to-come-by plane ticket out of the FREA, bound for South America. He dumped her over the phone and left the next day. As she'd done a thousand times by then, whenever she felt dragged down a path in life she hadn't planned on being dragged down, Oriana closed her eyes and thought of Lotto.

She thought of Lotto often in the year the bass player was gone. She thought of Lotto when Remy never came home from a quote-unquote business trip to Bassland, and when she and her mother were evicted from the casino and moved into a two-bedroom townhouse on the peninsula. She thought of Lotto when Caterina sold off Remy's antique furniture and oil paintings at a cheap auction house in Frankston and gave all the money to conservative political candidates. She thought of Lotto when the Tedeskis took her to an abandoned petrol station in far-north Cooksland, where she stood in as her stepfather's replacement, watching a convoy of motorcycles burn across the horizon, then meeting a gang of sunburnt theoretical chemists and learning about a new drug called F. Oriana thought of Lotto as she fed her new boyfriend vials of the stuff and then, as he sat hack-cheeked and stuttering on the rug, filled his notebook with new lyrics written in his perfectly forged handwriting (a useful trick that Sita had taught her). She thought of Lotto when the bass player came back and found her at a party by a shale-rock fireplace. She thought of Lotto as she sat, smoking, on a Chesterfield lounge while his band recorded another album. She thought of Lotto when they went on tour again, when she learnt she'd been flagged by the DID,

BIG TIME

and when she sat at the back of a bus, clutching a suitcase heavy with contraband, staring into the green-tinted eyes of a DIBM patrolman. She thought of Lotto as her childhood friend charged drunkenly into a human wall of military police, allowing her, and the bass player, and Charlie, and Sita to escape an ambush in Botany, on a night when the gum trees swayed with waves of explosive heat.

Wherever she went and whatever she did, Oriana found herself thinking about the Dalmatian. One day she would ask her therapist why it was that her childhood pet still evoked such a pendulous feeling in her stomach – why the mere mention of him felt like catching a hangnail on a shaggy piece of fabric. The pool ball in her throat. The pressure behind her eyes. Why it was that Lotto, still, was the only thing that could make her cry – not her partner, not her mother, not her father, not her country, not even Remy.

A dog has only the home you give it, her therapist replied.

Oriana thinks of Lotto every day, to this day – and some small part of her, a part very nearly snuffed out by the world, a slightly naive and childlike part, a part perhaps best described as *hope* – this part likes to imagine that Lotto is still out there even now, in that town beside the broken bridge, drinking cool water from the stream, sprinting through the beech forest, tail *pap pap pap*ping in fresh fields of snow.

16

Some hangovers have the power to change the way you see the world – diminishing every kindness you've ever known, leaving you knock-kneed and teary-eyed and dry-mouthed and mothball-brained, leaving you a single-celled, self-hating organism. And then there are the hangovers the band had the day after Xander died.

In their haste to dispose of every narcotic and pharmaceutical item in the penthouse, Ludlow had also flushed all the painkillers. There was nothing in the fridge except a creamy sewer of day-old piña colada mix, a half-empty pack of cheese slices and a solitary grapefruit. The taps throughout the hotel were coughing up brown sludge due to an explosion somewhere along the water main the previous night. This meant there was also incessant jackhammering just a few blocks away. It was twenty-eight degrees before the sun came up, so the Acceptables, their entourage and their scientist guests simply sat as still as possible, lights off and blinds drawn, too tormented to sleep, too hungover to move and too afraid to stray outside, no matter how badly their bodies screamed for sustenance.

After hightailing it across the city, splitting up their convoy, switching vehicles twice and hiding out for hours in an abandoned delicatessen, Oriana and Julian arrive back just as the afternoon heat is cooking the spilt blue curaçao on the rug near the kitchen, filling the suite with a malodorous, boozy tang. They find Ash in the kitchen, lying face down on the tiled floor; Ludlow in the conversation pit, massaging sections of their bare skin against the soft carpet; Abel, Edwina and Cleo trying to pry Minnie from

BIG TIME

the shower, which turned cold hours ago but which she refuses to leave; Fizz and Dante in the bedrooms, blinking dozily, dried tears and vomit on their cheeks and lips; and Skinner pacing around the dining room, lifting his chunky mobile phone towards the ceiling, trying to get a signal long after everyone else has figured out that the network's been jammed. Julian and Oriana tell them all about me – or at least, they recite the haphazard lie that Oriana had concocted on their way up in the lift. Something about going to get more F, a routine traffic stop, good old Wesley taking one for the team. Then the others tell them about Xander – or at least, the pared-down version: one too many drops and a poolside mishap. They leave out the dozens of onlookers, the fourteen-storey mercy dash, the psychotic episode currently being experienced by the PhD student in the sputtering shower.

Tammy's not here for any of this. She's out on the balcony in a deckchair, under the paltry shade of the potted palm.

'Were you with him?' asks Julian, shutting the balcony door behind him.

'We all were,' says Tammy, her clothes crisp with dried chlorine but turning wet again with sweat. She sucks on a spent roach she fished from the pot plant and cracks a beer. 'Last one,' she says. 'Wanna share?'

'No thanks,' says Julian. He leans on the railing and looks down at the pool. 'I wonder if he saw a shopping mall.'

Tammy laughs a big, throaty laugh that indicates her body didn't think she'd be laughing again this soon. 'He'd probably try nicking something and get chased out. Even in the heaven mall. Going to the shops with that guy was a fucking nightmare.'

Fourteen storeys down, a family pushes off from the pool's edge. A little girl on a crocodile floatie. Julian wonders if the groundskeepers changed the water. He wonders if Xander was even the first person to die in that pool. Julian hated hotels, as a general rule. He was a firm believer that spaces soaked up the energy of the people in them – that a room having too many occupants over time was like adding a thick, gummy coat of paint for each, until millimetre by millimetre the room got smaller, crowded, dense. Good or bad, Julian didn't want to wade around in other people's emotional run-off.

'You met Charlie,' says Tammy.

'I take it so have you.'

'Only once. But I liked him. Guy's a good talker.'

'He's not a good talker. He just talks a lot.'

'What did you talk *about*?' Tammy asks.

Julian looks at her. 'You mean you're not in on the whole fucking … caper?'

'Nope,' says Tammy, adding her beer to a pile of dead soldiers. 'Divided assets. Tail of the snake protects the head. It's like the recipe for Coca-Cola: left hand doesn't know what the right hand's doing. Left hand only knows that the right hand exists and that it knows what it's doing. Etcetera, etcetera …'

'Etcetera.' Julian sighs. Tammy mixed metaphors when she was drunk.

'I wish you'd told me, Tam,' he says.

'Sorry, man. But this shit is between you and O.'

Julian remembers the look Oriana had given him the night before. *Maybe I overestimated you.* He goes looking through the penthouse, but Oriana's split. Her green suitcase is gone, and there's a note on the kitchen bench:

I'll find you in Cooksland.
O xx

After the cellular network's restored, Skinner manages to get through to the label. Everyone agrees it would be prudent to push the Brisbane show to the following weekend. This time, with enough forewarning, Labyrinth assures them that the postponement will be properly advertised. Labyrinth also takes the opportunity to share that they've hired a team of set and costume designers to give the Brisbane show a little extra 'oomph'. (Audience feedback, from the surviving audiences at least, was that the Acceptables' stage presence was shockingly dreary compared to their support acts.) Skinner expects violent backlash from Ash over this, but Ash simply nods, grunts and returns to his spot on the kitchen floor.

Skinner extends the booking at the hotel. Everyone grabs their bags from their own rooms and moves into the penthouse, laying sheets and pillows on the stairs of the conversation pit. After a day of disruptions in the hotel kitchen (staff missing, injured, or stuck

BIG TIME

on the other side of the bridge, which had been blockaded by a small army of activists supergluing themselves to the steel struts, then to each other), they order room service: towering burgers of beef and wilted lettuce, thick chips dripping with canola oil and no-brand cola. The vegetarians eat deep-fried cauliflower dipped in aquafaba mayonnaise. Everyone's eyes sting with the gritty itch of F withdrawal. It hurt to keep them open, hurt more to force them closed. Fizz runs a dozen hand towels under cold, brown tap water and passes them around. There are bodies strewn on every surface, on the dining table and the kitchen bench, in the conversation pit and out on the balcony, wet towels across brows, convalescing like soldiers in a battlefront infirmary.

After they finally extricate Minnie from the shower, Abel, Edwina and Cleo wrap her up in imitation sheepskin rugs and put her in the master bedroom. She is trembling, hypothermic, even in the baking heat. She sleeps for twenty-four hours, dreaming underwater dreams, and wakes on Tuesday evening to find the others sitting in front of the television, watching a home renovation show. Abel seems particularly invested in the program, so Minnie finds a spot beside Edwina and asks: 'How was the summit?'

Edwina keeps one eye on the television, where a man and his look-a-like son are building a chimney while a stopwatch counts down in the corner of the screen. 'There was no summit. Abel and I went down to the foyer the morning of. Only about a quarter of the other delegates were there. The rest refused to leave their rooms. There was no sign of our guide. No bus, no drivers. A few people tried to make it to the convention centre on foot. Not all came back. The ones that did said the place was locked. Empty. Lights off and doors barred. The airport has no record of our return flight, and there's no embassy for us to go to. We can't even make an international phone call.'

The son drops a brick on his foot and fails to finish the chimney. The timer runs out. The father is ashamed.

'What are we going to do?' says Minnie.

'Stay calm,' says Edwina.

Even in his strung-out state, Julian doesn't trust public television. He picks up a guitar from the kitchen bench and sings:

JORDAN PROSSER

I would like to die lying down
So my soul has to stand before it leaves the ground
I would see the ceiling and my back would get my blood
I've never looked up enough

Yes, I would like to die sitting down
So that nothing will surprise me when what goes around
comes back around
I could keep my posture and my feet would keep my blood
I've never slowed down enou—

'Oh my god, SHHHHH,' hisses Ash.

Julian puts the guitar down. He's been waiting two days for Ash to ask him something, anything, about what really happened with him and Oriana on the night Xander died. But Ash never asks, so Julian never tells him.

The National Broadcast announces that the curfew will end on Thursday, kicking Skinner into high-stress, high-sweat organisation mode. Not a single person thought to get the bus repaired, so he plans on driving during daylight hours only, when the broken headlight will be less apparent. They'll leave at dawn on Friday, get into Brisbane by 3:30 pm, enjoy a luxurious soundcheck at the Fortitude Music Hall that afternoon before heading to the studios of FLEXX 101.7 FM for a peak-hour radio interview, play to a sold-out house on Saturday night, then begin the return journey to Melbourne on Sunday.

Skinner doesn't quite know how to broach the subject, so it falls to Dante to ask Ash: do they need to find a replacement guitarist? Ash says no; he couldn't possibly initiate and train some ring-in on the band's complex live arrangements in such a short period of time. He reminds Skinner, Dante and everyone else within earshot that he played every instrument on the demo tapes for *In the End*. He is fully prepared to step in and play Xander's guitar part himself. 'I can still feel it in my fingers,' he says.

Ludlow asks about Xander's funeral. They'd been thinking a lot about what they said to him on the side of the road a few nights ago, after he'd lost his brother, and worrying maybe they'd offered bad advice. Maybe they shouldn't have told Xander to – what was it again? – *give up, then begin*? Maybe they should have said something more along the lines of *hang in there!* or *chin up!* Or *it gets better!* instead. But maybe it wouldn't have mattered what they said.

Skinner says he'd been left on hold for a number of hours trying to get through to the coroner's office, before some wheezing intern picked up the line and informed him that they had all of Xander's paperwork – the death certificate, the autopsy report – but they couldn't seem to locate the body.

'The fuck do you mean they couldn't *locate* the body?' spits Ash.

'Well, um,' Skinner stammers, eyes pointing skyward as they do when he's glossing up some brutal truth, 'it appears that, what with all of the, uh, activity here in Botany the last few days, I guess you could say there's, ah, something of a backlog. A dearth of appropriate storage and a glut of, erm, people requiring it. Plus, with the electricity supply being so unreliable, there's been the need for some hasty relocation, um …' the eyes come down as he runs out of polish. 'Basically, the refrigerators in the morgue stopped working. So they had to move him. And they lost him.'

Minnie starts hyperventilating, stands up and heads back to the shower.

'Jesus,' says Tammy, shaking her head. 'His parents must be expecting the body soon, right?'

Now, Skinner's a pale fellow at the best of times. But in this moment, he turns so white he might as well be see-through. All the tension leaves his jaw, shoulders and hands. His arms hang flaccidly at his sides. His soul, if we're to believe in such things, may well have left his body.

'Skinner,' says Ash, taking one small but menacing step forward. 'Please tell us you've told Xander's parents that their son is dead.'

'On top of the other one they already lost,' adds Julian.

Skinner's lip trembles.

'Skinner,' says Ash. 'You are such a fuck-up.' Then he laughs morbidly and pours himself a bourbon. Picking it up off the bench though, he gags at the smell of it, his body still rebelling from the weekend's perversions.

Tammy plucks the drink from his fingers, downs it, then walks past Skinner and lifts his cell phone from one clammy hand. She takes it out onto the balcony, shuts the door behind her and dials.

JORDAN PROSSER

On Thursday night, as the curfew lifts, Cleo and Fizz announce they'll be taking the train back to Melbourne the following morning. Cleo says she has everything she needs to begin work on her new project. Had I been there, I could have smelt this lie a mile off – this was clearly a way to excuse herself from the grief and upheaval that seemed to stick to the Acceptables like gum to a sneaker sole. Cleo had begged to come along on tour so she could be where the action was – now she was desperate to get away from it all.

'I haven't been able to get through to Kyle,' she says, chewing a thumbnail. 'Hopefully he hasn't got a subletter yet. I figure I'll just get my stuff out of storage and show up at the house.' Then she remembers that her stuff is in storage with all my stuff. Cleo wonders, a little ashamedly, whether she can help herself to my things; I wasn't exactly dead, but I wouldn't be needing any of it, either. I had put her down as my emergency contact on a few medical admission forms in the past, and by Cleo's reckoning, that was as good as next of kin.

Fizz's excuse was a little more substantial; she'd landed a job as a director's assistant back in New Victoria on some First Fleet puff piece. Good for her. Had I been there, I might have been jealous. But there's no point in that where I am now. There's no status anxiety or ambition or envy. Amazing what that can do for your outlook.

On Friday morning, the girls pack their bags and shuffle towards the door – then Ludlow shuffles up beside them.

'*Et tu*, Ludlow?' says Ash.

Ludlow smiles sombrely. 'I'd like to be home with my family.'

'I thought we were getting a coffee table book out of you,' teases Tammy.

'Oh, you will! I've got plenty of great stuff already. And I'll be there for the Melbourne shows. Don't you worry.'

'I'm not worried,' Tammy says, going in for a hug.

Before they venture past the abandoned barricades, out into the battle-scarred streets and on towards Central Station, Ludlow asks for one more snapshot: a family photo. Or a funeral photo, in the absence of one. They prop up their camera on the kitchen bench, setting the timer and telling everyone to huddle in the conversation pit.

'Are we smiling?' asks Fizz.

'Obviously not,' says Ash.

Click-FLASH. The camera goes off and Ludlow will forever

BIG TIME

cherish the image it makes: on one level of the pit are Abel, Edwina and Minnie in a tidy row of three, deploying their best academic countenances. Behind them, Cleo and Fizz rest their temples on Ludlow's shoulders, and Ludlow smiles with closed lips, ignoring Ash's warning. Right before the photo, Skinner had lifted the hem of his shirt up (surprisingly well-sculpted abdominals, tracts of rough, laser-treated flesh) to wipe his face, so he's hovering in the background, pale, dry and wide-eyed, his clothes bearing incongruous sweat stains. Tammy and Dante squat on another stair, tongues out, fingers shaped like devil horns, trying to embody some decades-lost rock'n'roll paradigm. And on the right-hand side of the photo are Julian and Ash with their well-rehearsed promo photo faces, the ones they used to practise on each other in Ash's parents' basement, the ones they used to pull a hundred times a night for fans and photographers alike. Their expressions are cool smirks, relaxed and urbane, but there was something else – neither could have told you who made the first move, but as the light on Ludlow's camera blinked faster and faster, and the mirror tensed, ready to fire, Ash and Julian both lifted one arm, then those arms found their way to rest around each other's shoulders.

Many months later, while looking at the photo for the thousandth time, Ludlow would notice that behind the group, through an open bedroom door, you could make out the shape of Xander's closed guitar case.

A second after the flash goes off, Julian grabs his bag and heads downstairs. He never had any patience or talent for goodbyes. He marches straight to the back of the tour bus, throwing down a pillow and pulling on headphones, waiting for his old mp3 player to load. The first thing cued up is a Colombian folk song he'd heard and downloaded while he was away. Someone told him it was a children's song called '*El Puente está Quebrado*'. It went:

> *The bridge is broken*
> *How do we fix it?*
> *With egg shells*
> *Little donkeys in the meadow*

JORDAN PROSSER

Let the king pass
The king must pass
With all his little children
Except the one at the end

As the bus withdraws from Botany – downed power lines, broken windows, flooded underpasses, untended rubbish spilling from kerbside bins, pets left wandering and scavenging for food through the baking streets – Julian thinks about Inspector José Muñoz Rojas, what kind of man he was, and he wonders what kind of music *he* listened to while he was thinking about him.

17

The following day, en route to the Fortitude Music Hall, Skinner gets a phone call. Normally he would love nothing more than to saunter up and down the aisle of the bus, talking a little too loudly, punching out jazzy music-biz terminology for everyone to hear. (Ash had a theory that most of the time there was nobody on the other end.) But this time, less than an hour out from the Acceptables' Saturday night show in Brisbane, Skinner's phone rings and he legs it immediately to the back of the bus, leaving Dante to park Genevieve in a laneway near the venue. Julian, Ash and Tammy share a look. Skinner's gone some time.

'Everything okay?' asks Minnie. She's at the fold-out table with Abel and Edwina, all three of them dressed head-to-toe in Acceptables merch. After using Skinner's FreeNet burner phone to leave a dozen messages on the emissary's answering machine, the scientists had been left with a choice: wait in Botany and hope someone came to collect them, or follow the band to Cooksland, where Tammy said she knew somebody who might be able to help. Edwina had gone door to door at the Buchanan Hotel to invite the other delegates – at least, the ones who hadn't already taken their chances and made a run for it, leaving briefcases full of undelivered lecture notes and unpaid room service bills. For most of the attendees, the idea of following a group of unfamiliar Australians (whose companion they had watched drown from their hotel balconies) to yet another strange and likely hostile city was laughable. They naively insisted that help was on its way, or that the summit would proceed eventually. Edwina wrote down all their names, and took a small personal item from each delegate, something she could show their loved ones in Leeds, or Bristol, or Los Angeles, or Lisbon to prove that she'd been there with them. Proof of life, Edwina called it.

'Or *memento mori*,' Abel said.

So Abel, Edwina and Minnie hitched a ride to Cooksland, marvelling at the floodways, the stagnant city mangroves, the fecund overgrowth on abandoned buildings. They reeled from the tropical heat and the unseasonal monsoon weather. They burnt their research papers, threw their thumb drives in the river, dumped their tweed blazers in charity bins and disguised themselves as Acceptables super-fans. As Dante parks the bus, they're putting the finishing touches on a large, handmade cardboard sign that says *MARRY ME ASH* in Minnie's oddly childish handwriting.

'The more you can blend in with our fanbase, the safer you'll be,' Ash had advised when suggesting the sign. Julian suspected Ash was just annoyed that he hadn't seen many signs like this on the tour so far.

After waiting five minutes, Tammy finds Skinner stooped over in the wine cellar, ending the call.

'What's up?' she asks.

Skinner bangs his head in surprise and smiles broadly, but the man's sweat glands do not lie. 'Nothing,' he says. 'Just crossing a few i's and dotting a few t's.'

'You look like you just woke up from a coma.'

Skinner laughs outrageously, the fakest laugh Tammy's ever heard. When even he realises he's doing a terrible job of deflecting, he cuts himself off. 'Shall we?'

He barges past her, past the others and off the bus, leaving a chill in his wake.

Tammy turns to the scientists in their pink-and-red *Beaches* T-shirts. 'Why don't you three get Dante to show you up to the VIP section? Grab a drink. Try to relax. Skinner set aside some sweet booth seats so you don't have to, y'know—'

'Mingle with the proles?' finishes Abel.

'Your words, not mine. Dante?' Tammy gestures for the roadie to show them out.

Once it's just them on the bus, Tammy turns to Ash and Julian. 'Something's up.'

BIG TIME

'Like what?' asks Ash.

'Skinner's looked like hell all week, but he looked even worse just now.'

'Xander's folks?' guesses Julian.

'I don't think so.'

'Wesley?' guesses Ash.

'I doubt it.'

'We could always skip ahead and find out,' says Julian. 'Anyone got any F?'

'Fuck that,' says Ash with a wave of his hand. 'This guy works for us. Come on.'

Crossing the loading bay, Julian knows he's being watched. Sideways looks from hairy-armed tech crew, eyes ringed purple, stinking of guarana. He'd seen them yesterday afternoon at the soundcheck, and they'd been friendly enough – but that was before the radio interview.

It had started out innocently enough. Skinner chaperoned the three remaining band members to the inner-city studios of FLEXX 101.7 FM, where they'd been plied with inane questions about the trappings of fame and their wackiest tour anecdotes. But as the hour wore on, it became clear that Ash had grander ideas for the segment. Choice excerpts from his ensuing diatribe included labelling the DJs 'jesters in the court of the mad king' who would be 'first on the gallows' and the Acceptables' forthcoming album 'a howling indictment of the sickness at the heart of this country', while calling for 'nothing short of full-blown, white-fisted revolution' until 'the meridian crumbles and the Leader is dragged through the streets'. The broadcast was terminated at the height of Ash's screed, with the DJs throwing to an advertisement for Big Brock Burger's new Spicy Anzac Sandwich and Fully Loaded Federation Fries, followed by the radio debut of Wrecking Bones' new single 'Something for Everybody and Nothin' for Nobody'. People on their daily commute had tuned in expecting well-natured banter, cash giveaways and traffic updates – what they got was Ash's half-baked but full-blooded manifesto. Afterward, Skinner mentioned offhandedly that FLEXX's listenership was in the low millions – most of urban Cooksland.

At the stage door, Julian saunters past the doorman, who he'd shared a cigarette with at soundcheck the day before, and nods. The doorman spits on the concrete and doesn't nod back.

'Even the muscle hates us now,' Julian whispers to Tammy. 'That's comforting.'

A blare of sound reaches them from the auditorium. The warm-up act is in full swing.

'Skinner!' shouts Ash in the main backstage hallway, startling a caterer. A make-up artist swans over, but Ash shoos him away.

They go left – past the machine room then past the break room, a fluorescent cavern of vending machines and pleather couches. A group of half-a-dozen security guards with shorn heads, laughing and nattering only seconds ago, falls deathly silent and peers up from their card game as the band passes. Up a small flight of stairs is a whole floor of dressing rooms, three of them bearing the band members' names, assigned with hastily laminated A4 placards. Under the one that reads *ASH HUANG*, someone's added in Sharpie: *(IS A WANKER)*. Ash pretends not to see it.

'Skinner!' hollers Ash, and a pale bald head pokes out from a doorway at the far end of the corridor. 'You avoiding us, Skinner?'

'How are we all feeling?' Skinner babbles as the band marches towards him. 'Big crowd tonight. Packed to the rafters!'

Skinner backs into an enormous ensemble dressing room ringed by mirrors and tungsten bulbs in rectangular frames. Some of the mirrors still bear thick red lipstick kisses in their corners, scarlet ghosts left by wayward artists. Julian wonders where they all are now.

'Who was on the phone?' asks Ash, cornering the manager.

'Was it the label?' Tammy pulls up a chair.

'I— It— Yes. It was.'

'And?' says Julian.

'Just a little damage control after the radio interview. Nothing major.'

'What aren't you telling us, man?' demands Tammy.

'Nothing!' Skinner keeps eyeing off the exits, like he's preparing to shove the band aside and flee into the balmy Brisbane night. 'Let's talk after the show. I'd hate to bore you with tedious admin when you're supposed to be—'

'I don't think I could possibly go out on stage tonight knowing our manager's keeping something from us,' Ash says coyly. 'I think I'd be too distracted. Could be a total disaster.'

BIG TIME

Skinner winces at that last word.

'Same,' says Tammy. 'I'm feeling pretty fragile as is.'

'This could really throw us off our game,' Julian agrees. 'Fuck this whole thing up.'

'Please don't make me,' Skinner begs.

Ash widens his stance, folds his arms and waits.

Skinner hangs his head. When he lifts it again, his eyes are dull. 'Labyrinth is voiding your contract. The tour is cancelled. The album is cancelled. Tonight's your final show.'

Ash's right eye twitches. 'They can't do that.'

'Ash,' says Skinner, almost kindly. 'You know they can.'

After the interview on FLEXX 101.7 FM, the algorithm at Labyrinth HQ was adjusted. It was fed the results of listener surveys and audience feedback forms. It took into account door profits from the tour thus far, merchandise sales and pre-sales from the remaining shows along the coast. It was informed that the four-piece was now a three-piece. *In the End* had not yet been fully mixed and mastered back in Melbourne – the process was proving so insanely difficult, given the sheer amount of overdubs, the length of the tracks and their arduous complexity, that Nat the engineer had almost suffered a nervous breakdown and Solomon had quit the industry altogether to become a landscape gardener. The algorithm took this all into account. It assessed the likelihood of a Deluxe Edition, a Live Edition and a third full-length album. It took into account Ash's erratic behaviour, the bribes paid in Adelaide, the emergency kitty emptied out in Sydney, the enormous bill for room service and repairs to the penthouse suite that had become the band's wartime bunker. It then calculated the odds of Ash becoming ASH – and the graph it pumped out was an unpleasant picture of steady decline in both probability and profitability. Fifty-five minutes after the band had been escorted from the studios of FLEXX 101.7 FM, the algorithm had informed Labyrinth's parent company in the WRA that the Acceptables were no longer an acceptable risk – that in fact, they were a liability. Their lawyers drew up a breach of contract memo citing reckless behaviour and professional negligence. Someone further down the food chain was told to tell Skinner, and he was told to tell the band. He just thought he would wait until after the show.

'I am truly, truly sorry,' says Skinner.

Julian has a feeling in his chest he's felt only a few times before. Once on the day he left for Colombia. Once with Charlie Total. It felt like a door slamming closed in his ribs, leaving his lungs stuck on the other side.

Tammy's still sitting, shaking her head. Ash is pacing along the far side of the dressing room.

'Try to make the most of tonight,' says Skinner. 'Remember, they're here for you. They came to hear what you have to say. I hope you never forget that.'

Ash picks up a chair and launches it at the mirrors. The tungsten bulbs pop like bubble-wrap as he lifts another chair, then another, then another, working his way across the back wall. The room grows dark as he destroys every light source.

Skinner's edging towards the door, thinking he might be next in line, and Tammy's shouting at Ash, trying to get through to him, but Julian can't be here anymore. He can't stand this feeling, this wicked not-knowing. He lurches out into the corridor and gasps as though surfacing for air, retracing his steps. Back on the ground floor, stagehands are wheeling racks of guitars towards the wings, still eyeing him off, still staring just a moment too long, as if they know that none of this means anything anymore, that Julian's the bass player for the band on the *Titanic*, that they're all just going through the motions until they either freeze or drown.

'Dante,' says Julian, scanning the hall in both directions. 'Dante!'

He tries the machine room, where a grizzled mech who probably remembers the '80s is tinkering with a hefty remote control unit, griping to his younger colleague: 'What do you mean there's only three of 'em? We were told four platforms. What a fucking schemozzle.'

Julian checks the break room, where the security guards are gone but their cards remain spread on the table, a sad game of rummy with cough drops for gambling chips.

He bails up a stagehand. 'Dante, our driver. Our roadie. Have you seen him?'

The stagehand thinks he saw him stage left, but tells Julian: 'The support act's almost finished. You should really get ready.'

The Acceptables' support act in Brisbane was a Christian pop-rock five-piece called the Patronised Saints, who wore dark eyeliner and flowing white robes as they sang about what a cool guy Jesus was. As Julian steps through the sound lock and into the deep backstage wings, squinting and searching for Dante, the lead singer on the stage in front of him is belting out the chorus of their first and best-performing single, 'Golden Rule':

Do-do-do-do for each other what you'd have done to you
Th-that's the golden rule
That's the golden rule

The singer chokes briefly on a thick clod of stage haze as it rolls spectacularly from the wings, but he covers it well, rearing his Fender over his head and giving his drummer the nod to play a few extra bars. Julian steals a glimpse out into the auditorium. The crowd is massive. The crowd is drunk. Abel, Edwina and Minnie are up in their booth, looking utterly perturbed by the Patronised Saints, unsure whether this qualified as music or comedy, unaware that in the FREA there was very, very little of the latter. Other than the scientists in their fresh *Beaches* T-shirts, Julian can't make out a single piece of Acceptables merchandise, meaning no official fan club – although one large cluster of blokes at the bar are wearing matching, home-made singlets bearing a drawing of Ash's face behind a heavy red circle-slash.

'Dante!' says Julian, discovering the roadie lovingly polishing and prepping his saxophone.

'Julian, hey. You find your dressing rooms okay?'

'Have you got anything on you?' Julian asks a little too loudly.

'Have I got—'

'Have you got any F?'

Even over the din of the two-minute electric harp solo in 'Golden Rule', the stage manager's eyes flick up from behind her monitors. Dante shifts his weight, smiling nervously.

'Nah, Jules. You know we ditched all that back in Botany.'

'Don't bullshit me, Dante. If anyone's got anything, it's you.'

Dante's eyes dart around the wings. The SM, a lighting op and a pair of the card-playing security guards. All watching.

'Julian, can we talk about this later?'

'No,' Julian says, unblinking. 'You don't understand, Dante. I need it.'

Dante grabs Julian's upper arm – a polite but solid grip – and leads him back through the sound lock, along the ground-floor corridor where Julian swats away the make-up artist, past the mech room and the break room, through a double-doored fire exit and into a storeroom, where a bartender is loading two kegs onto a trolley and wheeling them front of house. He glances at Julian, narrowing his eyelids in distasteful recognition, but Dante shuts the storeroom door after him, sealing him and Julian in. It's cold in there, noisy with the hum of overworked refrigeration systems. The shelves are stacked with six-packs of beer, bottles of soft drink, pallets of potato chips, all ready to be marked up 300 per cent, sold to an idiot, then wiped up off the floor.

'You've gotta be cool about these things, man,' Dante says. 'Especially after Xander. What if Skinner finds out?'

'Forget Skinner. Have you got any?' Julian holds out a hand, palm up, ready to receive. He knows he's being obnoxious. But he feels like if he has to live another second in the *now* without knowing what it might turn into, he's going to seize into a ball and wither and die right there among the sour straps and post-mix. *What if it's a trap?* he's thinking. What if the security guards, and the bar staff, and the venue techs, and half the crowd have come here with the sole intention of humiliating them then chasing them from the theatre? Or worse, handing them over to some khaki-trousered fuck who's going to read a list of alleged improprieties then ship them off to Broken Hill with Pony and me and all the others? Then again, Julian wonders which he would actually prefer – to be lynched on the storm-slicked streets of central Brisbane, his body hung from a lamppost by an army of disenchanted fans, or to be condemned to anonymity, a life of hard labour and hard sun, a rubber-stamped number on some government record in a locked cabinet in a beige office building that no-one would ever retrieve or read or recognise again.

Dante hands him one of Oriana's perfume samplers.

Julian grabs the vial and holds it up to the light. Less than a quarter left. 'Wait. Did you already know I was going to ask you for this?'

'Yeah?' Dante shrugs.

'So why'd you bother pretending you didn't have any?'

BIG TIME

'I figured all I could do was try.'

'Admirable,' snorts Julian, who gets more arrogant the more anxious he is. 'You can go now.'

Dante says something Julian can't hear and makes his way out.

Julian jiggles the perfume sampler, lifts his left hand, pries the eyelids of his left eye open, sprays, feels a sudden, needling sensation on his cornea, blinks, swaps hands, pries the eyelids of his right eye open, sprays, blinks.

Julian didn't think his tolerance would be affected by only a week off from the stuff, but it hits him like a medicine ball in the solar plexus, technicoloured and violent. He slumps back against the shelves and manages to safely deliver himself to the concrete floor before he completely loses his balance. It starts to wash over him. His skin pricks up from every pore, one giant organ lifting away from his body in what feels like a wave, a freshly laundered sheet being flicked out in the sun. His jaw tenses. His skull is freezing already – *ice cream headache*. It makes his eyeballs feel enormous, and Julian remembers something Cleo told him once about how when you're born your eyeballs are already fully formed and your face grows out around them, all these tiny babies walking around with giant adult eyeballs in their skulls – shiny, dense jellies filled with light for the first time.

He gets an erection. Any time Julian came up on MD there was a ten-to-fifteen-minute window where all he could think about was fucking: the best fucks he'd ever had, the fucks he one day hoped to have, the fucking he wanted to be doing right now. Anyone and anything in his line of sight was a potential mating partner. The F does this too, but gentler. More persuasive, somehow. He'd like a tongue in his mouth and a finger in his arse right about now, please. Julian runs his fingers lightly up and down his own upper arms and feels the hairs dancing sensuously. *What if Skinner finds out?* Julian laughs, and for half a moment he recalls his manager's annoyingly well-formed abs.

Julian breathes in deep – his oxygen tastes like menthol cigarettes, harsh and sweet and tainted with chemicals, opening him up from navel to nape – and when he breathes out again: tsunami.

*

Julian coughs – loud but thin coughs that rush out of him in rapid-fire and force him to bend forward to catch his breath. He stands up off the floor.

'Ash!' he shouts, without knowing why.

Then he hears it again:

Ashhhh
Ashhh
Ashh
Ash
As
A

Echo, echo. That was the giveaway. Back in time – or rather, back in *now*, Julian understands he's seeing himself in the future. It always took a moment or two to get properly oriented, to really give yourself over to the trip.

Julian coughs again, so hard a hunk of phlegm comes flying out and hits the floor – so hard his perspective shifts and suddenly he sees himself, red-faced, runny-eyed, hard-cocked. Julian finds himself looking at himself looking back at himself.

While some people saw everything in their F-trips play out in first person, and others saw everything in third, Julian flitted between the two. It was as though his subjective perspective were an overlay, nested carefully atop his corporeal self, that had to be moved in delicate tandem lest it come loose and drift away. Peter Pan's pesky shadow. Julian saw this uncoupling of body and mind as a sort of design flaw he was constantly trying to iron out, as he would often get distracted, follow something interesting, leave himself behind and abandon his own timeline entirely to become a spectral observer, an omniscient narrator, seeing things it would never normally be possible for him to see, before snapping back to his body, snapping back to *now*, and realising he hadn't learnt a single thing about his own immediate future. And let's be honest – Julian only ever really cared about what was going to happen to him.

But now that he (they) knows (know) where (when) he (they) is (are), Julian sees himself fling the storeroom door aside and carve a path back down the corridor, through the fire doors and up the stairs. In the ensemble dressing room, a trio of cleaners are sweeping up the broken bulbs.

BIG TIME

Two doors down: *ASH HUANG (IS A WAN—*. Somebody, no doubt Ash, had tried to rub out the marker and left an oily smear. As Julian goes to knock at the dressing room door, his vision swims, rippling and blooming. One time, Ludlow took Julian to their darkroom, bathed in red light and stinking of hydroquinone. He liked the way Ludlow rocked the photo paper back and forth in those shallow plastic tubs. Sometimes that's how Julian felt on F; sloshing about in the dark, soft and blank, revealing more and more with time.

Julian shakes his head so hard his lips wobble, and suddenly he's back in the cockpit, right behind his eyeballs, gazing out.

Fuck knocking, this is important, thinks Julian. Then he's wondering *why* he's thinking this is important, another tiny causal loop that runs circles around itself and tightens too tight before collapsing into invisible paradoxical putty.

Julian shoves the door open. The room is empty. No flowers or champagne, just a pile of clothes in the corner, an open guitar case and Ash's old gym bag.

'Five minutes,' says the ASM, flickering past the door.

Julian murmurs, 'Hey, do you know where—' but they've vanished.

On a tinny PA system, there's the sound of three thousand Cookslanders praising the Patronised Saints while their lead singer screams: 'THANK YOU! THANK YOU! GOD BLESS YOU ALL! AND GOD BLESS THE FEDERAL REPUBLIC OF EAST AUSTRALIA!' Julian smacks off the speakers but can hear the cheering through the walls. 'NOW, STICK AROUND FOR THE ACCEPTABLES!'

We're the headline act, douchebag, thinks Julian.

Ash's dressing room expands and contracts as Julian breathes. He unzips Ash's gym bag and empties it on the floor: a hip flask; one of those hand-grip exercisers; hoodies and socks and a small disposable camera; spare guitar strings and an old tape recorder and a dog-eared novel, something lightly socialist, clearly redacted. Then there's Ash's songbook, the same battered, leather-bound tome he'd had since Julian first met him. Julian picks it up and unloops the leather cord. On the first page, he's greeted by Ash's tiny, familiar block lettering. Melody lines, rhyming couplets, simple stanzas about big feelings.

JORDAN PROSSER

Here's the page where Ash thought up the phrase 'Artificial Beaches on Every Mountain' (to which Julian added: 'Artificial Mountains on Every Beach'). Here's the page with the chorus for 'Miracle Boy':

Ain't it great how he looks
Ain't it great how he smiles
Ain't it great how he meets all your friends and
Slays them in the aisles
Miracle boy
Miracle boy
Watch his feats of strength and heart, and enjoy

Here's a page with a Polaroid stuck to it, taken by Ludlow: the band in a hotel room on the last night of the *Beaches* tour before everyone peeled off except for Julian, Ash and Oriana. Here's a page from a few days later, after Julian left for South America: murky, half-formed thoughts that never evolved into song. And then, after that, the book changes.

It's the snakes. At first, they're only in the margins. Harmless doodles, cartoon-like, stripy little pals with forked tongues, things a child might draw. Then they start creeping towards the centre of the pages, fighting for space with Ash's new lyrics. Here's 'My Futurist Bride':

I assimilate now
I join the parade
On our Honeymoon we burnt books in our bed
And looked through each other's eyes to the backs of our heads

The snakes become more detailed – patterned scales and slitted eyes and sharp-angled fangs. Ash's handwriting changes, becoming even smaller, denser, thicker. The impression of his pen is so heavy at times it nearly tears through the paper. Here's 'Misanthropatopia':

Are you happy now?
You will all be judged equally, utterly and unflinchingly
Anyone I consider waste
Anyone who triggers my distaste

BIG TIME

Here's a page where Ash can no longer even write between the lines, where the snakes have taken over entirely, writhing jaggedly with disembodied eyes and tongues that skitter like a zoetrope as the pages flick back and forth, consuming all the words, consuming all the lyrics except for one solitary phrase which, it appeared, was all Ash was physically capable of writing once the lyrics for 'In the End' had been locked in. In fact, since Julian had returned from South America, the only thing Ash had written, over and over, like a prisoner chocking up days in charcoal on a whitewashed brick wall, was:

He puts some thorn in the thicket and the ire back in fire he's an unbeatable poet and a first-class liar he puts some thorn in the thicket and the ire back in fire he's an unbeatable poet and a first-class liar he puts some thorn in the thicket and the ire back in fire he's an unbeatable poet and a first-class liar he puts some—

Julian drops the notebook. He doesn't know what deadline he's on, but he knows he's wasting time. He needs to see what he is yet to see before he can understand why he needs to go where he's yet to go. As Ash's notebook hits the floor of the dressing room, sighing closed and sealing off its secrets, Julian is struck by the realisation that in the months since he returned from overseas, he had neglected to do one simple thing: ask if Ash was okay. Because, of course, he'd just assumed. The new record, the doting fans, the girl on his arm, the life of every party. Ash was the man who would be ASH. But the notebook showed Julian something different – something divergent. Maybe that's what he was in such a rush to do – to find Ash and simply ask. To be a friend again.

'Jules! Ready?' Tammy's at the door in a glitzed-up version of her signature activewear and an improbable amount of eyeshadow. 'Skinner's about to throw a fucking fit.'

Julian grabs her. 'Did you ever ask Ash why he wrote the stuff he wrote?'

'What stuff?'

'On the new album! I mean, since when did Ash ever care about futurism? Or coal exports? Or fucking anything? Did something happen to him while I was away?'

Tammy speaks slowly, placatingly. 'No, Jules. Nothing *happened*. People change. Sometimes overnight. You'd know all about that.'

Julian leans in close, eyes narrowing. 'Was it her?'

'Who?'

'You know who.'

Tammy shakes her head. 'Man. You can be so fucking vain.'

A shame. That's the last thing she'll ever say to him – in this version of events, at least.

Tammy's out the door. Julian chases after but is waylaid by the make-up artist, who won't take no for an answer this time. He powders Julian's cheeks and attempts to comb his hair.

'Is that what you're wearing?' he asks.

'None of this has happened yet,' Julian answers robotically.

'I'll get wardrobe,' the make-up artist says.

Julian is escorted through the sound lock then down another flight of stairs into the trap room beneath the stage. There are four hydraulic pedestals at the ready, intended to lift the Acceptables up and through and above the stage, ascendant, for their terminal homily. One of the pedestals is empty. The grizzled mech is still arguing with his young offsider as to whether they can disengage it to prevent reminding the audience too pointedly of the band's absent guitarist. Skinner's there, suggesting the empty pedestal could be kept as a tribute, like putting out a bowl of milk for a dead cat. Tammy's already seated on her extra-large pedestal, testing the kick drum, twirling one stick around her fingers, and on the pedestal up front is Ash, his back to Julian, adjusting the neck strap on a brand-new guitar and rolling his neck side to side before a glitzy chrome vocal mic.

'Ash!' Julian shouts, but the ambient sound above them is enough to drown out even the temporal echo – the wailing crowd, the throbbing interstitial music, the quarrelling mechs, all reverberating in this dingy cavern beneath the stage floor. Julian makes a break for Ash but is intercepted by a solid wall of costumiers, tutting their tongues, peeling his shirt over his head, then wrapping him in a black sequinned tunic. They tug at his filthy boots and don him with chunky pleather sneakers.

BIG TIME

The lighting switches. The house music dies down. The vibe shifts. The sound from the auditorium gives way to a few expectant *whoops* and anticipatory applause. A bass guitar is slammed against Julian's chest, the costumiers evaporate and the platform beneath him begins to trundle magically upwards.

Tammy starts a low rumbling on her toms, and Ash whispers:

This is a cold drop of truth in both eyes

A trap door glides open and Julian emerges topside. He can see the stage itself is strewn with black balloons and metallic confetti, funereal and celebratory all at once. The platform rises, and rises, until Julian comes to a jarring halt six feet in the air. He would make a run for Ash right now if he could, but each of the band members are stranded on their own mechanical island, suspended in the atmosphere, blinking in the burning lights and drinking in the noxious haze. Xander's platform has been successfully disengaged, the trap doors above it sealed like a coffin.

Lean your head back and don't act so surprised

As his pupils shrink and he finds his balance, Julian takes in the crowd – the biggest they've ever played to. After the band's radio interview, the ticketing desk's phones had been overrun with people demanding their money back. But the tickets were non-refundable. *So what are they all doing here?* Julian asks himself. Were they here out of spite? Were some still true disciples? Abel, Edwina and Minnie seemed to be the only people genuinely excited, pumping their fists and dancing like carefree children in their booth. As his hands instinctively find their first notes, Julian looks for an escape route, should he need one – but an unplanned exit from the platform would mean ditching his bass and free-falling into a wasteland of monochrome party decorations.

Thought you'd be good but it never came right
Never even tried, you never even tried

No, Julian knows he's here for a reason. There's something he's meant to do. Something he's still yet to see, which will then become something he will have *seen*.

Just then, he does see something: two faces staring out from the mosh pit, only metres from the proscenium, clean-shaven, tight-collared, thick-browed and brown-eyed. Appearances carefully curated and expressions meticulously rehearsed so as to be entirely unmemorable – unless, of course, you happen to have seen them and fixated on them for an entire evening once before. The haircuts.

It's a sting, Julian thinks. The security guards, the stagehands, the make-up artists, the costumiers, all three thousand audience members: paid actors. There were no extremes the regime would not go to. The band was here, performing for their lives, and the second they stepped offstage, their lives would be forfeit.

Julian says: 'Ash.'

I'm not here to continue the tradition
I am here to hold your hand and dance you towards sedition

Ash was known for being incredibly intimate with microphones. He would wield them like weapons, clutch them like they were trying to escape, coil their cords around his arms and torso, caress their grilles with his lips. Tonight his hands are full, filling in (not by any means poorly) for Xander on guitar, so up until now, he is yet to even touch the mic. But a couple of counts after '*sedition*', the guitar goes quiet as the main beat kicks in, and Ash takes the opportunity. He reaches three inches in front of his face and seizes the microphone in his fist.

There's a sound like a depth charge. The drone of ancient electricity. Ash's whole body petrifies instantly – he ceases being flesh and blood and gas and gore and becomes a true solid. Marble. Quartz. Granite. Inanimate. Frozen and on fire at the same time. Alive with energy, then immediately dead. The circuit breakers explode somewhere behind them. The lighting grid fails. The smoke machines choke. The audience screams. The hydraulics give out. The platforms plummet. The two remaining living band members – and one body – come crashing through the trap doors and tumbling across the darkened basement floor. The drum kit disintegrates. The

BIG TIME

emergency lighting fires up crimson. Julian hits a wall. He is kicked and crushed by rushing feet. Shouts go up. Sirens blare. And out of the dark and haze, a familiar hand grabs Julian's hand.

'This is it. Come with me.'

18

Julian coughs – loud but thin coughs that rush out of him in rapid-fire and force him to bend forward to catch his breath. He stands up off the floor.

'Ash!' he shouts, and now he knows why.

Everybody knew some urban legend about some freak accident where some singer copped ten thousand volts through an unearthed mic. Julian hated to think about the wiring in this building – a hundred years old at least and sinking, like so much of central Brisbane, into a sweaty morass of waterlogged sedimentary rock. Every window in every building had a thin sheen of sweat. The carpets all reeked and the walls were all clammy. Basements opened up into underground rivers, and it rained two hundred days a year. Climate whistleblowers had predicted long ago that the entire Brisbane metropolitan area was at risk of being swallowed up by a single, Brobdingnagian sinkhole, and yet here were the Acceptables, hoisting steel-stringed guitars and jacking into three-phase power.

Julian coughs again, so hard a hunk of phlegm comes flying out and hits the floor. He's back, seeing through his own two eyes, coughing up a pocket of future oxygen. He knows exactly what's about to happen. He also knows the odds of him stopping it. Of the two hundred and fifty-plus F-trips Julian's had in the six months since he returned from South America, he's only ever seen one false vision: him and Oriana at the racecourse. One in two hundred and fifty. You wouldn't waste a dollar on those odds. Nevertheless, like Dante said: all you could do was try.

BIG TIME

Julian flings the storeroom door aside. He carves a path back down the corridor. He races shoulder-first at the fire doors and goes bouncing backwards, landing on his arse. The fire doors are locked.

Impossible. He's barely getting started, yet reality has already diverted from his visions. Julian rolls on his side, gazes up at the impartial, impenetrable bulk of the fire doors, and laughs. He remembers the restaurant in Adelaide, when his and Ash's competing hallucinations had been neck-and-neck, right down to the line. How had Oriana put it? *Now that we've gone down one branch, it's highly unlikely that the version we're in will dovetail once again with the false version.*

So maybe that was that. Just a real bad trip. Chalk it up to two in two hundred and fifty. He could tell the others about it on the long drive home. Tell Ash he'd watched him die.

Except now Julian has a very different, very real problem – there's five minutes until he's supposed to be on stage, and there's a locked set of fire doors between him and there. He pounds the doors with his fists, then hears:

'THANK YOU! THANK YOU! GOD BLESS YOU ALL! AND GOD BLESS THE FEDERAL REPUBLIC OF EAST AUSTRALIA! NOW, STICK AROUND FOR THE ACCEPT-ABLES!'

'We're the headline act, douchebag!' yells Julian, delivering a futile final kick to the doors. He'd have to go the long way.

Julian turns and ventures down the corridor, through a front-of-house staff room (stink of potato chips, spearmint vape, vodka cranberry), out another set of one-way doors and into the teeming crowd (stench of deodorant, smuggled weed, beer breath). He keeps his head down, making slow progress towards the green room door at the opposite corner of the auditorium, close to the lip of the stage. People are wailing drunkenly as the Patronised Saints overstay their welcome, blowing kisses and chucking guitar picks and making focused eye contact with specific boys and girls in the crowd they'd like to come find them later at stage door. They've already played ten minutes longer than their designated set time. The curtain comes crashing down like a velvet avalanche, and Julian imagines the pissed-off stage crew scurrying around behind it, rigging up the trap doors and scattering black balloons.

Julian knows people are looking at him. Hungry looks. He accidentally locks eyes with a young man in a sweat-soaked muscle tee, somehow balancing four full plastic tumblers even as he extends a finger towards Julian in trembling, gormless recognition: 'Heeeeeeey …'

Julian pulls a young couple, tongues down each other's throats, between him and the pointing man, and changes course, taking a long but necessary detour via the mosh pit. Then he remembers who he saw in there earlier (later) and freezes, scanning the backs of heads. The fire doors were locked, yes – things were different, yes – but that doesn't mean they couldn't still be here.

'Julian!'

He jolts, ready to flee, but then he sees Edwina muscling through the crowd, pulling Abel by the hand.

Julian remembers seeing them in their booth – a flashback to a flash-forward. 'You're not supposed to be here.'

Edwina tilts her head and shouts over the interstitial music ('Shut Up and Crush on Me', of course): 'You got us tickets!'

'No,' says Julian, 'I mean you're meant to be up there!' He points to the dress circle where Minnie still stands, clutching her homemade sign.

'We saw you down here,' Edwina says. 'You looked lost.'

'I'm …' Julian trails off. That's one word for it, maybe. He knew where he was heading in a geographical sense, but there were plenty of other ways to be lost.

'Do you believe in fate?' Julian asks Edwina.

'Absolutely,' she says. Zero hesitation.

'Why?'

'Because things only ever happen one way.'

'But how do you know that's how they're going to happen?'

'You wait until they've happened. Then it's obvious.'

'I think we're going in circles.'

'No, we're just coming at it from opposite ends. People think that fate is prediction. But fate is an outcome. Fate comes after the fact.'

Julian thinks: *like heavy chains, dragging across the bottom of the sea.*

Edwina yells in his ear: 'As soon as something's happened, then the odds of it happening that way were always a hundred per cent. You can't get any clearer than that. But fate takes patience.'

BIG TIME

'WHAT ARE YOU GUYS TALKING ABOUT?' screams Abel.

Out of the corner of his eye, Julian spots them: the haircuts. Khaki trousers, hands balled in the pockets of their light shower-proof jackets, sweat collecting in the folds at the backs of their necks.

Edwina follows Julian's gaze. 'Do you need them to not see you?'

Julian nods. Edwina smiles. A hand on his shoulder. 'Have a great show.'

Dragging Abel behind her, Edwina charges the haircuts and flings her arms around their shoulders, pulling off a very convincing impression of a fucked-up Cookslander. 'LET'S FUCKING DANCE,' she hollers, grabbing the men's hips. The DID agents politely resist, flushing red, while Julian bolts for it, covering the remaining distance to the green room door in a single zig-zagging sprint.

A security guard with a Southern Cross neck tattoo is standing in his way, shorter than Julian but twice as wide. Thick wrists twisted with vascular veins. A clear earpiece with a corkscrew cord jammed way too deep in his left ear.

'Hey mate,' Julian says casually, 'I'm with the band. Got locked out. Would you mind opening up for me?'

The security guard looks Julian up and down, then casts his eyes to one side. 'No lanyard, no access.'

Julian was afraid this might happen. 'I haven't got a lanyard. I'm meant to be on stage in like, two minutes.'

'Can't help you.'

Julian feels a hot flash of anger followed by a chilling wave of nausea when he remembers that he has, in fact, killed a person before – something he never considered himself capable of and was still squaring away mentally.

'Could you radio someone? Ask for my manager?'

'I'm gonna need you to step back, mate.'

'I can't do that, *mate*. This is our last show. Maybe ever. I have to get backstage.'

'Sir – *step back*.' The security guard puts a hand like a spatula in the middle of Julian's chest. He flexes only the tips of his fingers, but the force is enough that Julian goes teetering backwards.

People have started whispering, poking thumbs in Julian's direction. He's stayed in one place too long. He can feel more and more eyes on him, feel the orbit of sweaty, munted concert-goers bending slowly in his direction, as measured and relentless as quicksand.

Julian takes a step towards the security guard and half-lies: 'I've already seen this happen. I already know you're going to let me through. At best, you're embarrassing yourself. At worst, you're messing with the flow of time. Interfering with subatomic forces you cannot hope to grasp or bargain with.'

Whether this gamble on prophecy would have paid off or not, Julian will never know – because here comes Minnie in one of the Acceptables' original merchandise T-shirts, the same ones that had behoved Labyrinth to keep the peace with the unruly foursome, at least until they'd sold out of that print run.

'Look!' Julian shouts, pointing to his own face on Minnie's torso. A little younger, a little healthier, hair a little shorter – but it was him, alright. The security guard squints, looking back and forth between Julian and his screen-printed facsimile long enough for it to seem like he's giving the matter some serious, academic thought – then he opens the green room door and lets Julian through with a sniff and a scowl like he's done him a real big favour, and this is a one-time-only thing.

Once he's through, Julian turns back just in time to see Minnie at the cresting wave of froth-lipped goons that had threatened to envelope him at any moment. She raises one open-palmed hand in a simple, static farewell and mouths: 'Have fun.'

As soon as the green room door shuts, cutting out the roar and churn of the masses, Julian is seized by the make-up artist, who starts powdering his cheeks and attempting to comb his hair.

'He's here!' the man shrieks back over his shoulder. 'I found him!' Then, to Julian: 'Is that what you're wearing?'

Baby déjà vu. Should still be okay. 'This part's already happened,' Julian says.

'I'll get wardrobe,' the make-up artist says.

Julian lunges for a catering table and necks half a bottle of water. His vision swims a little, and for one brief moment his brain brushes up against a common fear of frequent F users: *What if I'm still in it?* What if you snap back only to find yourself in another trip? What if, when you skip ahead, you see yourself taking F – and then you see what *that* version of you sees? What if *that* version of you takes F *again*? And then *again*? How deep can you swim before you forget where the surface is?

Julian empties the rest of the bottle over his head. The soft spring water dashes the humid prickle from his skin just long enough for him to get a grip on his surroundings. *It's highly unlikely that the version we're in will dovetail once again with the false version.* All he had to worry about now was playing a good show – for Minnie, for Edwina, for Xander, for the band's legacy (such as it was) and for however many true fans may still have been out there.

Julian heads for the wings, then down to the trap room. Four hydraulic pedestals are laid out before him. A grizzled mech is arguing with his young offsider as to whether they can or should disengage Xander's pedestal. Skinner is suggesting it could be a moving tribute. Tammy's already seated, testing the kick drum, twirling one stick around her fingers, and on the pedestal up front is Ash, his back to Julian, adjusting the neck strap on a brand-new guitar and rolling his neck side to side before a glitzy chrome vocal mic.

'Ash!' Julian shouts.

Ash turns. His healing black eye has been concealered to oblivion. He nods and turns back.

Before he even realises he's moving, Julian's making a break for Ash, but gets intercepted by a solid wall of costumiers, tutting their tongues and peeling his shirt over his head.

Julian begins to panic. His brain has accepted this new version of events, but it seems his body hasn't. And when he really thinks about it – which preconditions leading to a fatally rigged microphone, in the version of the future he'd seen when he skipped ahead, couldn't just as easily be in place now? How did a locked fire door, and a conversation with Edwina, have any impact whatsoever on the venue's wiring?

The costumiers wrap him in a black sequinned tunic. They tug at his filthy boots and don him with chunky pleather sneakers.

In Adelaide, what possible impact did that theoretical fender bender have on the appearance of that theoretical van of troopers? Surely none at all. Ash and Julian must have seen two of an infinite number of possible outcomes that were identical up until that one critical juncture. And Julian had simply been lucky, as he so often was, to have seen the most accurate outcome, that and another two hundred and forty-eight times. But right now, out of a similarly infinite number of possible outcomes, all he had to go on was the version he'd seen when he skipped ahead and the version he was living through right now. Two out of infinity. Not a lot of data. Not enough to bet a life on. It meant that for all her experimentation, Oriana had been wrong: there must still be a chance, no matter how slim, that what Julian had seen happen *could still happen*.

The lighting switches. The house music dies down. The vibe shifts. Julian's bass guitar is slammed against his chest, the costumiers evaporate and the platform beneath him begins to trundle magically upwards.

Tammy starts a low rumbling on her toms.

A trap door glides open and Julian emerges topside, coming to a jarring halt six feet in the air, stranded on his own mechanical island.

Ash isn't singing – just nodding along to Tammy's drums. Tammy glances at Julian, then starts the measure again. Still, Ash doesn't sing. Tammy starts over for the third time.

'Hold up there, Tam,' Ash says suddenly.

Tammy lifts her sticks and a hush falls over the crowd.

Hands resting on his guitar, Ash says: 'Before you start demanding "What Time Is Your Heart"' – a small chuckle in the front row – 'I'd like to sing something else instead. Another old one.'

This seems to excite people. A smattering of claps. Julian blinks in the burning lights and drinks in the noxious haze. What did Ash mean when he said *before*? Had he seen all of this as well?

'It's a special show tonight.' Ash's fingers drum on his fretboard, his lips teetering inches from the cursed microphone. 'We're at the end of a very long road. So I want to look back and say thank you to the people who've gotten me where I am today.'

Julian's processing all this in real time. Ash's set lists were normally written in stone, but they were completely off-script now. Was this some ploy to deviate further from some terrible fate that Ash himself had seen? Or, after a week of sobriety and a bout of bad news, was he genuinely just feeling reflective?

Ash turns on his podium and extends one arm towards Julian.

'Julian Ferryman, ladies and gentlemen!' he says. Shouts. Whoops. Wails. 'My co-conspirator. And the best friend I ever had.

BIG TIME

This is something he wrote for our first album, and I find it very beautiful to this day. The man is an unbeatable poet.'

Julian holds Ash's gaze. 'Thanks, mate,' says Ash.

Then he turns back to the crowd and strums the opening chord of 'Genevieve'. The one about Julian's old girlfriend. Except Julian never actually had a girlfriend named Genevieve. Maybe Ash had finally figured out who the song was about.

The chord echoes and he sings:

Why so unkind, so unkind
Why wink one-eyed in the land of the blind
Genevieve
Feels like this city's falling asleep on me

It's hard to hold infinity in your head. Words and symbols are mere synecdoches. Julian hears his old song float back to him as he wrestles with every possible offshoot of the moment he's in, given what he saw before, given what he's seeing now.

You've got no clue
If I was the only one standing next to you
Would you touch me
And let me come alive, let me come alive, you're so unkind

Julian could scuttle the show. Scream for help. Leap off his podium and pull Ash down from his. But it might be all for nothing. He could freak out and ruin the Acceptables' final performance, be the laughing-stock of the crowd, loathed eternally by the few friends he had left. He could carry that shame for the rest of his life.

You are so uncouth
Did you think anyone would sleep next to you
It's a big town
But you're small inside, you're so small inside, I guess I had to
remind you

Julian's vision narrows, a shrinking iris on the back of Ash's head – the leather of the guitar strap, the glint of the microphone, only a kiss away. Astounding, thinks Julian, that even with the gift of foresight, still you could be so paralysed by indecision. There were never any sure things in life – only hedged bets at best.

And so, true to form – as he had done so often in his life before now – Julian Ferryman does nothing.

You've got no proof
If I was the only one left who even knew you
Would you think twice
And let the world rewind, let it all unwind, you're so unkind

In the live acoustic arrangement of 'Genevieve', the next line is sung a cappella. Ash plucks out a chord, then reaches for the microphone.

Julian says:

BIG TIME

Ash

But he's too quiet and too far away – slower than electricity and slower than fate.

The circuit breakers explode somewhere behind them. The lighting grid fails. The smoke machines choke. The audience screams. The hydraulics give out. The platforms plummet. The drum kit disintegrates. The emergency lighting fires up crimson. Julian hits a wall. He is kicked and crushed by rushing feet. Shouts go up. Sirens blare. And out of the dark and haze, a familiar hand grabs Julian's hand.

'This is it. Come with me.'

Oriana pulls Julian to his feet and up the stairs. He loses sight of Tammy, Skinner and Dante. She hauls him through the wings, out the stage door and across the loading bay. The sticky weight of Brisbane's permanent low-pressure system has lifted, and it's starting to rain. The wind picks up a hurdy-gurdy of trash from an open skip. Nothing like a cool change.

'Ash,' Julian cries as Oriana puts him in the passenger seat of a black four-wheel drive. She jumps behind the wheel and steers them away. Away from it all. Heading west. Towards a future unseen and uncertain.

19

Julian and Oriana don't say a word until they're well outside the Brisbane city limits. In the rear-view mirror, Oriana watches the thunderheads, purple like day-old bruises, roll in from the ocean and batter the town. She knew that if they'd left even half an hour later, they would have been cut off by the floodways and spent the night in the back of the four-wheel drive, bumper to bumper with their fellow motorists, waiting for the waters to recede, listening for the rumble of police dinghies or the snicker and swish of opportunistic crocodiles.

But by the time the riverbanks breach and the city grinds to its daily standstill, they're out near Toowoomba, the halogen blur of road-train headlights streaking past them in the opposite direction.

'Poor bastards,' says Oriana with a nod at the trucks, imagining the kilometres-long traffic jam slowly piling up behind them. 'They won't get far.'

Julian puts the heater on full blast.

'Are you crazy?' Oriana snaps, turning the fan down. 'It's a million degrees.'

'I'm freezing,' says Julian, hunched over in his seat. He's shivering, rubbing his arms to keep warm. Blue lips and sweaty palms.

'You might be in shock.'

'No shit.'

'I mean literally. Medically. Try taking a few deep breaths. There are sleeping bags in the back seat.'

Julian reaches behind and unfurls one from its silky cocoon.

Oriana drives. 'Did you …'

'See it? Yes. And before you ask, I tried to stop it. I tried everything I could.'

'I wasn't going to ask that.'

'Well anyway, I did,' Julian tells her, and tells himself. A hand of lightning grips the sky. He waits for the thunder, but it never seems to come. 'Where have you been, anyway?'

'Last-minute preparations,' she says, 'and a few loose ends. Not sure when I'll be back this way.'

'Does anyone else know where we're going?'

'Tammy. But not the specifics. She just knows she'll hear from me.'

'Do I get to know the specifics?'

Oriana rolls her window down to let out the heat. 'Do you actually want to know, or are you just being shitty?'

'I have a right, don't I?' Julian snipes, aware of how child-like he must look writhing about beneath the sleeping bag.

Oriana nods patiently. 'I've got tents, and food and water to last us a few days. We'll head north-west, towards Longreach. Assuming we don't run into any trouble – and haven't been followed – we'll stop there for supplies. Maybe a change of clothes for you.'

Julian shifts self-consciously in his chair. The sequinned tunic. The pleather sneakers. He steals a look at himself in the passenger-side mirror, powder and eyeliner and perfectly coifed hair. A fugitive clown. How fucking embarrassing.

'Then it's a straight shot to Mount Isa and Tennant Creek, before we head south again. We'll use the old highways around Alice. Stay off-road for a day or two. There's a motel in Petermann, not far from the border. Sita will meet us there. We'll switch cars and make the crossing.'

Julian looks out at the endless housing estates rocketing past beneath those same purple clouds: beige-brick, off-the-plan, four-bedroom, two-point-five bathroom, three-car-garage nightmares. Netted trampolines in every backyard. Utes in the driveway. Windows glowing silver from the internal spill of television. Someone's left their Christmas decorations up. Someone's put their jack-o-lanterns out too early. Every few blocks, a new build stretches from the earth. Cement mixers. Witch's hats. Storm drains. Wheelie

BIG TIME

bins. Kumquat trees. A 3D simulation of life. Lattices laced with too-red tomatoes, pumped full of hormones and dying on the vine.

A solid wall of sound barriers suddenly penetrates the view, so Julian looks at the road ahead instead. 'The haircuts were there.'

'I know,' says Oriana. 'After that radio interview, we figured it wouldn't be long.'

'Why not get everyone out?'

'Taking you's risky enough. Taking him …'

Julian senses a sore point and jumps on it. 'You mean you didn't want to save him?'

Oriana looks at him fiercely. '*Want?*' she spits. 'Of course I *wanted* to.'

'Then why am I here?'

'Because you're important, Julian. Even if you don't think you are. Even if you wish you weren't. You are. So that's why you're here and he's not.'

Julian desperately wants to keep needling. He could recline beneath the soft down of the sleeping bag and take pot-shots at Oriana all night. But he can see her knuckles twisted tightly around the steering wheel, her eyes forcing themselves open, unblinking in the onslaught of oncoming headlights, pupils small and hard.

'How long until Longreach?' he asks instead.

'Overnight. Get some sleep.'

They would have time to get into it, Julian figures. For all he knows, they have all the time in the world.

He must have fallen asleep at some stage, because the next time Julian opens his eyes, the world is unrecognisable. For one thing, it's day – caustic, bleached, white-hot day. The purple clouds and creeping vines of Brisbane, the swamp and fog and scum of it all, gets filed away with his uneasy dreams. Now they're on a desert highway going a hundred and forty kilometres an hour, without a single human structure in sight.

'Where are we?' Julian groans, wiping white from the corners of his lips.

Oriana wears sunglasses and a tank top. She smokes. 'The desert,' she says plainly.

Half an hour later, Oriana parks the four-wheel drive on the outskirts of Longreach. There are public toilets, where Julian tries to avoid his own funhouse reflection in the warped metal mirrors. Then Oriana tells him to stay in the car while she walks into town. She leaves the air-conditioning on, and Julian remembers a time, many years ago, when his mother drove to a TAB and left him in the back seat and didn't come back for fourteen hours. (She'd left him snacks – she wasn't a total monster.)

The sun's beginning to sink below the car's tinted windows by the time Oriana returns. She hurls a bulging plastic bag in the back: more food (chips, things in tins, nothing particularly nourishing), more water and a puzzle book 'to help pass the time'. There are also supplies from the pharmacy: electrolytes, bandages, antiseptic creams, sunscreen, painkillers and sleeping pills. Julian half-wonders whether Oriana had wanted to go in alone because she'd stolen all this, stuck up a small-town chemist, Bonnie going solo while Clyde fretted in the car – but he doesn't have the energy to interrogate her.

'I got you these, too,' she says, proffering a pair of cheap dollar-shop sunglasses. 'It gets pretty glary out here.'

'It's almost night,' huffs Julian, slumping down in his seat and putting them on anyway.

They set up camp a hundred metres off the highway. Oriana builds a fire, then douses it as soon as they've boiled water for tea. They keep their head torches and camp lights low. They eat spaghetti from tins and don't talk much. Oriana erects a small, two-man tent and lays the sleeping bags down inside, head-to-toe. The soft insulation cushions their backs against the red rocks underneath, still warm from the afternoon sun.

When Julian complains that his sequinned tunic is hardly appropriate outback attire, Oriana says she'd tried to find him something in a workwear store in Longreach but got a bad vibe off the security guard. At a petrol station the next day, while Julian pumps the four-wheel drive full of diesel, Oriana goes around back and kicks the latch off a charity bin, returning with an armful of stinking, mismatching, old new clothes. She pays cash at the counter and buys herself three packs of cigarettes. She says she's given up on vaping.

'Made me feel like a fucking teenager,' she says.

BIG TIME

That night, after a meal of canned stew, white bread and pub squash soda, Julian asks about the snakes. Oriana's lying with her head resting on a smooth rock, watching the embers of the dying fire, blowing smoke rings at the stars.

'I saw Ash's notebook,' says Julian. 'The snakes became a real preoccupation.'

'Ophidiophobia,' says Oriana. 'Which is different to the more generalised herpetophobia. Ash loved lizards. Just hated snakes.'

'That story he told onstage, about his father – was that true?'

Oriana crosses one ankle over the other. 'Would have been a weird lie.'

'And what about the other stuff?'

Her eyes narrow. 'When did you see his notebook? He didn't let anyone near that thing.'

Julian thinks how best to explain. 'I saw it when I skipped ahead at the concert, in Brisbane. I found it in Ash's dressing room. But only then. I never saw it when I snapped back. I guess you could say I never actually saw it in *real life*. Things happened …'

'Differently.'

'Yeah.'

'You took a little detour.'

'Yeah. So was it still real?'

Oriana just stares up at the sky.

'From the moment I came home,' Julian says, 'Ash seemed so certain of everything he was doing. I never stopped to think if it was all *normal*.'

'He was an artist,' Oriana says, a little bored.

'But there were things in that book that I could never imagine Ash writing. Not that he didn't have the talent, just … things I didn't think he even cared about. But I get it. I left. I was gone a whole year. So maybe I just didn't know him anymore.'

'People change,' Oriana says evenly.

'Not like that, they don't,' Julian says. 'Not that much, that fast.'

Oriana stubs out her cigarette and stores the butt in a small aluminium container. She was fastidious about covering her tracks, even out here. Then she lights another, waiting patiently for Julian to get where he's going.

'It was you,' he says.

Oriana's hands peel upwards and outwards in a theatrical shrug. 'I might have made the odd addendum.'

'While he was on F. The F that you gave him.'

'It's not like I was force-feeding it to him. He was obsessed with the stuff.'

'But while he was under, you ... what? You wrote those lyrics in his book?'

'To give him a nudge.'

'Then he snapped back, saw what you wrote and thought that *he'd* written it – that it came from him, from the future. He thought he believed it. But he never knew *why* he was saying half the stuff he was saying. You trapped him in a feedback loop.'

'Some killer lyrics though, no?'

'Do you think this is funny?' Julian growls. 'Because I think you drove him mad.'

'Oh, boo-fucking-hoo!' shouts Oriana, sitting up. 'About time everybody else got a fucking taste of it!' Then she puts her head back down on the rock, hating herself. 'I didn't mean that.'

Now it's Julian's turn to wait. The fire's died out, smoke dissipated into sky.

'I had a dog when I was little,' says Oriana. 'Did I ever tell you that?'

'No.'

'There's a lot you don't know. A lot of reasons why things are the way they are. I loved Ash. Fuck, I loved him. I know you did, too.'

Julian turns away.

'But things were only getting worse,' Oriana goes on. 'Something had to happen. And the band was blowing up. You went platinum, for fuck's sake! So I – we – saw an opportunity.'

'You and Charlie.'

'And others. We thought, hey – these guys have got the ear of this entire fucked-up country. What if, instead of shitty pop songs, they were saying something that actually meant something?'

'Hard to park your Lambo when the street is in the surf?'

'It wasn't *all* me,' Oriana says. 'Not every word. I just tried to point him in the right direction.'

Julian thinks about the hundred and thirty-two days he spent in that church in Belgrave, microdosing F just to get through a session in one piece, a frayed ball of nerves. It had felt like coming home to find that someone's rearranged the furniture. Solastalgia. When you're the same, but a place has changed. Now Julian knows why he felt like that.

He gestures around at the ocean-dark depths of the desert sky, the diminutive remains of the fire. 'Was this the direction you were hoping for?'

'Ash wasn't the problem,' says Oriana, slipping off her boots. 'The music wasn't the problem.'

'Then what was?'

'The people. Your so-called fans. We thought that if the band went one way, your followers would follow. But they didn't. They clenched up. They resisted the new in favour of the old. We thought that the Acceptables, as a cultural institution, was the perfect vessel through which to sow the seeds of dissent. Of meaningful social change. But we overestimated. Nobody wanted change. They just wanted you to shut up and play the hits.'

Julian shakes his head. He can feel the outback cold setting in. He wraps his charity bin cardigan tight around his chest. 'This is what I've been saying all along.'

'Don't let it go to your head,' says Oriana as she stands and heads for the tent. 'You were always plan B.'

Julian gets into the sleeping pills, of course. Oriana doesn't stop him. The world is one unbroken line of red dirt and bullet-peppered signposts. Julian looks in his side mirror and thinks he sees Ash in the back seat, one leg crossed over the other, foot tapping impatiently as it always did on interstate drives. Other times, he thinks he sees the Plutos brothers rolling joints from their home-grown stash, Xander correcting Pony's fingering on some interminable original song he'd been super excited to play for them. At one point he thinks maybe he sees me, how I might look like after a week's forced sobriety in an outback work camp – brown hair turning gold, the circles beneath my eyes and the puff in my cheeks lightening and tightening while the flesh around my waist begins to cling to my ribs. But mostly, Julian just rests his head against the dirt-streaked window and watches the world roll away, ochre and flat and empty. When they get out of the car – to piss or to nap, or to let some other car that was following a little too close for comfort overtake them – it's hot. Fan-forced, heat-of-hell hot, the kind of heat you can tell is hotter than your own blood. It glazes Julian's bare skin like heat-shrink, and his dopey breath feels like evaporative cooling on his lower lip. When he looks at Oriana, he imagines her a wax statue, cool and still but slowly melting, roiling sheaths of glossy plasticine. She smells like cigarettes and coconut sunscreen. She keeps her sunglasses on at all times, so Julian doesn't see her eyes for days.

He wakes up on a bed with the doona kicked aside. The fitted sheet is warm and wet from sweat. Oriana's sitting on another bed – must be a twin room – legs crossed like a Buddha, fingernails digging around beneath her toenails.

The room is dark but for three small, distinct glimmers: the first is Oriana's cigarette with its hot vermillion tip, travelling from her lips to her lap then back again with the morbid precision and regularity of an oil sump; the second is the offensive electric blue of a bug-trap that must have been hanging outside, throwing an incandescent pool under the door as if a UFO had silently arrived nearby; the third is the gap in the heavy, flower-stamped drapes which allowed for the lazy strobe of passing headlights to spill through, scanning the room left to right or right to left, hitting Oriana's face with a pupil-shrinking shimmer before fading again with the drowsy sound of engines pushing a dozen frayed tyres down unfathomably long and unfinished desert roads.

'Where are we?' Julian asks without lifting his head.
'Petermann,' she says.
'What time is it?'
'Around three.'
'Why aren't you asleep?
'Because somebody burnt through all the sleeping pills.'

20

Julian wakes from a dreamless sleep to the angry rush of a shower. His throat is coated with the smooth tastelessness of drug-induced rest, and his forehead feels heavy – heavy enough to keep the rest of his head pinned to the bed. He closes his eyes again and listens to the patterns of the falling water in the ensuite, using the noise like sonar to sculpt the negative space and placing Oriana in it. He's completely forgotten what it's like to be with her – even touch her – and the thought now arrives with a strange, anthropological sensation. Julian once put his fist through a drainpipe because Oriana couldn't make it to one of his gigs. Now, he likes to think he wouldn't care all that much if she walked from the shower straight out into the desert and never returned.

Julian sits up and extends his spine to its fullest length, then wiggles his toes. A nauseous vacuum stretches from his ribs to his hips. After days of tinned spaghetti, his stomach's howling for some real food.

Julian peels off his charity-bin singlet, soaked through with sweat but beginning to dry, turning light and salty like driftwood. In the open wardrobe, he finds a perfectly clean, perfectly crisp, perfectly white T-shirt, floating like a spectre on its cheap wire hanger. It must have been left there by the previous occupant. Julian pulls it down over his shoulders and feeds his arms through the sleeves. It makes him feel brand new.

He waits another moment, just in case Oriana's almost finished in the shower, but from the steady thrum of the water Julian guesses that she's sat down on the tiles, something she used to do a lot when they were together – just sit there for an hour or more, even after the hot water ran out. She never seemed to mind.

'The colder it is, the cleaner you feel,' she would say.

Julian ventures outside and immediately begins to sweat, defiling the white shirt. Hot sunlight leaks through a monolith of white cloud crouched atop a distant patch of mountains. Only a handful of cars are scattered across the parking lot, surrounded by the heavy brown brick of the U-shaped motel. All the other brass-numbered doors stand closed, and the same offensive floral drapes are drawn in every room. Julian sniffs the air: eggs, bacon, pancakes, coffee. At the far end of the U sits a slipshod truck-stop diner.

A rusty bell proclaims his arrival. A waitress in her late forties, with an apron held together by tomato sauce and syrup stains, gives him a nod. A greasy-looking fry-cook with shifty eyes and a pencil moustache, only just visible through the narrow porthole to the kitchen, cracks eggs one-handed onto an industrial fryer. In a booth by the window, a young couple, all teeth and freckles, pore over a map of Wakefield, deciding what to see once they head further south.

In the middle of the diner sits a man with polished boots, moleskin trousers and a tilted brown Akubra, his back turned to Julian. He holds a coffee cup aloft at a curious height, as though he were stuck deciding whether to drain the dregs or ask for a refill. There's a plate of scrambled eggs and bacon on his table, covering the corner of a *National Telegraph*.

'Take a seat, love. I'll be right with you,' the waitress says to Julian, delivering an ugly pile of baked beans to the couple.

Julian steps up to the counter. The waitress meets him there.

'Can I get two cups of coffee, some pancakes and one of those egg and bacon sandwiches for room eleven?' says Julian quietly.

'Don't do room service, love,' replies the waitress, whose name badge says *SHARON*. 'Take a seat.'

Julian can feel the young couple looking at him. And he hasn't heard the Akubra put down that coffee cup yet. 'I'm in a bit of a rush,' he says with a vague attempt at charm, 'and you'd be doing me a huge favour—'

'No way I'm carrying a tray of food 'n' hot coffee all the way to eleven. Not with my bung knee. Take a seat 'n' I'll bring it to you here.'

Sharon had assumed this would end the conversation, but Julian persists. 'You know what? I just realised I don't have any money on me.' He tugs theatrically at the sides of his track pants. 'My partner's got our credit card, and she's in the shower. If I could just—'

'We don't do room service. And we require payment up front.' Clearly Sharon's tussled with far greater hoodwinkers than him.

A single bead of sweat curls down the valley between Julian's shoulders. 'Then I guess I'll come back later.' He turns and heads for the door.

A voice says: 'Ferryman.'

Julian stops. Perhaps he stops too suddenly. Perhaps he shouldn't have stopped at all.

The voice comes from under the Akubra. 'That Irish?'

The man finally puts his coffee cup down and knits his fingers on the tabletop. 'You don't look Irish.'

Julian's frozen right beside the man's table. 'Not Irish,' he says. 'Just ... Anglo. My great-great-grandparents came from Norfolk or something. I'm really not sure.'

'It's a tragedy for a man not to know where he comes from.'

'I don't see how it matters.'

'How it *matters*?' The man removes his hat, revealing a rough, bald hemisphere of melanoma-scarred skin. It takes Julian a second to recognise him without any Kevlar.

'Why, it's all that matters,' says Officer Barnes.

In the burning daylight, face to face, Julian is struck by the shocking blue of the DIBM patrolman's eyes, two sapphires on the barren stretch of his leathery, weather-beaten face. His scalp and cheeks are closely shaved, and a small, four-pointed scar adorns his chin.

'Take a seat, son,' he says, nudging a chair with his boot.

Julian sits opposite Barnes, feeling his heartbeat in his feet, wondering whether the shower has turned cold yet, wondering whether Oriana's wondering where he is.

'Did you want that coffee?' Barnes asks. 'Something to eat?' With a jolt, Julian realises Barnes is wearing the same department-store cologne his father used to wear.

'Sure,' says Julian.

'You kids have been on the road a while, eh? Must be craving a decent meal.' Without moving his head or taking his eyes off Julian, Barnes calls to the waitress: 'Sharon, love, get this bloke his breakfast, would you? What was it – pancakes …?'

'And an egg and bacon sandwich,' Julian says, biting his lip.

'And a brekky sandwich,' repeats Barnes. 'Might as well put on a fresh pot, too. Add it to my bill.'

'Right you are, Frank.'

'Cheers, Sharon.'

Barnes picks up his newspaper, folds it to page three, then places it in front of Julian before leaning back in his rickety chair and folding his hands in his lap. 'Guessing you haven't seen the papers, either.'

Julian's eyes flick down to Barnes's *National Telegraph* – to a two-inch column with an old promo photo of Ash winking out at him. The headline reads: *LIBERTINE MUSO, WANTED BY DID, KILLED IN FREAK STAGE ACCIDENT, ANARCHIST TIES BEING INVESTIGATED*. He doesn't bother reading the article.

'I know what happened,' Julian says. 'I was there.'

'Still. Nasty stuff,' tuts Barnes. 'Your girlfriend must be pretty torn up about it.'

'She's not my—'

'Of course. My apologies. Looking through everyone's files, it can be a little hard to keep track of who's with who.'

The waitress shuffles over with a fresh, foggy pot of coffee.

'You can go ahead and set that down there, Sharon. We'll drink it,' says Barnes.

Sharon leaves the pot on the table and shuffles away again. Barnes pours a cup for Julian, then fills his, picking it up and sipping very slowly. Julian does the same, slurping at the thin rim of porcelain. He remembers reading something in a book one time about how mirroring people's body language could psychologically disarm them, something like that, so that's what he's trying to do now, moving and sipping in perfect sync with the patrolman. All he really does is burn his tongue.

'We can just natter for a while till your pancakes get here,' says Barnes.

BIG TIME

'What about?'

Barnes clicks his tongue. 'I've got to ask: why are you two so hell-bent on getting over there? What's over *there* anyway? What makes you think it'll be so much better than here?'

Julian can't think of a single reason not to answer honestly. 'None of this was my idea.'

'That's the thing that really sticks in my craw,' Barnes says plaintively. 'It's the lack of gratitude. See, I look around at this country – at everything we've built, everything we've preserved, everything we intend to pass down – and I just think it is so bloody beautiful. Now, I'm no poet or writer or what have you, not like you, so I haven't got any fancy words to express it. All I can say is that it really does move me. But when you look at it, you believe it's not enough. More than that – you believe it to be somehow *defective*. Yet both of us are looking at the same bloody thing! I don't reckon I'll ever wrap my head around it. We have to physically force you to stay here, when personally, I can't think of a single reason why I'd ever want to leave.'

'Why are you here?' Julian asks. 'And not in Botany?'

'Now, that's an interesting story.' Barnes grins, showing off a gold tooth. 'I knew there was more to you lot when we found you on that bus. I put in a call to the DID and had some very illuminating chats with the department blokes there. Heard some pretty interesting stories about your mate Ash and your girlfriend Miss Devereaux. But when they told me they were planning on making their move in Brisbane, I just had this feeling. Call it a hunch. Something told me there might be a little bit of spillage. And I was right, wasn't I? When I heard that you and the girl had bolted, I requested immediate personal leave so I could come up north and search for you myself. They've doubled the troops at the meridian, so there was never any chance of you getting through there. It was only a question of who would nab you – and where. The DID fellas, they reckoned you'd go far-north through Timber Creek, try to blend in on the highways. And my mates in the DIBM, they put their money on you going south, trying your luck on the Nullarbor. But I just had this feeling I'd find you smack-bang in the middle.' He spreads his hands proudly, wisely. 'And here we are.'

Julian blinks. 'You're here on *holiday*?'

Barnes laughs, a robust sound – charming to hear in a country pub, horrifying to hear in a holding cell.

'What can I say? I'm married to my work.'

'So it's just you, on your own?' Julian feels him out.

'Oh, no,' scoffs Barnes. 'I picked you up back near Davenport and called it in. There's half-a-dozen troopers on the highway half a click in each direction and a dozen more in the desert, just waiting for my go-ahead.'

He unclips a CB radio from his belt, waggling it theatrically. 'But why am I telling you this? Well, I'm telling you this so you don't do anything stupid, like try to make a run for it. That'd be a big bloody waste of everyone's time. Mine especially.'

The mid-morning sun is crossing the table between them. Barnes leans forward and knits his fingers again. The phalanxes between each knuckle are stocky, pale and rough, like oblongs of whittled wood.

'I'm telling you this,' he says, 'because you've got yourself involved with some dangerous individuals. And while I can be a bit of a stickler at times, I also believe that people can come around. I'm glad we got to have this talk, just you and me. Because I hope you'll see reason. I hope you'll go back to your room and have a frank chat with Miss Devereaux, maybe talk her out of doing anything … calamitous. This way, you can even take a moment – if it feels appropriate, totally up to you – but you can even take a moment to say goodbye.'

Sharon the waitress appears beside Julian, proffering an enormous stack of starchy, beige pancakes topped with a clod of half-molten butter. She slides it in front of him. 'Sanger's on its way.'

'Yummo,' says Barnes, eyebrows peaking.

Julian ignores the pancakes. 'If we're such a pain in the neck – such a blight on the Republic – why not just let us go? Have the whole place to yourself?'

Barnes wiggles one square-cut thumbnail between his teeth, loosening some bacon fat. 'The world is a zoo,' he says. 'I hope you'll indulge the metaphor – but the world is a zoo, and every country's an enclosure. Now, what's the primary function of a zoo?'

'Tourism?'

'Bit cynical there, son. Sure, tourism, maybe. But I was going to say: conservation. The job of a zoo is to *conserve* different forms of

BIG TIME

life. What would happen if a zoo just let all the different animals run amok and intermingle? No cages, no moats, no enclosures?'

'Well ...' Julian imagines it.

'Pandemonium and tragedy. Monkeys go wandering into the snow leopard enclosure? Whack! Dead monkeys. Snow leopards run afoul of the rhinos? Boom! Dead snow leopards. It would defeat the entire purpose of the enterprise. These are endangered creatures we're talking about here – if they're not kept in a controlled environment, they will die. Thus, the key to conservation is *containment*. You haven't touched your pancakes, mate.'

Julian glances down at his pancakes, slowly cooling and fusing together. Barnes lifts a pitcher of syrup from a condiment caddy and slowly, deliberately, pours a thick brown stream in one endless concentric circle over Julian's plate.

'It's only through containment that we preserve what's great in this world,' the patrolman purrs. 'Without that? Dilution. Chaos. And extinction. Animals need enclosures so that a hundred years from now, they're still around and they're still the same. This is also why we need borders. Now, you probably think that borders are nothing more than invisible, arbitrary lines on a map. But borders aren't walls or fences or bridges or rivers or barricades. Borders are people.'

He empties the last of the syrup onto Julian's pancakes. The stack silently implodes beneath its own sodden weight. Barnes replaces the pitcher in the condiment caddy and looks right at Julian with his bitter sapphire eyes.

'I am the border.'

After letting this hang for a moment, scanning Julian's face for some sign of either comprehension or terror, Barnes snorts back a huge hunk of phlegm. Julian hears it hit the back of the man's throat.

'Now go tell your girlfriend that if she's not out in three minutes, I'll be walking in there and executing her myself.'

The rusty bell rings. The sunlight flares.

'Julian?' Oriana stands at the entrance to the diner, cautiously studying the back of Barnes's bald head.

'Oh, g'day love,' the patrolman coos, turning to face her. 'We were just talking about you.'

Julian shoots up from his chair. The table rocks. The pancakes go tumbling. He grips the plastic handle of the half-full coffee pot, rears it back and swings it sideways at Barnes's head. It hits the man's ear and bursts like a glass balloon, showering the table in a hot glaze of caffeine and crystal. The jagged hemisphere remaining in Julian's hand lodges itself in the patrolman's temple. The glass hits skull, a dull breach that vibrates back through Julian's fingers, fist and forearm. Barnes's body spasms horribly, twisting and plummeting from his chair, hitting the linoleum, soaking in a sparkling pool of syrup, blood and coffee.

Sharon screams. Julian staggers backwards. Oriana grabs a hold of him and looks down at Barnes. What had he told her once? *You'll keep.*

The young couple are cowering in the corner of their booth, emptying their pockets, envisaging a hold-up. Julian's arms are frozen at waist height. He can't put them down, can't move them at all. They no longer feel like his.

'Jules,' Oriana says, shaking him. 'Our ride is here.'

Julian looks down at his white T-shirt – ruined. Rich reds and browns. An outback landscape. 'There are people out there,' he manages. 'Waiting for his signal.'

'Well,' Oriana says evenly, 'he's not giving any signals now. You bought us some time.' Her eyes flit between Sharon and the hyperventilating couple. 'But we have to go.'

She drags Julian through a *STAFF ONLY* door and into the kitchen, where the cook turns and watches them mutely, strips of unattended bacon fiercely self-immolating on the grill. Oriana heaves open a rear exit and they go stumbling, staggering out into the vacant desert, a picture split in perfect horizontal halves: a hundred and eighty degrees of limitless, smooth, Martian earth beneath a hundred and eighty degrees of infinite azure sky. And right at the centre of this dreamy, prosaic canvas, is a black sedan.

A woman gets out, dressed in department uniform. Julian recognises her from the cinema in Botany.

'Quickly now,' Sita says, guiding them to the back of the vehicle. She pops the boot. Inside are more sleeping bags, snacks and bottled water.

Julian mumbles: 'There's people in the desert.'

BIG TIME

'I've seen them,' says Sita. 'We'll stick to the old camel trails. It will take a few hours. I have a diplomatic pass, so they won't search the car.'

'Come on, Julian,' says Oriana, helping him into the boot. He nestles in deep, fumbling for one of the waters.

'I'll let you out again as soon as I can,' Sita says as Oriana climbs in after him. 'Just hold on. You're almost there.'

Julian and Oriana rocket through the desert, huddled in the nocturnal cool of the boot. The air is still and stale. The tyres grind invisibly, inches from their faces. The underside of the boot lid is hot to the touch. Julian thinks this must be what it's like re-entering Earth's atmosphere from outer orbit: cramped limbs, hot metal, blind faith. Oriana's thinking something similar, but neither of them share their thoughts. Julian spoons her out of sheer necessity and finds his nose nestled in the nape of her neck. A familiar smell.

'Do you think we'll make it?' Julian asks.

'Yes,' says Oriana.

'Do you think we'll ever come back?'

'Maybe.'

'Maybe?'

'That depends on you.'

Julian's watch hand is pinned behind his back, so he can't tell how long it's been – but shortly after leaving Petermann he feels the car grind to a stop.

'Something's wrong,' whispers Oriana.

'What do you mean?'

'It's too soon. We can't be at the meridian by now.'

Through the hum of the engine and the bulk of the vehicle at his back, Julian hears more tyres – maybe two sets, trundling to a halt on the road not far ahead of them. Car doors and combat boots. Muffled voices. Sita's door opens and closes. She offers some benign greeting.

'Old mate was right,' murmurs Oriana. 'They must be everywhere.'

The voices come closer. Sita is protesting. 'Full clearance', something something, 'department time', something something. She's a good liar, but even Julian can hear the tinge of worry in her throat. A male voice is talking back to her, placating her. Apologising, explaining. Something something 'manhunt', something something 'done in no time'.

Boots crunch by the passenger door, and the door sighs open. Gloved hands root around in the glovebox. Another pair of boots trudges down the driver's side, rounding the rear right tyre.

Sita gives it one last shot: something something 'speaking to your superior about this'. The other voice is unmoved. It barks out an order.

Oriana reaches back to hold Julian's hand, and he lets her.

A click. The boot yawns open to the afternoon sun, blinding Julian and Oriana. They breathe in sharply and force their eyes open. A DIBM patrolman in desert fatigues is looking right down at them, a rifle on his shoulder, dust in his hair and sweat on his brow. And what are the fucking chances? It's my old housemate, Kyle.

During the previous summer, while Cleo and I were hobnobbing with the Acceptables, sitting in on recording sessions, getting drunk, chewing pills, making art, swanning about at parties, experimenting with F and sunbathing naked, Kyle was spending most nights alone in his room agonising over a Department of Internal Borders and Migration enlistment form that his father had sent him. Kyle's grades at law school had been less than impressive; his internship at an inner-city firm wasn't panning out much better. He'd had two written warnings for showing up late to pre-trial meetings with heinously bloodshot eyes, reeking of skunk. His parents had expressly told him that if he lost his job and could no longer afford to pay rent, there wasn't any room for him back in the family home; his old bedroom had been turned into a study for his father to work on his retirement project, a nine-volume biography of Alfred Deakin. Hence the enlistment form – a not-so-gentle nudge. Something to build character, his father said on the phone. Something for the public good. Kyle would chew pencils down to the nub, staring at the form while Cleo and I came and went at all hours, stealing leftovers from the fridge and pinching his good bottles of booze. I suppose we should have noticed something was up with him. I suppose we should have just asked.

BIG TIME

When both Cleo and I announced we were leaving on tour with the band, that settled it. With all our stuff in storage, Kyle could simply sever the lease and slip away unnoticed. He knew that if we knew, we would have tried to talk him out of it.

The DIBM would never publicly admit this, but they were severely understaffed. It was difficult to maintain round-the-clock patrols at every state border, let alone man the full length of the meridian. There'd been a flurry of internal memos about a draft, or mandatory service straight out of high school, but nothing had been made official yet. This meant that the current timeframe between enlistment and deployment was unnervingly brief – Kyle submitted his paperwork the day we all left from that hardware store parking lot and was summoned to the barracks in Werribee the following Monday. After one week of basic protocol and arms training, he was shipped to Alice Springs – remote central Cooksland traditionally being something of a proving ground for rookies. In his three days on the job so far, he'd already impounded a smuggler's truck at the border, chased down and bagged a renegade abortionist from Ballarat, and turned around an elderly couple in an old Tarago who his commander suspected were trying to reunite with family in Port Hedland.

As a new recruit, Kyle was fair game for his older colleagues. He'd been spat on, slapped around, verbally abused and sexually humiliated. After being roughed up in the base camp showers, he'd wet his bunk and was forced to sleep out in the desert, naked. As he'd quivered on the blue sand, his teeth chipping away at themselves involuntarily, he'd forced himself to conjure up memories of our tiny sharehouse courtyard with its shitty fold-out chairs and cobwebbed festoon lights. Maybe he should have been more honest with his housemates. Maybe he should have just told them what was going on.

Now, Kyle's standing in another featureless stretch of outback on an old camel trail, a rifle on his shoulder and the sun at his back, looking in the boot of a black sedan and recognising two old friends. Not close friends, exactly – he and Julian had one really great night a few years ago when they found a backpack full of nangs in a toilet stall at a bar in Northcote – and he and Oriana had gotten into some deep, drunken conversations about courtroom ethics over the years.

They were ancillary friends, people in his orbit, people who would see him and smile at him and offer him a hug and a pat on the back and a beer. But now they're staring up at him like newborns, holding each other, shrivelling in the light, their eyes enormous and silent and afraid.

'Fennessy?' shouts Kyle's commander from the front of the car.

Kyle swallows. Every muscle in his body still aches from convulsing overnight in the desert. He wants nothing more than to put down his gun and take off his boots and climb in there with them – to curl up his weary legs and relax into Oriana's arms – to close the lid behind him and shut his eyes and just be there in the dark and cool – to be with old friends, to be with people like him – to be taken away from here and on to some new, better, unfamiliar place.

Kyle says: 'All clear.' Then he closes the boot.

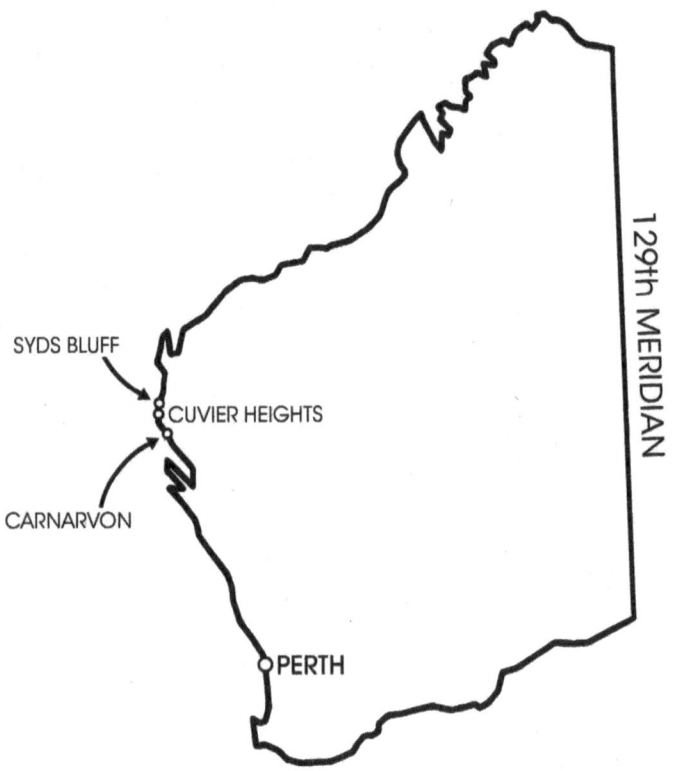

PART FIVE

THE WRA

21

Here's the track-listing for Julian Ferryman's first and only solo LP, *THE MOTHERF*CKER MANIFESTO*:

1. Quiet Boy Freak-out
2. Genevieve (Redux)
3. Hugo Valentine
4. The End of Days
5. Echo Hotel
6. Point Perpendicular
7. Cloudtown
8. Give Up Then Begin
9. Shark Teeth
10. Great Green Nowhere
11. Surprise Party for a Stranger
12. Plan B
13. Cul-de-sac
14. Big Time

At the moment Julian crosses the hundred and twenty-ninth meridian, he has the melodies and choruses for about half these songs already in his head. Some he began to write in South America, some he'd been tinkering with during the Acceptables' short-lived second tour, others he'd been keeping in his back pocket for years. 'Hugo Valentine' he'd almost shared with Ash during the initial jam sessions for *Beaches*, and he was quietly confident that

BIG TIME

if he had, it would have made it on the album. But Julian sat on it, perhaps sensing that one day he'd be making music on his own and not wishing to – as the saying goes – give it all away for free. The other half of these tracks will be conceived and scribed in the months following Julian's arrival in the WRA.

The first thing he notices as they approach the outskirts of Perth are the hematite skybridges – gargantuan grids of shimmering, elevated tollway feeding millions of daily commuters in every direction, hovering like splayed hands above the city skyline. Even higher than the skybridges are the sun reflectors, big black dots the size of football fields fluttering on the wind in a military-enforced no-fly zone some eight hundred metres above the tip of the tallest skyscraper, catching UV rays and sending them back into space, a Sisyphean task if ever there was one. (Track 7: 'Cloudtown'.)

The second thing Julian notices are the times – plural. Which is to say, in the WRA, there didn't appear to be just one. While the east had doggedly decided to stick things out with Coordinated Universal Time despite its increasingly suspect activity, on this side of the meridian the response to Eleuterio Cabrera's Anomaly and Yumi Atako's Heaven Tapes had been to frantically begin searching for a more reliable alternative. But people had yet to settle on one, so instead – for the moment – there were many.

While certain fringe groups had taken a somewhat radical approach to the problem – disappearing off-grid and burning timepieces in enormous bonfires in the desert – mainstream society was still in general agreement that it was necessary for our lives to be undergirded by *some* form of consistently progressing unit of measurement. First, people harkened back to ancient time-keeping systems grounded in the natural world. They built giant sundials in their gardens and miniature moondials to carry in their pockets, before naysayers gleefully pointed out that the sun was constantly burning through its ancient stores of hydrogen and was subject to unpredictable fluctuations, while the moon was slowly but surely drifting away from Earth at a speed of approximately 3.9 centimetres every year. Not an imminent problem per se, but there was no use going to the trouble of establishing a new omnipresent system that would only have to be reassessed and potentially scrapped in a few hundred years' time.

JORDAN PROSSER

With the moon proving unreliable, tide-based systems were ruled out as well, so people looked further, to the stars. They proposed the use of *sidereal* days as measured by Earth's rotation relative to fixed celestial bodies – but what guarantee was there that these bodies would be any more dependable than our own sun? Entire constellations might have blinked out millennia ago without us knowing it yet. The universe itself was in a constant state of flux, slowing, cooling and expanding – hardly something you could set your watch to. Plus, the satellite noise, space debris and surfeit of research stations in low-Earth orbit made astronomical surveillance increasingly difficult, if not impossible, for the layperson.

As soon as space entered the conversation, scientists from WRASA butted in and suggested adopting the Darian calendar – twenty-four months, each comprised of twenty-eight *sols*, with one leap month at the end – all the better to prepare humanity to juggle schedules across multiple planetary time zones. But a coalition of C-suite executives (mostly from toy, catering and greeting card companies) railed against the idea, concerned that celebrating Christmas only once every twenty-four months (and in the month of *Vrishika*, no less) would decimate their annual profits. The scientists said they were only trying to help and returned to their simulation stations in Antarctica.

A start-up in Toronto volunteered to oversee the global transition to decimal time, but schoolteachers drew up picket lines at the concept of a ten-day work week, and again, the private sector balked when labour unions determined that a ten-hour day would necessitate '3.333333333333 HOURS LABOUR, 3.3333333333333 HOURS RECREATION, AND 3.333333333333 HOURS REST'.

Arguments were put forward to adopt Unix time, which uniformly tallied the number of seconds since 1 January 1970, but no-one liked the idea of trying to remember that their dentist appointment was scheduled for 2368786183. In that vein, though, people figured they could measure time *since* just about anything. Some declared the discovery of the Anomaly to be the most obvious inflection point for a brand-new system and began to measure sun-cycles from that point forward. Others flipped the concept ominously on its head, stating it would be easier if the world were

BIG TIME

counting *down* towards something – the passing of a comet, the next ice age, the heat death of the universe – but using intervals on the petasecondal scale of giga-annums was not all that practical when trying to organise Sunday brunch with friends.

There was hexadecimal time and binary time, centiseconds, milli-minutes, kiloweeks and gigamonths, Incan time wheels and Egyptian merkhets, modes and methods of chronological measurement both ancient and fantastical. In the spirit of inclusiveness – and in a bid to prevent more citizens from giving up on society altogether, burning Breguets in the Gibson Desert – the WRA attempted to accommodate all these new systems simultaneously, stating that one's preferred method of time measurement was not merely a personal choice but an inalienable right, as singular and protected as any other aspect of one's identity. This meant that every timestamp throughout the country, from airport departure boards to restaurant opening hours to the screens in the stock exchange, had to be displayed in five, six, sometimes as many as a dozen distinct formats which fluctuated day by day.

However, not long after Julian arrives in the west, a misread train timetable will cause a violent derailment, killing forty-three people. It will be the 8:28 am / 3.52.77 DCT / 010110:100100:111110 BCT / 2286145680 UXT / 8843D090 UHT / 1349.3.52 SCSCT (sun cycles since Cabrera) / 6986.6.48 SCUHCT (sun cycles until Halley's Comet) / −5.4 GY PDSST (billion years pre-destruction of solar system) service from Perth to Mandurah. As a result, the president will announce a complete about-turn, ordering every time of every variety to be removed from every window, surface and screen, effectively rendering the WRA timeless. The government will assemble a think tank of industry and community leaders, who will then announce a multi-billion-dollar tender. The international consultancy firm that wins that tender will engage in a lengthy process of stakeholder consultation and market research in order to arrive at a new unilateral system that will allow the WRA and its citizenry to successfully mark and measure the passage of their lives. They will beseech the public to remain patient during this consultation period, estimated to take somewhere between eighteen and twenty-eight months – but of course, by the time they arrive at this estimate, the president will have passed their decree and there will be no legal or accurate means of expressing it. (Track 4: 'The End of Days'.)

During his first strategy meeting at Jianhong-Waterford-Sprouse, Julian remains almost entirely silent, sullenly kicking the carpet as he sinks into the depths of an Italian leather armchair at the head of a long table, hoodie pulled down tight, dollar-shop sunglasses firmly in place, twenty PR cadets grinning statically across at him. (Track 9: 'Shark Teeth'.)

Jianhong-Waterford-Sprouse had recently made international headlines when they became the first company to (apparently) successfully broker a sponsorship deal in the afterlife. They claimed that their client, the Canadian doughnut chain Froakley's, would henceforth have a shopfront in everybody's heaven mall. No-one currently alive had any way of verifying this – and Jianhong-Waterford-Sprouse drew the line at enlisting *Neue Götter* to do so – but their press release had been extremely compelling.

The people at the table want to call him 'Julian F'. They want to cut his hair just so and dress him in name-brand clothing. They've already begun seeding word of Julian's talents with a number of influential clients, politicians and celebrities – people who will pay top dollar for private consultations and then publicly vouch for the veracity of his claims. They've organised for Julian to have a recurring weekly guest spot on the infotainment news program *TimeWatch with Thomas Cabrera.*

Julian's ears prick up. 'Cabrera?'

'Yes,' says Jianhong.

'Eleuterio Cabrera's son,' offers Waterford.

'He's another one of our clients,' adds Sprouse.

'He was living here when news of the Anomaly first broke – and already working in television!' says Jianhong.

'As a floor camera operator,' says Waterford, 'but still.'

'Now, I guess you could say, he's carrying on his father's work,' says Sprouse.

'What channel is he on?' asks Julian.

Everybody at the table suppresses a delicate laugh.

'We don't really do those here,' Jianhong says.

Julian twists in his chair and faces out the window. The city stares back at him. He tries not to focus on the itch behind his eyes. Julian hates Perth. He feels overwhelmed by the skybridges, the sun reflectors, all the different times, all the gleaming titanium wearable tech affixed to people's eyes and ears and fingers and torsos. He feels overwhelmed by the smells of imported food everywhere, of international cuisine, of custom chemicals, of designer perfume. He feels overwhelmed by the angles of the architecture, the height of the skyscrapers, the density of the crowds, the brashness of the fashion. He feels overwhelmed by the sound of so many languages: Cantonese and Noongar and Bengali and Afrikaans and Portuguese and Farsi and Ngaanyatjarra. He feels overwhelmed by the different shades of skin – in the FREA, complexion-whitening moisturiser had been a hot item at pharmacies (even Ash had partaken on the sly) – but not here. Here, he's overwhelmed by the moving billboards with text crawling in every direction, the giant talking heads beaming in from distant countries saying words he doesn't comprehend about people and places he doesn't recognise. Yes, Julian had been outside the FREA relatively recently, but even in South America he'd avoided the cities wherever possible. He'd shunned marketplaces, band rooms, business districts and anything that seemed too alien, gravitating instead towards rural villages, where he slept in hammocks and on boats and beaches. He'd spent weeks in the jungle or on offshore archipelagos. Julian was naturally inclined towards simplicity and familiarity. Towards comfort. There was a little part of Julian Ferryman that was always trying to go backwards.

On their third night in Perth, Oriana tells Julian she has a surprise for him. (Track 11: 'Surprise Party for a Stranger'.) He follows her from the hotel, keeping his head down as they navigate the city grid. Oriana leads him down an alleyway to an unobtrusive metal door where a bouncer rocks back and forth on his heels, pretending not to hear a trio of young men, clearly too fucked up to be permitted inside, complaining loudly, citing their loyalty to this establishment.

'Evening, folks – how are ya?' the bouncer says, smiling warmly, opening the door for Oriana and Julian and waving them through.

'What are we doing here?' asks Julian as a bald woman with scalp tattoos charges Oriana two cover fees and stamps their wrists.

'It's been a tough few weeks,' says Oriana. 'I thought maybe you'd like to dance.'

Bass rumbles in Julian's chest. Oriana takes him by the hand, pulling him down another flight of stairs and into the belly of the club, into a crowd a thousand strong. There's a low ceiling of red brick above and an apron of sticky floor below, saturated UV blue. A group of shirtless men nearby are passing around poppers. They offer one to Julian and he shakes his head.

'Here,' says Oriana, pulling out a baggy of shardy, sparkly beige MDMA. Julian's heart rate hadn't dropped below a hundred and fifty for about ninety-six hours, so drug-wise, he could take it or leave it. But the music was good. A DJ at the far end of the basement was seamlessly splicing '20s pop-punk, early-'30s cutbeat and Korean trap. As Oriana taps the baggy on the rim of a glass of vodka and soda, Julian wonders when she even had the time to get this gear. She stirs the drink with a finger, downs one half of it, then hands the rest to him.

'Why don't you ever do F?' Julian asks her, straining to be heard over the music.

'Life's strange enough,' Oriana replies, shouting into the depths of his hoodie.

'It's less strange if you know what's going to happen.'

'Maybe I prefer to live in the moment.'

She proffers the glass again. Julian gives the room a quick visual sweep. Old habits.

'You know we're safe now, right?' says Oriana.

Julian kinda nods, kinda shrugs. Knowing was different to feeling.

He takes the glass and necks it, feeling that instant chemical tang on his gums, that ancient gag reflex arcing up then settling down.

Oriana's swaying, tapping one foot. She's looking around at the other women in the crowd. Julian remembers that she's quite a good dancer and suddenly feels bad for being such a downer. Maybe Oriana's been looking forward to this for months. A chance to let her hair down. To remember what all of it was for. Well – she'd only have to wait about twenty-five minutes.

'Sometimes I think about how one day none of this will be here,'

BIG TIME

she says. 'These people, this building, this city, this country. The entire planet. Does that make you feel sad? Or does it make you feel lucky?'

Julian thinks about his lengthier F-trips – how the further you go, the less you feel.

'It doesn't make me feel anything at all,' he answers honestly.

The music switches imperceptibly, shuffling off one beat and stepping into another. Something familiar. Julian's heart rate spikes as he hears Ash's voice, singing:

I got fifteen minutes to fall in love
Twenty minutes to hold you
Twenty-five minutes to start again
For the next thirty minutes it's all you

Tammy's drums had been stripped out, replaced with a slinking breakbeat, and Julian's bass had been tweaked, electrified and expanded with some booming 808s – but there's no mistaking it. The shirtless men begin to leap up and down, arms flung above their heads, sweat flying off them in sheets, chests wet and eyes wide as they scream and chant along:

What time is your heart
It's quarter to three
What time is your heart
Time for you and me

'You've got to be fucking kidding me,' says Julian. They'd never seen a cent from any international sales.

Oriana reaches out and slides off his sunglasses, flipping them around and putting them on her own face.

'Tell me the truth,' says Julian. 'Did Labyrinth fuck us?'

'Oh yeah!' Oriana dances. A staccato sample of Ash crooning *YOU AND M-ME-ME-ME-ME* echoes through the palatial sound system. Oriana drops low to the floor and glides up again, arms twisting, shoulders rolling. Her hair jerks in the haze and falls across her face. She flips Julian's hoodie down and puts her mouth close to his ear.

'But you're under new management now,' she says.

With that, Oriana slides over to the shirtless men, finding a natural position in the centre of their circle and punching the air, hopping up and down as they all shout:

Thirty-five minutes look what you've done
It'll take forty minutes to know you
Forty-five minutes let's have some fun
Now I've got fifty minutes to show you

Almost exactly twenty-three minutes later, Julian throws up in a bin. That's good, that's better. Sometimes that's what you needed to do. The oxygen in his lungs spreads in waves across his body, and the *now* begins to feel exceptionally small and focused. His jaw locks up and his ears start to buzz. His mouth feels extremely clean.

Oriana finds Julian cross-legged under a table, churning his cheeks, drumming a beat on his shins, looking out at the crowd.

'You okay?' she yells.

He says something she can't make out.

'WHAT?'

'Certain people just exist more than other people' is what he said.

'How are you measuring that?' asks Oriana.

'Through legacy.'

'And how do you measure legacy?'

'Memory.'

'And how do you measure memory?'

'Time.'

'And what do we know about time?'

Julian's fingers stop tapping as he loses the beat. He stops talking, as he no longer knows what to say. His eyes stop moving, as he no longer knows where to look. He lies flat on the floor and folds his arms across his chest like a mummy. Oriana goes, dances, comes back. She shakes him but he doesn't respond. She gets a security guard to carry him outside, where the three young men from earlier have given up trying to get in and instead smoke cigarettes in the gutter with their heads on each other's shoulders, talking about all the mistakes they've made and what they're going to do differently from now on.

Julian's locked himself away in his body – closed the door and drawn the blinds and turned the lights off one by one. He remains like this despite all efforts at external stimuli. At the hotel, Sita waves a penlight across his pupils. Oriana plays music from his favourite redacted bands, telling him they could listen to whatever they wanted now. (Track 5: 'Echo Hotel'.) After another three days of not speaking and not eating – three days of monitoring his breathing, changing bedpans, peeling off his clothes and redressing him in terry-towel hotel kimonos – Oriana gets him to a doctor, one sympathetic to their cause. The doctor diagnoses Julian with 'futureshock' and prescribes at least six weeks of supervised convalescence, somewhere quiet and calm, as far from the city as they could take him.

Cuvier Heights was just the place – an oceanfront housing development ninety minutes north of Carnarvon and nine hours north of Perth. Construction had begun more than ten years ago on what would have been the western-most suburb on mainland Australia, but it all ground to a halt when the east closed its borders. Freight companies closed their headquarters and shipping lanes dried up. The Lake Macleod salt mines went into administration, rendering Cuvier Heights' once-strategic location utterly redundant. Shortly thereafter, a tropical cyclone tore along the coast and the entire cliffside promenade went plummeting into the Indian Ocean. An appraisal by external assessors deemed the area dangerously susceptible to erosion, sinkholes and cliff collapses, and therefore uninsurable. The property developers, a pair of brothers who'd initially made their fortune in children's cosmetics, abandoned the project, filed for bankruptcy and moved back to their family home in Rockingham. They found their feet again shortly after, with a new concept for aged-care homes based on the design and dimensions of Japanese capsule hotels.

As you approach Cuvier Heights from the south, this is what you see: an enormous faded billboard with a picture of a girl and her mother standing in the ocean, beneath the words: *A LIFE BY THE SEA IS THE LIFE FOR ME – CUVIER HEIGHTS. ENQUIRE TODAY.* There are twelve blocks of half-built houses, alternating between the 'Janssen' three-bedroom/two-bathroom model and the 'Gaultier' four-bedroom/two-point-five-bathroom model – shuddering timber skeletons capped with rusted iron roofs. There are six perfectly laid and sealed bitumen roads connecting these houses, dotted at intervals with non-functioning streetlights and driveways leading to nothing. There are two completed builds, one Janssen and one Gaultier, which the developers were going to keep for themselves as investment properties. And on a cul-de-sac one block away from the ragged coastline with its fresh limestone wounds there's a fully fitted-out model home, front and back gardens of lush green turf kept alive by an automated sprinkler system that no-one knew the code to. The house runs on solar panels bolted to the roof and a lithium battery humming dulcetly in the garage. This house is a 'Marquis' – the five-bedroom/three-bathroom model – and Julian is in bed upstairs.

When he wakes up – which is to say, when his eyes look anywhere other than directly ahead and his throat emits sound for the first time in days – Oriana is sitting in the corner, drinking coffee.

'There you are,' she says.

Julian blinks and looks around his dwelling. Wood veneer furniture made in India, linen bedding from Bangladesh, framed wall decorations from Portugal, paper chandelier light fittings from Sweden, an air conditioner from Korea, incense from China, coffee beans from Indonesia, floor rugs from Burkina Faso. All the world boiled down into one lifeless six-by-four room.

'Where am I?' he asks.

Oriana tells him about Cuvier Heights – about how her 'friends', as she keeps calling them, swooped in and bought the entire subdivision when the developers were liquidating their portfolio. It was a strategic asset, far from prying eyes but close to working ports and inland airstrips. Oriana says they come here to regroup from time to time, making plans or lying low, normally inhabiting the Janssen and the Gaultier. The one they're in now, the model home, the Marquis – it was now his.

'And don't worry,' she says when his eyebrows twitch at the mention of the recent cliff collapse, 'we had our own people look into it. It'll be years before this block is in any real danger.'

Julian groans, propping himself up on atrophied elbows. 'Could you open a window? I'm freezing.'

Oriana crosses to a set of French doors, leading out to a tiled balcony with views of the hungry, grabbing sea. She cracks them open to a rush of ocean sound. Julian's nose crinkles.

BIG TIME

'It's the salt,' Oriana says by way of explaining the sudden, sharp smell filling the room. 'Syds Bluff, just north of here, was a stockpile for the mines. When the mines closed and the ships stopped coming, all the salt got left behind, cooking away. We use the jetty there sometimes.'

'I'll just rug up.' Julian lies back down and bundles the sheets around his neck. Oriana seals the French doors and the room goes quiet.

'I know you've been through a lot,' says Oriana as she sits again, 'but as soon as you're ready … we need to get to work.' She places a brass vial on the bedside table.

Julian looks at it. His eyeballs feel as though they're reaching from his skull and towards the table, like dying horses in the desert, desperate for water. But he's not going to cave that easy.

'About that,' Julian says. 'I've been thinking. I'm putting my mind and my body on the line for you. I've basically thrown my whole life away for you. Not that I really had a choice.'

Oriana folds her hands, patient as a saint. She must have at least half-expected something like this.

'So I have some new conditions,' Julian says, trying to sound self-assured.

'What makes you think you're in any position to haggle?'

'Because if I refuse to do what you ask, and you dob me in and I spend the rest of my life in a Colombian prison, you're back to square one. I don't want that, and you don't want that.'

Oriana listens.

'I'm going to do everything you ask,' Julian says, 'but your friend Charlie did say I'd be compensated. So I want something that's just for me.' He looks her dead in the eye. 'I want to make an album.'

Oriana nods as she thinks. A petty request, but not impossible. He could have demanded something far more ridiculous and difficult than this. 'I could have some recording equipment set up in the garage.'

'No. It needs to be done in a studio, with proper engineers. I'll need five session musicians, at least six months of rehearsals, three months to record and two months to mix and master.'

A small, bitter laugh escapes Oriana's lips. After everything she's been through the past few years, this is what it comes down to:

negotiating her ex-boyfriend's rider. 'Out of the question,' she says. 'Besides being an enormous and unnecessary drain on our resources, it won't be safe for you in the city once your profile begins to grow. We'd like to keep you here.'

'Okay,' concedes Julian. 'But I'll need the garage properly converted. Sound cladding and everything.'

'That can be done.'

'And five musicians.'

'Three musicians.'

'*Five,*' he insists.

'Three, plus you, is four. The best bands in history had four people in them. You'll make do.'

'Fine,' says Julian. 'Three musicians for six months of rehearsals—'

'One month to rehearse,' Oriana cuts him off, 'one month to record, one month to mix.'

'Three months to rehearse, two months to record, six weeks to mix,' parries Julian.

'Deal.'

Julian's mouth opens, preparing to counter, then closes when he realises he's won. 'Okay,' he says. 'Deal.'

'That's more than you had for *Beaches*,' Oriana says, standing. 'And I'm sure it will be just as good.'

She turns off the air conditioner then cracks the French doors again, flooding the room with salt air.

'You should try to get used to it,' she says as she goes.

Julian buries his head under the covers, hiding from the stench. This house will be the inspiration for the penultimate track on *THE MOTHERF*CKER MANIFESTO*: 'Cul-de-sac', a seven-minute ballad that begins with a simple vocal melody and guitar accompaniment before building in a propulsive percussion line (big toms and a stealthy, expanding snare) as well as one of Julian's only forays into strings (growling cellos and swooning violins). At the five-minute mark it feels like a fitting climax to the album. The song begins to move away from Julian's inward-facing musings and makes way for something bigger. The lyrics are haunting. The strings are ferocious. For a moment, it feels like maybe Julian's going to pull something truly special out of the bag. But then, in the final minute, it all dwindles and evaporates to make way once

BIG TIME

again for Julian, front and centre, on some myopic, falsetto jag. 'Cul-de-sac' ends much like the street where it's written – going nowhere.

22

For the next year, Julian divides his time more or less equally between the *now* and the *then*.

In the *now*, he remains holed up in Cuvier Heights. He oversees the renovation of the garage into a makeshift recording studio, watching more of Oriana's 'friends' staple-gunning foam eggshells to the walls. At first Julian assumes they're members of her militia, but then he figures maybe they're just contractors. The rebellion probably had better things to do. Thorn in the thicket, etcetera, whatever.

He writes the rest of his album. He takes long walks to the salt heaps for inspiration, a duo of nameless bodyguards shadowing him at a distance. He stands on the unstable cliffs and stares out at the Indian Ocean. If he simply started swimming, and could swim for weeks on end, where would he end up? Sri Lanka? Madagascar? He could look it up on the internet and find out for sure, but he'd logged on to the FreeNet (a name locals found amusing) a few times since arriving in the WRA and hadn't liked what he'd seen. There were platforms he didn't know how to use full of slang he didn't understand. There were news stories about hit albums written and produced entirely by AI. One article featured an embedded interview with an aging rock star who'd been big in the Brooklyn scene in the mid-'00s, saying that it wasn't such a big deal, saying that was what we'd all been becoming for the better part of a century anyway, all of us AIs, ingesting everything as data points, training information for the neural net so we could synthesise it and spit it back out in the hopes of making future generations understand how much it had all meant to us. Julian closed the article and disconnected the router from the wall, resolving to use the internet only for emergencies or special occasions. The one time he thought to look up 'JOSE ROJAS INSPECTOR COLOMBIA', he discovered that Oriana had set up the computer's parental controls to block the search results – her own mini-AusNet.

After a week listening to the audition tapes submitted in response to Oriana's fairly cryptic online ad, Julian signs off on a trio of accompanying musicians from Perth. They are blindfolded and brought to Cuvier Heights in an unmarked van for five-day-at-a-time recording stints. At night, Julian peers out at the Janssen and the Gaultier, imagining the musicians inside buddying up with his nameless bodyguards. He quickly clashes with all three musicians, fires them and orders their replacements. Then he clashes with them. Every week, some new ring-in is driven down the desolate roads of the unfinished housing development before being helped out of the van – their blindfold removed, pupils denouncing the sudden, bright sun – and shown to the garage. Some last a few weeks. Some last half a day. It's not that the music was particularly challenging; all fourteen tracks were in standard 4/4 time, and the arrangements were rudimentary at best. It's just that Julian refused to write down a single note or lyric and forbade the other musicians from doing so without ever telling them why. (He was haunted by the drawings in Ash's songbook and never knew when Oriana might be stopping by.)

Every Thursday, Julian himself is blindfolded. His ears are cuffed in white noise-generating headphones, and he is transported (he couldn't be sure, but he believed by air – there was a noticeable lurching sensation in his stomach every time, a feeling he hadn't felt since his flight home from Auckland) to an airless, windowless studio at an undisclosed location to film his weekly segment with Thomas Cabrera. The secrecy, he learns, is because *TimeWatch* is streamed worldwide, 24/7, via a number of unassailable, flawlessly encrypted pirate servers. There isn't a government on Earth that wouldn't instantly and savagely shutter the entire operation, bastion of reckless misinformation that it was, if only they could figure out where it was being broadcast from.

JORDAN PROSSER

Julian is buffed and powdered by a team of make-up artists, then wheeled in front of a lurid green screen live-composited with a shameless full-screen graphic of his new moniker and segment name: *THE SHAPE OF THINGS TO COME WITH JULIAN F.* He is the weatherman of doom, a prognosticator of everything from minor inconvenience to grand cataclysm. The first week, he predicts the outcome of a golf tournament in Dubai. The second, he calls the results of the upcoming Namibian election. The third, he apologises to Agnes Hawthorn of West Bromwich, England, for the imminent death of her beloved cat by automobile accident. The winning golfer is stripped of their title and the Namibian election is overturned, but at least Agnes Hawthorn got a chance to say goodbye.

Pretty early on, Julian has a revelation: instead of splitting from his own perspective during his lengthy F-trips and wandering the globe, seeking out newsworthy titbits, all he had to do was take Oriana's weekly dose of F on a Wednesday, skip ahead far enough to watch his own appearance on Thursday, then snap back, and on the day itself repeat whatever he'd seen himself say. It was a tidy closed loop that required minimal effort on his part but yielded startlingly accurate results.

People are, understandably, mystified. Even Thomas Cabrera himself – who Julian had imagined as some towering Svengali from the way people reverently whispered his name in the *TimeWatch* green room, but was in fact a short, lopsided man with thinning hair and crooked teeth – is endlessly impressed by Julian's predictions. Every week, after Julian wraps his segment, Thomas introduces him to some posse of rich, paranoid hangers-on, most of whom immediately schedule one-on-one consultations with Julian. He goes to their houses all along the west coast (also blindfolded, also possibly by air), drinks their champagne and eats their oysters, tells them their baby will be born with fragile X, tells them their cloud server (bursting with illicit images) will soon be compromised and held ransom, tells them it is most certainly not the time of year to be planting artichokes. Of course, all of these starfuckers, above all else, wish to know when they will die – but Julian has been explicitly warned not to share this information, even if he possesses it, for insurance purposes.

Nevertheless, the clients are happy. Thomas Cabrera is happy. The public seems happy – or if not happy, then at the very least hooked. *THE SHAPE OF THINGS TO COME WITH JULIAN F* is streamed onto giant outdoor screens in town squares around the world and watched by millions upon millions each week. After more bitter bargaining with Oriana, Julian is permitted to perform a small handful of shows at venues in Fremantle, Broome and Margaret River, ostensibly to drum up interest in his solo LP – but the audiences aren't there for the music. They only want to know what he's seen.

'This one's called "Point Perpendicular",' he says mid-set.

'Tell us who's gonna win *The Bachelor*!' someone screams from the crowd.

Data scientists try to poke holes in Julian's prophecies. Betting agencies amass staggering jackpots in anticipation of the day he gets something wrong – but he never does. Julian predicts landslides, mudslides, avalanches, earthquakes. He foretells the San Andreas fault line cracking open and swallowing San Jose. He sees planes falling from the sky, spaceships exploding in orbit, children taken from their homes. He implicates no less than thirteen people from seven different countries in capital crimes (three of them are executed). He recites, in his trademark monotone, the names of winning politicians, overdosing actors, scandalised businessmen. He announces the fate of entire nations in his private school Melburnian drawl and controls global stock markets with the cock of an eyebrow. Many international sporting bodies, having only just returned to some sense of normalcy in the wake of the Cabrera Effect, pre-emptively cancel their entire upcoming seasons. Julian predicts the death of Eleuterio Cabrera himself, only days before the man's seventy-seventh birthday, and announces it live on camera, right beside his son.

In the *then*, things are murky. Julian stops being able to tell the difference between his F-trips and his dreams. He sees himself teetering on the cliffs of Cape Cuvier, the limestone giving out beneath him and the entire housing development collapsing behind him, inhuming him at the bottom of the ocean – then he snaps back with a cough and a shout. He's in his bed, in the upstairs bedroom, an empty eyedropper in his palm, fingers of salted air curling round the cracks of every window. Bad trip or bad dream?

There are footsteps downstairs. Not the bodyguards who never talk to him. Not the musicians who hate him. Not Oriana. Some people have broken in. They're poring over his instruments and his effects pedals. They're looking for his lyrics. They're coming up the stairs. These are people who've been hurt by his predictions, people who've lost money or jobs or pride or love or self-esteem or certainty. People who want things to go back to how they were. They're Central Government assassins, sent by the FREA. Ex-ASIO button men from Old Canberran sleeper cells. They don't kill him, not right away – first they take his eyes. They'll sell one on the black market and donate the other to science. As the air-conditioned air fills up his skull, Julian screams out Oriana's name – then he wakes up. He's in his bed, in the upstairs bedroom. A bad trip *within* a bad dream.

Other times, Julian dreams and knows he's dreaming. He sees the friends he's lost. The life he had. The places he used to go. Xander and Pony's parents' place. The church in Belgrave. The tour bus. The Thebarton. The Enmore. The Fortitude Music Hall. Hotel rooms. Restaurants. Houses and apartments. What does it matter. Walls and floors and roofs and doors. Four corners, right angles, endless time.

Julian grows tired of these dreams.

THE MOTHERF*CKER MANIFESTO is finally finished – four months late, thousands of dollars over budget, and having claimed no less than thirty-four different backing musicians and seventeen separate sound engineers. Julian burns through eight different versions of the cover design, eventually settling, somewhat uninspiringly, on a black-and-white photo Oriana took of him out by the salt heaps, guitar propped awkwardly on one knee. He's squinting in the sun and you can barely see his eyes. The liner notes are much the same, a scrapbook of monochrome snaps of Julian around Cuvier Heights – posing on empty streets, reclining in half-finished houses, peering off cliffs, sporting a scruffy bushranger beard he was immensely proud of – interspersed with the lyrics to all fourteen tracks. As soon as the final master was locked, Julian had feverishly written them all down by hand. He never learnt to write in lower case, so it's all in caps – a booklet of piecemeal libretto shouted at you in photocopied biro. There's no mention of the title anywhere on the album, because Julian's still yet to choose one. ('*THE MOTHERF*CKER MANIFESTO*' will come later.)

BIG TIME

Despite *Beaches*' apparent staying power in the WRA charts, none of that goodwill seemed to translate to Julian Ferryman's solo career. He was sitting on a newly minted album that no-one was interested in playing, let alone buying. It wasn't like back home, where you could write a good hook, drum up an EP, get it played on one of three national stations and become famous overnight. Beyond the borders of the FREA, the music industry was a fickle, complex beast. When Julian laments all this during one of her weekly visits, Oriana coolly informs him that she's kept her end of the bargain. Julian had wanted to record an album – he hadn't stipulated how successful it needed to be.

Julian is reduced to sending handwritten notes, along with home-made versions of the record, to various promoters and record labels based in Perth. In these letters he frames himself as 'the last of the Acceptables', a sort of spiritual Holocaust survivor for the East Australian music scene, while omitting any mention of his day job as a world-famous TV doom merchant. The nearest post box is an hour and a half away in Carnarvon, so he has to ask Oriana's 'friends' to mail them for him – and Cuvier Heights never qualified for a postcode, so for a return address he uses an old warehouse at Syds Bluff, which still inexplicably has a letterbox attached to it, burnt bright blue and dried-blood brown from an infinity spent soaking up salt air. Twice a week Julian walks to the warehouse and checks the letterbox, and twice a week he walks home empty-handed, picking at the scabs beneath his beard, shouting insults at the nameless bodyguards who keep just far enough away to be able to pretend they can't hear him. *They'd like my stuff back home*, Julian tells himself, twice a week. *They'd get it back there.*

Then one day, there's a letter. Julian opens it with trembling hands. It says:

Dear Mr Ferryman,

We were pleased to receive your record, as we are always on the lookout for fresh talent. While we can't promise anything at this stage, we can tell you we're keen to hear more. The next time you perform live, we'll endeavour to send along a representative.

All best,
The team at Labyrinth Records

He sprints back to the Marquis, his bodyguards struggling to keep up, then waits what feels like an eternity (but was actually three hours) (but in the WRA could have been anything) for Oriana to arrive with her weekly F delivery. Except today, Julian refuses to take his medicine.

'Not unless you promise me another show,' he says. 'A headline gig. A thousand seats at least.'

'What's gotten into you?' asks Oriana, not used to seeing Julian this energetic. Normally he would take his F and slink off wordlessly to the rumpus room.

Julian waves the letter in her face. 'It's Labyrinth,' he says. 'They're interested! They said if I play another show they'll send someone along!'

'Labyrinth?' Oriana laughs. 'Labyrinth who withheld your international royalties and basically handed you over to the DID?'

Julian had barely registered that the letter contained no reference whatsoever to his long, fraught personal history with the label, opting instead to categorise him somewhat eerily as 'fresh talent'.

'That was Ash,' Julian says indifferently. 'His music, his agenda.'

'As soon as *In the End* came out, they were planning on dissolving the band and propping Ash up as a solo act. Did you know that?'

Julian doesn't even hear her. 'This is it,' he stresses. 'The last thing I'll ask for. After this, I'll keep doing the other thing as long as you need.'

Oriana scrunches her eyes, a sure predictor of an oncoming headache. She had so many things to worry about besides this – things she knew Julian would never care or even bother to ask about.

'Fine,' she says, sending Julian on a lap around the living room. 'I'll get in touch with the team that did the Fremantle show for us.'

'Thank you,' says Julian. 'Thank you.' He means it.

'As for *the other thing*,' says Oriana spookily, placing a fresh brass vial on the kitchen counter. 'It won't be long now.'

23

The Perth Concert Hall is a skinny mausoleum set two blocks back from the Swan River, dwarfed on all sides by reticulated glass skyscrapers. Tonight, the LED signage above the doors reads:

> ONE NIGHT ONLY
> JULIAN F 'UNPLUGGED'
> (AS SEEN ON *TIMEWATCH*)

Oriana had taken Julian at his word when he'd asked for 'a thousand seats at least'. He plays the new album in its entirety, from start to finish, completely solo, for a stony-faced crowd of seventeen hundred – all of whom remain firmly seated the entire time, in a venue generally intended for classical music recitals or end-of-year graduation ceremonies. When Julian half-jokingly demands that everybody get up and dance, the front-of-house staff immediately order the patrons to return to their seats, so as not to block any access points or fire exits.

Julian hops across the stage as he plays the rapid-fire arpeggios of 'Hugo Valentine'. He sits on a stool and sombrely croons the call-and-response chorus of 'Great Green Nowhere'. For want of a drum kit and strings, he wails the climactic stretch of 'Cul-de-sac' completely a cappella. Julian will never know that it's a fully papered house, the vast majority of the audience being rebel soldiers called away from active duty and explicitly ordered to sit through the entire show.

Julian sits alone in his dressing room afterwards. A stagehand rips his laminated name off the door without realising he's still in there.

'Sorry,' they grunt.

Oriana had left Julian a bottle of champagne, but no-one put it in the fridge – so it's room temperature warm, its glass dark and smooth when it ought to be dewy.

'Gonna drink that whole thing by yourself?'

Julian looks up. Skinner's standing in the hallway, a lanky vampire waiting for an invitation.

'Skinner!' Julian leaps from his chair, lunging at his old manager, wrapping his arms around his torso, feeling Skinner's arms wrap around his.

'Hello, matey.' Skinner pats him on the back. 'Congrats on the show.'

'Thank you!' Julian gushes. 'How are you? What are you– you got out!'

'A few of us did. Which is to say, ah, some did, and others didn't. But boy oh boy is it good to see you!'

Julian leads Skinner into the dressing room, clearing his sweaty clothes off a spare seat. Skinner sits.

'Have you got a tan?' Julian asks, a little rudely.

Skinner laughs. 'I suppose I do. Or rather, I got a very bad sunburn, which might pass for a tan in a day or two.'

'But you look well.'

'Thank you, Julian. I am.'

A noticeable but not unpleasant silence hangs between them, before Julian remembers the champagne. 'Sorry – did you actually want some?'

'Only joking,' Skinner says, raising a palm. 'Still not for me.'

'Of course. Sorry.'

'It's fine.'

The silence returns – still noticeable, slightly less pleasant.

'So you're a real one-man band now,' Skinner says. 'Quite the feat!'

Julian shrugs modestly. He's remembering the last time he saw Skinner. It was almost a year ago, in the trap room at the Fortitude Musical Hall, right after watching Ash's dead body hit the floor.

'So what are you doing here?' Julian asks.

BIG TIME

'I'm here for work, actually—'

'No, I mean, what are you doing *here*?' Julian gesticulates, indicating the entirety of the WRA.

Skinner's eyes go to the floor. He wipes two fingers across his damp brow, then folds his hands in his lap. 'It was a difficult time, after you left.'

Already, Julian wants to jump in and correct him – to make it very clear he hadn't *wanted* to go anywhere – but it's possible that Skinner's been curating this retelling of events for months. So he listens.

'Ash, well … Ash didn't pull through, as you probably guessed. There was a lot of confusion. They kept us in detention for a long time. Dante and I got off with a warning. Tammy, however – well, they had a lot on Tammy. Turns out I didn't know the half of what you kids were up to. So Tammy got sent away.'

'Tammy …' Julian's heart sinks. He imagines his friend, head shorn, freckles popping under the burning Broken Hill sun.

'No, it's okay!' Skinner says. 'She escaped.'

'She what?'

Skinner chuckles, shaking his head. 'She broke out with a few others and spent three months on the run, hiding out in the desert, before some, erm, some *friends* of theirs came to get them. She's somewhere near Townsville now, with her brothers. The most wanted woman in East Australia, apparently.'

Julian sighs contentedly; the moniker felt fitting. Of course Tammy would be the first person in the history of the FREA to actually escape from a work camp and live to tell the tale. He wishes he could sit down with her, fresh pint in hand, and hear every detail. Simply knowing she was safe would have to be enough.

'If she got away,' Julian thinks out loud, 'then what about Pony? Wesley?'

Skinner turns his palms up, empty-handed. 'Nothing, I'm afraid.'

Julian nods. Wishful thinking.

'Anyhow,' Skinner continues, 'Dante and I made our way back to Melbourne with the scientists.'

'Holy shit, the scientists. I totally forgot.'

'They send their regards. With a little help from the label, we managed to get Minnie on a flight back to Auckland. Abel, believe it or not, has decided to stay in Melbourne. Seems he's become quite fond of the FREA.'

'You're joking.'

'Sadly not. He's already made tenure at the state university, teaching physics. Or whatever passes for physics there. He said the student body's overall lack of critical faculties and general pliability actually suited him quite well.'

Julian snorts in mild surprise – then he never thinks about Abel Finnigan again for the rest of his life.

'What about Edwina?'

'She's here with me,' says Skinner.

'Here?'

'Well, here in Perth. She wasn't able to come along tonight, unfortunately. She's, ah, doing some last-minute packing.'

Julian is more disappointed than he thought he'd be at the idea of Edwina shunning his solo show.

'Packing – so she's heading home, too?'

Skinner shifts in his chair then wipes at his forehead again, this time with the full width of one hand.

'Yes. And I'm going with her,' he says sheepishly. 'We leave for Europe in the morning.'

'Europe,' says Julian.

Skinner nods.

'Wait. Are you and Edwina …?'

Skinner was prepared for the question and raises his palm like he's refusing more champagne. 'No, no, nothing like that. I'm flattered, but no. I'm fortunate enough to name Edwina Abbakar as one of my newest and dearest friends. That's all.' His heel taps against the leg of his chair. 'They say it's near impossible to make new friends once you hit forty. But you never know, do you?' Skinner looks around the dressing room with a sudden sense of appraisal, as though he were deciding what to buy. 'You simply never know.'

'And what's in Europe?' Julian asks.

Skinner's eyes flick back to his. 'Galleries,' he says firmly. 'Concerts. Restaurants. Ruins. Dying languages and ancient colosseums. Deep history. The opera. Music and ideas. I've missed those things.'

'So you're retiring?'

BIG TIME

Skinner smiles. 'Something like that. I've spent my whole life berating myself for being a dilettante. Now I'd like to give myself permission to be an aficionado instead.'

Julian cocks his head, a little unsure what this means.

Skinner clarifies: 'Not everyone can *make* things like you, Julian. But what is art without an audience?'

Julian gets it now. 'Falling tree, empty woods, etcetera, etcetera …'

'Etcetera.'

'And what about Ludlow? And Fizz? And Cleo?'

'Ludlow's well,' Skinner says, nodding thoughtfully. 'They moved to a place in the country. A big, old, goldrush-era sort of place with a dedicated dark room. Just their thing. In fact, they made that coffee table book, just like they promised. A tribute to the band. It was promptly redacted, naturally, but you can still find copies if you know where to look.'

'Ludlow,' says Julian, just to hear their name again.

'Felicia's doing quite well for herself, though no-one heard much from her after Cooksland. Seems one job led to another, and now she's fairly high up in the Department of Families and Propaganda.'

Classic Fizz. What a fucking turncoat.

'And Cleo?' Julian asks fondly.

Skinner bows his head, rubbing his wet palms on the thighs of his trousers. Julian feels his shoulders pinch.

'Skinner, what about Cleo?'

'She was sick,' says Skinner, forcing his voice to remain level. 'She had been for a while. That cough. She thought it was, you know, late nights, cigarettes … but it wasn't any of that. It was cancer.'

Julian is appalled. Cancer? In this day and age? Something so mundane for someone so exceptional?

'Ludlow saw her through to the end. Even helped her make a video diary of it all. So that was her, ah, final project. Ludlow was filming her when she, uhm.'

Skinner bites a thumbnail, tugging at the cuticle. The soft flesh comes away, and he bleeds. He sucks at the blood. What he doesn't tell Julian is that Ludlow had helped administer a substantial dose of F every day in the lead up to Cleo's death. Her final work – which would never be exhibited – was titled *Self-portrait Running Out of*

JORDAN PROSSER

Time (after Ren Hashimoto). During her F-trip the day before she died, Cleo saw a shopping mall. It was Christmas in hers.

Julian clears his throat and tilts his head back, hoping Skinner won't notice the shimmer in his eyes. All of a sudden, he wants desperately to be alone. 'Skinner, man, I just remembered there's someone from Labyrinth here tonight, so I should really—'

Skinner, seemingly just as ready for a change of subject, slaps his knee and spreads his hands like a carnival clown. Jazz hands. 'Ta-da!'

Julian chokes. 'You?'

'My final assignment,' Skinner says cheerfully, as though it was just the grandest coinkidink imaginable. 'When I arrived out west, my first order of business was tying things up with the old band accounts. You wouldn't believe the loose ends. But when Labyrinth said you'd contacted them, they figured: who better to go check out the ol' deserter's solo act than his ex-manager?'

Julian swallows. Something in the way Skinner said *deserter* hinted at an emotional process he hadn't previously believed the man capable of: disdain.

So Julian smiles, suddenly on his best behaviour. 'Fascinating,' he says, crossing his legs and tapping his chin. 'And ... what did you think?'

Skinner holds Julian's gaze for a long, long time. Then he says: 'Getting the chance to work with you, and Ash, and Tammy, and Xander, was the most fulfilling experience of my life. Now, I may be just an aging punk. And perhaps I was never really cut out for this industry. But I know a thing or two about beauty. And the four of you had something truly beautiful.'

Having rehearsed this line for twenty minutes in the foyer downstairs, Skinner hopes he landed it in such a way that Julian might remember it always – that he might carry those words as a talisman. Skinner wishes he'd had someone say something like that to him even once in his whole life.

'Back then, at least,' he qualifies, standing and buttoning his blazer. He glances around the dressing room with the same look of appraisal – although now it seems clear he does not wish to buy anything.

Skinner places a hand on Julian's shoulder. 'It's just not the same, is it?'

BIG TIME

Julian hadn't touched Oriana's F in days. Fool that he was, he thought it would be a novelty to experience his concert hall debut without having already seen it first. Now he can't believe that he would ever leave such a thing to chance – that he would let himself be blindsided by real life like this.

'Please,' Julian says. Suddenly he's crying, stealthy tears that roll off his chin and soak into the silent oblivion of the shampooed carpet. 'Please.'

Skinner makes for the door. 'Try to remember why you started out in this game in the first place. It was never for the money, or the fame, or the fans.' He pauses in the hallway and turns to face Julian, who watches him searchingly.

Skinner laughs once, then asks as though it were the most obvious and only real essential question in life: 'Are you having *fun*, Jules?'

Julian's lungs fill his chest and he screams – a gravelly bellow that he feels shredding his vocal cords even as they force it out. He leaps from his chair and slams the door in Skinner's face.

24

'Would you like to see?'

Oriana's lifted one of Julian's headphones. Her voice is in his ear. Behind it, there are chopping waves and rotor blades. Julian nods. Oriana removes the headset, then his blindfold. A stab of vertigo as Julian looks down, suspicions confirmed: they're in a helicopter off the coast of the WRA, ten thousand feet above the churning Indian Ocean. Julian looks out at it, unmoved.

Oriana's face falls a little. She'd expected more of a reaction. Then she realises: 'You've already seen this.'

Julian nods. 'Why do I get to look today?' he asks, going through the motions.

'It's a special occasion,' Oriana says, a little flatly. (Once you knew someone had seen your current interaction play out in an F-trip, there was very little incentive to get too fired up about anything. Even if you made a conscious effort to zig when you may have otherwise zagged, the version of you that this person saw likely had that same idea first. Wherever you went, you were already there.)

Oriana hands Julian a folded piece of note paper. It reads:

Thank you, Thomas. And greetings to everyone at home. Today I want to share with you the most significant events that I have ever witnessed in my journeys through time – events that will commence a few days from now and irreversibly change the course of history.

BIG TIME

Friends – I have seen the fall of the Federal Republic of East Australia. I have seen rebel movements gaining ground in every city. I have seen everyday people rise up and take to the streets. I have seen the scales tip from injustice to justice. I have seen the Central Government overthrown and each department disbanded. I have seen the Leader flee. I have seen the Leader captured and killed. I have seen the meridian wall torn down from both sides, and the reunification of this great country and its people.

I hope by now you all understand how seriously I take my duties here – how blessed I feel to possess this gift and how heavily the responsibility of my calling weighs on me. I would not tell you these things if I had not seen them with my own eyes. To my brothers, sisters and compatriots in the east: good luck. Your time is now. And for once, time is on your side.

'High drama,' Julian says.
Oriana leans in close. 'I'm not going to ask you how today goes. I'm just going to trust you.'
Julian feels their altitude drop. In the distance, on the far horizon, a rectangle of red and yellow steel juts out from the ocean.
'Is that it?' Julian asks.
'That's it,' says Oriana.

Just beyond the jurisdictional reach of the WRA, the Reverie floating liquefied natural gas facility had gone into administration following a series of catastrophic operational issues and crippling union action. After five years as one of the world's most coveted urban exploration destinations, it was briefly touted as an ideal location for an offshore casino, then an aquaculture farm, before it was snapped up by a vaguely named shell corporation and receded from the global imagination. That shell corporation happened to be owned by the same London-based far-right media conglomerate that funded and oversaw the production of *TimeWatch with Thomas Cabrera*.

From the helipad, a short walk down three flights of rusted steel gantries leads you to the main deck. One minute, Julian's looking out across the water in the direction of Jakarta – the next minute, he's being ushered through a set of fire-proof, sound-proof double doors and into the buzzing hub of a live broadcasting studio. This area is all too familiar; Julian's been here every week for the past year. He'd always imagined he was in a bunker somewhere in downtown Perth, or a paramilitary base in the hinterlands north of Albany. But instead he's here on a decommissioned gas rig, along with the harried TV directors, the loud-mouthed line producers, the slovenly camera ops, the energy drink-guzzling hair and make-up teams, the glossy-lipped daytime presenters and the hollow-eyed overnight anchors, smack bang in the middle of absolutely fucking nowhere.

TimeWatch aired twenty-four hours a day, seven days a week, as the modern global TV infotainment news landscape demanded. Thomas Cabrera personally hosted only one primetime hour per day. The remainder of the schedule was fleshed out with various acolytes, conspiracy theorists, televangelists and lengthy online shopping segments.

Right now, a woman named Mercedes Belle is previewing the next half-hour's top stories: 'Coincidence, déjà vu, or time loop? This man swears he picked up his keys *three times* before going to the shops.'

CUT TO: a turkey-necked man in a duplex somewhere near Port Hedland, vamping awkwardly for the camera as it noses around his filthy apartment. 'I was heading out to meet me sister for lunch,' the man says, 'so I picked up me keys and went to head out. Then when I tried to lock the front door, I thought to meself, aw! Where are me bloody keys? So I went back inside, and there they were again, in the big abalone shell where I normally leave 'em. But I swear I'd just picked 'em up! So I picked 'em up. I went to the door. But then I didn't have 'em again!'

CUT TO: a close-up of the offending abalone shell, unaware that at this moment it was provoking a whirlwind of online debate as to whether or not this event constituted an 'official' chronological anomaly.

> *The old fuck's gone batty*
> *It's like when you lose one sock – the other one must go somewhere*
> *How old do you suppose he is*

BIG TIME

> *We measure time through memory – if memory becomes unstable then time does too*

> *Look at this guy's fucking house*

> *Subjective time slip, not a proper anomaly*

> *Isn't it all subjective*

> *Our experience is, time itself is objective*

> *What about relativity*

> *If it's different in two different places then it can't be objective*

> *You're saying his front door and the abalone shell are light years apart???!!*

> *If he forgot them four times then maybe I would consider. Three times not enough*

> *I can't stop looking at this guy's fucking house*

This had become the world's new favourite pastime: picking holes in the continuity of existence. And this nameless, faceless, amorphous online community, many thousands strong, were the self-appointed gatekeepers and taxonomists. While the Cabrera Effect was widely recognised as the first officially observed anomaly – subcategory: *coincidence*; classification: *time loop* – there were also time slips, time steps, time holds and time folds. The classification process could get heated and messy. When one particularly juicy report of Laotian twins aging at different speeds was 'officially' disqualified (one of the children had a run-of-the-mill hormonal disorder), the moderator of that particular subthread had been found dead in their Copenhagen apartment beside a day-old pizza box laced with sarin.

Julian didn't care about any of this in the slightest, although one time when he ventured onto the FreeNet, he searched for his name in the sprawling online anomaly database, finding thousands of pages dedicated to his exploits on *TimeWatch*. In fact, Julian himself had been declared an anomaly – subcategory: *human*; classification: *prophet*. Julian liked that a lot.

Before retreating to the green room, Oriana touches Julian's shoulder. 'If they were here today, I think they'd be proud of what you're doing. Pony and Xander. Cleo and Wesley. Ash. I'm not saying this is the reason for what happened to them, or that it's all been leading up to this moment, or anything like that. But I do think that, after today, we can say that what happened to them didn't happen for nothing. Good luck.'

JORDAN PROSSER

It's the last thing she'll say to him for a very, very long time.

'But first,' says Mercedes Belle, tilting her head towards B-cam, 'we return to our rolling coverage on the disappearance of Helena "Helly" White. Horological hero ... or terrorist in time?'

Helly White was a Canadian physicist who had recently vanished from a nuclear power station near Gwangju in South Korea. When the police began to investigate her as a missing person, comparative image search results returned troves of archival photos from Three Mile Island in the 1970s, Chernobyl in the 1980s and Fukushima in the 2000s. Helly White had worked at all three immediately before their catastrophic meltdowns. What's more, she looked the same in every photo, not aging a day in more than half a century. This made her an anomaly – subcategory: *human*; classification: *time traveller*. The most popular theory online was that Helly White had been periodically sent from the future to sabotage our efforts at perfecting nuclear energy, in order to prevent some other, greater, future disaster.

'Helly fucking White,' a voice snaps behind Julian. His eyes flick up to a make-up mirror, and he looks past the reflection of the hairdresser plying his beard with mascara to where Thomas Cabrera sits in the opposite bank of chairs as another dutiful employee touches up his hair plugs.

'That woman's fucking killing us,' Thomas says to no-one in particular, though knowing Julian can hear him. 'The second we mention her, the message boards blow up. It's all pro-nuclear this, anti-nuclear that. They're digging up thirty-year-old research on renewable energy and it's alienating whole swathes of viewers. Plus it's just deathly fucking boring.'

A PA flutters past with some forms on a clipboard. Thomas scans them, signs them, then places a hand on the PA's thigh.

'Would you find me a coffee, love?' He grins, then shouts as they go: 'A *real fucking coffee*, aye?' Thomas had retained the indefinable accent of his youth – the supple *zh* sounds of an Argentinian father with the harsh consonants of a Scottish mother – all now varnished over by a nasal, open-ended West Australian twang.

'Helly fucking White,' he says again, sneering. 'Hopefully they find the meddlesome bitch in a trash heap somewhere with a pocket full of plastic surgery receipts. Then we can all move on. Find a new lead story. Something non-partisan, but something explosive.'

BIG TIME

Thomas angles his head left then right, assessing his own profile. 'Speaking of' – he winks at Julian in the mirror – 'got anything good for us tonight, pal?'

'I think so,' says Julian.

'Cryptic fucker, aren't you?' Thomas laughs, leaping from the chair and brushing down his expensive pinstripe suit.

Julian and Thomas didn't like each other one bit, but enjoyed a mutually beneficial working relationship. Julian furnished Thomas with the content he required to keep the paranoid rubberneckers of the world in a state of constant anxiety, thus keeping his program on the air and his pockets well-lined. In exchange, Julian had been kept out of a Colombian prison or an East Australian work camp. So he tolerated Thomas for the one hour per week they spent in conversation, even though sometimes, on the days when maybe he'd had an argument with Oriana or a stoush with his band, Julian found himself dying to ask Thomas Cabrera, live on air, whether he believed his recently deceased father would be proud of him.

As Mercedes Belle finishes her segment, the floor manager throws to a secondary stage where a pair of bronzed brand ambassadors exalt the benefits of the new Howzer-Halligan FleshWatch ('because your body knows what time it is!'), and Julian is shown to his lonely stool in front of the dazzling green screen. A sound op gingerly sticks their fingers up his shirt and tapes a microphone to his chest.

'Can I get you to say something for levels?' the op asks, twenty-six hours into a seventy-two-hour shift.

'Hi, I'm Julian F,' Julian says in passive singsong. 'Testing, testing, testing for levels. I put the thorn in the thicket and the ire back in fire, I'm an unbeatable poet and a first-class liar.'

'Bit more?'

'Testing, testing. I regret to inform you that a comet, seventeen kilometres in diameter, is on a direct collision course with Earth. When it makes impact in northern Siberia, it will instantly wipe out the populations of Europe and Asia, plummeting the rest of our world into a period of lightless desolation that will end human civilisation as we know it.'

The op's eyes flick up from their audio monitor.

'I'm just riffing,' says Julian.

The op scuttles away, leaving Julian under the baking studio lights, staring out at the dark hemisphere of camera crew. Thomas sidles up to his desk on an adjacent part of the set and adjusts every item on it to a precise right angle. He gargles something, swilling it between his cheeks, then hawks the liquid into a brass spittoon beneath his desk. Julian wonders how much money Thomas makes. He wonders if he lives here, on the Reverie, in a private suite above the old industrial gas condensers, where seven generations of sea swallows have lurked and bred and cooed and died.

'Forty-five seconds,' says the floor manager. The FleshWatch people on the far side of the studio are wrapping up their presentation.

'Do you think it changes you?' Thomas asks.

Julian realises he's talking to him. 'What's that?'

'The shit you put in your eyes. Has it *altered* you?'

'Altered me how?'

'I don't know. On a molecular level. Can't be natural, can it?' Thomas says with a grimace, like he's glad it's not him down there in the muck.

'Definitely not,' Julian agrees. 'But what is anymore?'

Thomas laughs this off. 'Ah, indeed.'

'Thirty seconds,' says the floor manager.

Julian peers out at the dark studio, his eyes adjusting to the gloom. A familiar silhouette strolls in from the green room and settles by a bank of monitors, watching.

Some part of Julian had resigned itself to appearing on *TimeWatch* every week for the remainder of his natural life. But then Oriana handed him that note in the helicopter, and all of a sudden there were *rebel movements gaining ground*. There were *scales tipping from injustice to justice*. The machinery of Oriana's uprising had clearly reached a critical stage back east, and tonight was what Charlie Total had called – what was it again? – *the defining spark to set the tinder box ablaze*. Julian realises that tonight is his swan song. After tonight, he'd have served his purpose. He'd be free. And with that realisation comes a feeling like the last hour of the last day of school, when you're on the precipice of a new chapter, bold and mischievous and utterly untouchable.

'Fifteen seconds,' says the floor manager.

'You weren't there when your father died, were you, Thomas?' asks Julian.

BIG TIME

Cabrera's jaw sets. His cheeks turn red beneath their thick mask of foundation.

'I told you exactly when it was going to happen,' says Julian. 'I'm sure you could have made it there in time. So why didn't you?'

'Ten seconds.'

'Don't you say another fucking word about my Da,' Thomas seethes.

'Was it because of your show? Were you an embarrassment to him? Is that why you let him die alone?'

Thomas slams an open palm on the desk. 'Listen here, you little fucking shite—'

'AND FIVE.'

The floor manager, powerless to defuse this confrontation in any meaningful way, holds up five fingers, then counts them down, mouthing: *FOUR*.

'Probably just as well he's not alive to see you now,' Julian says, rolling his shoulders back and facing B-cam.

THREE.

'After tonight, you're fucking through,' Thomas spits. 'You hear me, lad?'

TWO.

'That's fine,' Julian says. 'I quit.'

ONE, AND:

The red light on A-cam blinks pleasantly to life, and Thomas's entire face shifts from bitter hate to authoritative concern.

'Good day or good evening, wherever you are – I'm Thomas Cabrera, and this ... is *TimeWatch*.'

A spike of dramatic horn music. C-cam sweeps the studio floor and arrives for a close-up right as Thomas cocks his left eyebrow, a move some sycophantic PR underling once said made him look enigmatic.

'Today, I'm joined by Julian F for another enlightening – perhaps frightening – glimpse into the not-too-distant future. Thanks as ever for joining us, Julian.'

'Thank you for having me, Thomas,' Julian says.

'But first, let's recap. One week ago, sitting where you are right now, you issued a grave warning to the residents of Richfield, Utah, did you not?'

'That's right, Thomas.'

'And what did you tell them?'

'I told them, Thomas, that the serial killer known as the Richfield Ripper would claim another two victims in the days that followed.'

'And did he?'

'Sadly, Thomas, yes – he did.'

Thomas Cabrera cocks his other eyebrow. 'And of course, our deepest condolences to the citizens of Richfield. But what else did you predict?'

Julian dutifully recounts his previous week's testimony. 'I predicted that after those two final killings, the Richfield Ripper would be caught and unmasked, thanks to the diligent efforts of the Sevier County Sheriff's Department.'

'But you went one step further than that, didn't you, Julian?'

'I certainly did, Thomas.' (Julian knew all too well that there was something almost erotic about his exchanges with Thomas Cabrera, a sort of breathless, heated brinkmanship.)

'What else did you say?'

'I said that the Richfield Ripper was in fact Felix Middleton, resident of 296 West Sawgrass Road.'

'And what happened just yesterday, Julian?'

'Felix Middleton of 296 West Sawgrass Road was arrested and charged with all seven murders attributed to the Richfield Ripper.'

Another spike of horn music. Coloured lights sweep the studio, as though a million dollars had just been won and not seven lives miserably lost. On the bank of monitors, Oriana watches the live feed cut to news footage from the Sevier County courthouse steps, as a group of women from the local PTA hurl fresh eggs at a man in a plumber's uniform as he's escorted from the back of a police car and hastened inside. The man was Felix Middleton, and this had been the worst week of his life: first, his apprentice quit and moved to Los Angeles to become a stunt driver; then, some drug-pushing shaman on some shit-stirring pirate TV network announced that *he* was the Richfield Ripper. Felix's mother phoned him from her nursing home, distraught, and his sister stopped returning his calls. Every client he had that week cancelled their appointments, and undercover police cars started following him everywhere he went. Eventually they came to his door, arrested him and interrogated him for seventeen hours.

BIG TIME

Felix said he didn't know nothin' 'bout killin' nobody, but nevertheless, he will spend the next four years on death row before a Hail Mary pardon from the new governor of Utah releases him back into society, a pariah. He will pack up his house on West Sawgrass Road and move to remote central Canada, where in another six years' time he will be gored to death by a mother moose protecting her calves.

'Another incredible prediction come true – and another *Time-Watch* exclusive,' Thomas Cabrera summarises smugly before throwing to a commercial.

I've talked plenty about how distasteful Julian found his duties as a revolutionary – about how trivial he considered the slow-grinding gears of the uprising to be – about how unpleasant he found the world beyond the meridian to be – about how he resented Oriana, and Sita, and Charlie, and the nameless grunts who shepherded him around like some prized mafia accountant, unwilling yet indispensable. But to understand this next part, you need to realise there was at least one thing Julian had come to relish about his life of semi-captivity: the power.

Through his forced regimen of F consumption, Julian's mind was now a muscle that could stretch through time almost at will. His tolerance was sky high, and the level of lucid control he retained while under meant he could go just about anywhere and see just about anything. Though outwardly he scorned the punters at his poorly attended concerts when they demanded to know the results of the weekend footy or their dear grandma's diagnosis, inwardly Julian savoured the sway he held over these people. He loved having what everybody else wanted. Simple as that. He loved drip-feeding it or withholding it altogether. Julian had been cornered into doing what he was doing, yes – but in being blackmailed, wasn't there also some perverse kind of reverse empowerment? Once the terms had been set, it was all up to him. He could follow his instructions to the letter, but he could just as easily decide to burn it all down.

Charlie Total thought he had something on Julian? Now Julian Ferryman had something on everybody.

*

The red light on A-cam blinks back to life. Thomas turns to Julian. 'Over to you,' he says.

The crew members standing out past the halo of studio lights lean forward on their toes. At the monitors, Oriana crosses her arms, fingernails digging into her skin.

'Thank you, Thomas,' Julian says. 'And greetings to everyone at home.' He speaks from memory, except he'd memorised what he was about to say long before Oriana had handed him that note. 'Today I want to share with you the most significant events that I have ever witnessed in my journeys through time …'

Thomas, prone most weeks to playing on his phone or massaging his bunions while Julian was performing, listens intently.

'I'll miss this,' Julian says abruptly, going off-script. 'This is my final appearance, after all.'

Muttering in the studio. The message boards blow up invisibly in the bandwidth. Julian feels Oriana's hard stare. He looks to Thomas, casually seeking confirmation.

'Right, Thomas?'

The host plays along. 'Why, yes! A great loss to the *TimeWatch* family.'

Julian lingers, looking at Thomas, whose eyes go large, seeming to say: *get on with it*.

The studio is silent. Julian can smell the dust cooking on the lighting grid above. He can sense the sweat running down the backs of every crew member whose livelihoods and futures depended on whatever he said next.

'Today,' Julian says, 'I want to share with you the most significant events that I have ever witnessed in my journeys through time – events that will commence a few days from now and irreversibly change the course of history.'

Knowing that not a single person on Earth has the power to stop him, Julian pauses just long enough for his eyes to find Oriana, silhouetted in the shadow of the monitors. He looks straight at where her face would be. He looks long enough to know with absolute certainty that she's looking back at him. Then he says:

'Friends – I have seen my forthcoming, debut solo LP turn triple platinum within the first month of its release, breaking every known sales record in the WRA and landing in the top ten of every major album chart worldwide. I feel humbled, grateful and immeasurably blessed. Today, I feel as though time is truly on my side.'

25

Julian flies home alone, just him and the helicopter pilot, who stays mute for the entire journey, visor facing staunchly forward. When they arrive in Cuvier Heights the following morning, the entire development is deserted. The Janssen and Gaultier, normally host to a rotating roster of rebels, bodyguards and jaded musicians, are empty – stripped of every piece of furniture and every scrap of food. The garage batteries have been powered down and the cars are all gone.

'Hello?' Julian shouts into the Janssen, instantly reminded of just how hostile a voice can sound inside a vacant house.

Julian walks down the cul-de-sac, approaching the Marquis, and is relieved to find it still sealed and untouched. The blinds are drawn. The air-con hums. He goes to the fridge. It's morning, but a significant morning. A morning to remember. He cracks a beer.

'What did you do?'

Julian chokes on his first sip of lager and turns to find Sita, seething at him from the unlit dining room. 'You stupid shit. What did you do?'

Julian had expected this. He knew he'd have some explaining to do, so he starts reciting the line he'd prepared: 'I understand you're upset. I broke my end of the bargain. But the way I see it, I didn't have a choice. This was the only way I was ever going to reclaim any power in our arrangement.'

'I told her,' Sita says. 'You're a nasty little weasel. I tried to tell her all along.'

BIG TIME

'What you're overlooking,' Julian says as he approaches the dining room, hands outstretched, coming in peace, 'is how this benefits you and your cause, long term. I've put you in a tight spot. I get that. You and Oriana have a lot of work to do if you want to uphold the illusion that *all* my predictions come true. But rebellions need money, right? Well, I am but a humble artist. I'm willing to settle for 40 per cent. Leaving you with 60 per cent of the profits from the most profitable album of the year. It'll keep your outfit afloat for decades.'

'It's already been a decade. It was not supposed to take *more decades*.'

Julian can tell Sita's been crying. Now she's controlling her breathing, exhaling through pursed lips. Still, Julian feels she's not being quite as receptive as she ought to be, given the opportunity he's presenting her with.

'I know,' he says, feigning remorse, stepping right up close. 'And I'm sorry. But some things take as long as they take.'

Sita strikes Julian across his left cheekbone. His head snaps to the side. He feels the skin open up, a clean incision from one of Sita's bronze rings, and before he realises he's even dropped it, his beer is on the floor.

'SORRY?' Sita wails. 'You have no idea what it means to be sorry. You know no loss. You know no shame. You know nothing but your own tiny, pathetic ambition.'

'HEY!' Julian roars, his whole body shaking. 'I've lost plenty!'

Sita stabs a finger at him. 'Tell me the truth: did you actually see your "forthcoming, debut solo LP turn triple platinum within the first month of its release"?'

'I saw myself say it would.' Julian shrugs, like that's good enough.

'Exactly,' Sita hisses. 'You can move through time, Julian. You can see anything you want to see. But the only thing you care about seeing is yourself.'

'I couldn't go on like that. I had to do something.'

'People gave their lives to get where we are today,' Sita growls, advancing on him. 'But you ... you want to repurpose an entire revolution to promote your vanity project.'

'I did say there was money in it.'

Sita hits him again, with the other hand, on the other cheek.

Julian shrinks back, holding his arms up in a feeble boxer's stance, ears ringing.

'THE MUSIC IS SHIT!' Sita howls, a brittle sound halfway between a giggle and a scream. 'Even if we had the time, or the resources – THE MUSIC IS SHIT!'

Julian folds his arms, attempting defiance. 'Where's Oriana? I want to speak to Oriana.'

Sita laughs, gathering a few items from the kitchen counter – loose documents, maps, sensitive stuff. 'You won't be seeing Oriana again.'

This thought had not occurred to Julian. 'That's not good enough,' he stammers. 'I need to speak with her.'

'She's busy,' says Sita. 'Cleaning up your mess. Then she'll be busy starting over.'

'We're talking about the fate of a nation here, and she won't even grace me with a face-to-face?'

'Don't you get it?' Sita snarls, grabbing Julian's shirt and pulling him close enough that he can smell the coffee and nicotine on her breath, so close he can see the veins popping in her moist, bloodshot eyes. 'You broke her heart today. For the second time.'

'So what about …' Julian wonders how to ask. 'What about Inspector Rojas?'

Sita relinquishes her grip suddenly, hands springing open as though she'd just realised the lunchbag she was holding was full of maggots.

'Oriana's call,' she says. 'As far as I'm concerned, we've wasted enough time on you.' She begins to head for the door.

'I have to see her sometime!' Julian shouts, following after. 'I mean, what am I supposed to do now?'

Sita turns back to Julian, patience worn to the nub. 'Make another album. See the world. Write your memoir. I couldn't give less of a shit. It's got nothing to do with us.'

'Sita, hold up. This is crazy—'

'You're cut off, Julian. Our business is concluded. No more PR. No more bodyguards. You can stay here for as long as you like. But you're on your own.'

Julian's stomach drops like he's back in the helicopter. 'You can't do that,' he stutters. 'I'll die out here.'

BIG TIME

'Try not to, I guess,' Sita suggests generously, kicking the front door open and marching towards a waiting Humvee.

'This is *bullshit*!' Julian screams as he races out after her, battered by the wind and heat.

'Good luck, Julian,' Sita says. 'And from the bottom of my heart: go to hell.'

26

With Oriana gone and her cronies all gone – without his weekly trips to the *TimeWatch* studios, or eavesdropped updates regarding rebel movements back east – for Julian, it felt as though time was finally gone, too. The bedside clock radios died and the battery in the garage would blink on and off, so the digital clock faces on the oven and the microwave were constantly resetting. Julian never got a smartphone, never got the TV connected and had asked for the house's FreeNet connection to be severed. He cut up the wall calendar to make a set of solitaire cards. He traded his wristwatch at a roadside fruit stand for a carton of mangoes. He ate one, fell asleep, and the next morning found the rest flourishing with periwinkle-blue mould.

Julian had no more seconds, minutes, or hours. No more days, weeks, or months. What Julian did have was the sun and the moon, the day and the night, short days and long days. He had changes in temperature and switches in the wind – times when it swept in from the sea, brimming with salt tang, and other times when it carried the asphalt dust of his cul-de-sac back out across the thousands of kilometres between him and Madagascar.

Julian also had his own body – changing, calcifying, deflating. Decay created its own kind of time. He shaved his beard and dyed his hair so he wouldn't be recognised when he hitchhiked into Carnarvon, but knew roughly how long it took for his roots to grow out and his beard to grow back. After a while, he abandoned this ruse; his face and body had changed so much there was no longer any danger of being stopped for an autograph or a photograph or

BIG TIME

an impromptu augury. He felt his feet swell, his knees crumble, his chin sag, his teeth ache. Whiskers grew from his ears and nose. Skin tags grew in places he could not reach. The pockets of fat on his hips ballooned outward, even as his calves and upper arms shrivelled with malnourishment.

Occasionally he would receive letters to the warehouse at Syds Bluff, asking him to perform at weddings, birthday parties, bat mitzvahs, asking him to say something promising about the future, to grant a good omen to the lucky couple or boy or girl. He never replied to any of them. He had no good omens left to share and nothing nice to wear.

He retained a small number of personal clients – celebrities, bankers and career criminals – who were willing to overlook his final, failed *TimeWatch* prediction. They would make the journey to Cape Cuvier and sit beside Julian as he soaked in his bathtub, skipping ahead and snapping back and telling them the truth about what he'd seen. They left him offerings of tinned food, paper and pencils, matches and candles, a new set of sandals. And always more F, as elusive a commodity in the WRA as it was in the rest of the world. Without Oriana's endless supply, Julian told his clients that that was what he needed most – more than tinned spaghetti or colouring-in books or board games. He stockpiled litres and litres of the stuff, and when his clients visited again, he would ask them for more. Occasionally, they would gently suggest that Julian accompany them to the city, to go shopping for new clothes, to get a haircut, to see a doctor – they asked if he would like them to contact anybody on his behalf – but he turned it all down. So they left him alone, and eventually, stopped coming. The celebrities had become criminals, the bankers had become celebrities, and the criminals all went clean.

When he wasn't in town haggling for supplies to maintain his rapidly declining house, or draping a washcloth across his eyes and whispering prophecies to clients, Julian tried to see just how far he could skip ahead. There were only two times in Julian's life when he'd thought he was dying – once when his mother tickled him so hard he began to choke, and once when he'd gripped the frayed cord on a set of Christmas lights – so he was familiar with the sudden, jarring sensation of coming so close to your own mortality you could no longer focus on its features. But he never got that feeling taking F, no matter how far he went. Even as the months, years and decades passed by, and Julian began to approach the upper limit of a male human lifespan, never once was he afraid. In fact, he was eager for the day when he would see himself tumble down the steps from his solitary bedroom, or collapse from a heart attack out by the salt heaps, or break a hip in the shower and die slow beneath a cold stream of water, or be ambushed and arrested by Inspector José Muñoz Rojas, flown to Colombia, tried and sentenced, tossed in prison, his skull caved in by a gang of fired-up inmates who remembered 'Julian F', only to be instantly resurrected in the glass hallways of his own celestial shopping mall. But these visions never came. Julian skipped ahead weeks, months – on one occasion, he was fairly certain he skipped ahead at least three years, because after he snapped back, that's how long it felt like he was sleepwalking through life, following dazedly in his own footsteps.

Plenty of people say they can see the remainder of their life stretching out before them – an uninterrupted, unnervingly straight line that persists, and persists, then begins to putter and peter out. But only Julian had literally seen such a thing. The further he went, the more certain he was that there was nothing to be afraid of – but also not much to remark upon, either. Because the further you go, the less you feel. That's true of everything.

Julian visits the cliffs almost every afternoon, in the blazing sun or the cyclonic rain, willing them to crumble at his feet and consign his solitary spit of land to the silent sea floor. He spends an indeterminate stretch of his life attempting to write a piece of music with no time signature, attempting to free the thing he still loves the most from the thing he likes the least. Convinced it will be his magnum opus, Julian handwrites hundred-thousand-word dissertations on the subject and mails them to academic institutions. He calls upon world-renowned experts in musicology and chronophenomenology to join him in this grand experiment, but receives no reply.

His waking hours become unmoored from day and night. He thinks himself a bear – prone to annual bouts of hyperactivity and hibernation. When he does sleep, he has a recurring dream in which he is invited to perform at the Palais in Melbourne. A solo show. A

BIG TIME

sold-out house. Just him and his guitar in front of a thousand rapt strangers.

I'm here, he says to them. *I know what you want.*

When he's awake, he practises his stage banter in front of the mildewed ensuite mirror: puffy eyes, greying beard, liver-spotted scalp of thinning hair. *Everyone's so scared of things happening the same way twice*, he jokes for his home crowd. *But that's all I've ever wanted!* Laughter, applause. *It's so good to be back. I think* this *is what the party really means.*

Julian pawns off most of the recording equipment in the garage, but keeps one guitar. He plucks a string and it kicks up a straight line of dust, suspended in mid-air for one perfect split second. Words come to him – the last lyrics he'll ever write:

I guess the things you said don't sound the same when you're older
And I guess the things you loved don't look the same over your shoulder
And I guess it all ends feeling a bit smaller and colder—

He's cut off mid-sentence, distracted by a seagull.

Later that day, Julian announces his official retirement from music to the empty housing estate. He dismantles the guitar and uses the wood for a fire. Then he draws himself a bath, delivers an even stream of petrol-sheen *trypto-lyside glutochronomine* to each eyeball and watches the next rotation of the Earth unfurl.

27

Elena Rojas was in her sixties when she found the man who killed Brayden Byrne.

She never planned on becoming an inspector, and her father never asked her to carry on his work – but we inherit all sorts of things from our parents. Some when we're born, others when they die. When she was born, Elena inherited her mother's hair, coiled and untameable, and her father's eyebrows, heavy and quizzical. Eyebrows that could make people talk. When her father died, Elena would inherit his final obsession.

She'd wanted to be a sculptor. She had grand plans to spend the break after secondary school working in her Auntie Gabriela's shop before travelling north, spending a few months in Mexico City then trekking up to America. Los Angeles. She wanted to sculpt the monsters she would sometimes see in her dreams, enormous alien figures of bronze and brass. She imagined a red-brick loft in Koreatown, second-hand invites to parties at rappers' houses, champagne, ribbon-cuttings at galleries, a retrospective coffee table book. She could see it so clearly. Her parents still thought she was going to study medicine, but Elena figured she had time to gently sow the seeds of her true ambitions with them.

One night, a few weeks before finishing school, she and her friends took their scooters around the city, whisking through the streets of El Poblado, bodies carving through the still mountain air. Elena sat behind her boyfriend, Angelo, hands wrapped tight around his waist, savouring the feeling of his slender deltoids and the smell

BIG TIME

of his cheap teenage deodorant just a little while longer. She would have to sow those same seeds with him at some stage – but not tonight. They weaved through the scattered late-night traffic. When they stopped at a red light, Elena looked in the back of a taxi cab and saw a young man, some gringo with jagged hair and leather bangles and a loose-knit sweater, looking out at her as though he'd found her in a museum. Elena held his gaze and smiled. That night, she had nothing but love for him, and for all the inhabitants of her city.

Her father didn't come home from work the following morning, and didn't come home that night, either. Another full day passed before he finally returned, slipping off his boots and unsheathing his tie and dropping them by the doorway, wordlessly downing a full cup of coffee in the kitchen before taking himself upstairs to bed. The coffee helped him sleep; twenty years of homicide, half of that night shifts, had entirely inverted his metabolism.

An Irish tourist had been killed in La Candelaria, not fifteen minutes from where Elena and her friends had spent the night on their scooters, kissing the balmy air and soaking up the ultraviolet petrol fumes. Her father had spent two days canvassing the neighbourhood, knocking on doors, asking after suspicious characters, requesting access to CCTV footage from petrol stations and convenience stores, all to no avail.

The young man's name was Brayden Byrne. Early twenties. On a post-graduation jaunt with his mates from the University of Galway. They'd all seen him earlier that day, when he'd announced he was going to get groceries. Later, after Elena's father deployed his infamous eyebrows, they sheepishly admitted that he'd gone to get more gear. Par for the course with their kind in that city. But what kind of gear he'd gone to get, and from where, his mates didn't know and couldn't say. Honest to God, on their mothers' lives, they said – they didn't know.

The coroner ruled it an accidental homicide. There was a single trauma wound on the side of Byrne's head – not enough to do the job on its own, but he'd likely passed out from the impact and subsequently bled to death. A toxicology report found traces of cocaine in Byrne's bloodstream, as well as some other, unidentifiable substance present in the aqueous humour of both his eyes. The coroner took samples and sent them to Bogotá for further analysis.

JORDAN PROSSER

When Elena finished school, her father held her tight and kissed her forehead and told her he was proud of her, then immediately returned to work. The Brayden Byrne case had become an all-consuming affair, and Elena's father was under enormous pressure from the Ministry of Defence to find the perpetrator(s?). The murder rate in Medellín remained a sticking point for the international media, and the last thing the General of the National Police wanted was to appear to be standing idly by while some gang of thugs bludgeoned upper-middle-class European tourists to death.

Brayden Byrne's friends were interviewed again and again, their every movement, purchase and proclivity since the moment they arrived in Medellín scrutinised incessantly. Their passports were confiscated until Elena's father was satisfied they held no further useful intel, at which point they were released and put on a flight back to Dublin. After that, it was back to their parents' houses, then their university dorms, where they drank yard glasses of lager and cried their eyes out over the mysterious death of their awkward, loveable friend. Brayden. Strawberry-haired and scrawny-necked. Bony-shouldered and blue-eyed. Drug-loving but booze-averse. He'd wanted to be a maritime lawyer.

After Byrne's friends left Colombia, no new suspects filled the void. Elena would glimpse her father in his study at 2 and 3 and 4 am, scrutinising the autopsy report, cross-checking the location of the public restrooms where Byrne was found with reports of known gang activity. He would return to the alleyway in La Candelaria, sometimes at dawn, sometimes in the thick of night, to appraise it from different angles and in different light. He hounded the lab in Bogotá for news of the substance found in the dead man's eyes, but they'd failed to match it with any known pharmaceutical, legal or illicit. Soon they'd have to release the body to be repatriated across the Atlantic, and it would take its secrets home with it.

Elena asked her father about the case one night over dinner, when her mother had finally managed to lock her husband down to belatedly celebrate their daughter's graduation. Elena's father had always hated losing things – keys, socks, trinkets deeply sentimental or utterly disposable – it didn't matter what it was, he couldn't stand the thought of something still existing somewhere just beyond his reach. Things don't just *stop existing*, he proclaimed after a few too

BIG TIME

many Apóstols. That's the law of conservation of matter. You must have learnt about it in school, Elena. That means people don't just disappear. Nothing's ever really lost. Things persist, just past our perception. Beyond consciousness, or outside of time. Every lost thing we resigned ourselves to losing. Every culprit in every cold case. They're all still out there, hidden. An infinite string of missing things. If only we had the right tools, and enough time, to find them.

The weeks wore on. The school break came and went. Elena failed to mention anything about Mexico, or Los Angeles, to her family. Time dulls even the sharpest plans. She worked in her Auntie Gabriela's shop, often coming home to find her father napping on the couch, or passed out in one of their worn leather armchairs, or pacing in the study, forming a rut in the rug as he smoked his pipe, turning on his heel, further considering the impossible. He was sent to Ireland as a special envoy from the Colombian government to accompany Brayden Byrne's remains. A gesture of good faith. A sign of penance. A symbolic apology for sending one of their countrymen back in a box and a silent scapegoat to stand in the corner at the funeral before milling about uncertainly in the home of the Byrne family, sipping tea and Jameson's with a view of the Celtic Sea.

When he returned home the following week, Elena asked her father what Ireland was like.

'Cold and green,' he said.

A year later, Elena's father suffered a massive stroke in the fruit and vegetable section of their local supermarket. He was still stuck on the Byrne case, but it was his day off, and he'd resolved to make an effort to help his wife with the meal prep for the week ahead. He sagged suddenly to the left and dropped his shopping basket, scattering half-a-dozen limes across the polished tile floors. He gripped the side of a goldenberry display to steady himself, but his legs gave out, meaning that was the last image his brain formally formed and recognised: the soft orange spheres of the fruit, static and ripe, soaking up the supernatural supermarket lighting.

The stroke was a by-product of two earlier heart attacks he'd had in his late forties, which in turn were by-products of a weakened aorta, which was a symptom of the same condition that had led to the surgical complications that killed *his* father at around the same age and would likely kill Elena one day. A hereditary quirk of the bloodstream. Dumb luck and circumstance. Must we inherit everything?

They kept him on life support and surrounded him with flowers, turning him into a shrine to himself. Elena sat with him and held his hand, singing a song he used to sing to her when she was little:

The bridge is broken
How do we fix it?
With egg shells
Little donkeys in the meadow

Let the king pass
The king must pass
With all his little children
Except the one at the end

Even after they switched off the machines and the hospital room drowned in silence, Elena had the sense that her father was still there, somewhere just out of reach. Beyond consciousness, or outside of time. Strange, thought Elena, how something that killed thousands of loved ones every year could still hit you as though you were the only one.

That night she lay atop her bed, listening to the rain soar in from the mountains and breach the gutters on the roof. The light from her laptop screensaver painted the ceiling a sickly, dancing blue, a meaningless kaleidoscope changing colour every minute.

Then her screen blinked to life with a message in a nondescript window:

> *Sorry for your loss*

Elena stared at the message, resisting the urge to immediately assume this was her father's chosen means of contacting her from the afterlife. Once she'd played out every permutation of that scenario in her head and set it aside, she wrote back:

Thanks.
> *It's hard to lose a father*
Elena typed: *It is.*

BIG TIME

Then she waited. She waited so long she fell asleep, but when she woke the next morning, there was a new message:

> *I know who did it*

Elena scoffed, then yawned. A sick joke, then. Some idiot kid pulling a prank.

He died of a stroke, estúpida.

The cursor moved.

> *Not your father – the Irish boy*

Elena sat up quickly, feeling the night's fitful sleep pooling and stiffening in the muscles of her back.

> *I'll tell you one day*

Tell me now, typed Elena.

> *I'll tell you when you're ready*

How do I make myself ready?

> *Up to you – I'll be in touch – time is on our side*

The next morning, Elena took a bus to Bogotá and joined the police academy.

These mysterious messages would find Elena Rojas intermittently throughout the decades that followed – as she graduated from the academy, as she moved back to Medellín, as she climbed the ranks of the *Dirección de Seguridad Ciudadana*, as she got married and divorced, then married, then divorced, as she miscarried one child and aborted another, as she watched her mother die and watched her own hair turn grey and watched countless murders go unsolved, and got suspended without pay and suspected of corruption and investigated by internal affairs and eventually cleared of all wrongdoing, and adopted a cat and then found the cat dead and then cried for the cat even longer than she'd cried for her mother, and managed to get away on just one decent vacation, just once, on her own, to Puerto Vallarta.

In the midst of all this, when Elena asked what she should call them, the messages replied:

> *Call me Mal Vivante*

Like Malcolm? wrote Elena.

> *No – it's a joke*

Mal was Elena's phantom pen pal. They would talk about life. They would talk about fathers. Mal would offer Elena advice –

sometimes vague and philosophical, other times frighteningly specific. It was Mal who gave Elena the tip-off that ultimately cleared her of any wrongdoing in the death of a fellow inspector. It was Mal who then gave Elena *another* tip-off unequivocally implicating one of her *other* colleagues in the murder. *That* colleague happed to be Elena's second ex-husband. She chalked this up as a win for her instincts.

When Elena grew impatient and was reminded of Byrne – after a case involving a dead foreigner, or on nights when she woke clutching at dreams of her father – she would hassle Mal, threatening to cut them off if they didn't tell her what they knew.

> *It won't be long now*, Mal replied carefully, a promise which became increasingly true as life passed by.

One week after her retirement from the force (flaccid coloured streamers, half-inflated balloons, a sodden *tres leche* cake in an air-conditioned ballroom, not quite enough close friends present for a person who's lived a life), Elena's phone pinged on the coffee table.

> *Happy retirement – here's a little gift – I'm sorry it took so long*

Elena waited, then saw a video tab appear on-screen. Pressing play, she watched a loop of grainy footage from the alleyway in La Candelaria – the alleyway her father had paced countless times in the year before he died. In the footage, a familiar, scrawny-looking tourist loped into the public restrooms. Then a second man appeared from the opposite direction and went inside as well. A minute passed. The second man left in a hurry, but the first man – Brayden Byrne – never came out.

> *Bonne chance*, wrote Mal Vivante, signing off forever.

A rudimentary facial analysis made quick work of the video. With 99.99 per cent certainty, it identified the man in the footage as Julian Ferryman, better known as 'Julian F'. Decades ago, Ferryman had become notorious for making a string of unnervingly accurate predictions on a pirate infotainment network that had been raided and shut down not long after he stopped appearing on it. Prior to that, Ferryman had been the bass player in a bygone East Australian rock outfit called the Acceptables, whose debut album had become something of a sleeper hit around the time Elena was finishing school and her father was working the Byrne case. She remembered that period well – the Cabrera Effect and those so-called 'Heaven Tapes'. Back then, every day brought fresh reports of freak occurrences and unexplained phenomena. New branches of science were springing up overnight to question the nature of our reality and the omnidirectional flow of time. People were consumed by it. In her first few years on the job, Elena tended to countless homicides where the perpetrators' only motive was a devout suspicion that the deceased was a 'hostile traveller' or a 'loop gremlin', or had caused a supposed 'misalignment in temporal flow'. These armchair chronophenomenologists had picked up this vocabulary from commentators like the disgraced Demetrice Pham, or from programs like *TimeWatch*, osmotically absorbing that day's delusions then regurgitating them back out into the world. And it had all been underscored by that one band's catchy, innocuous pop ballads.

But live long enough and you realise people can get bored of anything – bad news, good music, anything. That era's obsessive, incendiary analysis had eventually died down to background static, and the niggling question of time's fidelity became just another daily worry, rank and file with all the rest. One more thing to keep an eye on. Something to be dredged up when politically or socially convenient, but more frequently overshadowed by some other new, more exotic, more persuasive and more profitable perceived threat.

Elena considered herself more of a spiritual person than a religious one, but it's possible some of her mother's lifelong piousness had rubbed off on her. Because during those years when the world was shadow boxing with chance, quaking at the slightest whiff of serendipity, Elena had never joined in, never once partaken in that glorious global communion of fear. She'd looked at all those dreaded 'anomalies' driving everyone ragged and mad, and thought to herself: *Imagine being so ungrateful for a miracle.*

These days, Elena mostly heard the Acceptables' music played on pianos in lounge bars, over speakers in department stores, or in the roar of a drunken office worker's Friday night karaoke, its edges smoothed over and its verses forgotten – nothing left but hooks and choruses. The homogenised graveyard that all success points to: comfortable nostalgia for strangers.

JORDAN PROSSER

*

Immigration records indicated that Julian Ferryman was born in what would become the Federal Republic of East Australia. He visited Colombia in his mid-twenties and departed on the day Brayden Byrne died. Six months later he popped up in the Western Republic of Australia, playing a handful of solo concerts around the same time he started appearing on *TimeWatch*. A year after that, he dropped off the face of the Earth and hadn't been seen or heard from since – almost half a century later.

Elena wasn't stupid. She knew that in all likelihood, Ferryman was long gone. A wanted fugitive from a notorious rogue state who'd spent a full year broadcasting prophecies that ruined lives and destabilised governments? There must have been millions who wanted him dead and even more who couldn't care less if he was.

Elena sat on her sofa, cracking her knuckles, slugging the last of a bottle of *aguardiente*, eyeballing a bursting scrapbook's worth of clippings and printouts she'd arranged chronologically across her living room floor. Next to some grainy enlargements of Ferryman's face in that cursed La Candelaria alleyway was the coroner's report, including the mysterious toxicology findings that her father had once sent to Bogotá for analysis. She'd called in a few post-retirement favours and gotten the lab techs in the capital to rerun their archived samples, and what had once been unclassifiable was now clear as day: the substance in Brayden Byrne's eyes when he died was *trypto-lyside glutochronomine*. During his run on *TimeWatch*, 'Julian F' had been the drug's unofficial mascot, but to this day it remained all but impossible to acquire anywhere outside its purported place of origin: the FREA.

Elena had spent the last ten years suspecting, even anticipating, that she would drop dead at any minute. She was still one heart attack short of her father at the same age, but figured it couldn't be too far off. That might have been why she'd never married a third time, or bothered to get another cat; if there was one thing a life in homicide had taught her, it was how much paperwork death brought with it. She'd just as soon spare somebody else the trouble a little down the line.

If searching for Julian Ferryman was the last thing Elena Rojas ever did, she'd have to make her peace with that. And so, with a mountain of evidence at her feet and a floundering heart in her chest, Elena packed her bags and booked a one-way ticket to the WRA.

In Perth, Elena was quickly reminded, then reminded many times over, that she was a retired foreign police inspector with no jurisdictional authority. She was stonewalled by government officials, sent in circles by automated assistance kiosks, left on permanent hold by music-industry PAs and banned from multiple libraries and archives when she tried to illegally copy or smuggle out materials. For months, she attempted to locate Julian Ferryman's old friends and bandmates – but those who hadn't literally perished on stage had likely died in work camps, along with many of the FREA's artists and activists. A small handful of his associates had fled the country and disappeared for good, while others remained to fight for the resistance. One of Ferryman's ex-girlfriends currently held the record for the longest active Interpol red notice and still ranked high on every major global terrorism watch list.

There was a well-established cottage industry for adventure tourists hoping to sneak into the FREA, to steal concealed-camera pictures of the work camps and emaciated citizens, to eat the strange, tasteless foods, to marvel at the byzantine technology. Elena tried to arrange similar passage, but the people smugglers and brokers she engaged either disappeared in action or took her money and vanished.

Six weeks after arriving in Perth, Elena found herself drunk on Margaret River cabernet in a hotel bar, vaguely repulsed by the crooning sounds of the cover band occupying the corner stage, but feeling too woozy and too old to make the journey back to her room. Just as she was mustering the energy to ask for the bill and haul herself upstairs, a fresh glass of wine appeared in front of her. The downlights shone through it like a fishbowl, projecting the crimson liquid across her hands. Elena had mopped up and tiptoed through enough blood in her lifetime to fill her own body up twenty times over, and sometimes she still saw it everywhere.

'From the lady,' said the bartender, gesturing to a woman seated on the far side of the bar. She was ten years Elena's senior, with a spectacular mop of shimmering grey hair. Her face was scarred, but the wounds looked decades old, healed and smoothed. She drank vodka from a rocks glass which she raised in Elena's direction. It was a busy night in the bar, but they were easily the two oldest people there. Elena squinted. The woman looked familiar. Minor celebrity or ancient mugshot? What did it matter. Elena raised her wine, nodded in thanks and drank deeply.

The cover band launched into a barely recognisable rendition of some decades-old slow jam. Elena had been in her forties when she finally understood why every generation inevitably came to loathe the one after. It wasn't superiority, but jealousy – the simple fact that they would get to see what happened next. In another thirty years, this cover band would be mangling songs written the day after Elena died and calling them classics.

Ten minutes later, another wine appeared. Elena clicked her tongue in thought. She'd never been with a woman and wasn't in the mood to try it now, if that's what this was. But the silver-haired woman made no move towards her side of the bar, gave no indication that she wanted to speak or interact at all. She seemed content simply to have Elena there.

In this way, they spent the night together – many metres apart, silently appraising the young occupants of the hotel bar with a mix of knowing fondness and resigned indignation. A backpacking couple in the corner tried and failed to break up. A tied-and-blazered businessman confided in his colleagues that he hadn't been happy for a very long time. A gaggle of teenagers arrived right in time for happy hour, drinking and shouting and scheming, the world at their feet.

The woman bought Elena another glass of wine, compelling her to stay. Elena's head swam from the booze, and for a second, she forgot where – even when – she was. She imagined she could step outside into the warm Medellín air and hop on the back of Angelo's scooter, cling to his waist and slice through the night air together. That was how she'd felt once: like a knife warm off the anvil, gleaming and true and impossibly sharp. Now she felt kept at the bottom of the drawer: rusted, warped, of little use to anybody.

She wondered if the woman on the far side of the bar might understand this feeling. She had a sudden urge to buy her a drink in return and ask – to get off her stool and close the distance between them and tell her about her life, tell her about her father – but when she looked again, the woman was gone.

BIG TIME

The lead singer of the cover band segued into their next track with the classic introduction: 'This next track needs no introduction.'

What time is your heart
It's quarter to three
What time is your heart
Time for you and me
Ooh-ooh-wee
Ooh-ooh-wee

Elena wondered if the bass player in this hotel bar knew that, right now, he was mimicking the precise fingering of a man she'd been searching for her entire life. But how could he? People forget people. People remembered music.

After a pre-dawn vomit and a breakfast of black coffee and breath mints, Elena found a record store in Fremantle – one of the last remaining physical media music stores in the country – and sauntered inside. There were private booths with headphones and walls lined with thousands of albums forged in every imaginable format. She paced along a row of vinyls, moving backwards alphabetically. *F, E, D, C, B, A*. Acceptables, The. She picked out a fiftieth-anniversary remastered re-release of *Artificial Beaches on Every Mountain / Artificial Mountains on Every Beach* (featuring five never-before-heard tracks). She flipped the sleeve over and there was Julian Ferryman, staring out at her from the band's hyper-stylised group photo.

Elena took the record up to the young man at the counter. 'Excuse me,' she asked in broken English she'd picked up from American crime procedurals and a three-month fling with an exchange student from Vancouver. 'Do you have any other music by this band?'

The young man looked at the album, then smiled knowingly. 'You're in luck,' he said. 'Their second album – the only other album they ever made – is getting released next week, for the first time. It's being shipped *as we speak*.'

'Okay,' said Elena.

Clearly the man had hoped for a bigger reaction, so he elaborated: 'It's one of the great lost albums. After Ash Huang, the lead singer, died – supposedly an accident, but don't get me started – after he was killed, everybody thought the second album was destroyed. But then it turned up in a vault somewhere after their old record label went bust. Unbelievable stuff.'

He stared wistfully at the record jacket. 'I was actually born over there, y'know. In the east. My old man, he used to run a venue in Adelaide, and one time, they played there. The Acceptables. They played *that album* in *his theatre*. My dad, he said there were coppers trying to bang down the door and stop the show, but he held them back until the band finished their set. *Not today, pigs!* he said. He spent the rest of his life hoping to hear that music again, and now I get to hear it in just a few days. Then I'll know what it was he stuck his neck out for that day. What he believed in. Crazy, hey?'

Elena nodded along, only catching every second word. 'So no other music?' she asked bluntly.

The young man's lip was quivering. He felt raw, opened up by his interaction with this old stranger. 'You're not a cop, are you?' he asked suddenly, words laced with the promise of misconduct.

'No,' Elena said with a laugh, lacking the language or inclination to explain the technicalities of her reply.

The young man disappeared behind the counter for a second, then reappeared holding a second record.

'I'm not supposed to have this,' he said furtively, 'but I know some people who know some people back east. It's another lost recording: a solo project by the bass player, Julian Ferryman, and it's only getting released over there. I'm not into it, personally. Pretty naff. But it's a curio for sure.'

Elena took the vinyl from the young man's hands – twelve inches by twelve inches of black-and-white cardboard, with a golden sticker in the corner of the cover declaring it *THE MOTHER-F*CKER MANIFESTO*. There was Ferryman again, this time on his own, a guitar propped awkwardly on one knee, squinting in the sun. Still young, but discernibly changed by the time between the first album and this one. Behind him were two huge, indistinct piles, like pyramids of fake snow, or pristine white sand.

'Where is this?' Elena asked, tapping the album cover.

The young man shrugged. 'No idea.'

BIG TIME

Elena squinted at the photograph again. Not snow, surely – the ground around it seemed bare and hot. Like desert. She pointed at the towering white piles. 'Do you know what this is?'

The young man leant in, properly analysing the background of the image for the first time. 'I'm really not sure. Sorry, lady. I mean, to me, it almost looks like salt.'

28

On his last day in the *now*, Oriana comes to see Julian. He's upstairs in the ensuite, running a bath. He has a stoop. He has arthritis. His body bulges at unhealthy angles, a fading homunculus in a threadbare bathrobe.

'You look good,' says Julian.

'You look old,' says Oriana.

She's carrying an aluminium box. Her hair is silver, shimmering, long – longer than he's ever seen it. Her face is lined with age and scar tissue, and she walks with a limp from some wartime misadventure he'll never know about. She's lived a whole life without him.

'Ash and I used to play this game,' she begins. 'A thought experiment: how could we use his music for the revolution – not just artistically, but materially? We joked about writing songs as acrostic poems that spelt out the locations of secret military bases. Smuggling coded anti-FREA messages into the liner notes of albums, or fixing lyrics so they'd recite bomb recipes when you played them backwards. It wouldn't matter what the actual music sounded like. True fans want what's *behind* the music. And they tend to leave no stone unturned.'

The bathtub is full. Julian turns off the taps, then leans against the vanity with a wince. Two months earlier, he'd gotten into a scrap with another drifter somewhere on the highway and taken a boot to the kidneys, and his back still ached.

'This is what you never understood,' Oriana goes on. 'You were meant to be a delivery system. You were never the message – merely the microphone. But I will give you credit for one good idea.'

Oriana unlatches the box, reaches in and pulls out a record – twelve inches by twelve inches of pristine cream cardboard. A tracklisting on the back and a single image on the front of a human eye, open, ringed with fine eyelashes. The eyeball is adorned with the markings of a clock, complete with a big hand and a little hand jutting out from the pupil, marking five minutes to midnight.

'About a year ago, things took a turn back east,' Oriana says. 'It wasn't looking good for us. We were broke. Then somebody remembered that stunt you pulled on *TimeWatch* all those years ago. You thought you were doing us a favour, bankrolling the rebellion off the back of an LP. Well, it never would have worked, Jules. Not with yours, anyway.'

She unfolds the record jacket. Inside there's a collage of tour photos taken by Ludlow, scanned, digitised, recreated in ribald colour. Like it all happened yesterday.

'Do you remember?' Oriana asks. A sweeping question with infinite avenues in and out. For a split second, Julian wishes there'd been someone around these past few decades to ask it more often.

'I do,' he says.

'Labyrinth Records used to use a proprietary algorithm to forecast the likely success of new bands and their upcoming albums. During your final tour – well, you remember. The algorithm condemned the Acceptables to the scrapheap. These unfinished tracks were sitting in a vault. But the label made this decision only hours before something else happened.'

'What's that?' asks Julian, fully aware of the part he's meant to play in this exegesis, that of awed recipient.

'Ash died,' Oriana says with a pinch in her throat, like maybe it really *did* all happen yesterday. She slips the record from its sleeve. It is vacuum black, black-hole black, so black it absorbs most of the bathroom's pale morning light.

'Also a year ago, Labyrinth's parent company was on the ropes, looking to liquidate its assets. With what little money the rebellion had left, we offered to buy the Acceptables' entire discography along with an archived version of that algorithm. Can you guess what it said when we updated its data set to account for Ash Huang's untimely demise?'

Julian could figure. 'You had a hit on your hands?'

'Like you wouldn't believe.'

Oriana explains that with *Beaches*, the Acceptables had been shrugged off as a group of harmless one-album wonders. But when the world heard about Ash's death and the tragic tale of this group of fearless musicians who'd been hunted down and persecuted by a hard-fisted regime, they became the de facto poster children for the worldwide anti-FREA movement. Songs from *Beaches* were sung at charity concerts in London, and an NGO promising to 'Save the Children of East Australia' used a slowed-down ballad version of 'What Time Is Your Heart' in one of its fundraising commercials. Rumours that a second album had been recorded, but lost to time, only compounded the band's cultural mythos – and *In the End It's All Okay, and If It Ain't Okay, It Ain't the End* had become an artistic artefact of intense speculation worldwide.

Julian didn't know any of this. Even if he did, he wouldn't have cared. By now, he'd spent half his life lying naked on the salt dunes, strung out on F, sending his mind to the bottom of the ocean to observe the migratory patterns of tropical rock lobsters.

'People forget bad behaviour,' Oriana says, turning the record over in her hands, the black disc scraping silently against her fingertips. 'They forget messy press and disastrous PR. But people remember music. They remember the way something made them feel.'

'You once told me nostalgia was a conservative contrivance,' Julian grumbles. 'A worthless affectation.'

Oriana shrugs serenely. 'Fire with fire, enemy of my enemy, etcetera, etcetera ...'

'Etcetera,' he concurs.

'I came here to give you your contractually mandated artist's copy. And your cut.'

Oriana pulls a cheque from her pocket and places it on the vanity. Julian needed glasses but hadn't been to an optometrist, so he can't read what the cheque says – he can only make out the shapes of multiple zeroes.

He waves a hand at the vinyl, saying: 'I've nothing here to play it on.' He'd bartered off the turntable and all the audio equipment what might have been a quarter-of-a-century ago.

BIG TIME

'You don't need to play it,' says Oriana. 'Do you remember the first lyrics off the opening track?'

Julian does:

This is a cold drop of truth in both eyes
Lean your head back and don't act so surprised

Oriana twirls the record once more, then tosses it like a frisbee, straight into the bath. Julian shambles aimlessly backwards – as though he had any chance at all of intercepting it – then pauses and looks in the water.

He used to dye silk with his grandmother. They would fill enormous tubs under the laundry taps – ice cream containers, paint buckets, whatever they could find – then sprinkle in the dye with eyedroppers. Julian used to stare as the ink unfurled from one small drop into a writhing blossom of colour, feeling its way through the water. He would add as many colours as he could, just to watch them intermingle – a handheld lake of porous, swirling rainbow. Looking in the bath now, he sees something very similar: the vinyl is dissolving like a breath mint lodged beneath a tongue, its curved plastic dissipating in the water and converting into sheaths of roiling colour, oily and vibrant.

'Ash was always banging on about the FREA's trade obligations,' says Oriana, 'the lucrative little lifelines that it just couldn't cut, no matter how self-sustaining it tried to be. To this day, one of those lifelines is polyvinyl chloride. Every year the FREA produces more than two hundred thousand tonnes of PVC in its New Victorian work camps. More than half of that is exported to the WRA. And six months ago, we infiltrated the supply chain.'

Julian drinks in the sight of the vanishing vinyl and the radiant, psychedelic tub water. Then he begins to laugh. The laugh becomes a cough. He needed medication for his lungs but hadn't been to the doctor.

'This was partly Ash's idea,' Oriana says.

'You mean you tricked him into *thinking* it was his idea.'

'No, we imagined this together. We wrote those opening lines together. Awake. Sober. Totally clear-eyed. One of our thought experiments. We never believed it could actually be done.'

Julian presses his knuckles into the rim of the bath. There's an industrial amount of F in there. He can picture Oriana's army of zealot chemists in far-north Cooksland, putting the finishing touches to the potion. Powdered and plasticised to be dissolved and reconstituted. Liquid to solid to liquid once more. He can't imagine what the street value might be, how far it might stretch, how many individual doses the by-product of a single vinyl might provide.

'We always knew that F would be central to our struggle,' says Oriana. 'The most important scientific discovery of the modern era, and it happened right there, in our fucked up, sealed-off little part of the world. And it happened right then, in our time of need. That couldn't be just a coincidence.'

Julian's ears prick at the word. 'You're saying it was meant to happen?'

'No. Fate's a lazy thing. It was good timing, sure – but we're the ones who made it mean something.'

The record is gone. The bathtub fizzes with slick, glossy hallucinogen – the medium and the message both.

Julian says: 'Who buys vinyls these days anyway?'

'Oh, plenty of people. Nostalgia still sells. This is the Deluxe Version. And I've got a feeling, once word gets out, everyone will be wanting the Deluxe Version.'

'How many copies did you say you'd sold?'

'Worldwide, a million so far. The first shipments left from Perth last week.'

'Well, congrats,' Julian growls, trying to muster some sarcasm. 'You're an international kingpin. Very impressive. But you know it won't last. People will figure out what you're doing.'

'Eventually, yes. But by then it won't matter. By then, the whole world will have access to what we invented, and what's been a trickle for so many years will have become a flood.' Oriana rolls one hand through the air, rhapsodising. 'You know, we were going about it all wrong with you – stockpiling that power, manufacturing scarcity when it ought to be for everyone. This is the great democratisation of time! Charlie Total always said you can't build a better future until you can imagine it. Better yet – until you can actually *see* it. So this is us, showing people the future on a massive scale, with an enormous sample size. It only takes one person to put it to better use than you did. One in a million, Jules. For once, I like those odds.'

With enormous effort, Julian turns to sit on the edge of the bath, facing Oriana.

'Is everything just a means to an end with you?' he asks.

'Well, everything ends. So technically, that's all anything is.'

'People will die from this.'

'People died because of you.'

'No, they didn't!' Julian splutters.

'Julian. They did.'

He stands, arms waving, knees cracking. 'I never wanted any part of this! You're the one who dragged me into it. You're the one who brought me here!'

'And you profited every step of the way.'

'Profited!' Julian chortles. 'That's rich coming from you. I'm enjoying this, you know, this whole "democratisation of time" schtick. Very noble. What's the price tag on one of these Deluxe Versions, anyway?'

Oriana watches him darkly. 'It will finance the rebellion for another century.'

'You are your stepfather's daughter.'

'We've weighed the cost. There will be collateral damage, just as there was when we started seeding it back east. But what choice do we have? Look at me, Julian. Look at us.'

Julian resists the urge to steal a glance in the mirror above the sink. He doesn't have to. He knows what she's getting at.

Oriana plants one hand on the vanity to steady herself. She'd come here to lecture him, but realises she really does want him to understand. 'I spent my entire life trying to change people's minds the gentle way. Trying to nudge them in the right direction. Trying to sway public opinion. I tried suggestion, inspiration and incitement. I tried appealing to their taste and better nature. I tried to speak their language. I tried to hold their hand while they got there on their own. I tried, and I tried, and I tried, and I tried. But it didn't work. None of it. I'm tired of waiting for all the variables to line up. Strip them away, and what's left?' She jabs a finger at the tub. 'That right there. Pure and simple. Chemistry and commerce. Do you mind if I sit?'

Julian clears a pile of musty towels off a stool, and Oriana perches, catching her breath. She had a degenerative hip but hadn't been to the physio.

'Sorry,' she says. 'It was a very long drive.'

Julian sits again. Oriana feels him watching her.

'Go ahead,' she says, exhausted. 'Think whatever you want of me. I tried every other way, Jules. I promise, I tried. I thought that we could get there gently. But the gentle ways have taken too long.'

Julian remembers Oriana in the rose garden at the racecourse. He remembers her smoking on that Chesterfield in the church. He remembers spooning her in the boot of that car, speeding blindly towards the meridian. If you told Julian that he died in that boot, and that everything since had been nothing more than the synapses in his brain firing and failing, a death dream grab-bag, a convoluted neurochemical farewell, he might have believed you. He might have even been relieved.

'This is how you stop the world going backwards,' Oriana says, swallowing painfully. 'You force it forwards.'

'Not the whole world, though,' Julian says. 'Not the FREA. They'll never sell Ash's album there. Besides, like you say – the people, the fans, they didn't want it then. I can't imagine they'll want it now.'

'No, you're right,' Oriana concedes. 'For that, we used yours.'

She bends down and pulls another record from the aluminium box – twelve inches by twelve inches of black-and-white cardboard with a photo of Julian as a young man standing out by the salt heaps, guitar propped awkwardly on one knee, squinting in the sun. A photo Oriana took. The original cover design had no title treatment, but the one she's holding now has a foil sticker plastered in the top corner. In chunky black lettering, it reads: *THE MOTHERF*CKER MANIFESTO.*

'It needed a proper name,' Oriana explains. 'Jianhong-Waterford-Kumar-Carmichael-Sprouse had a bunch of suggestions – but this was an old joke Sita used to make, and it stuck.'

Julian is conflicted. He wants to lift the record from Oriana's hands and pore over it like the holy text it is, but he's repulsed by the golden sticker and its insidious wording.

'People are buying this back home?' he asks.

BIG TIME

'They're gobbling it up,' says Oriana. 'It's vapid. Apolitical. Inane. Utterly toothless and completely unredactable. In fact, it's about to go platinum. Thank you, Jules. It was just the thing. Here's another cheque.'

Julian's half-blinded by tears and cataracts. He ignores Oriana's growing pile of cheques and the growing number of zeroes. He reaches for the record – his record.

'They really like it back home?' he asks, delicately removing the vinyl from its sleeve.

Oriana sighs. She decides to let him have this. 'They really do.'

Julian holds the record up and angles it to the light. It glitters with the same distinctive multicoloured hue. Buried futures in black rainbows.

Julian presses his eyes into the sleeve of his robe and cries. He's crying for Ash, his old band, his old friends, his old home – but mostly he's crying for himself, for his scuppered life and his broken body, for the ideas he had that no-one ever heard or wanted, the songs he never sat down to write, the goodbyes he never gave. He's crying over that imperceptible switch in life when you stop imagining what might be and begin to toll what never was.

'Have you been alone all this time?' Oriana asks at last.

Julian feels dizzy. He places the vinyl on the basin, then reaches out for the towel rail, hands fumbling, stabilising himself as he comes to an unglamorous seat on the grotty tiled floor.

'I don't really know. I skip ahead. I see things. I go places. I meet people. Then I snap back, and I never actually do any of those things or meet any of those people. So I guess I never did any of it. They're still out there, though, these ... *lives*,' Julian says, as though he could almost catch one in his fist. 'Entire existences, floating just out of reach. I've seen them, walked through them, but I never know whether they're real or not.'

'There's a lot more lives you didn't live than the one you did,' says Oriana.

Julian gets a sudden premonition she's about to reach down and hold his hand. Then she does. Maybe there were no more surprises. Maybe he had seen this already, every last moment of it, someplace else, a long time ago, and it was all just a drop in an ocean on a world somewhere behind him.

'I thought I would have seen it by now,' Julian says, the words catching in his throat. 'The shopping mall. I've gone so far, but I've never seen it. I'm afraid I never will. What if it isn't there for me?'

Oriana nods, like a priest forgiving a list of common sins. 'Edmond – up in Byron Bay – he never saw anything like it either,' she says. 'He saw tens, maybe hundreds of thousands of years ahead, but he never saw his own death. So it means what it means. A closed loop. We discussed this internally, and our working theory is: people who see their deaths and go straight to that place, it's like they took a shortcut there with the fuel that they had. But if you've never seen it … that means that, eventually, you go the long way. I think you haven't seen yourself die, Jules, because technically – metaphysically – which is to say, chronologically – it's possible you never do.'

'The long way, you say. Eventually.' For the first time ever, Julian feels exactly as old as he is. 'When?'

'If you're wondering when, the answer is now. The moment you're waiting for is the moment you're in. Do you remember?'

'Yes. Yes. God. I remember.'

Oriana lifts Julian's unsheathed copy of *THE MOTHER-F*CKER MANIFESTO* off the basin and hands it to him. He grips it with trembling hands and holds it close to his heart.

'My dear Julian,' she says. 'Don't you think it's time for you to see how it ends?'

'How what ends?' he asks.

'Everything,' says Oriana.

29

Elena Rojas took a car to the desert. She drove north for nine hours, staying overnight in the township of Carnarvon. Lying on the motel bed, she felt her heart thump in her chest. Perhaps she'd been unkind in her assessment of it – maybe it, just like her, was doing its best. Maybe she actually had more time than she thought. Maybe once this was finished – once she'd found Julian Ferryman, or at least found out what happened to him – she could stop dreaming about her father pacing that alleyway in La Candelaria, stop dreaming about Brayden Byrne's blood drying dark pink on those tiles. She could move to Mexico, then on to America. She could finally try sculpting something. She was old, but her hands still worked, and she longed to use them for something other than filling out death certificates.

A helpful young woman at one of the libraries in Perth that Elena hadn't been banned from had concluded that the white piles on the cover of Julian Ferryman's solo album were indeed most likely salt. Taking into account the age of the photograph, what little Elena knew of Ferryman's movements and the library's records pertaining to the West Australian salt industry, the young woman used archival satellite imagery to provide Elena with a possible location: Syds Bluff.

The following morning as she approached the location tagged in her car's GPS, Elena saw a grimy billboard appear on the horizon. In sun-bleached letters, it read: *A LIFE BY THE SEA IS THE LIFE FOR ME – CUVIER HEIGHTS. ENQUIRE TODAY.*

Elena took control of the vehicle and made the turn, soon entering an open maze of cracked bitumen roads. It looked like an entire suburb had been scooped up by a cyclone and tossed into the sea, leaving only its footprint. A few half-built timber frames slumped into the red dirt. Rows of rusted streetlights wavered like alien antenna. There were two neat piles of brick and wood, possibly completed homes that had long since collapsed in on themselves. But at the end of a far cul-de-sac, teetering metres from a crumbling coastal cliff and a vertiginous thirty-foot drop, a single rundown house still stood, its front door flapping in the hot wind.

Elena parked and got out of the car. There were tyre tracks beside hers in the dust. Someone else had been there. Someone had only recently left.

A sprinkler system spewed brown water across a dead front lawn. Elena approached the house, sidestepping the streams, holding the front door in place and knocking on it. Not knowing any other way to explain her presence or introduce herself, Elena called inside: '*Policía*!'

There was no reply. When she knocked again, the door came off its hinges. As good as an invitation, she figured.

Inside, salt air blew in through the broken windows. Every fixture and piece of furniture was painted with a solid coat of either dust or rust. Every surface was piled high with used food containers, empty soda cans and stacks of books on music theory, many of them stolen from the same libraries Elena had been kicked out of. Every wall was covered with pages torn from pop culture magazines: photos of Julian Ferryman, Ash Huang, Tammy Tedeski and Xander Plutos. All so young. One double-page spread from a faded *Rolling Stone*, tacked below a group shot of the band on their first ever tour, asked: *WHERE ARE THEY NOW?*

'Hello?' Elena called out.

A drop of water hit the floor beside her, turning dust to mud. She followed its trajectory upwards to where a thin pool of liquid was gripping the underside of the ceiling, rippling with tiny, shimmering stalactites.

Elena took to the stairs, wondering how long until this house caved in like the others, praying it could hold out just a few minutes more.

BIG TIME

She turned to the bedroom. Towards the ensuite on the far side. Towards the sound of a steady drip. She pushed the door aside and kicked up a miniature wave; the floor was flooded with an inch of water, translucent but somehow teeming with colour. In front of her was a bathtub, full to the brim, leaking gently around the rim as the rusted taps continued to drip. Slowly disintegrating on the ensuite floor were two empty record jackets – one with the familiar photo of Julian Ferryman by the salt heaps, the other with a hand-drawn image of a single eye, its cornea a clock, staring unblinkingly out at Elena.

She took two steps forward and peered into the tub.

There was a man in there, fully submerged, eyes open, freshly dead. She'd missed him by maybe an hour. Maybe even less. He was older than her, craggy and misshapen, his rough skin and untreated sores now softened and blanched by the water. Elena gazed at him through the heavy liquid, which seemed to dance from hue to hue as it moved through the morning light, an aqueous kaleidoscope.

Even before she picked up the sodden sleeve of *THE MOTHERF*CKER MANIFESTO* to compare the young man in the photo to the old man in the bath, Elena knew it was him. Because people don't just disappear. Nothing's ever really lost. It just takes the right tools, and enough time, to find them.

Elena Rojas called the police station in Carnarvon and waited on the muddy lawn for the ambulance to arrive. They drained the bath and took the body into town, where a local church offered to hold a simple ceremony. They would have to keep the casket closed, because they couldn't close his eyes; too wide as they were, too full of the future.

30

Put your hands by your sides. Breathe out. Force the sigh. Now tilt your head back, and open your eyes. Submerge and saturate. Don't act so surprised. You're free to roam now. Go wherever you like.

The sun sets and rises. Sun sets and rises. It's the world's high hat, rhythmic and tight.

There's the cliffs by the seaside, giving way at last, adding to the ever-expanding underwater mountain ranges. Maps redrawn. Coastlines redefined.

There's the crunch of autumn leaves and a shipping container full of bodies at Amsterdam airport. A Boiler Room set by a prominent DJ that lasts one full calendar year. Strange vibrations in the regolith. A prime minister choking on a chicken bone.

Winds from the desert. Cries in the night. Bombings at the Reichstag. Bad communication. Silicone eyedrops. An upside-down palace. A plague of dancing. Rocks like crayon. A resurrection cult with proven results.

A woman watches her mother take the wrong medication and says nothing. A perfect circle forms on the surface of Jupiter.

Unfamiliar piers. Carved wood and terry towel. Honeysuckles plucked from the side of the road and the very first one-way mission to Mars.

The Metaversal Financial Collapse. Digital mortgages bursting by the billion. Full moon on a leap day. Super Bowl on a Monday. Unidentifiable insects. The Beijing Spring. A private highway stretching over the Darién Gap.

BIG TIME

The transit of Venus. Trade-route Tetris. Bitcoins run dry. Halloween at the White House. Crescent moon and supermoon. Meals among friends. The satellite graveyard at Point Nemo breaches the surface, and tourists flock in boats to see.

An at-home DNA testing kit reveals unknown chromosomes. The second one-way mission to Mars, cancelled. A country held hostage. The Digital Pool of Infinite Worry™. Chicken steaks and cherries on death row in Ohio.

Genocide. Repatriacide. A wedding at a waterfall. Songs sung at storm clouds. The world's slowest monk.

Landlords hanged. All debt erased. New debt created and all debt indexed.

Strange hallways. An interdigitation. A betrayal. A fuck. A killing on the markets. The Amazon Desert. The Aerospace Massacre. Blueberry cheesecake. A story written with water.

The screaming of megafauna. The crumbling of leather. Warm toffee collapsing. A drop of semen on a stomach. Secret jokes and made-up names. Desire paths, all covered over. Pluto reaching aphelion. Libraries turned to ash. Man-made lakes too suddenly unmade. Deep-fried MARS Bars. Soft hotel pillows. Broken teeth. Fossilised graffiti. Birthday pancakes. Glow-worm caves. Penguins in Ulaanbaatar.

A tower in Old Canberra, still stabbing at clouds. Cities on the high seas. Communities in caves. A body floats down the Chico River. A soldier on the front line fills out his own death certificate.

Jungles full of woodsmoke. Babies born faceless. Dogs learning Mandarin. The New World Cup. The triple-ring plane crossing of Saturn.

EMP warfare. Blue dot. Red dot. Scottish Independence. Catalan Independence. Californian Independence. Australian Reunification.

The Cascadia Subduction Zone. Mass graves in Greenland. 3D-printed missiles. A life-sized gingerbread house. Trillions of terabytes of memories lost.

Halley's Comet fails to appear and nobody knows why.

A clock ticks high on a mountaintop in Nevada. No more beaches. A wet, wet world.

Voyager 2 changes course and nobody knows why.

The roaring earthworm trade. The bursting of the earthworm

bubble. Forests fill the Gobi. The last animal in the last zoo escapes. A woman falls in love with her clone.

Cosmic Call 1. Cosmic Call 2. The fingers of radio frequencies grasp at distant stars. Ancient alphabets updated. Absolute panmixia. The remains of museums. The last family of fireflies.

Planets align. The stars grow brighter. Twenty-five hours in a day. Cities in the deep. A new North Star. The Nubian Plate and the Somali Plate. Emoji nuclear semiotics. The dust of Great Pyramids. The Mediterranean Ranges. All-new fossil fuels.

We flee to the poles. We return to the oceans. We feast in the Arctic. We die by the billion. The Great Gamma Ray. The Seventh Extinction. Pangaea Proxima. A tube worm sucking on an ocean-floor vent – then that's that.

Supernovas burn in the daytime sky. A switch of the seasons. Sand in the Arctic. Echoes on Venus. The fourteenth zodiac. The Sun's hottest day. Greenhouse to icehouse to greenhouse to icehouse. The oceans run dry. A time traveller appears – a grave miscalculation – and evaporates instantly.

Mercury sacrifices itself to the Sun. Faraway moons smash each other to pieces. Planetary pinball. The final eclipse. Mars eats Phobos. Sun eats Earth. Soft gamma repeaters. New rings on Neptune. The kiss of solar winds. Red dwarf. White dwarf. What does it matter.

Curtains of energy. A dark dance of positrons. Black holes sprinting at the speed of not-light. Spacetime unspooling. The beginning of the end. Stars running empty. Milky Way spillage. The Great Cool Down. The Black Hole Era. Proton decay. Infinite scale. Zero per cent nothingness. A liquid universe. Blessed redshift. Unobservable everything. A horizon longer than time. The Big Bang's final echo.

It finishes as it began – one perfect, all-consuming rhyme. Spatial decline. Terminal vacuum. Thermodynamic equilibrium. Catalysed fusion. Maximum entropy. The universe has finished breathing out and won't breathe in again.

Julian Ferryman had been right about one thing: we leave traces of ourselves wherever we go. If a new creature were to come into being now, this is what it would inherit. Pockets of pure, untethered emotion. Leftover longing, leftover regret. Ghosts of ancient timelines. Particles without people. Feelings freed from context. Cosmic

BIG TIME

floating thought cloud. Pure objective vortex. There is subatomic sentience still, bobbing on the black-matter spume.

And in these things, all of us are there. Everyone from everywhere, even you and me – see, heaven is the end of time. That's where we all will meet.

EPILOGUE

There are sniffer dogs at Auckland Airport, weeding out errant apples and plums. They sniff the wheels of the stretcher as it rolls past, and one of the beagles' paws catches the corner of the coroner's sheet. Suddenly a socked foot is sticking out, exposed – a dead foot in the middle of an airport food court.

Trevor watches this from his seat near the Froakley's Doughnut Shop, its roller door shut and its neon lights off. Just as soon as he'd seen all the passengers safely off the plane and answered the police's questions, he'd come to sit here and watch the scene unfold.

It's late. One of the cops is yawning. A few passengers are crying. They'd all been given vouchers to the tune of two hundred and fifty New Zealand dollars to help them find accommodation for the night, as a number of them had missed their connecting flights.

After the stretcher disappears and the hubbub dies down, Trevor rests his head in his hands and cries – an acceptable amount for a flight attendant dealing with a high-stress, mid-air calamity, but not so much as to draw any unwarranted attention. A garbled page rings out over the PA. An attendant from another airline struggles with, then mispronounces, some tardy traveller's name. A cleaner glides past on a ride-on floor polisher.

'*Viaje seguro*,' he'd said to the boy in seat 46D. Trevor never caught his name. But he'd liked him, so he'd left him the vial, and he must have taken too much. Didn't have the tolerance. Body chemistry, dumb luck and circumstance. Trevor feels a sudden, excruci-

BIG TIME

ating stab of jealousy, even through his tears. He wonders just how far the boy had gone. He wonders what he'd seen.

But the feeling passes quickly. Trevor blinks and wipes his eyes. He'd get to the airport hotel, draw a bath and get drunk from drinking three bottles of minibar rum in rapid succession. He'd watch TV, drift off to sleep and dream. Those dreams would be murky and misaligned, but they could be shaken off tomorrow, much like all this.

As for Trevor's aspirations of fame, he decided they could wait. There were worse things than the graveyard shift at thirty thousand feet. He would keep his world small, manageable, understandable. It didn't need to be any more complicated than that. He didn't need to be anything more than a man in a room. A brain in a body. A shape on a sphere in a circle in time.

ACKNOWLEDGEMENTS

This book was written predominantly on the unceded lands of the Gadubanud people of the Eastern Maar nation, and those of the Wurundjeri Woi Wurrung people of the Kulin nation. I acknowledge the Traditional Owners of these lands, and pay my deepest respects to their Ancestors and their descendants.

Thank you to Sarah Walker and David Finnigan, creative confidants and co-conspirators. Thank you to everyone at the Peter Carey Short Story Awards. Thank you to Aviva Tuffield, Ian See, Lauren Mitchell, and everyone at UQP. Thank you to Harriet Hirshman and the team at Dead Ink Books. Thank you to PJ Crimmins for the football insights, Luke Shields for the musical know-how, Ness Roque for the Japan tips, and Have/Hold for letting me sit in on their sessions. Thank you to Rebecca Giggs and Melissa Manning for their sage advice. Thank you to Izzy Roberts-Orr, Carly Jacobs, Mike Greaney, Sarah Kimball, Kim Prosser, Jarrett Prosser, Sophie-Anne Stanton, Sam Burns-Warr, Ben Hamey, and all the Shieldses. Thank you to Hartie the kelpie for the knowing looks, the chin on my knee, and showing us all how life ought to be. And lastly, thank you to Jessa Shields, first and dearest among readers; a dog has only the home you give it, and you gave me mine.

ABOUT THE AUTHOR

Jordan Prosser is an author and screenwriter from Australia. *Big Time* is his first novel.

About Dead Ink

Dead Ink is a publisher of bold new fiction based in Liverpool. We're an Arts Council England National Portfolio Organisation.

If you would like to keep up to date with what we're up to, check out our website and join our mailing list.

www.deadinkbooks.com | @deadinkbooks